SAFE HAVENS: SHADOW MASTERS

SAFE HAVENS: SHADOW MASTERS

A SEAN HAVENS BLACK OPS NOVEL

J.T. PATTEN

Escape Your Reality Press

A Donovan Black Holdings Company

J.T. Patten Books in conjunction with Escape Your Reality Press,
A Donovan Black Holdings USA LLC company
1212 So. Naper Blvd., Suite 119-239
Naperville, IL 60540

Please visit our website at **www.jtpattenbooks.com** or follow us on Twitter @jtpattenbooks

ISBN 978-0615950471

This manuscript has been submitted, reviewed and approved by the Central Intelligence Agency Professional Review and Department of Defense Security Review.

To my wife, my safe haven

Acknowledgements

I would like to thank my wife who shoulders the burden of work while I steal away time to write, wherever I may be. I love you and appreciate all that you do.

Thanks to Sean, who threw down the gauntlet and challenged me to write a book. Brother, I think I was bamboozled, but what a great feeling now that it is complete. Thanks for your encouragement and friendship. To my writing mentors and friends, Mark Greaney and Kevin Maurer. Thanks for your time, your assistance, and occasional swat to the head. If I ever grace the bookshelves where your bestsellers reside, you'll know I rigged it. I owe you both.

Thank you, Carie, for sharing your publishing insights and for introducing me to editor Molly Wojda. Molly, you did a fantastic job improving the story and the writing mechanics. Thank you for your professionalism and patience. I hope you are ready for the next one.

To the Quiet Professionals of the special operations and intelligence community. Respect. Thank you, PRD, for a painless process. And to my recruiter. I hope you are enjoying retirement. Thanks for your advice and guidance so many years ago.

"Certainly there is no hunting like the hunting of man and those who have hunted armed men long enough and liked it, never really care for anything else thereafter. You will meet them doing various things with resolve, but their interest rarely holds because after the other thing, ordinary life is as flat as the taste of wine when the taste buds have been burned off your tongue."

—Ernest Hemingway, "On the Blue Water," *Esquire*

Prologue

Under cover of darkness, the last member of the kill team felt the reassuring clicks and finger tension from the Schlage cylinders as they tumbled into place. No light was needed to assist the lock-picking tradecraft now being done in a reverse technique. With a twist of the hook and a pull of the lock pick rake, the metal inter-workings slid into their nest. The steel bolt eased back through the reinforced doorframe.

The remaining crew had exfiltrated the target site perimeter as their mate finished manipulating the deadbolt components to relock the door from the outside. They all melted quietly into the moon-cast shadows like demons of the night with captured souls in their clutch and firearms at their grasp.

Dew formed on the lawn they now vacated. Droplets of moisture hitched a ride on the bootie-covered combat assault boots that were fast on the move. The trampled grass blades would unbend back into place by sunup with new condensation visible to any discerning eyes.

No trails. No trace.

Aside from the satisfaction of completing their mission, the assault team never gave a moment's thought to the death they had left behind them in the house. At the forefront of their minds was disposing of the edged weapons and the bloodstained gloves and coveralls, ditching their vehicles, and blending back into their lives after a debriefing.

But they would never make it out of the after-action meeting. These men were loose ends and the masters who had sent them on this assassination quest would kill them without remorse in a remote warehouse later that morning.

Their abandoned carnage within the secured home was exposed mere hours after sunrise. Its discovery was also part of the plan to set the stage.

****

"No, sir. I'm not going back in there. Can't do it."

"Roberts, you can and you will! I know it's hard. Step up." The superior police commander was empathetic to young Officer Roberts, but had to be firm. This certainly was not a normal law enforcement call. The commander had to maintain control of these fledgling officers in a situation like this. This was different from the typical suicide or gang violence response calls.

"Just take a few breaths and get back in that damn house, son."

"It's just too messed up. Give me more time."

Another officer nearby was hunched over, legs spread apart; both hands palmed a tree trunk for support. The patrolman gagged and retched some more on the shredded cedar mulch below. He had been the first one on scene after an anonymous tip to police had dispatched him to the home. An hour inside the house was too much to handle. A minute was long enough. Emotions nudged out professionalism.

For God's sake, he had his own kids that age.

Many of the officers present had reached their threshold of what they could do on scene and had begun congregating outside. The press and all their cameras would be here soon sharing with the world this middle-class neighborhood horror show.

Lars Bjorklund walked up the concrete sidewalk passing all the officers. Traffic had been bad but the Starbuck's drive thru line was unbearably long. He drained his coffee with a large gulp before entering the house and tossed the cup on the vomit-wet mulch. The knee-weak officer, now hovering above the litter and his emptied stomach contents, viewed the act as contempt. Lars knew that by tossing it outside, he saved the cup from being tagged as potential evidence.

Within the non-descript residence, converging pools of dark red silhouetted the lifeless bodies, concluding the fatal process of catastrophic blood loss. The foul smell of death and involuntary bodily waste release was setting in now, and it established a foreboding warning to those entering the home.

Crime scene investigators had been called in to capture the extent of the event and process the house for evidence and answers, which were few.

The projected, cascading blood spatter was everywhere. Cast-off stains on the ceiling, walls, and furniture created numerous arcs of blood droplets from the repeated pulling back of blows to the victims.

One forensic analyst lost count of the number of blows determined by the blood arcs. He wiped his face while squeezing his eyes shut as if to clear the frustration and overwhelming effort. He started over with a deep breath and a mental reset.

Another examiner kept rambling to criminalists about exsanguination, hypovolemic shock, cardiac tamponade, and asphyxia. Young pup officers near their more senior counterparts raised their eyebrows, not fully grasping the forensic medical jargon. It sounded to them like medical-ese bullshit. Death was an international language. It was abundantly clear to the new guys what had happened in this home and it shook them to their very core as they grappled with the thought that some savage was capable of such inhumanity.

A specialist was probing a wound for any residual weapon trace. It appeared that an arsenal of metals was wielded across the flesh. The specialist nodded to a field serologist—a "goo guy"—who was not watching his crew. A young team member was trying to lift a body before examination was complete. The serologist would need to give more professional direction to the evidence handling procedures to avoid a paperwork nightmare later.

"Bad practice, Leo," the serologist addressed the young examiner. "You need to wait a few. Couple more tests before the body can get back to the shop for further analysis. I need about another ten minutes on that one."

"OK, boss, but what else can we even do?" Leo realized he was not going to get an answer. He stood up and walked away, pretending that he had something else important to do in an attempt to save face.

Lars, still passing through the scene, casually stepped over the corpse roughly brushing by the newbie. He answered Leo, the paid intern, as if it was as simple as rudimentary kindergarten arithmetic.

"The combination spatters are going to take priority so we can get some sense of directionality and sequence of events. Your team still has to look at possible transfer patterns. Clots, contraction, and separation from the past few hours should help some."

"Oh, yeah, sure it will help tons," another technician replied sarcastically.

"There's gotta be over twenty liters of blood volume here, Lars. We really need to do a volume test?"

Lars wished his senior analysts could step up and assert themselves as leaders and mentors. *Bueller, Bueller?* Nothing. *Do I really have to do everything?* "Guys, focus on the cast-offs and textures of the stains and patterns. Make sure to note the origins and direction of blood travel in your log." Lars glared, sending the flying daggers from under a furrowed brow, at his most senior man, Ted.

"Ted, take care of your shit. Your guys need better guidance. Clearly, they must have cheated on their certifications. Wonder if you did too. Need some continuing ed this month?" Lars stood dominantly over the shamed group, daring anyone to open their mouths.

The men around Ted lowered their heads out of both embarrassment and boss avoidance.

Other forensic examiners snapped their flashing Nikon cameras throughout the scene making incessant clicking sounds like dueling typewriters. The light exploded in bursts of white from all corners of the room.

As Lars strolled through the middle of the room, it looked like paparazzi coverage at a red carpet event as the investigators carried out their zone search—close-ups, mids, and overview shots for the photo log.

The bodies lay as they had fallen, or so they appeared—except for the ones who had crawled seeking something, someone, for help.

Help that never came.

A Spider-Man action figure lay on the floor. It was still in reach of its owner's small hand. Likely clenching the toy until the very end. Such a bitter emotional symbol when clearly a real superhero had been desperately hoped for. The blood on the action figure's nylon costume made it look like he too had been part of the massacre. As if Spider-Man, like the others in the room, had succumbed to a mortal wound in the melee.

There were four corpses being covered. They had once been a family, not the blanketed heaps that they were now. At first glance, the victims appeared to be a woman and three children based on their sizes and the age-appropriate clothing now shredded and soaked, adhering to the bodies.

"We found another vic upstairs!"

Five.

Little Mexican vacation statuettes adorned a knick-knack table between small tabletop pictures of the household's greater Latino family. Happy moments.

A wedding picture hung on the wall. It was likely not more than five to eight years old judging by the sequence of photo milestones in the room, the ages of the deceased lying about, and the unchanged hairstyle of the bride. The groom's hair had remained the same throughout all of the photos in the room. Closely cropped. High and tight.

The man was not here among the dead.

Where is the dad? The thought puzzled Lars as he rescanned the room for any more meaningful clues.

Chief Forensics Crime Scene Investigator Lars Bjorklund had been scanning the full sickening aftermath of horror, and he understood why the police-secured entryway and front bushes were a combination of freshly ingested coffee and bile-egg-breakfast sandwich-donut vomit. Few of these newly hired men would ever encounter such a scene in their careers.

Bad crime scene to cut your teeth, but they still need to step up. If they can get through this, the next twenty years will be cake.

Lars, on the other hand, had seen far too many death scenes. His stomach growled from hunger. The morning's lox and capers on top of cold leftover pizza was enough to get him to the scene but not enough to hold him over. He'd be here for hours, provided there was no interference with his work or authority.

The examiners could likely rule out the post-event taint from potential evidence, but the cleanup may wipe some potential footprints and other forensic trace from the foyer.

Damn, what a mess. Can't worry about contaminated evidence in the front at this point. Need to write it off in my notes.

"Did anyone capture the shoes from the first on-scene uniform?"

No response. No eye contact.

Lars called again out to no particular police officer in the room.

"Does anyone know where the husband is?"

"Afghanistan," a uniform replied. "Neighbor said Mr. Gonzalez, or whatever his rank or title is, was supposed to come home in a few weeks. The Department of Defense'll get him home right away now, I suppose."

The officer's voice trailed off as he now looked to the ground, shook his head and muttered; "*Now* they'll get 'em home. Shit."

Someone else said under their breath, "Welcome home. Thanks for your service."

Glaring, disapproving eyes honed in on the officer who made the remark.

"What? I am not saying anything bad. This is bullshit. Guy is serving the country, we're supposed to watch the families, and this shit happens. I'm sorry. It goes down as our watch. How do you look that guy in the eye to give him the news? We had the easier of the jobs. No one mortared our station last night. Car didn't blow up in front of my house when I got the paper. It's messed up."

The glaring looks left the officer and returned to the graphic scene with slight nods in agreement. How *will* this soldier be told?

The incessant typewriter-like sounds of the photo duel continued. Flashes in accompaniment to the camera snapping still ruptured the already numbed human senses. Some officers winced at the light from the stressing sensory overload.

Lars Bjorklund exited the room. He walked through the kitchen and opened the sliding glass door to the patio. Spotting a comfortable looking plastic deck chair he brushed off the seat with a kerchief clearing some water-pooled dirt and debris, then sat down. He closed his eyelids, hoping his mind's eye would guide him through the seemingly disorganized murder scene back in the house. Lars was trying to enter the crime scene again from this vantage and reflect on what he had missed.

I have to piss.

Refocus.

It is a planned offense. That makes it organized not disorganized. The attacker or attackers must know the victims. That's organized. Were there signs of aggressive acts prior to death? No use of restraints. Wait. There was redness and bruising on the mother's wrists above the point where her hands were severed. Had her wrists been bound? Check that. Why kill the kids? That's power display. No weapons present, that could mean organized. Shit. Had to be more than one killer. A goon and a thinker? With that many people in the room controlling the acts, three killers would be ideal. Could there be more?

OK, the perps are in the house. How do two or three guys come in? Where would…

"Chief?"

Begrudgingly, Lars opened his eyes. He regarded an officer with the residual stain and wetness of vomit on his uniform breast and black low-top assault boots peeking from the house's back doorway, "They thought you may want to see this. Can you come back in? Right now?" The officer paused. "What are you doing out here anyway?"

Lars clenched his jaw in irritation as he threw a brief mental tantrum.

As Lars fought to extract his large frame out of the chair while re-taking in the officer's soiled attire from head to toe, his eyes continued in a downward assessment and noticed a small piece of paper on the brick patio stone a couple inches from the entryway stoop.

What do we have here, little fellow?

Taking a branded FBI Behavioral Sciences Unit ink pen from his jacket, Lars walked over, squatted down, and gently touched the receipt with the pen's metal tip.

The paper was dry and clean.

Two days ago it had rained. Then the weather had cleared enough to dry things up a bit but this paper, had it been discarded or blown here more than twenty-four hours ago, would have been soaked and potentially stained from dirty rain runoff and pooled water.

This scrap has been recently dropped or blown. Lars looked at the yard from the ground to tree tops. He saw no movement in the wide spans of back-to-back yards adorned with towering oak, elm, and maple trees. The chained play gym swings also remained motionless in the calm of nature. There was no other debris on the patio. No grass clippings, no dead leaves, no clothes dryer lint or pollen spores. Partially dried bird droppings were scattered around the area which ruled out a spray down. *Wouldn't have blown here in the past few hours.*

Lars regarded the royal blue ink print on the receipt as he remained squatting down. He read the word 'Mexico' on what appeared to be a border ticket. *Mexico? You are a long way from the border here in Chicago.* As a seasoned detective, this wasn't passing the sniff test. *Evidence eye candy? Maybe, but why would something be planted? From Mexico nonetheless…*

Damn. Stuff here in the house is from the Mexican border. That statuette on the table. Was that Jesús Malverde, the angel bandito of the poor? Need to look at that again.

Lars had recalled asking about a similar figurine when he was in Mesa, Arizona for a bachelor baseball vacation to watch Cubs spring training. He had felt compelled to pay a visit to a law enforcement friend in the Nogales-Tucson area. His buddy had a similar statuette on the desk and said it was the Mexican saint of Sinaloa's narco-state.

"Hey, Chief, you coming?" the officer persisted while hovering over Lars in the rear entryway.

"Yeah, can you step back so your pecker sack isn't hanging over my head while I am looking at things down here. Get one of my guys to snap this and bag it for the lab. I want it documented. Have them put me in for discovery chain of custody notes. I want this whole back area captured. Document any of the details that could potentially change with time."

Lars was pissed now that he may have tainted some trace evidence, impressions, or any other physical forms that would have aided in recreating the crime or identifying the perp—or maybe perps, given the management of killing so many people.

On the other hand, could one person herd all of them in the room jumping around from one to another like a crazed maniac? No. Impossible. Lars feared regretting his careless crime scene actions later. *Shit. I come out here to play Forensic Yoda and end up throwing off the case myself.*

One o'clock baseball game today. Crap. Won't make it.

The officer stepped back to give the investigator space but couldn't contain himself any longer.

"They found a shitload of drugs in the basement. Heroin. Coke. Methamphetamines. Scales. Bags. Another vic with a head severed. Unbelievable."

Six.

"Head was lopped off and propped on the table with a penny taped to her mouth. Pretty fuckin' weird, if you ask me. Like voodoo shit. Looks like mama and this other lady were payin' the bills distributing while daddy was away in the sand. Maybe the dad was shipping heroin from the sandbox. Maybe it's like that Haitian voodoo Santa Ria Santa Rita stuff. I think that's what it's called. Is that Haitian?" He stopped when he realized he was talking only to himself. Nevertheless, contained himself for only a moment.

"What's that, Chief? Is it paper you're looking at?"

Lars tilted his head, gazing at the officer. His patience was long gone but his outward temperament remained direct, yet controlled. "I have a million and ten smart ass responses to all your questions. Get one of my guys, get out of the way, and shut the hell up."

Lars stepped through the door and realized he didn't know where he was supposed to go or what he was supposed to see.

Some crime scene Jedi I am today.

He turned around to see the officer with one arm crossed over his protruding belly tucked in an armpit and the other arm halfcocked extended with a finger pointing to a door.

"Thanks. Sorry," Lars said sheepishly. The man pissed him off, but Lars had a job to do. It was about the job. Most importantly, it was about answers and about making evidence stick when his ass was on the line.

"Dick," the officer said matter-of-factly under his breath.

Lars gave a final look back towards the living room before going downstairs. His probe sought the cluttered tchotchke table and the little ceramic man sitting upon it. Plain as day, that little mustachioed bust was Malverde. And among the other items was a tribute drawing of Juan Soldado, the patron saint of illegal aliens, as well as the boy pilgrim Santo Nino de Atocha, saint of prisoners and travelers. Also on the table was a candle of St. Jude, patron saint of lost causes.

Damn five and dime criminal shrine. Gotta be drug cartel.

Although not fully surprised at his own deduction, the reality of an apparent drug-related massacre of this magnitude being in Chicago was still astonishing, even for an investigator with as many years under his belt as Bjorklund.

And this homeowner was a soldier too? Sweet Jesus.

"Hey, Chief! FBI is here. They want to know who lead investigator is."

Shit.

Chapter 1

TWO YEARS LATER.

With head low and dark eyes darting in all directions Sean Havens fought through the early morning market crowd.

Ah yes, another glorious, muggy morning in the fine Republic of Yemen. Sea, sweat, and shit.

A slide show of filthy places and unpleasant operations played in his head as he shuffled past merchants hawking their wares.

Kenya. Fucking Kenya. We shouldn't have staged from the river. Should have just pulled smoke and bailed.

He navigated the dense waves of crowd as a sea captain reads and drives through the chop. His movement flowed gracefully through the sporadic pace and rhythm of pedestrian traffic in the souk, Arabic for market. But while he moved with purpose, he appeared to walk in a benign manner that blended with the surroundings.

Syria. Same thing. What a nightmare that was.

Havens noticed that an approaching souk patron's eyes appeared locked on something, and then witnessed a very slight nod. Was there something or someone now behind him to worry about? Havens wasn't sure if the look was a true 'tell' or just a misread out of suspicion. Had to be just a case of the jitters. Sean was clean in this country. Regardless, the odds now increased of a tail present. Havens was careful. Beyond careful. That's why they sent him alone when discretion and precision mattered most to his country.

The Sana'a district souk was full of patrons this Friday morning, which made full motion video tracking a bit more difficult from a satellite. All of the patrons seemed connected as they were eagerly exchanging morning greetings, sharing the latest gossip.

Sean Havens, while walking among the Yemenis and cursing his surroundings, was indeed under watch. His master was also at the souk, albeit virtually through cyber feeds, viewing from somewhere safe as an eye in the sky, high above the city out of view, sitting in a government-purchased faux leather chair, drinking filtered bags of Folgers coffee from a stained ceramic NSA anniversary mug.

Far from such air-conditioned comforts, Havens knew what he had to do today. He was to hunt down someone else's master. It would be a bad day for that principal target. For that matter, it would be bad for just about anyone who got in the way of the mission.

Havens' direct orders were not actually to kill. They were never quite that explicit. His commands were to follow his instinct and direct his own missions as appropriate. In this case, he was to create an effect for display as part of a careful orchestration to send this city into strategically planned disarray through a combination of sectarian and tribal civil conflict.

Havens had been unsuccessful in developing a quick turnaround puppet proxy to do the deed in his stead. Unfortunately, the buck stopped with the operator on the ground to make things work. Therefore, Sean was left holding the bag.

In theory, his targeted attack would be enough of a catalyst to cause a surge of social discontent and finger-pointing in the city, which would create opportunities for other follow-up missions, no doubt in the works, but out of Havens' need-to-know.

Stir the pot and kick it over. Let someone else clean up the mess.

Al Qaeda's Yemeni membership was among the largest in the region. The ongoing strife in Yemen had specifically provided Al Qaeda in the Arabian Peninsula, or AQAP, a safe haven for their base of operations. For AQAP, that meant it could plan, recruit, train, and operate with near impunity. The exploitable Yemeni social differences of sect, tribe, and class, combined with weak central rule and ungoverned spaces had fostered a complex enablement system for both separatists and jihadist rebels.

Impunity went so far. Now they had an adversary walking on their terrain bidding to do them harm. Sean Havens was good at strategically starting fights.

This trip to Yemen, for Havens, was about smoking out a few of those high priority targets located in the Sana'a, Abyan, Shawba, and Aden provinces. The end state objective was to stoke more requests for the U.S. to re-establish a greater presence in the country. That allowed the U.S. to have more say in the Yemeni government and could increase support for more military staging to monitor regional activities. Politics as usual, but that was the name of the game.

Havens contemplated again how his makeshift plan would go down. He was compartmentalizing his mind to focus on the mission while keeping vigilant of the prospective tail pursuing him.

It's got to be a superficial wound. Go with a belly slice first. Thin cut. Target grabs his belly instinctively. Shirt soaks with blood fast, stains hands, makes it look worse. That enough?

Havens watched people as they passed, looking them up and down identifying their viable attack points that could be applied to his primary target if he decided to change his mind again on where to strike.

I still need to go with the head. Rapid slash on the forehead. The brow's bright red blood flow is best due to shallow blood vessels. Traumatic image for witnesses. That will be good. Blood flow will also blind and confuse the victim. Complete sensory shock. Overwhelm emotions and stage an effect for the crowd. Good, good.

Satisfied with his choices, Havens continued observing his surroundings with all senses alert.

Why must they eat things in the morning that smell like ass? They should fry up some bacon. That would taste sooo good right now.

A wry smile crossed Havens' lips. Pork here in an overwhelmingly Muslim population was a stupid thought, even for self-talk.

OK, turkey bacon.

He continued along the route that he had reconnoitered the morning before. And the morning before that. He needed to change his route some to see if he was actually being followed. His instincts said he was clear, but his training ordered him to make sure.

Need a crowd opening near a good blocking object so I can spot any bogie on my six.

Most passersby hurried along minding their own business. Havens mirrored the direct smiles and occasional nods of the men walking by.

"Sabah al-khair." Good morning.

"Sabah an-noor." *Right back atcha Ali.*

"Salaam," a particularly toothless individual greeted, upon a casual but innocent bump in the crowd.

Havens replied back with a smile and a nod bringing his hand to his heart, "Wa alaikum assalaam."

He wondered if they were greeting him or actually acknowledging his traditional shilan headwear that, by its symbolic design and colors, signified his family lineage to a local. Something as simple as headcover to feign a particular sect, geographical area, and social status coupled with other carefully selected details and mannerisms gained immediate legitimacy with a glance.

Havens had planned for most every contingency in such a manner. Seconds counted, and he would take all the seconds that he could get in order to buy time to act or react.

He noticed fewer of the younger males wearing headwear since the last time he was here four years earlier. Many were now even wearing western hats.

You hate us but want to wear our hats, he said to himself, spotting a Somali immigrant wearing a Detroit Tigers cap. *Magnum P.I. Sammy style. Nice.*

A group of merchants brushed past, almost knocking Havens into the large vats of spices that lined this area of the souk. He did a casual body check visually and with his hands to see if he had been pickpocketed, shot, or stabbed.

It was instinct.

The flock of jabbering men didn't apologize for the accidental hip check. They appeared to be arguing, but Sean Havens knew this was typical chatter and debate. It was one of the many cultural intelligence nuances he grasped. It was a necessity to understand people he dwelled among or hunted.

Havens stopped to examine some fresh dates on display. He moved around the stall so he could get a look to his rear. A professional tracking him would already have broken the pursuit to feign an innocuous activity. A thug killer would freeze and stand like a deer in headlights.

It was the same the world over. He scanned his rear. No deer behind him.

Coffee would be good right now. Maybe around the next souk market stall there will be a big green Starbucks sign. Nope. Golden arches perhaps? I'd even drink a foofie latte.

What does Christina drink? White chocolate…mocha…non-fat. Skinny. Tastes like dessert. His wife and he had opposite tastes. He preferred bitter. Havens slowed his gait for a moment as he turned.

Is that him? Need a better look.

He turned to another row of stalls and vendors just off the cobblestone path.

Qat was just arriving in one of these areas. Bundles of the basil-like plant were sliding down a makeshift human conveyor belt to be distributed in the market and throughout the town for the day's upcoming social chew.

Havens cut through a line of parked delivery trucks adjacent to the stalls and emerged at a small arms stall displaying Kalashnikovs on the walls. Other obsolete and antiquated Soviet gear, WWII-era British Lee-Enfield bolt-action rifles, German H&K G-3 rifles, and 1970s vintage multinational arms were strewn about the small shop. Boxes of ammunition lay all around. Some weapons were bashed, most scratched, and all seemed to have never been touched in terms of maintenance or serious cleaning by their users.

These guys should clean 'em up and make a mint on eBay as collectibles. Unbelievable how many weapons still flow here without interdiction. As he passed, he looked around the stall out of amused curiosity to see who may have a laptop for enterprising profit.

No computer. Guess no one feels too entrepreneurial around here.

Illicit arms schemes occurred in and around the Aden complex in the south, al-Hudayda along the Red Sea coast, Al-Mukalla in the east and al-Mukha and al-Salif along the Red Sea. It was a hornet's nest of activity but the really bad guys had gone quiet. The United States needed to get things cooking again. Citizens back home didn't understand the world's threats like arms flow and dangerous nation states or religious alliances unless they could graphically visualize the ramifications on their televisions or iPads. That meant seeing blood, death, and street-filled revolts. If mayhem was not apparent, someone like Havens needed to make it more visible.

Havens turned again.

Someone else passed between the trucks.

That someone walked with less purpose than the other workers near the stalls. To Havens this meant a surveillance asset was on him and it probably was not an assassination attempt. It eased him back into relative comfort for just a moment or two more.

Nope, no McDonalds here either…Not that I really want McDonalds…But pancakes…That could be good...That would be real good…Oh, I wish I hadn't thought of that…Change thoughts…Smelly ass old man cooking chai and stinking ass breakfast food? Mmmm…sorghum bread...that actually does smell good…Where was that bread smell coming from?

Where is this asshole? Can't engage my target with a hot tail. No one should be following me. Shit! I don't need this today.

Now distracted, Havens slipped up on his field tradecraft and lifted his left arm to look down at a watch that wasn't there. He knew it was almost time but cursed himself for the novice error.

This whole op's been a shit show from the get-go.

Really? I'm supposed to ID and penetrate the Yemeni underground in a week? Never mind any complex social aspects, personalities, money flow, or ideology not worn on every Yemeni's shirtsleeve. I'll just walk right in to the big black bad guy house on the corner labeled 'No good guys' on the door. Just knock with a shave and a haircut code and say, "Hi guys, playin' cards? Can I play?" Boom!

Never mind the fact that military intel or the other spooks couldn't do it. Just send fuckin' Havens. He's smart. He can do it. He doesn't matter. He's got nothing to lose.

Ridiculous. Got your Saudis funding Yemen's Sunnis, Iran giving cash and guns to Zaydi tribes. Bad horse pick either way you go.

God forbid anyone read what I reported on this over a year ago. We could have actually planned something.

Despite the task in Yemen being against the odds, Sean Havens was a natural at doing it right and getting away with it.

Sean ducked into a dark tight crevice between stacks of boxes and crates to see who was following. He pulled his own engineered device, a half-sized field syringe with a squeeze pump instead of a thumb stick plunger, and a quarter inch needle vice the longer traditional ones of a doctor's shot. It could be pushed at all angles and still deliver the barbiturate mix of Azaperone and Immobilon tranquilizers.

Lights out.

This calls for a little Dexter Morgan spec ops style.

His concentration was shattered for a moment as the inner ear cavity communication sounded off. "Blackswan 6 we lost your movement on overwatch. How copy?"

Havens reached into his ear and pinched enough of the latex with his fingernails to withdraw the device. He dropped it on the ground and crushed it under his foot. He didn't care if it was found. It was French-made. Procured for that very purpose.

Fuck overwatch. Screw the French.

Havens worked alone. No babysitters. No distractions. No mess-ups that could not be fixed quickly.

His tail was draped in traditional garb that cloaked what appeared to be a large frame as he passed less than a minute later. Havens couldn't make much more out without being obvious. Too tough to tell who it could be. As Havens hoped, the tail stopped for a moment to reorient position and target location. The tail started again heading towards Havens' hidden position. The man would pass right by in seconds with any luck.

I need you off my ass for good. No more cat and mouse games.

Syringe in hand, he swiftly grabbed the tail from behind and drove the needle into the man's tricep while squeezing the homemade venom into the meaty arm. It wasn't an ideal injection point but it was close enough for the potent drug cocktail. Havens wrapped his arm under the tail's chin in a half-sleeper hold and twisted his own hip for leverage while he lowered his center of gravity by bending knees and dropping ass as the knockout drug took its effect on the victim.

C'mon, c'mon. Work, dammit! Let it go. Holy shit, you're stronger than I imagined.

The tail tried to struggle and push back but Havens was firmly rooted and stabilized to thwart any resistance.

Ahhh. There you are.

Good night, John-boy!

Chapter 2

As the target went limp, Havens couldn't help the feeling of exposure and uneasiness as he settled the man to the ground gently without raising too much attention from those walking around him.

Three things were just not right in his mind. One, the tricep he dosed was firm and well developed. In this town of scrawny men, firm and developed meant security, military, or foreigner. The guy's back was solid muscle. Two, the back of the man's haircut had been recently squared and his neck had been shaved. That validated his hunch that the dude was military. Three, this guy didn't smell bad. Everyone in Yemen smelled, even Havens, but this dude smelled of French milled hotel soap and deodorant. Foreigner. Maybe Havens' own tribe—an American.

Despite his mind jesting and complaining of the environment, Havens had immediately felt remorseful in another compartment of his brain right after his initial musings about the Arabs left his mind's tongue and touched his inner soul.

His soul still breathed the richness of life amidst the heavy scarring of his professional career. He kind of liked the Middle Eastern market smells and often missed those aromas when he was back CONUS.

Home in Chicago.

And sure, the smell of perspiration, stale dust, heat, and ethnic spices were at times less than appealing, but admittedly, he liked that too. It was different. It was what made the world and people interesting to Sean Havens.

He really didn't feel disdain at all for the Muslims walking around him seeking deals, buying specialty items of the day, or just walking about to see or be seen. He loved them. He understood them. He respected them, their history, and their customs. Their habits both amused and intrigued him.

That was all part of his job—to plan, understand, anticipate, adapt, execute, and vanish. Therefore, he had selected a location for his and his family's residence that was far from the shadow world. Far from military affiliation. Far from black helicopters and black SUVs carrying sunglass-adorned suits with bulging side masses from the artillery they carried to protect themselves and their cargo.

Havens exited from one of the little souk "mall" areas back to the street. Mopeds, motorcycles, bicycles, and wheelbarrows weaved in and out of the ethnically diverse crowd. The noise of the small engines and vehicles beeping were particularly annoying on this day.

There he is. Havens spoke to himself in Arabic to shift back in character should expressive thoughts enter his head and reflexively exit his mouth.

Get your head in the game, Havens. Let's make sure.

OPSEC to men like Havens is about paying attention and being aware of the surroundings. It was routine, but as necessary as a pilot's pre-flight check.

Is anyone with him today? This is a wide open area. Get him before he goes back into these catacombs.

Random distracting thoughts would now have to wait.

Game time.

Deftly, Havens reached past his lightweight traditional Yemeni shirt and embroidered futa skirt.

His hand moved across his body like a cat stalking an unaware robin probing for worms in the quiet of a summer morning.

His grasp was now nearing a not so ceremonially edge-honed jambiyyal dagger tucked at the waist belt. His edge was personally honed to be razor sharp. He would have preferred having his Emerson CQC-7 blade, but that would be a clear tell to any observer.

He closed the distance.

Havens took another panoramic view of his surroundings for potential threats. His mind rapidly processed with hyper-vigilance a mentally engrained checklist of feasible sensory alarms.

Is anything out of the ordinary?

Is anyone else watching me?

Is anything blocking my way of escape?

Am I making any assumptions?

Am I going to get caught?

Am I going to get dead?

Assured that his situation was clear or at least manageable, he re-gripped the ivory handle of the knife while simultaneously setting a fabric basketball pick with his left hand and shirt bottom to conceal the weapon's withdrawal from its decorated scabbard.

Something stood out in his periphery.

His senses signaled something was off. *Where?*

What the hell? Where did this come from?

Havens froze mid-stride.

Dammit!

A bead of sweat rolled down his inner arm. His lip tasted of salt. His grip hardened around the knife handle. He started to count the men.

Outnumbered as usual, Havens.

Let's do this.

Chapter 3

Back home on another continent, the Chicago Police Department was convinced that fifteen-year-old Maggie Havens had been lured earlier in the day by an internet predator to the spot where she was sexually assaulted.

They had told Maggie's mother, Christina, that the man representing himself on the social website was not likely the sixteen-year-old misunderstood music lover and humane society volunteer that had been represented in online posts. It was much more likely that this individual was in his mid-twenties or thirties, based on Maggie's description of her attacker to the responding officer.

What troubled the police, and now both Maggie and Christina, were the threatening texts she was receiving on her cell phone, having been instructed prior by the assailant to "not fucking talk to no fucking cops or I will cut you from ear to ear."

Further troubling was the sophisticated layering of cutout communications from IP addresses to cell phones that blocked the police from identifying and tracking the messages and internet traffic history. Techno geek rapist, maybe, but the threats seemed much more aggressive than the typical profile.

The police did not share this aspect with Mrs. Havens, but were consulting a few department experts since this no longer seemed to match the MO of a typical perv, power rapist, or angst-filled teen.

Maggie had initially convinced herself that she could keep the incident to herself, more frightened of her parents, who would no doubt kill her for meeting someone that she neither knew nor had permission to meet.

She continuously processed the ordeal while stumbling home sobbing. She started to get light-headed. It was so bright out. She squinted her swollen eyelids. Rubbing them caused more irritation from the salt residue of dried tears.

Everything hurt so much.

Her head throbbed, her legs felt weak, and she felt her hands get cold and clammy.

She knew she was going to faint and tried to fall on the grass.

A cyclist had stopped, immediately dialing 911. The good Samaritan had inadvertently exasperated the situation as soon as the police had arrived.

A watcher had notified the rapist who sent the text immediately.

U FUKD UP!

C U SOON BICH

While the rape kit and prints were being analyzed, debate ensued among a group of officers sitting on their desks in a traditional morning huddle. They couldn't wrap their head around whether this was just an internet geek who wasn't getting any and needed to prey on a teen or something more, as others added their two cents in the station's makeshift verbal circle jerk.

"I bet we find out it was the Albanians."

"No way. They would have taken her for prostitution or cut her. I saw that movie. CIA dad comes to the rescue."

"Yeah, it was on that show *Castle* too."

"Dude, it's on every show where a girl gets kidnapped. They always blame Albanians now. What else? Something good."

"Does she have a boyfriend or history of meeting up with guys on the internet?"

"She could be one of those Chris Mathews lures where he comes out of the pantry and the dude shits his pants when he sees the cameras."

"Yeah, I've seen that. Did you see that school teacher who got pinched? I keep waiting to hear how many of those guys blow their heads off or find a rope in a closet."

"Guys, she is a sixteen-year-old girl who the mom says keeps to the books."

"Well, you know those quiet types."

"You keep quiet if you have nothing constructive to add."

"Then it must be like a Russian mafia thug."

"Enough with that shit."

"Wait. Let's see where he goes. Go on…"

"Don't they have hackers and a network of soldiers who do this?"

"Homeland Security says the Iranians can do the same thing."

"Maybe it was someone who the girl double crossed or her parents. Did they have gambling debt? Any enemies?"

"Where was the dad?"

"His wife said he is away on business and is still traveling on the road between…let me see here. She claims he is in Slovenia and Greece."

"See, I told you it could be the Albanians. Maybe the dad is involved with them in his business. Is anyone checking on that?"

"Wait, I didn't think Albanians lived in Greece."

"They don't, idiot. They live in Albania."

"Maybe they are sex slaves."

"Not the kind of Albanians we are talking about and why would the dad be doing business with human traffickers?"

"So what does that have to do with Greece?"

"Oy vey, shut the hell up. You make my head hurt. Where did you say you went to school?"

"Western Illinois. What's the big deal?"

"Somebody get me a map."

"You don't know where Western is?"

"No, dumbass, a global map. Never mind, the dad doesn't work for the Albanians, the Greeks, or the friggin' Russians. He works for a consulting company doing some freakin' MBA business stuff."

"Dude, Western sucks. No wonder you don't know geography."

"They are solid for Criminal Justice."

"Oh, yeah, I can see that. How you doing on this case?"

"Bite me!"

"What does the mom do?"

"I'll tell you what the mom does…" The officer looked down to his crotch nodding.

"Puleeze. Don't waste my time."

"She is a therapist."

"Oh, we should check that out. Maybe one of her whacked out or pissed off patients did it."

"She is a speech therapist for little kids, not a shrink."

"Thhhwelll."

"Dude, that ain't cool. That's like mocking a kid."

"Thorrry," another officer chimed in, but was met with a middle finger.

"Dude, really. You can't mock disabled kids like that. It's like the same rule that you can't call them retarded."

"Dude, way uncool. My kid goes to speech."

"Sorry."

"Tell you one thing, whoever it is—Albanians, Russians, Hells Angels, friggin' Stone Cold Steve Austin, or an army of Bruce Lee's—I'd kill whoever touched my daughter."

A number of officers nodded in their first agreement of the morning.

"OK, so we know that Mr. Daddy Havens is probably a pussy with no enemies who leaves his family to make shitty companies in shitty countries do business better in some emerging market."

"That's what it sounds like."

"What else have we got for possibilities?"

The officers looked around at each other then down to their shoes as if the answers would be looking up at them.

"LT's coming ladies. Let's get to work."

"Hey, Daniels. Come here," the lieutenant called to an officer. "Close the door when you come in. There's more. I think I know this dude. And if it's the guy I am thinking of, it may be worse than we thought."

Chapter 4

Completely unaware of his daughter's recent assault thousands of miles away, Sean Havens stopped moving in the Yemeni souk.

Like a tailor of men, Havens worked in the rich fabric of socio-economic human systems and their exploitation. He operated at or below the classified Special Access Program level to remove oversight scrutiny, meaning he had intel clout. Clout that was supposed to keep him informed of anything and everything he should know while in the field.

He didn't know about these men now in front of him, but he should have.

Havens watched with concern as two over-muscled Caucasian men were trying, but failing to contain their giggling and tomfoolery as they stole various small goods from the vendor tables and hanging rods.

For as much as they stuck out among the native crowd, surely people would be watching them closely. Unless, of course, they were regulars in the area.

Havens thought it odd that contractor presence did not come up in the intel reports he had received or even during the surveillance of the area that he had personally conducted for the past week.

He watched as one man would block the other from view while blabbering to the market hawker. For being so boisterously silent, if there is such a description, he was impressed that they were able to pull it off…

Nope. Havens noticed some men advancing towards the petty thieves. He could see that, while in plain clothes, the local men were armed authorities.

Someone's in trouble. Oh, this day sucks.

Havens sized up the unwitting contractors in their 5.11 military cargo pants and black performance t-shirts. In one man's hand was an out of place local artisan bag, likely with stashed stolen trinkets.

Did the storeowners just ignore them as if they were bullies coming through sweeping milk money off weaker students' desks?

They appeared to be young former Marines or Army Rangers who had been in Iraq or Afghanistan but had now signed up as hired guns, enticed by private military corporations' money, over re-enlisting. Havens didn't fault their choice; he faulted their immaturity and current behavior. They had forgotten that they were soldiers and should still be acting like professional warriors. It would be worse if they just didn't care. Clearly they were drunk, but at this time in the morning were they just starting or finishing? And where were they partying, and what commercial contracting outfit was running the risks of giving their guys booze here in Yemen without better monitoring?

Havens knew they were private contractors, but with whom and for whom, he did not know. Nor did he care.

He did care about why they were off the reservation this morning screwing up his plans. He had carefully assessed where military, police, contractors, etc. would and could be that would potentially be in his path on that day. And why were these fools armed? An incident like this would end badly, especially if the contractors shot someone.

More anger towards the West. Just what we need.

Arresting or killing some wayward soldiers violating local laws and cultural codes could be unifying for a people who did not want armed foreigners in their midst. That was not what Havens had in mind. That did not fit his morning plans. He did not want this place unified.

Perhaps the locals were waiting for just the right excuse.

"Hmmm. Maybe this is my lucky day," Havens said to himself, now operationally going mobile again.

Luck is what happens when preparedness meets opportunity, Havens often said, and he was about to seize this opportunity as it unfolded before his eyes.

Havens reached into his own artisan's bag. He discretely extracted an Israeli Defense Forces stun grenade and eyed a spot to pitch it. Havens gave a quick tug of the primary pull ring and tossed it towards an alleyway that was devoid of people.

He threw another armed stun grenade backhand ideally to go just further than the first, but heard a small crash as opposed to the combo thud and tumble sound he was expecting.

"Allahu Akbar!" he shouted hoping to draw upon the fear of a martyr suicide bomber or rebel attack.

Heads abruptly turned towards the call. Others blindly dove for cover just before the detonating flash-bang blasted the marketplace.

In four great strides Havens withdrew his dagger, and through a full economy of motion cut one arching slash up and across the first contractor's thigh, then up the torso across the cheek and over to the second contractor across the forehead flowing in the motion down across the contractor's lower thigh above the knee before continuing the circular motion and then hammering the knife down to the first contractor's boot just below the laces and before the potential steel toe.

Nice boots. New Oakley ¾-height assault. Very nice, you fucking punk. May as well be walking around with 'Death From Above' Ranger t-shirts, dip cans in your back pocket, infantry belt buckles, and damn cowboy boots. Way to blend in. Clearly not ex-Special Forces.

The contractors let out screams, unheard during the second grenade detonation, as Havens' ceremonial knife parted flesh and found bone at an angle and level of pressure that would scar but not severely damage long term.

Havens was lightning fast with fluid motion, like an artist painting a grand circular brushstroke across a six-foot canvas. The artisan operator shifted compression and angle as he neared arterial threats and eyes.

Now, as he was in a low crouch having completed the slashing superficial circle of wound, his right leg sweep kicked the second contractor's left leg just to the side of the knee but with only enough force to damage cartilage and tendon as opposed to breaking the bone.

As the first contractor was reaching down towards Havens, he snapped up the knife torpedoing upwards from the stabbed foot that was starting to bleed through the tan mesh of the Oakley.

Havens struck the lower jaw of the contractor with the butt of the knife causing the man's head to snap back and his body crumbled from underneath.

The contractors would be in the infirmary for the next few weeks, but at least they would be out of the picture and do no further damage in this country.

Havens tried to stay in some mental character while attacking his fellow countrymen, however stupid and juvenile they were. He recognized that this attack was rather unconventional even for his taste, but he was going for effect and these oafs were perfect scapegoats at the perfect time. Not his greatest performance, but perhaps enough to get a little something going and salvage his outing. It might even save their lives. Hopefully, it would save his.

As Sean Havens spun towards the previously approaching authorities, he noticed they were now confined by a crowd of people rushing to gawk and put out a fire that had caught a shanty stall ablaze from the grenade's flame and high heat detonation. The authorities were still trying to part the crowd and break free towards his position.

Oops, didn't mean to toast that shop. Looks like you guys are jammed up for now while I scoot. Exit stage left.

Havens turned his attention back to the contractors. As they were dazed and a little slow on the draw from Havens' shock and awe combination, Havens directed a low volume but audible statement to the men, delivering perhaps the greatest shock yet to their system.

"Sorry, dudes, but you were in the wrong place. Don't make a move. Believe it or not I just saved your lives. Sorry about your new boots."

In the bloody mess, the whites of their surprised eyes looked almost cartoonlike to Havens, popping out. *Aooga!* sounded in his head as Havens recalled the familiar sound that accompanied shocked animated Saturday morning characters with their eyes shooting out of their heads in astonishment.

Pull smoke, Havens. Time to bail.

Havens started to make an exit dash towards an adjacent alley when he literally ran into his originally intended mark.

Still moving with conviction and thinking in rapid adaptability mode, Havens said quickly in Yemeni Arabic, "Help these men," and he handed his target the bloodied knife while wiping his bloodied hand on the mark's shirt.

The mark, stunned, stood with his arms now widening open in utter confusion but nonetheless took steps towards the men just a few feet away.

Another man from the crowd pointed to the mark and yelled out to others, "That man. There. He has stabbed those men."

The crowd shouted at the authorities now making their way out of the crowd into the space of the scene with weapons drawn.

"This man has tried to kill us all with his bombs. He is Aulaq! He has stabbed them. Shoot him!"

Like good public servants in a hostile crowd, despite knowing this man was innocent, they opened fire to the demand and jeers of the crowd. On the other hand, he did look like he was from the Aulaq tribe who was granting safe haven to AQAP mujahideen.

The report to their superiors would be of a crazed jihadist attacking the capital's market in a separatist rebel act, and despite a threat to their own lives, they confronted the man and were forced to kill him.

They would be heroes.

Others could then start rounding up the usual suspects and engage the military to head to the Aulaqs.

As the innocent mark fell back riddled with bullet holes, he dropped the knife and looked up to the fine wisps of clouds, still not comprehending what happened before he died.

Havens felt some remorse for the man who was supposed to be scared, not killed. Scared was the plan. Havens shrugged and continued on his way.

Do I smell pancakes?

Ugh, need to see what is up at home too. Hope it isn't the air conditioner or something expensive like that. I wanted to buy that BMW SUV for Christina. So close.

Bet she keeps calling because I left a dirty coffee cup and sandwich in the basement that started to smell. Crap, I promised I would try harder to clean up.

Did I pay the bills before I left or are they still on my desk? Shit.

Take your pick, Sean; it ain't going to be pretty.

Chapter 5

Havens got to the safe house with minimal street interactions. He cut into the dank alleyway between earth toned brick buildings tightly nestled together. A slight glimpse of a figure in a black burka caught his eye. He entered the rustic wooden side door. The loud creak had been welcome days before as an economical anti-personnel warning. He could hear the creaking from his apartment above. The noise was a vulnerability now that he was unsure if someone knew of his temporary lair.

He paused in the hot musty entryway at the bottom of the staircase to get a sense of his environment.

The sounds and smells were the same at this point.

Havens climbed the old stairs slowly and opened the door to the apartments' shared hallway. A dusty long handloomed rug lined the hallway with numerous small unlit sconces mounted along the wall. The trapped heat in the hall burned his lungs. Everything appeared to be in place. His tradecraft counter-penetration traps and tells along the route and around his door remained untouched. Havens looked down the hall again and seeing that all was clear he pulled out a small ultraviolet light. He shone it up to the overhead panel that opened to a small segment of the rooftop. The panel's orientation and screw head positions were designated with an ultraviolet marker. No one had entered from this point either. It appeared safe to enter his apartment. After a quick glance around the inside, it was the first good thing of the morning.

Havens walked to the window for a small breath of any fresh airflow. He peered from a crack in the closed window coverings first. The surrounding outside area seemed relatively calm. Normal traffic, normal loitering, normal patterns of life for this third world country. It appeared safe to open the window and curtains a bit. Maybe he would get a slight breeze. Doubtful, but he hoped.

He would wait a few hours to unwind, change, and get out of Dodge. Now was an opportune time to dial his wife's dedicated throw away mobile phone.

Sean Havens' tradecraft was exceptional for a man who was not officially trained in the same CIA Farm-type field tradecraft that stood out to other operators and foreign intelligence services. He had more of the old school spycraft traits of Cold War days over today's more tactical operators. Like other skilled operators with years of tradecraft and kinetic targeting experience in country, Havens' mind was honed. His senses alert. His emotional intelligence could be as one with his surroundings. But on this temporary duty assignment his wife kept calling, and that above all things was really what was irritating him and causing such distraction in his day.

Maybe his tradecraft was not so exceptional carrying a personal mobile phone on a field operation that could reach his wife's location directly, but he was contracting now, and his wife was really being a pain in the ass about this trip. To a degree he was able to incorporate this into his cover. It was real life. Not a poorly fabricated cover legend secured to be vetted only one layer deep and glaringly sterile to anyone with an ounce of counterintelligence experience.

Havens couldn't put his finger on the situation. His marriage was solid—or as solid as it can be for those deploying with a moment's notice while keeping secrets at all time. His daughter was not giving him the problems that were forecasted to him about having a teenager. Everyone in the small family of three knew the routine when he traveled and could fend for themselves. The family was in a domestic battle rhythm that was working, contrary to the lives of similar men and their families in this line of work.

Still, he wondered why his wife was so irritable and on edge. Then again, when he was last in Somalia running a discrete operation, his wife was constantly trying to get in touch when their refrigerator had been moved for a counter top repair. The move subsequently broke the water coil that leaked onto custom Brazilian hardwood floors which had to be torn up along with the subfloor and drywall ceiling in the basement—all while he was away. She blamed him for not being there to handle the situation. After all, she had a job too, a house to take care of, and everything else.

Life doesn't just stop for the family when Dad is away going after bad guys playing David Bourne all around the world, or at least that was how Christina once described it. He corrected her saying, "Jason Bourne is the operator, and David Webb was Bourne's real name." He should have shut up. He was right, but she defeated him with a look regardless.

Sean found it all so frustrating. It was as if he was expected to have a list of home improvement contractors and plumbers in his back pocket while staying in a filthy safe house in a hostile country trying not to get killed. The rant was always the same, adding in having to stay at a safe house that some shitty young DC case officer who couldn't get promoted or screwed up in clandestine service probably set up for him. Did she think he was hunkered down at a fancy Westin with internet service at his fingertips after his day stopped at 5PM? Did she really think he could just make all the domestic calls from his plush hotel suite to fix the warped floors while he had room service bring in a French dip with a liter of seemingly complimentary water that would cost $7 on the checkout bill? Maybe he would just have to skip the OnDemand movie in the room tonight. What the hell did people think while they were tucked away in bed, safe from the real world?

With the tirade ending there, she would calmly say, "If you are so worried about not getting killed and living in unsafe environments, maybe you should stay with us to ensure we are safe and taken care of. Maybe your priorities should be reviewed. Why don't you think a bit about that?"

When the arguments happened at home, she would then walk away to do something upstairs knowing there was nothing else he could say. He, in turn, would retreat down to the man cave where he could pour himself a slow stream Guinness in a pint glass.

In Havens' view, all would be right again in the world for just a moment in time and then he would go up and apologize.

Shit, I forgot to return the Red Box flick before I left. Now a one dollar movie that sucked anyway just cost me ten. Bet that's what this is all about.

All right, Sean, let's get this over with.

Sean's wife, Christina, answered on the first ring with the requisite "Hello?"

He noticed the subtleties in tone, volume, and intonation. Whether an operator or an attuned husband, her voice sounded off. *Less cheery. Less multi-tasked.* She was waiting for a call. *Apprehensive.* His mind processed everything said and not said. Every pause, every enunciated word.

"Hey, Christina, what's up babe?"

"Where have you been?" her speech rose. Intensity was increasing. "You need to get home now. Right now! Sean, didn't you get my messages? Where were you? I have been texting and calling you for two days. What the hell is wrong with you? Don't you check messages or carry your phone? What's the purpose of the phone if I can't reach you?"

His wife started crying, escalating into a complete breakdown of emotion.

This was not normal. He had misjudged this one.

Havens ruled out the sandwich in the basement and floor guys. He knew this was dialed up a few notches on the drama meter and was fearful to hear what this was going to be. This was code orange for sure. Swearing, yes. Blubbering, never.

"What's going on? Why are you so out of control? Just relax. Talk to me." He tried using some of the same techniques his wife used to help him cope back to reality when operational stress returned home with him like a shadow.

"You relax!" She screamed. "Your daughter has been raped and is now being stalked by the psycho that did it! Don't tell me to get control! You...f...fucking…asshole!" Christina was full out sobbing now.

Havens' stomach had dropped. His throat was tightening. He felt a bit out of body and light-headed. He found himself biting his lip near to the point of pain.

The best he could muster was, "What?"

"She was raped. She was raped, Sean. Raped! You got it now? Raped while you are running around who knows the hell where. Raped and now this son of a bitch is after her because we talked to the police."

She paused, but he didn't know what to say. "Where were you, Sean? Where *are* you? You better fix your priorities back to us right away. Don't give me any mission bullshit either."

"OK, OK, OK, I am so sorry." Tears welled in his eyes. "Can you please tell me is she OK? What happened? Who is after her? I assume that if they are still after her she is OK?"

Christina knew Havens' daughter was everything to him. Despite their personalities being so different, there was the undeniable bond between father and daughter, and this was no exception. Her empathy for her husband's emotions now was the only thing that settled her. She had had time to process this all and realized the shock that was hitting him. She would be there for him now. It was his turn to absorb it all and deal with the feelings of helplessness, sorrow, and guilt.

Ever since Maggie was born, Havens had his daughter in the jogging stroller all along the lakefront and anything else with a path or pavement. He would push her in the stroller to the store, to restaurants for evening carryout, and take her to sports events she was too young to understand or care about. Christina knew her husband was broken now and her anger quickly turned to calmly informing him and assuring him of her improving condition.

She knew his mind was reeling and detailed what the police had shared.

She expressed their current state of concern with the text threat that they had received. The threat element broke Havens out of his helpless trance. He watched a spider crawling up the cracked plaster wall. He could hear his wife's voice but didn't know what she was saying. His daughter was hurt. Hurt by another man.

"Sean, we need you home right now. When can you be home? Get those people to get you home now. I know you will do whatever you can, but get home now."

Still in utter shock, Havens assured his wife he would start his journey back immediately and would keep her posted. He was concerned that the police were not keeping a closer eye on his family, but evidently their concern did not warrant a protective detail. It occurred to him that in the entire special mission unit and intel entities' OPSEC they didn't consider the families left behind while the husband was away.

Havens would make a few calls and get his own protective detail over to the house. He would call some hunters to get started on the rapist. His fears turned to fury. Sean Havens flipped the switch back from father to hunter and the predator would become the prey.

I am going to turn the whole motherfucking world over on you. You're dead. You're fucking dead! I will fucking rip you apart. Kick in your door and fucking tear you up, motherfucker.

Havens dialed another number. The line picked up.

"Get me out of here NOW!"

Chapter 6

Havens waited alone with his thoughts, fears, and guilt for about a minute before he broke out paper and a pen and started outlining what Christina had shared with him.

Three hours had passed before there was a knock at the door. In that time he had detailed the scenarios by which he could kill the rapist and lend plausible deniability to himself. It was a good plan. He just needed to learn who did it or get a whiff of a trial. The rest could be augmented and modified on the fly.

The original exfiltration plan was to use the same false persona cover legend as when he entered the country from Saudi Arabia to Yemen, but now departing from the new Sana'a International Airport in Yemen. The logistics plan would preserve continuity of country customs entry and departures. It would also harden his cover for his next trip to the region, should one be required.

Havens, holding an 18 round Russian 9mm OTs-27 Berdysh pistol as he approached the knocking, coughed twice out loud and uttered, "Two seconds, please." It was audible enough to be heard on the other side of the door, but while doing so he was crouched low and to the side of the door in the event he was blasted by a bullet assault from the hallway from an uninvited party anticipating someone approaching the door.

"I am sorry, sir, but there is no tour today," the Arabic reply stated in response to the cough.

Havens called out to the closed door. "Can you accommodate me for next week?"

"Certainly, sir, but perhaps we can discuss the details for a different tour activity."

Havens opened the door to see a thirty-something-year-old light-skinned Ethiopian man standing before him in local apparel. Sean's gaze met the Ethiopian and gestured to his left and right with his eyeballs. When he received a negative nod, Sean felt things were clear and summoned his guest to come in.

Havens extended his hand to the Ethiopian, "You are not quite what I expected. I am Mick."

The Ethiopian shook it vigorously. "Not expecting? What did'ja expect…uh, Mick, a white dude in a pin stripe suit and bowler hat with a big booty bitch on each arm?"

"Whoa," Havens offered a smile, "Where are you from? You're American."

The Ethiopian, who introduced himself as John, laughed. "Yeah, I'm Americano. I get that a lot. From DC originally. Moved to Maryland later, came back to DC area, went to school at Georgetown. That's the story and that's all you get. I'm just the bridge between you and my guy."

"Understood."

John threw a twined cloth package on the small dining table, which Havens knew would be a new set of clothes.

Still amused, Havens was ready to transition from personal to business. He had things to do. "Well shit, had me fooled."

"Yeah, that's the point, right?" John looked around the room. He started walking towards the bedroom where local news radio was playing from somewhere in the back to drown out and confound potential audio surveillance.

"Whad'ya have for me?" Havens was anxious to get on his way. He knew John was just doing a cursory check and paid it no mind.

John called back, "I have a ticket, few credit cards, passport…"

"Whoa, buddy. Passport? I don't need one of them." Havens cut John off and grabbed the small leather fanny pack that John had thrown on the clothes package.

Havens shook his head in utter disbelief. "No way. No frickin' way. What are you guys thinking? A black passport? You are handing me an official diplomatic passport? How did you get this so quickly and with the name of someone I have never heard of and one that singles me out as official? I have a blue regular guy passport that I am using. Are you kidding me?"

Havens started to pace the room. He started flipping through the passport that typically indicates those traveling for strictly diplomatic purposes and who hold diplomatic immunity. A nicety, but not for those who are not looking for scrutiny and identification as U.S. government.

"This passport you got here is even brand new. It cracks when I open it. Thread is tight. No stamps. Cover isn't creased from any use. It is dated last year. Where did you get this and who the hell put this shitty ass kit together for me? I trust you have nothing under organizational cover or a cover organization?"

"Say, Mick, may want to not shout this to the whole country if you are so worried about being clean. I'm just sayin'."

Disregarding the warning, Havens continued his rant. "If I am a traveling government official with regional diplomatic activity in this area, do you really think I never traveled anywhere before as it shows on this flippin' brand spanking new passport? God forbid I encounter biometric scrutiny!" He threw down the passport. "What the fuck?"

John backed up, raising his hands defensively. "Not me, man. I am just delivering the goods. One of your dudes at the blue building downtown here gave it to me to give to you. So don't bring your shit on my shoes."

"Blue building? What blue building?"

"Yeah, right. You know, where all you…you…c'mon, you know…your kind comes when they are in Yemen for action. I ain't a shooter, man. I street lurk, but ain't no hunter killer. I just stop by the blue building if I have to drop something off or get a kit to stash at a house so you snake eaters have their toys 'n shit. You really don't know?"

"John, look. I never heard of a blue building. To the best of my knowledge there are no shooters in some place I don't know about. If you are in the game you know I can't play this hand unless

I know who this guy is, what he does, why he is supposedly here, where he entered the country from and when, does he have a physical and digital or virtual footprint. I could get burned real quick."

"Look man, I feel ya. Here is the bottom line from where I am standing. There is a ticket, a passport, some cash, and probably some other stuff. We're understaffed here at this station. Sometimes the dudes that come in here to help are just contractors or old military dudes with the right tickets punched for clearance. They ain't smart, Mick. They just cleared. Doesn't mean they know what they are doing just because they were lucky enough to have a full scope lifestyle and CI poly, but chances are this will get you seventy-five percent of the way. Up to you to fake the rest. They train us Farm chickens like that. You do know the Farm?"

Not needing to be convinced and not willing to indulge the snarky question, Havens was already trying to solve the problem. "Where is this blue building? I will take care of things."

John started backing up towards the door, and with his hand on the knob said, "Yeah, right. Man, if you don't know where the blue building is, you ain't supposed to know where the blue building is. It ain't even really blue. Anyway, I said too much, so forget I said that. See ya, wouldn't wanna be ya. Write your congressman and get some funds appropriated if you don't like what's going on here in the Yem. Continuing resolution just boinked you in the ass, Pops. Don't miss your flight. Gotta go. Leave your shit here and someone will come get it after you leave," John's voice slowed and trailed while now eyeing the pistol Havens was tucking in his waistband.

With that, John exited the room to go back to the streets he worked each day for the intelligence community. Low man on the totem pole caught shit from all sides. Today was just another day. He thought about having a qat chew, but now he had one more task before Havens could leave town. He'd have to move quickly. A text message would save time, but it would also leave a trail. No trails.

Fuckin' cowboy shooters. How can you not know the blue building if you are a hardcore. All the hardcore ones go there. Shit, they own the night here.

As soon as John left, Havens briskly walked the room as if in search of something, hands on hips with a constantly shaking head. The risky cover legend was compounding the stress. Havens wanted to kill someone but knew John had done his part and was not at fault. John was right. He was trained to adapt and make the best of it. Carry on. He never got rattled. But with today's news about Maggie, he was.

Havens opened the ticket, figuring he had a better than a fifty-fifty chance of pulling this ruse off. He had to get home as fast as he could. No time to bitch and moan.

Four more hours before his flight left.

Havens scanned the ticket, hoping that he would see a lucky mid-point transit that could give him some hope of passing checkpoints and the scrutiny of his background.

C'mon Dubai, c'mon Dubai.

His gaze stopped on the destination.

Kuwait. Well, that's going to have to work.

Chapter 7

Havens called Christina again to inform her of his basic itinerary and that he was expected to be home in two days. It was the best he could do and she never challenged it. She knew her husband would pull out all the stops to get home as soon as possible.

He asked to speak to his daughter. Although she was sitting in the other room just socializing on her computer, his only child refused to talk to him.

"Give Maggie her time," Christina had told a disappointed Sean. "She has been through a lot, and in fairness to her, you were not here when she really could have used you. We have to rethink this whole travel thing while she is still with us at home. I'm not throwing this in your face. It's just what we are dealing with."

"I wish I had woken her before I left. I don't even think I kissed her goodbye."

"That makes two of us you neglected to kiss goodbye."

"Shit. Sorry. Well, at least you're talking to me."

"This time. Just leave her be for now. You are making it more about you than her."

Sean was hurt, but understood. In truth, he really didn't have anything to say to the poor girl. He was ashamed that he had let her down and was simply trying to extend some sort of olive branch. The travel thing came up again. He would have to make some changes again for both of his ladies. If Christina was asking this of him, he knew it was important. She was a more than fair wife and would not impose undue demands unless she really needed his help. He would oblige her request without another thought. They were a team although she shouldered the brunt of the responsibilities, and he recognized this.

His daughter received the message loud and clear too. While she refused to get on the phone and put up her distant angry face for her mom, she was typing on her Facebook wall, "My dad is coming home tomorrow :) I am so happy."

Somewhere in cyberspace, the message was received on another computer's pop-up display. The user opened a software program with secure instant messaging capabilities. He clicked on one of the usernames and typed, "HE'S ON HIS WAY."

Christina had informed her husband that the police were now downplaying the threats. They believed the texts were likely just a time saver for the rapist to stall any investigation and an attempt to hush his victim. There had been no other text messages, threats, or indications of further aggression. It was an eerie but welcome calm. The police stated that they would continue the rape investigation. The local television stations even showed a three-minute feature story on the attack during the evening news with a sketch and a hotline number for any information that was potentially available on the attacker.

Christina had said the lack of additional threats had calmed her down some and the police's rationale of why a rapist would have made such a threat now made more sense. She told her husband that they should discuss it when he got home and to hold off on sending his own band of merry men to the house. "I don't want a bunch of your friends here, Sean. I want you."

Christina loved her husband and respected his work, but he was a bit different from some of the other men that he associated with. She had heard that those sorts of men were called "rough men" in some circles. Not her circles. But it made sense. Most of the guys were not big muscular Stallone or Schwarzenegger types. They are more like that Jason Statham guy, she'd think to herself. They were nice, quiet, and good looking, but they had an edge. A rough edge specifically.

They were respectful to her but struck her as having a certain indiscernible look. A look about them and a way they would actually look at her. The look was not an uncomfortable sexual look like one she would receive from admiring eyes on the street. These men were looking at her or rather inside of her with more of an introspective probing. Sometimes she felt as though they were cyborgs constantly scanning, assessing, and ready to react or attack at a moment's notice. They reminded her of a big dog you trust but would never leave unattended near a child, and yet the dog would probably save the child's life in a moment of danger.

Then when the men would go downstairs to the man cave, she could hear their laughs, chiding, and camaraderie that could only be described as a fraternity or, in some cases, a family bloodline.

As the night would go on, the laughing would get louder, the empty bottles would clank more often in the garbage can, the profanity would increase, then hush down in a constant flow of party party shhh shhh party party shhhh.

By two in the morning, they would be gone.

And oddly, so would all the trash. It struck her on more than one occasion that when Sean would hand a man a beer, they would take it from the bottle cap, slide it into their own coozie, open the top and put the cap in their pocket. It was as if they never wanted to touch the bottle or leave them behind. It would have been easier if they just wore gloves.

She never asked her husband much about it as it was indeed a rarity for him to have these men over. Her husband was not really like them. Most had military training. He did not. Not formally. Not that she knew of. She knew he had been to a number of trainings over the years that could extend beyond a week but never more than two.

Sean didn't have that same look either. He was much more casual and had much more levity about him. He didn't have that hawkish look for prey; he had a constant look as if he wanted to make a new friend. Anywhere the Havenses would go as a couple, he could chat someone up. Weddings, restaurants, taxi cabs, Sean was chatting away. He was interesting to others and yet exuded that he was more interested in others and in their interests. She liked that about him, knowing that really he was an introvert.

Every now and then Sean would even surprise her as she eavesdropped on the conversations he was having outside of her likely earshot. He would throw out some foreign language phrases to the person he was speaking with—often of a foreign heritage. When she asked him about it, he would reply it was just a different type of Arabic but basically the same. She was a speech therapist and had an ear for subtleties in language. It was not always just a different Arabic dialect. Sean knew stuff that he didn't share with his wife, and she was OK with that but never gave him too long of a leash.

He said that he was more of an intelligence analyst, who would help the military on some out-of-the-box plans and stuff, or so he would describe to her when he could, so she let him keep his little secrets so he could play James Bond with the big military boys.

He was her little Cliff Clavin know-it-all geek. A geek that was trim and chiseled with lean muscle mass—athletic but not brawn. Even his "martial arts training," as he would call it, didn't seem like the tough guy type. She would sometimes tease him when a Mixed Martial Arts commercial would come on the television.

"Sean, isn't that what you do, oh, no sorry your cage matches are with cranes and tigers and snakes. Do you guys hissss and grrrr when you make animal hands? Do they turn out the lights so you can make shadow characters?"

She would start to giggle, mocking his Kung Fu. Some days he would give her a protective glare, defending his hobby. Other times he would play along and start to go after her. Sometimes when he would come up from the man cave she would jump out at him in a karate stance and caw like a crow with hand pincers or meow like a cat and gesture slapping a pretend air toy. She would playfully slap at his face.

"C'mon toughie. Let's see what you've got."

Of course, there was that time when he actually did do some crazy whirlwind move that ended up crossing her arms, twisting her around, and putting her on her back with him bracing her fall before she knew what had happened. She was a bit taken aback. Not sure if she was scared or impressed. Maybe there was something behind that quiet, friendly husband of hers. Soft power, she thought to herself as he gently kissed her lips and released her wrists.

But despite that one incident she knew the real action heroes in the basement left when the drinking was done. They would cut through the shadows to their cars, usually pickup trucks and rental SUVs. She assumed they drove or flew back to their lairs with their bags of empty bottles and trash, while her husband came up to bed drunker than he should be at that age.

He probably had a harder time keeping up with his 'bubbas' who didn't have so much family baggage. Although she was secure in herself that Sean never saw his family as baggage. He was genuinely happy to be at home.

And on those nights that he would stumble up the stairs after a night with the boys, she would kiss his forehead and let him snore it off as she nestled on his arm and rocked as his chest rose and fell in deep slumber. She would whisper to him hoping he may wake and take her. She felt so secure in his presence.

As her mind raced in sleeplessness she would shift to wondering what she was thinking. After all, he was a consultant, a volunteer coach for the Park District, and a guy who just reads a lot and makes a bigger deal about traveling to third world countries than he probably should. She wondered if he even knew how to shoot a gun.

Hurry home, Sean. I miss you.

You also left a sandwich downstairs just sitting out. But you will never know that I find that endearing about you and it makes me feel that you are still here with us when you are away. We have a lot to talk about and a young woman who really misses her dad. Safe travels, my love.

Chapter 8

Havens had consolidated his non-travel gear in the apartment and left it for the cleanup crew who would sanitize the safe house sometime after his departure. They would not come too soon in the event he had to return for some supplies or safety. Someone else would run the countersurveillance and technical security checks this time to make sure the hide site was reusable for the next dark pilgrim.

Sean was bugging out and would be all eyes in front at this point.

He would mail his other passport to an address by his home in the event he was detained for some reason. In his experience, it was never good to be found with another passport depicting another identity. It was much easier to get out of a situation by having too little information than too many identities.

As a business consultant, his best weapon when confronted was Joe Average attitude, frustration, and open threats. An individual acting too calm and too patient under duress was a red flag to those looking for behavioral clues of deceit and subterfuge.

Havens had identified a FedEx location where he would send off his triple wrapped contents. It was lucky for him that UPS and FedEx had lifted their recent ban on package service from Yemen. It had been suspended after two explosive devices originating from that country were found on cargo planes.

After his conversation with Ethiopian John, Havens didn't feel comfortable going to the U.S. Embassy in Sana'a and having his creds sent back home in a diplomatic pouch. It sounded like they were having an interagency human resources mess.

Hell, they will probably tape another guy's picture over mine and give the passport to him for a quick fix cover for action or status. Unbelievable.

He made a quick call to a friend who did not pick up the phone. *He's probably in a SCIF and left the cell in the car.*

Havens left a message asking a small favor to keep an eye on the house for a day or two until he got home. Christina may be opposed, he had said in the message, so if she doesn't let you in, camp out until my return. Please park out front and you will be graciously rewarded in the future. *Please get this message.*

Sean grabbed some small benign items that he would need, showered for the first time since his arrival, and put on the clothes John had brought for him.

My belt, where's my belt? I need my Bat Utility Belt so I am not completely screwed if I get pinched.

A friend and colleague who had spent a career in DoD special projects and a bit of a gadget guy, thus earning himself the name of "X" (a dirtier James Bond "Q" he would say), had sent Havens a present for his fortieth birthday.

Havens had opened the shipping box to find a nylon-ish belt with nice leather detailing to dress it up a bit beyond completely camping casual. The leather trim in the front made it appropriate for slacks or casual khakis. It was a nice belt. But it was a belt. Who sends another man a belt?

At the time it seemed odd that he would just receive a belt with a note 'Happy Hunting,' but a nice gesture nonetheless. Maybe X realized that Sean liked to travel light and may need a belt for all travel occasions. Doubtful. There had to be more to it. Was it from a country that X was in? No, it had a little white tab near the buckle that read 'Made in USA.' What was he missing?

He had pulled the tissue out of the box. Nothing. Shook out the tissue. Nothing. It was like shaking an opened Hallmark Happy Birthday card from Grandpa and Grandma hoping money would fall out.

Shake the card like there is money hidden. Shake the belt. Rub the buckle and the genie will come out. X didn't just send me a cutesy GQ Orvis belt.

Upon closer inspection, Havens noticed three four-inch hidden compartments—two on each hip side and one nine-inch internal pocket where the small of the back would be. Inside the first front compartment was a black ceramic razor blade. The second pocket held two quarters and a fifty-cent piece. Havens wondered if this low profile survival kit included change for a pay phone, but the fifty-cent piece would not work. He continued to play with them and realized they were all laser cut male and female ends that secured a small compartment that could fit a SIM card or other micro data card.

Nice, X! He smiled every time he looked at it.

The back compartment held two key style handcuff shims and two black plastic nylon handcuff keys.

The belt itself proved to be constructed of Type 13 webbing with forged steel buckles and had been sewn with parachute weight thread to yield a probable 5,000 lb. breaking strength.

Good ol' X, always looking out for me, Havens thought at the time.

Now in Yemen he knew it. X had been the one to increase the dosage of the tranquilizer. Enough to put a big man down but not enough to be lethal. The last silencing cocktail Sean had used overseas, supplied by Science and Technology, wasn't enough of a dose. It cost a fairly innocent man his life when Havens had to finish the job with the only thing available. A deathblow. Chin punches and sleeper holds only worked in movies to knock a guy out. When seconds counted in a game playing for keeps, lethal choices had to be made. Choices that would stay with a man for a lifetime while the rear echelon gadget guys slept peacefully with clean hands.

Sean would let a guy like X come over to watch a football game any day. Even if X might bring a shitty six-pack and drink all the Black Label scotch or the good beer Havens kept in the fridge. X was a brother and they had one another's back. He could have a real friendship with a guy like that. Lifetime bonds tended to come easy, but enduring personal friendships were hard to come by. It was a close hug but arm's length community.

Sean found the belt still in a drawer from the night before. He whistled a sigh of relief.

"Don't want to forget this bad boy," he said, weaving it through the belt loops of his pants, and left the apartment.

Havens was hoping for it to be the last time.

What else am I forgetting?

Chapter 9

As two young men walked down the sidewalk of a middle-class Chicago neighborhood, the residents of the block slept peacefully with the belief that their higher property taxes were enough to keep the riffraff out. Among those sleeping were Maggie and Christina Havens.

It was quiet on this street. No police cars with flashing lights racing past responding to calls of violence and criminal activity. To the two men, it was eerily quiet. They were accustomed to the constant commotion of gunshots and sirens in their neighborhood less than a mile away.

Two different worlds only a matter of blocks apart.

The tall mature trees added to the young men's cover of darkness by providing a canopy of oak and elm leaves to block out the crescent moon. The moon shone with its fullest intensity as if trying to illuminate the area in anticipation of the imminent threat, but to no avail.

"Sixth house here, yo. Turn lef. Gotta cut through here."

Donald and James Hayes may have been out of their gang's territory, but this initiation phase was a breeze. Rivals would pose absolutely no street threat to their quest to full membership. Reward was in their grasp.

They had been informed that one of their "homies" was locked away on the third strike by a female judge who lived at the address given to them.

To climb to the next tier in the organization, they were to kill her and her daughter to make a statement and throw off further prosecution of their crew under her watch. The judge, they had been told, was also a closet racist and was trying to get a few new housing developments built over the public basketball courts that

Donald and James played on. More turf encroachment from rich whitey condos.

"Man, fuck this bitch, bro. Gon' cap her sorry ass like a muthafucka."

"Fuck yeah," Donald countered, pumping himself up. "Cold bust this shit."

They were told that alarms could sound upon entry so they would have to move fast. They each were given two nine millimeter handguns and were supposed to split up in the house. Above all they were to make sure the victims were dead.

Failure was unacceptable if they were to keep progressing in the food chain to more wealth and power on the street.

"Ready to get in the mix and light these bitches up, yo?"

"Let's do this."

Donald picked up a patio bench and threw it through a double long window. They athletically jumped in with both weapons now drawn in each hand and raced through the house guided by the dim light of appliance clocks and a neighbor's back porch light casting a narrow path of light on the kitchen floor. Both men moved swiftly towards the stairs leading to the second floor bedrooms.

An automated voice was announcing to the house "Glass pane break. Glass pane break." The crash woke Christina from an already light sleep. She instinctively grabbed the phone, hit the panic button on their alarm system, and raced to her daughter's room. She slammed the door behind her and locked it.

James spotted the movement and heard the door slam.

Donald went to the master bedroom to see if anyone was left.

Christina dialed 9-1-1 and threw the phone under the bed with no intention of wasting time with an operator. She ordered her startled daughter to a corner.

"Judge probably went to the little bitch's room. Kick it in."

The wooden jamb splintered and the door was easily kicked open and slammed into the wall, the knob sticking in the drywall. All was dark in the room but the suppressed cries of the women were audible to the intruders. James' heartbeat quickened and his blood raced with adrenaline. The beating in his ears muffled their sounds as he panted and probed the black void before him.

James pointed his gun in the direction of the voice on the phone. Before he was able to pull the trigger a heavy object struck him across the forehead down the bridge of his nose. Christina hit him again with the laptop, swinging it as many times as she could while simultaneously kicking at his legs.

Donald sensing the struggle started firing wildly from the gap between James and the doorframe.

A final swipe with the laptop knocked the already dazed and disoriented intruder off balance. James instinctively jerked the trigger as many times as he could before stumbling directly into Donald's wild line of fire.

Donald fumbled for where a light switch should be. He knocked upwards against the wall with the butt of his gun. Success. He squinted at the brightness to discern what had transpired.

James was on the ground bleeding profusely from his nose, right arm, and shoulder. Christina was also bleeding out on the floor. She tried in desperation to drag herself to Maggie. Her shrill screams not waning as her body failed to respond to her will. Still, she kicked out in futile thrashings towards the men in an attempt to defend her home. She continued fighting like a wounded mother bear doing everything in her power to protect her young cub.

Maggie remained sobbing in the corner holding her knees, shaking her head from side to side while pleading with her attackers and crying for her mother who was now attempting to pull herself across the room, despite her grave injuries, with undying parental commitment.

Donald fired more rounds that hit the wall but traced closer as he continued to pull the trigger towards his target. The final bullet snapped Maggie's head back, ceasing her pleas. Christina howled in agony at the sight of her only child's lifeless expression, head cocked back at an unnatural angle. She rolled her body over to face the attacker and struggled to elevate herself—still determined to counterattack—but only collapsed again, depleted.

"Damn you," she cried helplessly. "Damn you to Hell, you fucking monsters!" *Damn you, Sean. Damn you.*

Donald fired again despite being much more emotionally bothered by the display now before him than he could have ever imagined in his post-assault mental fantasies of how this would all go down.

He recalled from years back the screams of his mother and sisters when a stray bullet entered their house striking and killing his little brother who was innocently playing in the living room with a toy airplane. He knew he had to finish this for fear that he and the brother who now lay beside him in a pool of blood would suffer the same fate by failing to deliver on their task.

The new round of fire met Christina, compressing and hiccupping her body from the floor. In her final moments, Christina continued her laborious quest to reach her baby girl for a last touch of love and a guilt-ridden need for forgiveness. She grasped Maggie's limp hand and craned her neck in a concluding effort to nestle her cheek on her daughter's bare ankle. A final tear rolled down her face as her last breath expired, her broken heart now still.

Sirens began to sound in the distance, growing in volume as they neared.

A new voice was audible through the speaker of the security system in the home. "Hello, hello, are you OK? This is your security service. We have been alerted to a glass break. Please provide your password."

"Sorry, man. You OK? We gotta go now. Man, this was bad. Aw shit, this was bad. It was not supposed to be like this. C'mon! I can't be here, man! This is all fucked up."

"Man, I'm trying. You go; I'll be behind your ass. Go to the car and start coming to me. Dat same street. It's gonna be OK."

Donald dashed down the stairs, ran through the hall and leapt out of the window they had entered from catching part of his clothes on the wood and glass shards. He caught a foot on the window base and fell to the plant bed below. Recovering he looked up to see a man in the darkness a few feet away.

"Run, you fucker!" the man commanded in a low hushed voice.

"Who the fuck are you?" shouted Donald now scared shitless, his face wet with tears of remorse and panic. Donald started to run through the backyard looking back in time to see the man enter the house.

The cleaner rushed in to see James hobbling down the stairs.

He leveled his suppressed sidearm, shooting James twice in the head. James bucked backwards and slid down the rest of the stairs until he folded dead at the bottom. The cleaner deftly passed him and mounted the remaining stairs to the room where Maggie and Christina lay lifeless. He quickly scanned the scene. Assessing the job was complete, he grabbed the laptop and turned to go.

As Donald had turned away from the dark man and started off through the backyard, another man emerged from the side of the Havens house running at full speed.

"Stop!" the man ordered.

Not looking back and assuming the police were closing in, Donald kept running picking up the pace greatly to gain distance and freedom.

"Stop or I will blow your fucking head off!"

This new dark man on the scene gave chase to Donald at an alarming pace. This man knew he could easily put two bullets in the runners back and one in the head even at this fast pace. That, however, would be pushing a favor for his buddy Sean Havens, when he wasn't really even sure whom he was chasing.

From his car outside the Havens house, Red had heard a crash. As he unlatched his gun to investigate further, he heard the all too familiar popping that was never a good sound in his profession.

He was heading to the garage door to punch in the codes Sean had given him so he could enter the house. With two digits hit, he heard abrupt grating sounds and muffled voices in the back yard. Racing around the house, he saw a man running through the yard and pursued him.

Now gaining speed with his powerful muscular legs the fleeing boy was within reach.

A police cruiser with lights flashing sped down the street with another coming from the opposite direction no doubt to cordon off the area. Havens was his buddy, but not so close of a friend that he would risk being shot by authorities while in pursuit of an unknown assailant.

Red quickly tossed his firearm into the bushes just off the sidewalk and lunged towards his unsub. He slid down the legs of the runner, catching a heel in the jaw, but held strong to the pants and toppled the runner who loudly hit his face on the pavement with a thud and a scrape as teeth met coarse concrete.

Police cars screeched to a stop where the men lay on the ground panting. Guns drawn, "Freeze! I want arms out, palms up!" they shouted.

"It's cool; I am government, Special Agent. I am a friend of the Havenses'. Just saw this guy running after I heard shots fired. I pursued."

"Get up and walk over to the car slowly. I need to see some ID." Another officer with a gun pointed at the man said, "Hands on the car, what's your name?"

"Red. I mean Trevor Peterson. My Federal ID is in my shirt."

The other officer had instructed Donald to get up. Donald complied but was not speaking. With his mouth bleeding and his broken teeth left on the pavement, Donald Hayes was handcuffed and roughly shoved into the back of the police car with a forceful kick to his hip before the door slammed shut.

The squawk box on the police radio was informing officers of the gunshot victims found in the house with multiple 'GSWs.'

Gunshot wounds confirmed. Red pleaded, but with a firm voice of authority, "Please, I need to go to the house and see if they are OK."

"Get in the car, we will go around the block and go in the front. If I let you run back you'd likely get shot by the other officers on scene."

"Cool. Hey, I need my gun. I threw it in those bushes when I saw you all driving up. Didn't want you to shoot first ask questions later."

"Smart, Fed. Get it and let's go."

"On it." Red jogged to his firearm and crunched Donald's teeth underfoot.

Red knew this whole thing was going to be bad.

The cleaner peered around a house. Seeing that all was clear, he ran across the street to another row of homes and cut through the back, staying in the shadows. From an area nestled in a high hedge, he made a call.

"Targets all down. One bad actor eliminated. Stage is set, but one of our other shooters was picked up."

The voice on the other end of the line asked, "The older one?"

"Yeah, believe so."

"Where is he now?"

"Back of the cruiser."

"Can you get to him?"

"Affirmative."

"Set that bird free. Confirm when you are back hot."

"Roger. I also have the comms."

"Good, copy. Bravo Zulu."

"Tango Mike. Out."

The cleaner hurried back to the street where Donald was in the back of the police car. He saw the officer had walked over to the bloodstained sidewalk to take a picture for evidence exonerating police violence against the suspect. He prepared to engage.

The cleaner pulled his dark sweatshirt hood back and emerged from between the houses firing two shots in the back of the officer's head. He noticed lights were now on in bedroom windows along the street.

Perfect. Just need to spread the pattern like a street hood for the audience. Turn the gun sideways to cement perception. Cliché, but that's what they want to see.

The cleaner jerked on the trigger and spread his pattern to quickly put a few random bullets in the officer's vest and car window. For effect, he looked up at one of the lit windows where a head ducked back. He fired two shots above the window four feet apart.

That looks like what one would expect from a gangster.

The cleaner opened the door and reached in for Donald who had scrunched as far away from the open door and the reach of the cleaner as possible.

"Whatchu want with me man?"

"Get out and run. Leave your car, take these keys, and cut through the next block. You will see a rusted maroon Toyota Camry. Get in. Go home. Straight home. You did well."

Donald accepted the praise cautiously. Home sounded good right now.

"One more thing. When you get home, park in the back alleyway and do a quick wipe down. You can just leave the car there. I have some cleaners in the trunk. DON'T FORGET to wipe the wheel down with the cleaners in the trunk. You have the keys now. Your guys will move the car for you. Go."

"Where's my brother, man? He was coming too."

"I sent him in another direction. He told me to tell you you guys were going to be 'in' now, whatever that means."

Yes! "Cooo man, thanks. You friend of Skinny? He didn't say nothing about no white man helpin' us."

"I said run."

You bet I'm gonna run. Clean the car. Get inside and take a two-hour shit 'til my nerves get all back. Feel like I'm gon' shit my pants now.

The cleaner pulled off his latex prosthetic face accessories and blonde wig as he now ran between another set of homes towards yet another stashed car's location.

I'll be seeing you later kid and put a nice little bow on this op.

The Latino operator stuffed the mask into a zippered pocket of his jacket and moved out. He didn't want to be far behind Donald. There was more business to take care of. No loose ends. His boss demanded that.

Chapter 10

As Red and the officer pulled up to the Havens house, there were already four squad cars and two ambulances. An ambulance sped away as the other was loading a covered body.

"How do you know this family?" the officer inquired.

"Please, can you just unlock this door and get me in there? The husband called me long distance saying there was a potential problem. Please. I will answer all questions. Please get me the hell out of here so I can check on them."

"You know it was an act of revenge from that guy who raped the girl, don't you?"

"What? Raped who?"

"The kid. The kid was raped. Then she went to the police and the rapist threatened the family."

"Shit. I had no idea."

The officer opened the back passenger door. Red, with his Federal ID around his neck, was already making his way into the house when the officer yelled something indiscernible.

As the officer started to walk after Red, a call came over the radio. The officer stopped to listen. *Officer down on Elmore Street? That's where we just were…* "Mikey!"

Another uniformed officer heading out the door in response to the officer down call saw the FBI badge of the man running into the house and just shook his head. He was amazed how quickly the Feds got to scenes.

"It's over, Agent. Is this a federal case now?"

Red bolted past the officer and bound up the stairs where he was halted again.

"Sorry, Agent. Unless you all have some jurisdiction, I have a crime scene here. We got an officer down call now so nobody is doing anything for a few."

Red halted. He could see the aftermath in the room. He was too late. He had failed his friend.

"They were my buddy's family. They were…friends," Red mumbled.

"I'm sorry, sir." The officer looked down to break eye contact in the uncomfortable moment. "Agent, if you aren't official, I'm not sure you should be here."

Red scowled. "Uh huh. Not leaving. What happened?"

The officer realized this man wasn't going anywhere without answers. "From what we can tell, there was a break-in, and the women either ran to the room or the mom came to the room and tried to help her daughter. The assailants kicked in the door…"

"Assailants?" Red interrupted.

"Yeah, must have been at least two shooters here. One guy is dead downstairs. Body you likely had to step over. Looks like his partner shot him. He was pretty shot up. He was hit up here. Blood trail goes downstairs to their point of entry. Heard on the radio another suspect was picked up down the street."

"Yeah, I chased him down."

"Why were you here? Were you inside?" The officer squinted a bit and took a step back, instinctively moving towards his firearm before remembering he was speaking to a Federal agent.

"No, I'd just gotten here. The husband said there may be a problem. Officer downstairs said the girl had been raped and then threatened."

"These gangbangers are something else. Wonder how they crossed paths with a girl down here in Beverly neighborhood."

"I'm not sure either, but I sure as hell am going to find out."

Red turned back. "Hey, sorry about your fellow man who just took one. Hope he is OK."

"Yeah, thanks. Just happened a block over en route to this scene. Standing by."

Red went down to see the other shooter.

Another officer approached and looked down at Red's credentials. "Is this a Fed thing?"

"No, so no need to stand down. I mean, no, I am here on a personal matter for this family."

"Oh, well in that case. This guy was definitely shot…"

"No shit," Red said sarcastically as he moved around the body.

"Well, right, but what I was going to say was, and I am no inspector, but looks like this guy was shot in the back upstairs then shot in the head down here. Maybe they got in an argument. Like maybe one guy wanted to have at the women and the other guy was like, 'Naw yo, I want these bitches dead cause they saw my face,' ya know? Then the one guy shoots him and runs away after killing the women but then he comes down to get the other guy who turns around and shoots him in the bean. Right?"

"Right. You are no inspector." Red smiled and patted the officer on the shoulder. "Keep workin' on it."

Red could tell something didn't happen right, but he was not going to commit to any hypothesis at this point without more information.

Maybe the guy he tackled would have more information…if CPD would share it. And usually they would. They were a great outfit. Even those who were a bit overzealous in their initial assessment were trying hard. He respected that. Many here in Chicago could be stereotypical, but they were all on the same team. Team guys understood that. They just needed a little time and a little patience. Red had neither right now. This was a mess. How was Sean going to react so many thousands of miles away? It could certainly cause someone a problem.

Chapter 11

Havens headed out to run his last minute errands to close out Yemen before bugging out for good.

One stop was to a small hotel owned by a Turkish family. He had previously identified them on another trip and did some investigating as to their social ties. He concluded that they could be fairly trustworthy. Using a Turkish alias, he had booked a room for a future date and confirmed that he would send bags and a package to avoid baggage surcharges by the airlines. They had agreed to hold the items until he arrived to claim them for his stay. Unfortunately for them, today he would not be staying due to a change in his business itinerary. He would just collect a few of his things.

The suitcase full of clothing would be left in the street after he ripped the liner out to retrieve some paperwork. The bag had seemingly innocuous toiletries with additional disguise items concealed in pop out compartments. Were they to be discovered, it may raise questions but nothing to alert authorities over. No one would be running DNA trace here.

After a few other stops, he made his way to the airport. He didn't want to be too early and allow wandering eyes to check him out, nor did he want to be late and miss his flight in case he was delayed. Surveillance detection was an afterthought. His momentum was forward bound.

He stopped for a bite to eat in close proximity to the airport. His food, a traditional lamb stew with an assortment of sweet breads, arrived promptly, much to his dismay. Food was unappetizing at this point. So was the annoying proprietor who wanted to make conversation with his only guest of the day. He paid his bill and decided on a quick walk to keep moving. The owner was still loudly chatting away at him as he moved further and further away.

Havens dialed a secure number to X. "Hey, cell phone 2 going silent. Activate 3 with routing point in Germany."

"Roger that, cell 2 dead turning on 3 for lederhosen. Will be dead as soon as I get a connection."

"Good, copy. All good on your end?"

"Yip," said the other voice on the line. "We killing your wife too?"

Havens smiled at the play on words. "Nah, I'll keep her around for another year and renew her contract."

"Yeah, yeah, you know. Can I cut off her throw away too?"

"Yeah. I told her to pull the card and pitch it."

"Has she figured you out yet? She sure puts up with a lot of your shit."

"Yeah, but that is the price she has to pay when you marry a guy like me over slumming for a guy like you. Who marries a guy with the name of just an alphabet letter anyway?"

"That's not what she said. Like to bust your balls more, but I gotta do this now if you want it shut off. I have to leave this site too. Getting hot, and as you know, they don't know I am here. Talk to you later, bro. Out."

"Mick!" Havens heard a voice behind him. Before turning around Havens remembered that due to the passport screw-up he was no longer Mick.

"Mick!"

The urge was almost too great, but Havens was going to give it a little more time. He kept walking, looking for anything reflective that may show who was behind him. He thought he recognized the voice.

"Alright, you passed. I am just playing with you to see if you would respond wrong, Will-iam."

William was Havens' new name.

It was horrible security and tradecraft protocol having him use this cover blindly. There had been virtually no briefing on this persona, no background bio, just a pat on the back good luck sucker send off. Dudes got burned in the field with this kind of shit play. Even though government may support Tier One, he always felt better getting covers from the high-speed boys over the Feds. High-speed operators, himself included, knew the duress that an individual would be under while covered, so they took it very seriously. Especially since a team guy knew he may have to deploy to recover a field-burned bubba.

Havens knew now that the voice behind him was spooky mission support asset John the Ethiopian. With the proper name being used, he turned around. John stood there clapping for the successful Tradecraft 101 ad hoc field test.

Havens looked around to see who was watching or nearby.

"It's cool, man."

"What are you doing here, John? I'm not in the mood to be fucked with by some asshole playing games."

"I have a present for you. Well a trade."

"Do I dare ask?"

"Trust me."

"For some reason, I do. Despite that dumb ass test you just did out in the open. This isn't a role play, and I don't like fucking around when I am in play."

"Well you shouldn't trust me and you don't have to like me, but in this case, I have your '6.'"

John looked around discretely and from his front pocket pulled a diplomatic passport. "I'll need yours now."

Havens nearly swiveled his head around 360 degrees. His eyes widened in shock. "Jeez! What the hell are you doing? Can't you at least put it in something? Holy shit, you are going to burn me before I get through the doors. Fuckin' A. Let me see this first." He closed the distance to block any surveillance or casual glances by the right people who could screw with his day. It was the best he could make of the situation. Clearly, John didn't play high stakes each day. Maybe he was high.

Havens took the passport and opened it. It was the same name as the passport he was given earlier, but now official status with visa entry stamps.

"John, I don't know what the hell you all are up to, but this is not a game."

"Look man, I heard what you said and was in a position to make it a little better. I'd say now you are at about 80% chance of not getting detained. Most places you are going to will just see the cover, roll their eyes, stamp you, and move you out of the way. I want you to go to check in with the guy furthest to the right. He's a bit of a fat ass and will have a blue topped ink pen in his left breast pocket."

"John, this is just…"

John waved off Havens.

"I know bro, too A-F-U or amateurish, or whatever you are going to bitch about next. You could use some TC brush up yourself. Saw you in the souk. Know you were followed and that you put that big boy to sleep. I been following you for a while. But bottom line, I tried to make it better, you need to be somewhere quick, so go to the airport, get checked in, and trust that maybe we are not the Varsity team, but you getting busted will actually make it worse for us. So consider that our selfish self-serving motives are stronger than just caring about you. Done!"

"OK. Thanks. You know who that tail was? Was it you guys?"

"Nah. We think it was our long lost sister organization. They've been re-funded. Hard-edged man. Dirty muthers."

"Long lost? What sister org is that. You don't mean precursor. Some OSS thing?"

"Naw, man. Fuckin' Pond."

"What's Pond?"

"Man, for a guy who bitches at everyone and who don't know the blue building, the Pond, shit, I think half the guys in blue building are Pond. Thought you were too at first. You may not be as old school as I thought. You need schooling but best you take your shit and get out of here. I don't want Pond on my ass. One thing if it's you."

"You really don't care about me?" Haven smiled.

"Nope, not one bit."

"Not even a little?" Havens had his eyebrows raised playing around in a moment of softness for John who was trying his best.

"Maybe a smidge. Man you snake eater door kickers are weird."

"John, I am a snake charmer, door picker. Big difference. Thanks again."

"Methinks maybe you are a bit more than that. But anyway. No sweat. Be well." *Pool, pond, pond'd be good for you.* John smiled as he thought of old movie lines. He stopped smiling when he thought back on what he heard the Pond was doing on their turf. Bureaucracy, he thought to himself. But the Pond was scary. The Pond made people disappear. For good. Poof.

As Havens headed back towards the airport, John turned down a side street. A blue and grey Daihatsu Terius SUV rounded the corner heading in the opposite direction of John's travel. Only a kilometer from the airport, John heard the 4-cylinder vehicle revving its engine as it was gaining speed down the narrow side street. John turned towards the noise of the speeding Terius just as he stepped up to the sidewalk, aware that he should move to safety from the typically frenzied Yemeni drivers. As he viewed the driver hunkering over the wheel with his target in sight, John knew it was coming for him.

That's no Yemeni. Can't fool me.

John had no time to move as the vehicle was just feet away from impact.

"Shit." John resolved himself to his looming fate. *Man, fuck this business.*

The SUV slammed into John tossing him into the air over the Daihatsu. His head hit the windshield as his body tumbled from hood to roof to ground. The blood splatter and smear on the spidering splintered window glass would tell the tale of an anonymous fate as his rag doll body tumbled on to the dirty road.

Another seemingly unintentional traffic accident in Yemen. Another dead man who could tell no tale.

Perfect.

The operator behind the wheel dialed a number and looked to ditch the vehicle down by the port. "Langley, boy down. Out."

Chapter 12

With a pre-processed exit visa, a long wait in the line for passport control, and a slight wink from the heavyset CIA-funded customs security officer, Havens passed through the first leg of security without a problem.

Needing to catch his breath and settle the nerves, Havens entered the toilet facilities to relieve himself and splash some water on his face. The bathrooms had been substantially upgraded since his last visit. He hated squatting over the holes in the floor and was pleased to see upon entry at least a moderate attempt at better sanitation.

Half a dozen steps in and Havens saw that the holes had been replaced by toilets, but apparently not industrial strength ones. The smell and foulness of the human waste was enough for him to be convinced of holding it until the plane. His palms were sweaty. His eyes felt sunken. *Just get to the plane.*

As Havens exited the restroom, two AK-clutching security guards were blocking his path.

"Excuse me," the first guard said in English, "I will need to see your passport please."

Havens noticed the international language of micro-expressions on the guards' faces. One was blinking a bit more rapidly and another Havens could see had unusually dilated pupils given the current light source.. A third officer a bit further back from the others was holding a smile unusually long. The officer in front of him furrowed his eyebrows in a concentrated manner.

Timing is all off on these guys. I'm blown.

As Havens paused slightly in a natural reaction to the confrontation, he continued to witness clusters of behavioral movements leaking the true emotions of the guards—fear, preparedness, hostility, anger, and uncertainty.

Havens was becoming a bit uncertain himself, but would not let any asymmetry of expression act as a visual tell.

"I already cleared…"

"Your passport!" the guard interrupted now starting to clench his weapon.

"Sure, what's the." Havens decided compliance was best. "Yes. I have it right here." Havens handed over the official U.S. diplomatic passport as requested.

"You are American government worker?"

"Yes."

"Please come with me."

"Certainly, may I ask if everything is OK? I am trying to get home to my family and don't want to miss my flight."

"You will miss your flight."

The hell I am.

As anger and panic raged through Havens he maintained full control, saving his questions for whomever they were taking him to see or for whatever room away from the other passengers he was being taken to.

They walked down a short hall, turned to another nondescript hallway, and then another turn, finally stopping at an unpainted metal door. He noticed the locks did not lock from the outside. It wasn't a holding cell. Good sign.

A small desk with two chairs on opposite ends was in the middle of the room with two other chairs arranged in the corner.

"Please remove your clothing and place them and any items in your pocket on the table. You will have one minute to complete this."

The guard motioned for another one of the guards to also enter the room while Havens disrobed. When Havens finished placing his clothes and items on the table, the guard rapped on the door and the others entered again.

Havens didn't enjoy being completely naked, but he had to feign embarrassment and modesty. SERE training had taken that away from him years ago.

"Can you please tell me…?"

"What did you steal from your embassy?" the guard interrupted again while sifting through Havens' personal effects. The guard remained looking at the items on the table.

"Steal?"

"Yes, what is it that you do for your embassy?"

"Sir, I am just a staffer here on a brief rotation. I have not stolen anything."

"We will see. We were informed that you had stolen a particular item that does not appear to be here, so we must find out where you have placed it or who you have given it to."

"Sir, can we please contact someone from the embassy and I am sure this can all be cleared up."

"We have already been contacted by the embassy. That is why *we* are trying to clear this up."

"Can you tell me who called you from the embassy?"

"This is not important for you. Please sit down."

Under normal circumstances in a stressful situation, Havens would have been making light of his predicament in his mind, likely curious as to how many other bare asses had been on this chair, but now he had to maintain composure and above all not miss this flight getting him closer to home.

"Sir, I am more than willing to cooperate with you to come to some sort of resolution. I fully respect your position and authority but do not believe I have stolen anything, so if there is anything more that you can share with me so I can resolve this matter, I would be indebted to you."

The guard continued sifting through Havens' personal items as if he didn't hear him.

No, this is not how a government employee would be acting if they needed to get home. This is not how an audacious American would behave if they were not guilty of something. This subservient attitude is not going to gain respect.

"Listen you pieces of shit!" Havens switched to Yemeni Arabic and quickly got the attention of all in the room. "Get me your superior or kill me now, because when I get out of here, I am directly contacting Abu Rashad Al-Aghbari who is a personal friend and he will completely goat fuck you all! And I will not miss my plane!"

Upon hearing the name of the renowned Vice-Prime Minister for the Affairs of Defense and Security, two of the guards' eyes widened and jaws dropped.

The first security officer sensed a bluff, but the fact that this individual spoke local dialect, was clearly now explosive, and was knowledgeable of an individual who should cast extreme fear into the hearts and minds of security personnel, he was certainly going to proceed with caution.

The guard had been informed by his superior to detain this man upon entry but despite informing the other guards, this man had somehow cleared processing.

"I will be right back. You will wait here."

Havens started to dress.

"You must not..."

Havens did the interrupting now, "FUCK YOU! I am getting dressed, walking out that door, and getting on my plane. I have violated none of your laws which makes this an international incident if you do not release me or get someone from my embassy here. Shit, call the embassy RSO Kent Williams!"

The guards were still looking at each other hoping for some guidance from their superior.

"I will be quickly. You will wait for the moment and I will return quickly. Please. You must wait."

The guards exited the room closing the door behind them. Havens could hear rapid chatter among the guards, questioning the situation to which the head guard had no answers. But he was certainly going to get some.

As the guards were exiting, Havens followed them with impertinence until they slammed the door behind them. They failed to notice, however, as he looked to be naturally reaching for the door knob in an effort to come along, that he had retrieved and palmed the black ceramic razor blade from his belt. He was just able to insert it in the jamb between the frame and door lock when he slammed his fist on the door with all his might causing the guard to instinctively wince and release the door handle. When they saw that no crazy American was coming out the door, the guards continued on.

Havens waited until the conversational noise left the area and slowly opened the door, putting the blade back in his belt pocket.

He has seen upon his guided walk to the room that there were no security cameras in this area nor were there any other offices that may prove risky with increased foot traffic. Knowing what was to his left, he walked to his right not quite knowing what he was going to do. His plane would be boarding in the next thirty minutes, which would still give them time to detain him again if caught. Havens stopped and went back to the room's door which unlocked from the outside with a key. He pulled two toothpicks from a zippered pouch and jammed them into the lock before breaking them off. It would at least buy him some time knowing they would expect him to still be in the room.

Havens slowly retraced his steps through the hallway back to the terminal area. Still no sign of the security guards.

Havens saw a male backpacker with a Chelsea Football Club warm-up jacket enter the bathroom after stepping away from his boarding gate in an apparent last minute decision to use the toilet. Havens quickly followed from behind, careful to check that no eyes were tracking him.

If I kill him and take his ticket his body could be discovered and they will shut down the airport. Would they shut down the airport? I should know those procedures.

I could knock him out and make it look like a robbery. With more planning I could make it look like an overdose. Looks like a good kid out exploring the world getting high and sowing his oats.

Think.

"Shite!" the backpacker said as the sight and odor hit him. He was waving the air when he noticed Havens close behind him.

"Excuse me," Havens said. "Wondering if I could make you an offer?"

"Uhhh, no, I don't think so, mate. Plane to catch."

The backpacker guardedly stepped back, unsure of the kind of offer he was being solicited.

"I need to trade an airline ticket quickly."

"Uh, no, no way, I don't think so, mate. Look I have to be on now."

The backpacker, sensing something was awry, tried to get past Havens quickly.

Havens outstretched his arm but not too threateningly. He didn't need to raise any further scenes. "Look, if you don't have to be anywhere in a hurry, they won't check passports at this point. I will give you a thousand dollars for wherever you are going. My ticket is heading first class to Kuwait. You can likely get another flight from there and still have a few hundred dollars in your pocket. Looks like you didn't check your pack, so I am guessing no luggage? And if you are interested in a really great place for a chew, the Yemeni community in Kuwait has some great spots off the beaten path for a chew despite the area's drug control. They usually have some football matches on TV; they bring out great food while you are chewing. It's like a combination of the Barcelona's Ramblas and the Red Light District of Amsterdam."

C'mon kid bite, I know you are here for the qat chewing and some adventure. I can't bluff like this all day. I see you thinking, what part are you contemplating? No time for low key elicitation.

"Where are you going, kid?

"Dubai."

"Fifteen hundred. And Manchester United can sod off."

The backpacker grinned. "You play footie or a fan?"

"Fan. Used to play, now I coach kids, but really I prefer Arsenal best. I do like Chelsea. They play with such heart and speed. C'mon whaddya say?"

"Cheers. Fifteen hundred…U.S.?"

"U.S. I didn't have time to exchange," Havens smiled.

"Right. Well, looks like you are in a bit of a spot, and by the way you are looking around and talkin' all low-like, probably in some hot pursuit situation."

"Bit like a Jason Statham flick, but I have hair instead of the hot girls and smoking fast cars that Statham has."

"Right. Fifteen hundred. Best move on. Door may be a shutting 'Mr. Hairy Jason.'"

"Cheers, kid. How about another $500 for the backpack?"

"You must really be in a tight predic. But anything to fook the man," the backpacker said raising his hand and fingers like a gun in his best attempt at being a combo mafia, hood gangster, hipster-something that was so ridiculously awful it gave them both a quick chuckle and head shake before Havens emerged yet again from the bathrooms.

The young man added in an attempt at a casual afterthought, "Oy. You may want to stay clear of the dogs." The backpacker gestured with his eyebrows, hinting at the backpack.

"Thanks, chief." *Great, go from stealing something at an embassy I wasn't at to now drug trafficking.* "Do me one last solid. If you see any security right when you walk out, give a whistle or something. I'll be coming right behind you."

"Cheers. No problem."

When the coast appeared clear, Havens dropped his light jacket on the ground near some chairs kicking it to a corner and grabbed a thin long overshirt, put on some non-prescription glasses, and hefted the backpack over his shoulder. He spit in his hand and put a small dab of toothpaste in his palm and mussed it through his hair.

He hurriedly walked straight to the Dubai flight gate, handed over the ticket, and proceeded to board. With no intention of keeping the kid's backpack and whatever contraband he had in it, Havens would wait a bit to see what else could be of use in case the kid was caught and they discovered that Havens was in Dubai. Whoever "they" were.

John, I knew that passport was too good to be true. What did you do to me and why, you little shit?

As other passengers boarded, Havens reached down between his legs as if untying his shoes for the flight.

With his thumbnail under the sole of his shoe, he bent up a Vibram edge rotating it past the heel clockwise to the toe so he could retrieve another passport that was hidden within the package he had previously sent to the Turkish-owned hotel.

Now stuffing it into his sock so he could get at it later from the bathroom, he started to process what all had happened and how the hell he was going to get out of Dubai with no more surprises.

He wiped his forehead, hoping the plane would pull away faster. An Indian man in his fifties sitting next to Havens already started to unpack some homemade snacks. Havens wasn't hungry, but did like what the man was eating and had eaten it numerous times before. They made brief eye contact and the man offered Havens some of his thin flat yellow tortilla with green flakes.

"What is it?" Havens asked, reaching out for some with a curious smile. "My name is…" Havens casually looked from his left eye at the backpacker's plane ticket still in his left hand, "Nigel."

Sheesh. What have you gotten yourself into Havens?

"Very nice to make your acquaintance Nigel, I am Rajiv. What we are eating is..."

The plane pulled away with no incident. Havens listened to Rajiv for the rest of the trip while he silently willed the plane faster to the West. To home. To his wife and daughter.

I am so sorry, Maggie. Things are going to change. Maybe Christina and I can talk about adopting again. I think I could be better the second time around.

The director of Sana'a International Airport security hung up the phone and ordered his men to keep looking. He had been informed to let this man from the embassy just sit for a while in a locked room. He was supposed to be detained long enough to miss his flight with no interaction from the guards.

Apparently, from what little the director understood of the reason for detaining the American, there was some internal U.S. counterintelligence issue about whom the man may be meeting in Kuwait if he made his flight. After an hour or two they were to come in and apologize for the error and confusion.

It was a good thing that one of the guards had decided to go by the room to listen to the caged American animal and heard nothing other than silence. When they had finally unjammed the lock and entered the room to check on him, he was gone. They quickly checked to see if he had boarded his flight and learned that he had not checked in.

Where was he?

No one else had any record of another ticket being purchased, and if the U.S. Embassy was telling the truth, there were very limited flights now going to Kuwait.

The director was somewhat remorseful that his senior man did not keep a guard at the door, but after all they were just supposed to hold him. Why should airport security have to babysit a relatively non-threatening staffer? He suspected that perhaps his security team had gone for an hour chew. It occurred to him a chew would be good right about now. A few more hours.

The real Nigel exited the airport and texted a friend. He was going to go to the market for some qat, upgrade his hotel, get some clothes and hang out with some friends new and old. Perhaps he would stay another week. He wanted to bang that pre-med girl from New Zealand who had arrived in town a couple days ago. She would be with everyone this afternoon. Perhaps he could play a sympathy card appealing to her proclivities towards helping her common man. That's it, he thought. "I was robbed on my way to the airport and roughed up a bit."

Nigel saw a series of stone stairs. Without giving it a thought, he hurled himself down the steps pulling his arms and knees against some of the rough edges of rock as he fell. When he landed at the bottom he admired his abrasions and the prospects of the evening.

Chapter 13

The cleaner located his second stashed car a few blocks away. The quiet Chicago neighborhood was quickly coming alive. He had to get moving before Donald got home.

From the trunk he grabbed a sawed off Mossberg shotgun which he had loaded earlier that day and double-checked for shells. The shotgun was placed in the rear passenger side foot well for easy retrieval. A thin blanket was tossed over it in the event of a fast visual police check.

The cleaner's record would be spotless as his alias had been seasoned now with only the occasional parking ticket or traffic ticket that was promptly paid in full to augment the fictitious cover as true life.

He tied a blue bandana around his forehead and donned dark sunglasses before checking the GPS transmission reading from the device he had placed under the vehicle Donald was now driving.

Right on target, Donald. Keep going. Don't slow up, homie.

It wasn't the cleaner's position to ask questions but this job was nagging him a bit. He thought the killing of the teenager was overkill for a judge's assassination. On the inside of the house there hadn't been any legal certificates or diplomas in the den area walls. That wasn't typical for a judge. Why would he need to take the girl's laptop and not the judge's computer or thumb drives? There had been a few jobs now like this that were nagging at him a bit.

He remembered being a soldier. He had liked that so much more. He even missed the work and his team in Kabul. He had to keep reminding himself that his new employer was the boss, and his boss made the Clean the Streets missions of the Silver Star program a success. They were all apparently taking out crime at levels that were typically not touched, or they were unconventionally executed to draw pressure onto other criminal elements. That part he did not like, but life was not fair.

The cleaner pulled from his wallet the one piece of cover contraband that he allowed himself. A picture of his wife and children.

How he missed them so.

It still boggled his mind how his wife, sister-in-law, and still missing brother-in-law could get involved with the drug trade and Mexican cartels while he was away in Afghanistan. He didn't even have family in Mexico and certainly no family involved in criminal activity, to the best of his knowledge. They hardly had any Mexican friends where they had lived. Even the Mexican restaurants they frequented were national chains and not Mexican-owned. Nothing made sense about their slaughter.

The police had said his brother-in-law had "allegedly" been involved through Air Force connections overseas that transported drugs back to the states through military channels. The hit that left his family dead and sister-in-law decapitated in the basement was part of some turf battle and his brother-in-law was likely either part of it or in hiding.

Maybe his wife had just been helping her sister. He wondered how she could have let this come into his home. For God's sake he had been hunting Taliban funded heroin traffickers in Afghanistan risking his life to fight this drug's illicit economic expansion when he was called home. A couple years had passed, but the pain felt like it happened this morning.

He had made people pay.

His new employer had recognized him from the headlines, taken him in, got him some emotional help, and came up with a job he could hold down exacting revenge against the monsters who had butchered his family and that had let criminals out of prison to kill again. The judge was supposedly another one in the kill chain that needed to be terminated.

Once the cleaner could emotionally get through a day without breaking down, his employer had provided him with intensive, unconventional urban tactical training. He took to the training well and it complemented his previous military experience.

Upon its completion, he was handed a file identifying the murderers of his family. He was provided a small team to exact his revenge. They entered nearly ten different homes, apartments, motel rooms, and a restaurant, all the way from Chicago to St. Louis to Texas and Arizona, and just over the border in Mexico. They would burst in to each location as a killer assault team, wreaking havoc on those he was told were responsible for his own personal losses.

They had torn apart the murderers and drug traffickers with automatic weapon fire. In its final zenith, his employer had recommended beheading the dead to throw off authorities, send a message, and above all, pay back his children's likely last wishes for their father to come to their aid. It had brought the cleaner to his knees initially, but he knew he had to do it for his family honor and final vengeance.

From that point his heart turned cold. Yet underneath that compassionless void, he would on occasion hold the photo of his beloved family, looking wantonly at their lives that once were. It had been a good day when the picture was taken.

The cleaner decided as he drove to Donald's location that he would address these recent missions with his employer again. On one such mission, they had happened upon some Somali whores locked in a storage room strung out on heroin with only a couple soiled mattresses and a sink. No doubt they had been trafficked and held as sex slaves. Their orders were to kill them as well to paint a deceptive story of criminal rivalry. The first time the cleaner addressed his opinion on this he gained little more than a quizzical look from his handler who asked him if he was going soft. The handler had scolded him telling him to act like a soldier. To act in accordance of a man who had been given a new family and a new chance at avenging his family's murder without fear of reprisals. Who else would be given such an opportunity in a similar situation? How could he think there could be no innocent lives taken for the greater good to get after the heads of the snake? Who else could still be doing all this good for the public and still be working for the United States government?

It shut the cleaner up for a time, but as a lifelong Marine who had done some covert ops work in the past, he knew this was not the work of the United States government. Policy would never allow it. He knew, despite not yet fully coming to terms with reality, that he was being exploited by someone in the military or intelligence apparatus who had some temporary relief from oversight and accountability. He would have to find out who that was. His boss knew he wasn't happy. And that didn't make the boss happy.

Donald's car was now in sight as it pulled into the dimly lit neighborhood on the South Side of Chicago. The cleaner pulled up just behind and to the left next to Donald, who still looked a bit jittery walking to the trunk. He glanced up at his front porch to see under the dim lighting the bullet pock marks in the wood that had trailed to the living room window and killed little Darnell.

The cleaner lowered his glasses. "Get the trunk open and start cleaning the car."

Not recognizing the cleaner initially from the change of hair and latex prosthetics, Donald recognized the eyes and did as he was told despite fumbling a few times for the keys. He popped the trunk.

"Huh? What is this?"

Donald reached for the brick-like plastic-wrapped bundles in the trunk. There were five of them. There were no cleaning supplies.

Donald turned towards the cleaner who was still in the car with the passenger window rolled down.

Drugs. "Is this what I think it is?"

The impact of the shotgun pellets hitting Donald in the chest knocked him halfway into the trunk. The second impact to his torso created less dramatic movement but misted the trunk with blood. The houses would bear witness to yet another violent neighborhood fatality but would remain silent. Such was the code of this neighborhood too, but as a matter of survival.

The cleaner drove away. It was time to ditch this final car and report in. The cleaner called a number.

"Is it all taken care of now?"

The cleaner replied in the affirmative.

"Where are you heading now? Are you certain you have not been followed?"

"Yes, I'm certain," the cleaner said smugly. "I'll run another SDR just in case."

"Good. Excellent work."

"You know you have to find someone else on this block to take out?"

"Who? That was it for the assets I'm tracking and running."

"Think. You freed Donald and shot the cop. That makes three. Finish the story. Tie up all loose ends to make the story connect to a typical pattern and end it."

My God this doesn't stop. "You are right. Sorry. I should have thought of that."

"Yes, you should have. If you want to stay a trigger puller all your life you won't need to think like I am trying to train you to think. It is your choice. Remember, I am here for you and we have been here for you the whole time."

"Hey, thanks for the Hallmark card. I'm a big boy." The cleaner felt like he was being scolded by a parent. His smart ass remark received the same reaction that his father gave when he was little. Silence.

"Fine, I will take care of it now."

It was resolved with the cleaner as if he were just told to go upstairs and clean his room.

"I have someone in my sights now. Approaching to assess viability as surrogate tie-in."

"Good, copy."

"One last thing. Are we still going to meet this week? I have something I would like to discuss."

"Sure. We'd be happy to. Have you discussed it with anyone else from the team?"

"No."

"OK. Yes. Happy to discuss whatever is on your mind. We will call with a time and location."

The receiver hung up and the cleaner felt a sense of ease.

Another call was made unbeknownst to the cleaner.

"All is nearly completed. He has one more stop. Do you have him in sight?"

"Coming up on his location now. We had a tracker so we could stay back."

"Roger that. Hold until after he engages new mark, then proceed."

"WILCO. I can't believe he was really threatening to go to the press with our unit and had pictures of us. I never saw him take them."

Of course there are no pictures.

"Let's not discuss here. We really need to implement a policy on our open line communications. Myself included. Throw aways or not. Point of the matter is that he did have evidence on the team. Another team has located the photos, the notes he had made, and destroyed them. This was my bad. Turns out he really was involved in drugs. You guys are now clear. Take him out. Finish the story to paint the picture. Go back to his apartment and give his old identity back to him. The artifacts to stage the apartment with are in the bag you picked up from the shop. Then ditch your phones."

The cleaner pulled parallel to a hooded street punk who was clearly out too late for any good, but he was alone walking down the dark sidewalk. That was good for the cleaner.

"Yo, bro," the cleaner said.

The hooded gangster kept walking. Hands were in his hoodie stomach pocket.

"Yo, how do I get to the expressway?"

The gangster turned towards the voice. Seeing through the darkness a protruding pistol barrel bulge sticking out of the punk's sweatshirt, the cleaner said out loud, "Perfecto!" having found the ideal candidate for surrogacy and fired the shotgun at his final mark for the mission.

Quickly getting out of the car the cleaner wiped his own 9mm that had killed the policeman earlier and Donald's brother. He placed it in the now dead gang member's hand, fired a shot in the unlikely event gun residue would be assessed, let the gun fall out of the dead man's grasp to appear as it would naturally in a death fall, and with a kerchief took the gangster's Smith & Wesson snubbie .45 as his own now.

Back in the car he had taken off his headband, glasses, and was throwing the shotgun in the rear seat now that he was at a stoplight. Hard to tell if sirens would start approaching the area. This neighborhood was a regular shooting gallery throughout the week. Before he repositioned his hips and body back to the front of the car, he noticed a brown paper bag in the rear driver side foot well.

I didn't put this there.

The cleaner knew without opening the bag that it would have drugs in it. He saw the headlights of an SUV quickly approaching and punched it through the red light. The red Blazer coming up from behind never slowed for the light. The cleaner's car gained speed but was no match for the vehicle now at its side.

In a flurry of glass breaking, impacts from the ammunition, and audible shots ringing about, the cleaner kept his foot on the gas pedal. Forgetting the context of tactical driving ramming situations he tried to smash into the Blazer but only drew himself closer to the guns.

Looking down at his wounds he knew they were worse than those he had sustained in either Iraq or Afghanistan.

The cleaner, for the first time since his family's death, knew his wife would not have been involved with drugs. Yet another plant. If cartels really were involved, the scene would have been different.

He was set up. His family had been set up just like he was setting others up.

The brother- and sister-in-law spin was to take the proxy cover-up two to three layers deep to throw law enforcement off in a simple and logical conclusion. It had all been orchestrated by men. Men like him now.

He felt ashamed of dishonoring his family and the Corps by his actions, emotional reactions, and naiveté. He had played right into it and allowed his rage to transform him into the assassin they needed for off-the-books targeting. Had men like him killed his family or did they involve other surrogates who were manipulated to murder?

"What have I done?" he cried out, tears streaming from his eyes. "I am sorry."

Before his bullet-riddled body's reflexes waned, he unbuckled his seat belt and accelerated the car. He grasped within his shirt the pendant of La Virgen de Guadalupe for past crimes forgiveness. Bullets still permeated the car door skin and glassless windows as he drove the vehicle into an old oak. His unsecured body met the windshield upon impact.

The Blazer pulled alongside and out hopped an operator. The SUV drove off as the operator sanitized the scene of the cleaner's disguise pieces, moved the shotgun back to the front seat, ensured prints were on the grips, and looked for any other pieces of tell among the glass pieces, seats, and dash upholstery that would create questions at the scene.

The operator opened a wallet and saw the picture of the kids.

"Beautiful." *Finish the story.*

"We just tied you back to your wife's nasty drug business you fucking traitor."

The operator removed the cover-issued driver's license, replaced it with an old true-name driver's license, and inserted an Arizona taxi business card in the man's wallet next to the picture.

Gunnery Sergeant Miguel Gonzalez was again in the same place as his family.

There were many more men who had and would share the same fate.

Chapter 14

Havens disembarked the aircraft in Dubai with an offensive mental mode activated. He proactively scanned for any suspicious situations or behaviors in the terminal that indicated any deviation from normalcy. He looked for any overt or covert law enforcement and security personnel showing signs of apprehension or response to an incident. The area appeared clear any suspicious indicators or abnormal details that would trigger his internal warning mechanism.

Feeling comfortable with his surroundings, Havens switched off the enhanced sensory cybernetic organism mode of his mind and switched on the hurried business traveler manner. True to the character and his current pangs, he did what most typical people would do getting off the plane and dialed home.

Answer Christina, you should be using the phone located in the cupboard now. Pick up.

Havens dialed again to no avail. Although he assumed all was likely normal and Christina may be out and about, Havens broke security protocol and dialed her personal mobile phone. Again, no answer—only voicemail.

Well, as long as I am bending the rules, let's just try Maggie.

Havens hands became a bit sweaty as the phone continued to ring. His teenage daughter would rarely, if ever, not answer a phone, including times while in the bathroom, shower, at dinner, and endless other occasions where Havens would either hear or see her pick up the phone with the sense of urgency that rivaled his own profession's responsiveness to obligations.

OK, maybe a text. No, I don't want her having communications with this number since I am not buying her throw away iPhones.

"Red," Havens said to himself under his breath. Havens dialed a number that would relay to Red. Red would see the number and dial from another phone.

He and Red had experienced more than one encounter over the years when, in the moment, death looked imminent. They both had given one another that knowing look of being proud to have served with one another and to have each other's back, but they also weren't going to sit around waiting for fate to happen. Men of action defied fate to make a looming demise a time of valor and victory. Death to those who challenged their heart and will.

C'mon Red, hit me back.

Havens stared at his phone as if his intent gaze would cause the phone to ring faster, willing Red to pick up.

Shit, it is hot in this terminal.

He exhaled to center himself knowing the apprehension was triggering his physical sweat and emotional discomfort. He felt his bowels dropping with a wave of gastrointestinal cramping.

The phone rang.

"Domino's Pizza. Will this be pickup or delivery?" Havens answered with a smile of relief at having received Red's call before diarrhea further complicated his situation.

"Hey brother, where are you now?"

"Ah jeez. If you don't mind, I'll plead the fifth on that one. Suffice it to say I am still in the old world but heading westward as fast as I can. Had some odd hiccups that I hope are behind me now. I'll feel better when I land in Frankfurt."

"When will you get there?"

"About 8 hours if my plane is on time and I make it though security with no more problems."

"OK, so you are in Dubai, right?"

"Dick."

"Well you are the one sharing so much on the line, I'm just doing my job teaching you not to burn yourself by making dumb ass mistakes like that on the phone."

"You are right, I am just a bit stressed on the home front. Were you ever able to find anything out? I tried reaching them but no one is picking up." Havens was convincing himself that it was nothing unusual. Deep down he knew it was not normal. He was scared. His phone was hot. It was slippery from his hand's sweat.

Red paused uncomfortably as he struggled to find words that would express the situation to his friend.

"And…?" Havens pushed.

"Sean, I got your message late. There has been an awful…I have awful news, Sean. I am sorry to have to tell you there was an accident. Well a break-in, and Sean, someone, um, Sean, your family is gone, buddy."

Silence filled the lull.

"Sean, are you there? I am so sorry, bro. I did everything I could and well, they got the guys who did it. They killed 'em. I mean the guys who did it are dead now. I chased one down and they got him and the other was killed and the guy I was chasing is dead too, and one guy that was also there that I didn't see is also dead now in addition to the others. Shit brother, I am so sorry."

Sean Havens absorbed the news. In the twisted fantasies he had had of what it would be like to ever receive news like this, he never imagined it this way.

He felt nothing. It was not even emptiness.

He had almost anticipated this news, but why he did not immediately know. He recalled that something subtle had been triggered when Red started talking. Ever since Havens and Red served together in a Tier One Special Mission Unit, Red always replied to Havens' Domino's Pizza intro with, "I picked up your wife and made a delivery to your mom."

His head was floating. Suspended on its own. He was unaware of whether he was standing, walking, or holding a phone. The news was disassociated with his personal life. It was as if he had just heard of two deaths on the news. They were not his family. His family would not be gone.

Images of his daughter smiling at him sitting on the couch played before him. Family outings. His wife bringing food to the table like June Cleaver from *Leave It to Beaver.* Their trip to Costa

Rica. No, his family was not gone. He could see them. They were here.

"Sean. Man, I am sorry, can you say something so I know you are still on the line?"

"Where are Christina and Maggie, Red." Cain, where is your brother?

"Sean, what do you mean, like where are they now, like now?" Red didn't know if Sean meant the morgue or hospital, or if he was even grasping it all.

"I meant what I said, Red. Where are they?"

"Sean, c'mon. They're at a funeral home for now I suppose. Christina's brother, Lars, has been helping out a bit. He's gotten a lot of the initial arrangements made until you get back. I didn't even know she had a brother before this. Certainly not a Chicago cop. I mean, detective."

Images of family moments shifted in Havens' mind to visualizations of them on stainless steel gurneys, pulled out of body storage refrigerators, and in glossy wood coffins with white decorative upholstery. He visualized a crime scene. Reality was hitting him.

"What happened to them, Red? Who did it? Was it that guy who raped Maggie?"

"There were a few gangbangers who were in the house. We don't know why they were there. Nothing was missing. One was shot at the scene. But he was killed by his own guy. I don't know why, maybe he was deviating from the plan or had second thoughts. He had been wounded upstairs."

"Gang members? That doesn't make sense. The girls were fighting back?"

"Well, it seems that the guy who was wounded upstairs had been shot by his own guy up there too. The girls were um…They were not touched, Sean. They died painlessly."

"So they were put together and killed? Were they executed?"

Oh God, Sean, how could you have let this happen? You failed your primary mission to protect your own.

He envisioned his wife and only daughter kneeling on the ground, maybe reaching for one another's hand in the last seconds. Looking at each other for hope and solace.

"No, it looks like Christina got to Maggie's room and the killers kicked in the door. Sean, we can talk about this later? Man, I hate doing this on the phone like this."

"What the fuck other choice do we have, Red? I am here, you are there. What the fuck can I even be doing here?"

For the first time in minutes, Havens realized he was standing in the middle of the walkway area in the terminal. Passersby glanced at him but he was completely oblivious to their need to move around him.

Havens walked over to a seating section at another gate and collapsed into a chair. He dropped a small bag that he had taken from the airplane and filled with some items to get him through a couple more days of travel. As he released his grip he felt the tightness of his clenched fist and a slight pain as he extended his fingers. Color began rushing into the whiteness that had taken over his digits.

"Sean, we figured you would be going through Germany, so your company will be flying you in their plane. I have the details. I am going to meet you in New York. The Gulfstream will get us closer to your home."

"My company knows about this?"

"Yeah, the relay on the house alarm pinged security. They of course knew you were TDY and sent a CI guy over to the house."

"Red, this isn't a counterintelligence issue. It was a law enforcement issue. They were supposed to be watching them. Somebody is supposed to be watching them when I am away. Who the hell is looking out for our families when we are deployed? Someone didn't do their fucking job and now my family is dead."

He hung up the phone with such anger he half expected his thumb to go through the end call button and out the back of the phone. He could no longer control and process all of the emotions closing in on his sanity. Havens' mind was unable to find a compartment to hide these feelings of such an unjust loss due to his perceived inaction. His head flopped back in the chair hitting the wall behind him. He needed Christina. Christina helped him through this. It was coming back. The stress. Christina was gone. More than a best friend and lover, his bedrock was gone.

"Oh, God." He closed his eyes.

They were dead. And his baby, she was gone too. They would have been praying for his help that would never come. His daughter would be begging in her mind that her father would not let her down and save them before certain death. They would have been scared. They would have been terrified. They were alone.

Havens wept inaudibly to others, but in his mind he was wailing. His role of husband and father pushed his inner warrior to the corner where he would be called upon later. For now, the parent would mourn the family he had fought so hard not to lose in his years of special missions. Missions tasked to create outcomes of death that made other families cry. Not his.

He watched a family walk by dragging luggage and mini-roller backpacks. Overcome with the pain in his chest and head, he felt the need to attack someone. Repeatedly.

Chapter 15

The Crystal City, Virginia office building looked like every other structure on the block. Harrison Mann walked past the office complex's lower level Italian restaurant, went to the elevator bank, and upon entry pushed the sixth floor button.

Exiting at the sixth floor, he showed a badge to the armed security guard, and crossed to another elevator bank where he pushed a button for the tenth floor. On the tenth floor, he walked fifteen feet to an open staircase and climbed ten steps without acknowledging the guards in tactical advantage posted at the top of the stairs. At the top of the stairs he locked his mobile phone in the small metal lockers resembling post office boxes. He pocketed the key.

"Good day, Mr. Mann," said a guard with a KRISS Vector submachine gun strapped across his chest. The guard was much less comfortable giving a nod after a lifetime of requisite salutes to leadership. He bobbed his head acknowledging the Deputy Program Director of the supposed DoD Counter Terror Foreign Collection Task Force.

As far as the guards knew the high security requirements were due to the Task Force's need to house and receive human intelligence reports from non-official cover military assets globally tasked with targeting foreign threats.

For the most part this was true, except for the fact that this particular shop was focused on *domestic* intelligence collection with a mandate not to share or deconflict with other agencies or law enforcement elements. Direct action follow on activities—a nice way to say violence—associated with the intel collections may be, as it was often described to insiders, "a bit outside the scope of DoD," not to mention the restriction on military action on U.S. soil.

Mann simply gave each man a half nod acknowledgement of their presence and greeting.

He swiped the door pad with his badge and entered the office of the Domestic Support Activity, or DOSA as it was called by the select few bureaucrats and defense czars who even knew of its existence. DOSA was layered under a Pentagon basement program where Mann's boss, Prescott Draeger, worked as Program Director to a number of interchangeable programs with ever-changing names. The czars thought they owned Draeger and assumed with all practical reason that he was one of their own. Like so many secreted programs, even the employees were often seconded to someone else.

Internally, DOSA called themselves the pilgrim preachers, or the "Preachers" for short, as they were now the domestic version of an element that had travelled the world doing "God's work" ridding humanity of whomever made the naughty list.

Even Draeger, who was a career military and intelligence community member, was covered on the books as a technical contractor overseeing process improvement to special operations logistical supply. Secretly, and unbeknownst to even those working around him, he worked for an individual simply referred to as PASSPORT. PASSPORT, by his own right, led the operational activities of a U.S. intelligence rival of the CIA called the Pond.

The Pond was long thought to be disbanded. In fact, it could not be a better living organization for shadow masters such as Prescott Draeger or PASSPORT.

While his closest operator friends outside of the program could see Draeger's lips moving and hear what he was saying about his new low speed job, few bought in to this benign story knowing of Draeger's accomplishments in places such as the Congo and the Balkans. Guys like Draeger don't improve organizational process as he claimed. No, a man like Draeger helps destroy process and all things organized.

Draeger certainly wasn't a business guy; he was initially a skilled HUMINT collector and ex-Special Forces indigenous forces instructor who later served on a special activities unit running surrogate operations. He took a desk job and found his way into technology after a freak lunch break accident while playing soccer behind their compound where he re-ruptured an already damaged vertebra.

The damaging cheap hit came from one of the small community's members, Trevor "Red" Peterson, who always fancied himself as the founder of full contact rugby soccer. Red's overaggressive play was a result of wanting to end the tied soccer game quickly so he wouldn't miss the Friday lunch dessert buffet, where even the most health-conscious hunter killers would deftly palm a cookie from the table near the exit when leaving the chow hall on their way back to their respective squadron's corridors.

In years to follow, Draeger would snap when anyone referenced Red, calling him the "oaf who broke my back for a piece of fucking carrot cake." Most who knew the two men never brought the names up together, assuming they still didn't talk. A sour man like Draeger wasn't quick to forgive. One thing his peers all agreed on was that you can put Draeger in a suit, but you can't stop the man from convincing any guy on the street to go kill someone.

Doubt aside, no one ever pressed for more information from Draeger about his new job. They knew he also wasn't a techie, commo, or hacker lead. Draeger was a hacker of men's minds. They all knew that someone somewhere was dying and killing by the marionette puppet strings of Prescott Draeger. This tight nit community was used to odd stories of what people did for a living. Few cared that the newly created positions, units, or task forces didn't always correlate to skills and experience. Even fewer ever asked. If you were in it or read on to the program, you knew. If you didn't, you had no need to know or inquire. Amateurs asked. Professionals stuck to their beers and made other conversations.

Similarly, Mann also came from the world of off-the-books black special projects. Mann, however, had started out as an academy graduate Navy SEAL and later ended up with a Drug Enforcement Agency role with their Special Operations Division. DEA had him chasing down traffickers globally undercover, but as part of task forces that increasingly moved from the white overt world of law enforcement and oversight to a more nebulous grayish shade where parallel construction and investigative lines were crossed, criminals were kept on payrolls, and the reputations of operator units grew as notorious in the underworld as their targeted cartels and mafia families.

Mann was well suited for his role, having been the son of a tough New York Bronx cop. His father was well respected on the force and it was assumed by family and police friends that Harrison Mann would one day be working with his father. As such, rules were often bent so young Harrison could hang around in the precinct or go on patrol squad car ride along with "the boys."

The job was initially appealing, but Mann wanted to get away. An avid swimmer, he crossed the New York neighborhood's cultural lines one day and asked some of the firehouse guys across the way if they could teach him how to scuba dive when they went on Search and Rescue trainings. The fire chief, a crusty old Vietnam veteran who had served as a SOG SEAL, was more than happy to try and convert an up-and-coming police officer to the firefighter side.

Recognizing Mann's potential, even a dedicated firefighter who had a fresh recruit in his clutches, saw different opportunities on this boy's horizon. The old SEAL vicariously pushed his newly trained scuba diver to the open arms of the Navy, and sealed the deal with a few phone calls and cache of favors that would expire when his cancer-filled lungs finally gave in.

Mann's father, who had often reminded his son that the Navy was for pussies, was shot in the line of duty and paralyzed from the waist down while Harrison was at the Naval Academy. Quickly turning into a raging alcoholic in an increasingly obese condition, the father became unbearable to live with. Siblings quickly left the house and Mann's mother, who was no longer able to cope, shot herself in the head with her husband's revered service revolver. Her dying wish to herself was that his beloved gun would now be taken away as potential evidence in her suicide. With a split family, Mann became immersed in his profession with ties neither holding him back nor bringing him back home. His family was the job.

Mann now dialed his boss on a DSN secure red line for news.

"I don't have any more news on the investigation of your international 'preacher's' family. Everything else is cleaned up on our end. When does he get back CONUS?"

"I am sending him back on one of our planes so we can give him the warm and fuzzy treatment. He is going to take some time. This guy isn't our typical pinch. I am going to have to really work him from the sidelines as his friend and make the slow introduction to you."

"And you are certain he has no clue where you are in the Pentagon and who we are working for?"

"No, and it doesn't really matter. He is rarely in DC, and when he is it is around Arlington or Langley. He'd never know that I am running this program. We are safe from that standpoint. Foreign Collections Deputy has all contact with him, so he still has no clue that he has been working for me, nor will he when we transfer him to domestic. He's used to working that way. And I have a feeling he is going to stay put in Chicago for a long time after this. Bit of a shame, given my relationship with him and his family, but war has its casualties, and we need him to fight. His daughter was going to be a problem for him in the years to come anyway. I read the file on her texts. Social media posts and associations were starting a pattern. I think she was getting to the point of exploring outside her world and Dad's sheltering. Whore in the making. We had to play the screaming rabbit card to get his attention. The rest just had to be done to solidify his commitment."

"Yeah, well whatever. Job had to be done. Just like the rest. We have the laptop all rigged up now and will get it back in the house. We wiped down anything leaving traces and all the evidence plants are set. Took a while to get the surrogate set. I'm not challenging you, but this idea of a predator rapist and hood burglars was a bit off. I think this whole scheme is a pretty damn long stretch. Too many parts to orchestrate. Too complex."

Draeger let Mann continue to see if it was a rant or a real issue.

"With all due respect it leads to fuck-ups. I had to convince this maniac that the girl had printed out a picture of him from the registered offenders so he would act on her. I think he got off on it. Guy is freaking now off meds. I think your boy Havens will see that he had a lonely kid and that will feed his guilt and then we will tie our surrogate to the issues DHS has been having with the Eastern Euro car thefts and heroin networks. Once we get Havens up and rolling we will release him and make him up a pretty intel package. I still don't see how those gang members fit in. You turned about three different fairy tales into one."

"You just stick to the plans. As for the stretch, cut the DHS and Eastern Euro segment. It's overkill and too much to deal with. I have another team working that from a different angle."

"Roger that. Oh, I will also make sure that we cover the wife and girl's funeral expenses by the foundation. I have a guy who can do it so I don't need to touch anything."

"Sounds good. Can you make it look like a suicide and clean up our rapist? Psycho stalker guy was in love but then when the girl was killed he can't live anymore?" Draeger cringed realizing that one would hit close to home with Mann. Still it was a decent plan to tie up these loose ends.

There was silence at the other end. Contrary to Draeger's thought of a major faux pas, Mann liked the idea and was simply thinking of how he would convince Draeger to let him do it as opposed to using one of the surrogate team operators.

"Prescott, I think that will be tough to do in the time we have. I know it is risky, but let me handle that. You have too many lines of effort running into this one and since I had to cage this guy and take him off his meds, I can at least make sure there's no screw up."

Draeger didn't care for the idea but wanted to think for a moment. This activity was supposed to draw all connections away from their organization. It would be too risky, although Mann did develop this asset and built trust. And the plan Draeger had given him was outlandish and rather fucked up to say the least.

Little did Harrison know, Draeger was testing his deputy with as many far-fetched ideas as he could come up with while still making sure it could be pulled off. He was training his men to push their limits of creativity and manipulation. He was also tugging on strings so his guys would tug back. That in time would lead to autonomy. Autonomy led to plausible deniability for Draeger. Now his man wanted to keep his hands in the mess. Draeger would ensure there was plenty of mess to play in.

"I'm still thinking."

When you are running wolves, you have to let them make the occasional kill, Draeger thought to himself. He expelled a breath in contemplation. Mann, like a good salesman, knew to remain silent and not interrupt the customer's thought process. He would wait for an objection and then aggressively rebut it.

"God help you Harrison if this goes south. I respect your wishes and hope that you will respect the Activity's work and that you are not simply satiating your own desires. I know you are a professional. This is a soldier's duty. You are a soldier and you will execute by orders, not personal interest. Do you understand?"

Harrison understood Draeger's point. It was worth the slight chastisement by the boss so the underling would still get his way. So far they were a good team and Harrison respected Draeger as the commander in that he was not afraid of the unconventional, even though Draeger was a spoon feeder of intel and ops plans.

Harrison, however, did recognize that Draeger was yet another one of this country's toxic, narcissistic leaders who wouldn't accept criticism, didn't accept new ideas, and had likely built a career and reputation on exaggerated achievements. It was self-interest, but Harrison could tuck that away as par for the course and think of his interactions with his superior as an objective and tasking order fulfillment. Even if he clicked his heels in deep satisfaction when it was finished.

Harrison also knew Draeger walked a fine line between effective operator and veritable psychopath, his leadership style aside. Acute self-awareness told Harrison that he too was increasingly going to the dark side of behavior, but at least wasn't a psychopath. Maybe a slight sociopath. While it slightly concerned him as a matter of diagnostic labeling, he was actually having the time of his life. He looked forward to the challenge with Havens.

"Hey, boss, give me some more gouge on Havens. I read the files but I want a better feel."

In his office, Draeger rolled his eyes. He wanted to be thorough but detested the thought of having to ramble through the highlights of Havens' career. "Havens is a hunter but is also a homebody. He is always looking for good sources like one where you scan a table for a specific corner or color jigsaw piece in a grand cardboard puzzle. But he never looks for sources near his home. Home is hands off. We just gave him a big bitch slap. He's going to be dazed from this blow. What else? If he can keep the job away from his life, he loves it. Guy loves the idea of being able to walk among others without casting any initial or sustained suspicion. And he is decent at it. As you see in the file, he is usually used to establishing and overseeing surrogate infrastructure contrivances and schemes that support clandestine indigenous operating forces. Like us, he does it in places where the United States holds no military title authorities. The good news for you is he isn't a killer, per se. Clean black support. Procure safe houses, non-attributable vehicles, black hole sites, and cutout payment schemes. Kind of pussy stuff. He's the geek that finds storage sites and escape and evasion routes with friendly support or plausible commercial covers. While he isn't a death merchant as a primary trade he can fall back on it. Havens won't kill if it doesn't serve a purpose. That's also a weakness. He will risk himself or others to disable a man if it can serve a purpose. He has solid restraint. Probably why the risk-averse lawyers that approve Tier One missions like him. Ironic, because Havens as a softer approach still makes for spillage, which is why he is perfect for this. He isn't a meat eater, nor is he just a plant eater. He's more like…a stir fry…with extra hot sauce.

Enough of this. Why don't you fly in next week again? We can discuss more then go saw a steak at Ruth's for dinner. I am not going to stall Havens with any other obstacles."

"I can expense it right? No per diems? No orders?"

"No one said this isn't without its perks, Harrison. You will be rewarded and you will be reimbursed."

"OK. Thanks. How did you end up delaying him?"

"Don't worry about it. All handled. Check in to the Ritz by the Pentagon."

"Fine."

"Just don't use your military ID for a cheaper rate."

"Can I use my rewards card for the points? I mean it worked in Italy for those CIA folks a few years back, right?"

"Easy on the sarcasm, I am serious. We have to play this tighter than we ever have before. This is where the gloves come off and we really make a difference, but we don't have get out of jail free cards. We have to keep things compartmented and air tight against blowback. You've done a great job these past couple years, but now that we have tested the program we can start going after the fatty part of the snakes, but we don't want to cast a trail."

"Aye, aye."

"Aye, aye, my ass. Out."

Prescott Draeger sat back in his faux leather chair.

Harrison can be manipulated, but he isn't stupid. He wants his own lane to work in. That will actually work well for the bigger plan.

Draeger switched his thinking from Harrison to Havens. Courting Havens would not be easy. He would stay away from the funeral citing temporary duty restraints in Djibouti. This was going to be a tough chess match, but if Draeger could just keep at arm's length with Mann as the primary handler things would go fine.

Draeger never told Mann that they had lost Havens for a bit and were still unsure as to how he arrived in Dubai. It was just part of the wild card they would be dealing with in Havens. He too would take enough rope to be hung with later. Havens was dangerous, but he was not as ruthless as PASSPORT. The decision was easy. He would do what it takes to achieve what was asked.

Taking out John, one of the Agency's case officers after requesting Agency help had been risky, but fortunately there was a stay-behind Pond singleton asset still in place that could be tapped for the opportunity and made it look random enough. PASSPORT came through big time on that as he always did. Fucker had a finger everywhere.

Play the story, tell the story, and make the story stick. All would go fine. At least he would not have to have any more basement beer parties at Havens'. Wine was much more his style. He could go for a glass right now and certainly not in a wood paneled man cave with those Neanderthals. Such men were not his friends. They were beneath him. They were his tools.

Draeger felt that he had paid his dues in tents, shanties, and freezing cold or scalding hot safe houses in so many shit holes of the world. Each one of those shit hole places ended had criminal problems that always ended up on U.S. turf. And here the U.S. was looking to cut defense spending further?

Deployments were a waste of time to him when the root problems were here domestically. Why chop at the tail when you could whack the heads? Why live with uncertainty? In short time he would help change that.

To Draeger, the military had failed to understand that the human dimension of conflict demanded too much in lives, resources, and sociopolitical will for this nation to stomach. He believed that true 'left of bang' was found by creating opportunity before tensions turned violent or before there was a surprise event. Men like Draeger and Havens could raise tension and move nations towards conflict but also use surprise to give the offense the most options. Of course their specialty was to make it look like the bad guy was always willing to attack but not quite ready to. The key to having the most policy options, lowering engagement costs, and minimizing the loss of American lives was to punch first. Even if it meant punching Americans first through minions.

And his minions, if Draeger had it his way, would be the best utility that operators could offer—dependability and expendability. He may have to tweak their lives a bit, but that was all part of the assessment, recruitment, and handling of men. Havens, among others, was an end to a means.

Draeger's band of domestic merry men would get this fight going and then they could take it to all ends of the earth. Amplify and accelerate. Be agile, resilient, and compete more effectively than your adversary is capable of. Be merciless with no social or value limitations. His men wouldn't have to want to destroy; they just had to be influenced to the point of being willing to destroy. Destroy for him. And Draeger had no limits. Havens would be the perfect proxy under these circumstances. And he could be left as the mess for someone else to clean up or take out.

It was finalized in Draeger's mind. Napa 2011 blended red, The Prisoner, tonight. Not real fancy but real good. Worthy of his palate.

Chapter 16

Havens composed himself as best he could in the situation and shook off his stinging hand. A mid-force jaw punch dropped the rude and hurried German businessman quickly in the bathroom two terminals over. It was unlike Havens to ever pick a fight that was not associated with an operation. His blood was boiling and he was having a hard time controlling himself. Christina had been so good at talking him down and keeping him focused. They had been working on it now for several years. It helped him deal with things. Things he never talked about.

He called Red back. Red, fully understanding, had waited patiently in his office for the return call that he knew would come when the time was right. Sean couldn't let things fester. He was soft that way. On the call Sean did a lot of rambling but asked if Red would be around during the weekend. Sean thought the need may arise to just talk some things out amidst the turmoil.

As Red hung up he took a moment to put himself in Havens' shoes. *Talk?* Red was also a father though he was no longer married. Even when he was married, he rarely considered himself as the head of a family unit. Red's unit was on the East Coast. Everything else was a personal window treatment for what people said was important in life. He would actually be happy if someone killed his ex-wife and had often thought of doing it himself. For that he was envious of Havens to be rid of that baggage.

In Red's heart he knew killing his two girls' mother was certainly not in the best interests of his kids whom he loved in concept but never saw. In truth, he really didn't miss being home or away from his kids, it was the concept that he should.

Sean had given up work on the teams so he could be home more often and for longer periods of time. Sean also wanted to live remotely from the teams, the military, and the life of an operator. The team hadn't been happy about Havens' decisions but they understood. Red really couldn't understand. There was the mission, and there was the mission. It was a commitment that most men had signed up for long before they complicated things with family affairs.

Red struggled with the thought that he would need to be there for Sean and at the same time as this weekend's rare custody visit with the kids. He really didn't even have plans for the kids. He just knew it was his weekend for a change and his wife owed it to him. The kids would just watch TV and text their friends while they were at Red's house. He was free to come and go.

If he called his ex and said he had to change weekends, she would let the kids pack their bags and then tell them at the last minute that their father was not coming and blame him for the insensitivity. He never understood how a mother could be so cruel to her own. Even if she was a whore who slept with his teammates while he was overseas.

Screw families. It was the brotherhood he loved. No need to talk. Hanging out and BS-ing worked fine.

Havens was going to continue his travel plans and pick up the next leg in Frankfurt. He was on autopilot now, emotionally at a low simmering flame after mentally slowing his adrenaline-heightened body. Any added fuel would cause him to boil over. He kept breathing through the heaviness in his chest.

Stay cool. We have to get through this. Need to find out what went wrong. Keep moving, one foot in front of the other. Don't shut down. Just get home.

Havens dialed another number. When his handler Jason answered, Havens informed him that he wanted to change the plane ticket for a direct flight from Germany to Chicago. He appreciated the offer to go on the Gulfstream but he simply did not want to talk.

"We need you to be on the Gulfstream. I know it is difficult but it is the only way we can debrief you on your trip. We are very sorry for your loss, but we don't have an alternative. We can keep it short; you can take a break. Your buddy Red said that he would even make the trip with you from New York to Chicago on the jet. There will only be an hour difference or so, and we can be done to let you carry on with family business."

Family business? My family is dead because of you. "Who was watching my family while I was away?"

"C'mon, you know that is not our protocol. You are paid extra and given an extensive budget, not just for your overseas work, but for your domestic support infrastructure. I don't want to go there with you now as I know you are grieving. I humbly cannot tell you enough how bad I feel for your loss. Security for your family falls to you. We intervene when it involves you. We have to cut the line somewhere."

"You did not just say that to me."

"Hey, blame the people who killed them, blame the criminal activity that surrounds your family and neighborhood, blame the world we live in, but please don't blame the people you work for who are trying to make a difference out there like you are."

Jason rarely said more than a few words to Havens even when they were face to face in secure, controlled environments. If Jason was taking this posture maybe there was something to it. Havens felt bad for the finger-pointing when the finger ultimately came back to him.

"Sorry. You are right." *It is my fault. I wasn't there. I didn't take precautions.*

Havens noticed some security guards coming his way. *What are you guys up to?*

Jason continued. "Listen, get on the plane. Use the itinerary we have set up for you, and no funny business."

"Funny business? You should talk. What the hell was all that in Sana'a?" Havens lowered his voice. "And do you know anything about some mugs who are approaching me now?"

"See, we have a lot to talk about on the plane. Wait. Wha'd you say? No one has been authorized on our end for contact. What's up?"

The guards stopped. One was looking at Havens while the other radioed and looked back down the terminal walkway.

"You there? Get on that flight. And one more thing. I will see if I can get Red authorized to bring you a file on the assault and some individuals that we have confirmed are involved. You really shouldn't be privy to this but given the situation and your background I know you would want to know and be somewhat involved. I will have that on the plane in New York for you."

"OK. I will be there. I gotta figure out what is going on here."

"Hey, there are no ties to you for anything. I'm not saying you are seeing ghosts, but it could be the stress too. You are practically home free now. Just get to the plane."

"Hey, you there?"

A Caucasian man had now run towards the guards. They nodded in Havens direction. He looked familiar. Perhaps from DC. He was coming towards Havens. Havens looked around for others surveilling him or closing in. Tensing like a jaguar ready to spring, Havens remembered he was a business guy again. No, he thought to himself. He really didn't know this guy after all. He looked like the State Department guy, who looked the same as every other State Department guy.

He tried to remain calm. Business guys do not jump at their potential adversary with Baguazhang punches to the sternum or Jujutsu attack to the larynx. Business guys worry about missing their flight, taking a shit on a clean toilet, brushing their teeth after a long flight, and checking their email.

The man approaching was now smiling and slowing down, a bit out of breath.

"Hey," he said, outstretching his hand to Havens. "Glad I found you. I am an attaché here. Defense. Just got word that you were coming through here instead of Kuwait."

"Um, what's your business? I am guessing you didn't just drive over from Kuwait for me. I don't know you. Who are you and what do you need? I don't know anyone in Defense or know what an attaché is aside from a briefcase. I work for..." Havens stalled. He never forgot his cover legends. His mouth was still open as he was thinking.

Who the hell do I work for? What passport am I using now? Fuck.

"Hey, OK, no matter. I gotcha. It's cool. Word is you are trying to get home quick. I was instructed by someone who was instructed by John to get you back with no hassles. I work with DSS and the CoS here some. We pulled some strings to get you through quickly. C'mon."

"Wait. No. I have a very specific itinerary that my company has set up for me. I am not sure why you are involved due to some favor for John. I think John knew where I stood about more involvement from outsiders."

"Don't worry. My office knows all about it. Consider us 'insiders.'" He winked knowingly at Havens while making quotation gestures with his fingers.

The wink Havens had gotten throughout his career was usually when someone didn't have a need to know but were assuming that they could be included in the secrecy. More often than not, it meant a breach. The field was too deadly for breaches, especially when wannabes and posers tried to get groupie-close to ops.

"Who is your office?"

"DIA, brother," the attaché whispered as he looked over his shoulder in a horrible display of being discrete.

"OK, this ends here. I appreciate your help but I really need you to leave me alone and let me get on my way."

"Nah, it's cool. We have you covered and I am declared here already. I'd like to talk to you about Yemen a bit while we walk."

Havens swiftly stepped in to the man's space, grabbing the so-called attaché's tie with his left hand and grabbing the man's balls with a lower right iron clutch squeezing immediately while holding up the man's posture with the convenient neck noose.

"You will fucking back away from me now. I appreciate any gesture from John, but I have found that you guys do more harm than good where I am concerned. Stand fucking down and keep anyone else away that you all have in your pocket trying to help me. Understood?"

The silent gasping affirmation of rapid head nods and tears was accepted as a "Yes."

Havens continued on his way nodding to the security guards as he passed and thanking them by saying, "Shukran jazeelan."

They nodded and replied, "Aafwan."

At least this American spoke Arabic to them and had formal courtesies, they thought to themselves. The guards walked away with nothing further to say to this annoying embassy man whom they believed to be American CIA. They figured all Americans here were probably CIA. *And they all needed favors and asked too many questions, in English nonetheless. It was offensive. The Americans were guests here and treat us so inconsiderately. They need to learn their place. They should go home to their own problems. Let this other guy go. At least he was going and not staying like the others.*

The next leg of Havens' flight was torturous. He couldn't sleep, didn't want to eat, and most certainly did not want to talk or be talked to. He kept to his own thoughts while parrying all conversations coming his way, and soon his own thoughts were a menace to his well-being.

He grabbed a newspaper that had been stuffed in the seat pocket. Usual budget crisis and job loss issues. He saw that there was an attack on the tomb of Lincoln that was evidently affiliated with the killing of a State Representative from one of the House intelligence committees who was vacationing on a boat in Lake of the Ozarks, Missouri. It stated that the explosives were HME, British military, and were set off by a magnesium based detonator timed by the bilge water in-flow. Pretty heavy action for the Midwest.

Who the hell kills a no-name Rep in Missouri? Probably banging someone's wife or daughter.

Chapter 17

The doctors at Northwestern Memorial Hospital continued to work on both the head and body wounds of an intubated Maggie Havens. Wounds in both regions had passed through the body with the head trauma still life threatening. She had been found with barely a pulse when they went to body bag her.

Maggie's surgical team had been working against the intracranial and intracerebral hematomas through a craniotomy while simultaneously working against the mounting cranial pressure on the other side of the wound. IV fluids and transfusions continued to flow to maintain fluid balance while clotting concentrates now worked against the persistent bleeding sites.

C'mon kid. Hang in there. Fight for me.

The neurosurgeon worked a closed suction drain. A neurologist continued to monitor the hematoma evacuations.

"Stay with us Maggie," a surgical nurse continued encouraging. "You can make it kiddo."

A medical intern observing her first brain trauma surgery looked around the room for any eye contact that could reassure her of the likely outcome.

Is this girl able to even make it? Why are you working so hard if she is going to die in the next twenty-four hours anyway? Breathe, Andrea. You can do this. Don't let them see you freaking out. Breathe.

A surgical fellow looked over to check his intern, Andrea. He saw her wide distant eyes and recognized the concern. "She could still make it." He knew he had to reassure these interns. "What do you think? Still on board?"

"Will she even be able to function?" replied the intern.

The neurologist looked up and over, "Now that the bleeding has subsided, we will watch the pressure for the next day or so. She will likely be in a coma and if she regains consciousness could lose basic and or complex motor skills. Her behavior could become modified as well. She will certainly need long-term care and rehabilitation. But I have a good feeling about this one. She's fought for hours here on the table. She's died twice."

Life support monitors began to sound. The room filled with warnings. Doctors stopped what they were doing and frantically started new procedures.

"We're losing pressure. She is crashing. I am losing pulse. C'mon kid, keep fighting!"

Chapter 18

After landing in New York, Havens was escorted to the private jet hangars by an attendant who said nothing other than, "Sir, you will follow me please." They walked through the terminal rapidly.

Havens saw some young soldiers, perhaps reservists toting large duffels and rucks. It was clear they were going overseas. Havens regarded their shoulder patches to discern their unit affiliations. General infantry. Big Red 1. They looked so young.

The men paid him no notice as they passed. He had so much knowledge that he could share with them. No time now. He hoped someone had properly prepared the men. He thought of the contractors in Yemen. Wayward souls. Someone should have mentored them better.

He looked back as they moved on down the terminal. Straps were dangling down like a dozen air assault fast ropes.

The attendant reminded Havens of the time constraint. She could tell he was lost in thought.

"Wait a sec." Havens dropped his own small bag at the attendant's feet.

"Sir, we have to go."

"They'll wait for me," he said as he left. "Hey guys!"

The soldiers turned around looking to the ground to see if they had dropped something. Havens ran up to the young men.

"Guys, you need to secure these straps better. Here. Tuck them in so they don't catch on anything. Lift this here. Private, get some duct tape if you don't have it and fix that strap. It won't bear your load with that rip. Get if fixed ASAP."

"Thanks, sir. You a soldier?"

"Of sorts." Havens tugged another strap to make it tighter. It raised the load a good couple inches and relieved some pressure off the soldier's lower back. "Better?"

"Better. Thanks."

"OK guys, I gotta run. Be safe. And hey, get to know your terps. Bring them a gift. Be considerate of them and ask a lot of questions. The interpreters will be your lifeline to knowledge. Don't make them promises you can't keep, like helping their families come to America. They have been doing this for years now and know you can't do shit about that stuff."

Havens shook the men's hands and ran back to the attendant who was now on the phone assuring someone they were on their way.

"Sorry. I had to. They needed my help."

Boarding the G650 ultra high-speed jet, Sean immediately saw Red who was outstretching a Starbucks coffee black with sugar, no cream, the way Havens liked it, and a Heineken. Havens didn't care much for Heinekens and Red knew this. Havens knew which one was his, and for the first time in what seemed like days he had a brief happy moment.

"A sight for sore eyes, my friend." Havens reached for the coffee. *And to think that all that time in Yemen, I would have just had to call Red for a Starbucks.*

"Who's a sight for sore eyes? Me or the coffee?" Red smiled. He knew it was inappropriate to joke, but in uncomfortable situations he had to make light of things. He knew Sean did the same.

During one particularly hairy situation that he and Havens found themselves in, silence was absolutely required to avoid detection from a heavily armed sentry patrol. They had to remain absolutely still and quiet for safety. After nearly a week's worth of in-country boiled goat and lentils, Red decided this would be the perfect time to fart, rendering himself and Havens helpless to their suppressed laughter and the horrific smell.

Red managed to get out "I think they *passed*" and choked out "no pun intended" before receiving a kidney punch from Havens to cut it out. It was a story that rarely went untold in the presence of a few beers and friends who, despite having heard the story dozens of times, couldn't wait to hear it again. It was obligatory to tell the tale when someone passed gas in the company of others. Humor had managed to stave off death for both men to this point. Now was as good a time as any for a little levity.

"Both you and the coffee. Even the Heineken looks good." Havens managed a smile back.

The smile faded upon seeing Jason and their counterintelligence officer, Rusty. This meant business. Back to reality.

Havens looked back at Red for a moment. It struck him as funny.

Red and Rusty—couldn't have planned that if they wanted to.

"Hey, do you two firebushes know each other?"

Havens received two freckled fingers flipping him off.

"Sean, have a seat, finish your coffee, and we can get started in a bit. Then I will get out of your hair."

"Did you pack a parachute?" chided Havens nodding to the window.

"Funny." Jason paused. "Sean, I…"

"I know," Havens said, waving off the condolences.

"No, I don't think you do. Red, can you inform Sean on the somewhat positive news?"

Sean Havens looked at his friend. *Give me something good, brother. I need it.*

"Sean, this is no promise, and it could go south on us, but for the time being it appears that Maggie is alive. She wasn't dead on scene. There was evidently a pulse. I saw only the buses driving away. I saw one body bag and no one said she was being rushed off with any hope."

Seeing Havens about to talk, Red raised his hand for Havens to wait.

"Now let me finish. The intruders shot Maggie in the head and abdomen. Doctors stopped the abdominal bleeding and they are comfortable with the head trauma, short of swelling for now and of course any potential brain damage. The doctors lost her on the table a number of times and she is now in a coma. We will just have to wait and see. I didn't know she had even made it that far."

Thank God. My baby. You've got to pull through.

Astounded by the news, Sean acknowledged their efforts. "OK. Thanks. Thanks, guys. OK. I can work with that." He gave pause again. "But Christina, she's..."

"No, Sean, they were not able to save your wife. She's gone."

"I understand. Long shot. You know how it can be when you just don't leave something right with someone. I left it bad with her."

Havens let out a long exhale.

"Fill me in with what happened, who did it, and where they are in the investigation. Red said they called my brother-in-law as a next of kin while I was away. Is he looking into this?"

Jason had a quizzical look on his face. "Sean, why would your brother-in-law get involved?"

"He's a forensic specialist. Chief Investigator for CPD. Hell, if it was any further north in the city he would have potentially been called to the scene direct."

Jason looked at Red who shrugged. "What? I thought you knew about Lars. What's the big deal?"

Jason looked down at his hands, his fingers bent to touch the palms. They were moist.

Havens caught the movement.

Jason looked up at Sean.

"I just never saw it in your file and was surprised that no one had mentioned this before. I heard some brother-in-law was coming in from Arizona, which was another surprise. I certainly didn't know he was in Chicago. It really could have helped us to ensure the investigation was properly handled with someone who has a vested interest."

Havens informed Jason that his brother-in-law was on vacation in Arizona to watch Cubs spring training.

"You probably never saw it in any file because Christina had a different last name when I married her. She had been married for a very short time but kept the married name. Guess she hated the name Bjorklund more than her ex and held on to the bastard's name. Most of my background checks were done when I was single. They must not have hit it on the last SCI clearance periodic review. Maggie is mine, though."

I always do that.

Havens wondered why he always had to add siring ownership to Maggie when he told others about Christina having been married before. Though not an insecure man, Havens still took some slight issue or embarrassment with Christina's past marriage. It wasn't her fault, nor was it really the fault of her ex. They were just young. Too young. They thought they were in love and didn't think the pulls of the world could tempt a young couple still in college.

"No biggie, Jason. You probably just didn't have the need to know. That information comes above your pay grade. You'd need to be a GS-12." Havens smiled at the fun little jab to his government grade 15 boss.

Havens' supervisor, Jason, was making less than his subordinate, Havens, who was now "officially" a contractor. Pay and grade scale were an issue for Jason, who didn't want to leave government and was hoping for a DISL senior executive service level promotion. It was further off than Jason expected. He was too nice of a guy, always going with the flow. Indeed, nice guys did not get ahead in this business. The nation's capital was a war zone of type A personalities fighting their way to the top.

Jason brushed off the jab. "That's fine. We just want the best. We are trying to keep our arms around those who could help."

Havens appreciated the sentiment.

"Not really, Jason. If this ended up being a CI issue, we would rather everyone keep away." Rusty's interjection was quickly met by Red's counter.

"Aw shit, Russ, I chased that boy down myself. He wasn't any KGB, GRU, SAVAK, MOIS, whatever. He was G-A-N-G banger. Now what the hell he was doing there, I have no clue, and we will likely never know now that those guys got all capped and dead when they got home to the hood. You spook chasers think everything is a fucking conspiracy. Maybe the CIA was involved…wooo." Red wiggled his fingers like ghosts were about.

He continued, "No offense bro, it just seems like a stretch. And I know us beautiful red heads have to stay together, but I don't see it and don't see getting our pants all up our ass about it."

Jason was silently relieved by the deflection. He had heard something in the Pentagon office while in DC that involved the Havens murder case and his boss, Prescott Draeger. It seemed that Draeger wanted to ensure nothing went awry in the case, and Jason was unsure as to whether this brother-in-law would help or hinder an investigation. Since he didn't know who Draeger was on the line with, it was probably best to leave it alone.

Jason essentially liked Havens but was rarely at ease around him. Jason felt like an outsider coming from the NSA as a technical intelligence systems expert, despite the fact that he had been with a group of covert technical intelligence operators in Afghanistan as a fiber optics guru working with the "shooters." Draeger had been his boss for a time with "Orange."

It felt like high school for Jason when Havens was around. Jason, who was more of a techie geek, who on occasion was befriended by the popular guy whom everyone liked to be around, didn't resent Havens. He just wanted to be Havens. Jason never wanted to be Draeger; he just knew Draeger could get him far, so he followed.

Red was excused to another compartment of the jet while Havens debriefed his supervisor about Yemen. Jason had provided feedback that the desired outcome had been achieved with some small uprisings already occurring that would stage as a nice cover for this week's follow on clandestine activity to strike suspected terror cells, renditioning financiers, and gain more funding support from Washington based on the clearly unstable country.

Jason had admitted a problem with their Agency support and apologized for the passports and legends. They all knew this was a challenge to their operations but certainly better than operating in true name. "Add it to the list of things to fix when op tempo slows," he said. "Chances are, the current federal cuts will make it worse before better, anyway."

It also appeared that Jason was completely unaware of why Havens was detained at the airport and was genuinely surprised when Havens had turned up in Dubai.

Rusty took Havens' third throw away phone, tucking it into a plastic bag and assured he would call "Tech" and have the relay disconnected and the phone properly handled. Rusty gave Havens another phone to use domestically for the week if Sean was unable to retrieve his personal phone at his own residence. Havens didn't keep his personal phone at home, unbeknownst to Rusty. He took the phone nonetheless. It wasn't like the old days of isolation and cleansing of all items that could get the team into trouble. No one on his team was even allowed to have a tattoo, lest it give them away as Americans if caught.

Upon landing in Chicago, the group settled on a day and time for a follow-up conversation to discuss any ramifications of the Havens' home invasion on their covert operations. Rusty pulled Havens off to the side in what appeared to be another CI lecture.

CI was always in the guys' shorts about something.

"Hey, Sean, I know you want to go, so I will make this real short. We were never that close or anything and I know I left you high and dry on a couple occasions. Especially Iran."

"Rusty, this is not the time."

"No, man, hear me out. Most guys don't know that my wife and kids were killed by a drunk driver one night while I was deployed not too long ago. We're coming up on almost a year now."

"Shit, I'm sorry. I had no idea."

"Yeah, man, I know, but what I am trying to say is, I've been there. Let me know if you ever want to talk. I got some help and am getting through it. It's harder than you think it will be. I'm kinda sorting things out myself. Losses like that aren't supposed to happen."

"Hey, Sean, you coming?"

"Yeah, Red, hold on. Be right there."

"Thanks, Rusty. I appreciate the words."

"More than words, man. Let me know if I can help. For real. I'm going to look long and hard into this situation."

"Thanks."

"Be well, my brother." Rusty reached out and the two briefly embraced in a short bro hug with the one hit shoulder pat. "I'm in the area every now and again, so ring me up if you need."

"Roger that, Russ."

"Hey, everything OK?" asked Red. "Never thought you and Rusty got on."

"We don't. Or, didn't. Things change."

Red dropped Havens off at the hospital. Havens promised to give Red an update either that night or first thing in the morning. Havens thanked Red for his help and being there and offered the recommendation that Red call his own kids that night.

"You read my mind, brother. I have been thinking of them nonstop."

"I will talk to you later and update you on the services when I call Christina's brother."

"Sounds good. You hang in there."

"I'm hangin'." Havens took a deep breath and exhaled through his nose. He shut the door, gave the top of the car a couple pats as a final send off, and went to find his daughter.

Havens was led by a nurse to his daughter who remained in intensive care. The nurse shared what she knew about Maggie's condition and the overall "unofficial" prognosis, but promised to call the doctor upstairs for a full update.

The tubes, machines, and bandages were illuminated in the darkness of the room by a florescent light on the bed's side. The post-surgery life support scene was overwhelming for Havens but much more welcomed than the news he had originally received of her death.

Havens had yet to go back mentally and start the coping process of losing Christina. He knew that feeling would still be there, but tucked away for now so he could take care of his daughter. He felt that Christina was somehow there with him and that as parents they were doing what was right. She would understand.

Havens entered the darkened room and immediately felt another presence. A presence beyond his daughter in the bed. He followed his senses to the back corner of the room, fully cast in shadows and darkness. A hulking mass sat in a chair waiting, not in vigil, but for Sean Havens' return.

Chapter 19

The mass in the room was snoring. That same snoring mass could be heard every few weeks in the family room of the Havenses' residence after everyone had locked up and gone to bed. He would sit in the darkness with one hand on the remote control asleep while Sports Center daily recaps continued on. He could outlast his hosts but never worried about outstaying a welcome.

The mass was among family at his sister's house. An abrupt snore would wake him to be quickly replaced by momentary disorientation. Lars Bjorklund would wipe his mouth from residual drool, turn off the T.V., quietly grab a glass of water in the kitchen, take his tweed Irish Donegal cap from the closet, set the house alarm, and lock the doors before climbing into his car and driving northward to his Bridgeport, Chicago bachelor pad.

Sean now gave his brother-in law a gentle kick and shove with his foot.

"I'm not sleeping, Sean. I heard those loud footfalls a mile away while you were talking to the nurse."

"And the snoring?"

"A ruse to keep intruders in their comfort zone."

"And you would then pounce on them like a cat?"

"More like a mountain lion. A ninja mountain lion. I am spry under this façade of layering and big-bonededness."

"Is big-bonededness a word?"

"Been using it all my life. If it wasn't a word, I made it one to suit my structure."

"Structure, huh."

The mass shook in silent laughter as it got up from the chair. The darkness made Lars Bjorklund look even bigger. Lars slowly walked over to Havens like a bear on two legs stretching out of hibernation. Tree trunk-sized arms opened like a giant condor wingspan before enveloping Havens in a heavy embrace.

Havens had witnessed those same arms swinging a wooden bat at a 16" softball and effortlessly sending it well over 400 feet. The man was a yeti.

Lars' hug lifted Havens from his feet.

"I'm so sorry Sean, I am so sorry."

"Easy Lennie, you are crushing me."

Lars, a 6'6" roughly 350 lb.-Swede chuckled, "OK, Georgie."

"Lars, I am sorry about Christina. I should have been there for her."

Havens saw Lars amidst the glowing medical lights wipe the tears rolling down his cheek.

"No, Sean, you always took real good care of my sister. This was not your fault. And I am going to raise holy hell at the station again tomorrow too. I haven't been to the house yet, but I am going to make sure they didn't miss anything. They said the perps have all ended up dead but I want to look that place over top to bottom for anything. It doesn't make sense."

"Thanks, Lars."

Havens knew Lars was going to do whatever he wanted anyway so there was no point reasoning with him or trying to stop him at this point. Frankly, Havens wanted Lars' view on it all anyway. The whole situation didn't jive how gang-related street thugs were linked to the rape. He had learned on the plane that the thugs weren't even hard core gangbangers.

The rape. I completely forgot she was raped.

Having broken from Lars, Havens grabbed Maggie's taped and tubed hand. He bent to kiss his daughter's cheek, not knowing if a kiss on the head could hurt anything more.

"I'm home, baby. I'm home. I'm here for you. You keep fighting and I will be here with you. I'm not leaving. Ever. I'm here." *Finally.*

Lars too had walked up to the bed and was holding Maggie's blanket-covered big toe as he had done since she was a child. He gently squeezed and wiggled it.

Lars added in a voice spoken to a baby, as if she were his own, "Uncle Lizzard loves you too sweetie pie. And if I have to go the cemetery myself…"

Lars let go of the toe, his voice transforming abruptly to one of deep-seated anger, "…I am going to make sure those fuckers who did this are buried face down so they see the fires that await their souls. Sean, I'm going to the house. Call me if you need anything."

Havens said nothing but watched his brother-in-law leave the room. Havens looked at Lars' hands as he left, half expecting to see a massive caveman club clenched in it. Nobody messes with Lars Bjorklund's family, Havens said to himself. His sister was the last of his next of kin.

Chapter 20

"Thanks for the update, Jason. After the funeral you need to inform Havens that we need him in DC for the next couple weeks."

"Sir, he won't go for that. Not while his daughter is still in the hospital. He's going to need some time off."

"You can let him know that this contract his company has him on offers a one week bereavement time off. Then we will either need him here or he will have to seek other employment."

Draeger looked at his fingernails while on the phone in casual indifference to the call and the topic. He bit a hanging cuticle and spit it to the carpet.

"I don't have to tell you what his answer is going to be."

"Jason, you don't have to tell me anything. I served with him. You just have to tell Havens what his orders are and what his allowable absence will be."

"Then what? He's going to blow up on me."

"Handle it. Then we start transferring him to domestic."

"And the brother-in-law?"

"We have him all taken care of already, but I appreciate your information. That was a good catch on your part."

"I thought you would be surprised."

"Some things certainly get past me, but fortunately, we were in a good position on this one. I will be taking it from here once you cut Havens off. Be understanding and don't burn any bridges with him. Be a friend."

"We really aren't friends, but he is a good guy."

A good guy, my ass. "We'll take care of him; we just need him to consider some new opportunities that will be better suited for him given the recent tragedy."

"Then why can't you just tell him that you are going to transfer him?"

"First, and never forget this, we are compartmentalized. Buck stops with you in this chain of the network. He is still, and will remain so, unaware of my involvement. Second, I need this to unfold on his terms, not ours. Or so he will think. I'll handle it from here."

"Roger that, chief."

"Talk soon. And solid job on Yemen. Place is unraveling just as we were hoping. Serious operational win there."

"Thanks. Havens was pretty pissed at the bona fides he was working with that the Agency passed him. Sounded like he also had a real serious issue with security. I told him that I would follow up on that."

"Well let me start with the first. Those guys don't know what they are doing, but we have to use them. Second, thanks again for bringing it to my attention. I will handle it. No need to discuss further with Havens since we are rolling him out."

"Roger that."

"Speak soon."

"Out."

Out. Draeger sat back in his chair. *Man, we definitely have to find a way to use less military jargon in our communications. I am sure we will come under scrutiny or surveillance at some time. Have to think about who we are supposed to be and not who we are. Eh, still have time. Too many bigger fish to fry and we can always just make our tapes disappear.*

He was fidgeting with the seat swivel below. He liked being a man of power and the leather chair, fake as it was, still gave Draeger the feeling of authority. Master gamesman authority at that.

And welcome to papa, Havens. I need you to get these amateurs to the next stage so they don't screw things up and then we can pin some of it on you.

Going to have to pay you a visit. Also have to figure out how to keep you and Lars apart. Didn't count on that one, you sneaky fuck. How did I never catch that even at your house? What to do, what to do.

Lars could have an accident, but that would look suspicious.

The rape and murder was bad enough. Still a stretch, but it will have them guessing for years.

Can't let Bjorklund pick up on anything there. Maybe get him locked away for something that would piss off Havens.

Prostitution? Gambling? Nah, he's single. No one would care.

Draeger put his feet up on his desk. He was looking around the room to fuel his creativity. He liked playing God with other people's lives. Manipulating others was far easier than managing his own exterior life and feelings of powerlessness. He was increasingly becoming an introvert when dealing with people eye to eye.

Clandestine work in Southeastern Europe, Somalia, Syria, and Lebanon had rattled his nerves. Iran had pushed him over the edge.

Havens seemed to have managed a bit better, no doubt with the help of Christina. She had helped Draeger too at times, though she didn't know it. Sometimes she helped him by her simple inquiry as to how he was doing and actually meaning it. She could sense that there was a hole in Draeger and felt bad for him. While she didn't know what was wrong, she knew he was an emotionally wounded warrior and genuinely wanted to know if he was OK.

He'd miss her. He loved when she would touch his arm. But he needed her husband more. It was just business. Since he couldn't have her, why should anyone?

Draeger still retreated to the closet for good sleep. His panic room would be finished in another month. The new panic room would have top of the line electronics and the personal comfort of a dial-a-mattress. He still chose to make the final construction of the doorway to the secured room through a small 3′ x 3′ opening in his closet.

The closet was always a fast retreat if they came for him. He remembered the pounding on the hotels and apartment doors while operating discretely overseas. He never knew if it was the ruckus of guests and renters or if it was the secret police.

He was so tired.

Playing these games drained him more. He wanted secure sleep.

Games! Ha, sports bookie gambling debt on the games, that would be no surprise for Lars Bjorklund. But now we gave him too much money for that to be a problem. How could we ironically have a guy on the payroll who is family to another? Fucked that up but good.

Kiddie porn? Nah, I don't even want to go there. Too low. Have to sort this out.

And Maggie, God bless you, you little fighter. You have created the perfect thing for your dad to hold on to without completely losing it. Hadn't counted on that part either. Genius move. What is the chance of that happening from a kill shot to the head? This ended up perfect. Fate, faith, and a lot of luck!

Draeger bit into an apple that he pulled from a small nylon cooler. It cracked with crisp freshness.

Can't have you wake up, but need you to hang on for another few months. I think Mr. Mann has a friend that will help us out with that. Get you all strung out if you don't die here real quick. Speaking of which, wonder if your boyfriend is in the house yet. Harrison should have that taken care of soon.

With another bite the apple remained held in Draeger's teeth as he typed on his laptop and then reached for his encrypted cell phone. He sucked the juices and saliva until his hands were freed and finished another bite with a satisfying crunch.

Damn, this apple is good. Pick up, Harrison. Shit, I shouldn't bother you. I'm sure things are fine. I'll wait.

Draeger took another bite. Every bite as loud and juicy as before.

The girl at the store was right, Fuji apples were great. He wished he had spoken to her more. He knew he could have taken her to bed. The night terrors and panic attacks were killing his opportunities for sexual conquests. He was too humiliated to let anyone into his life. They wouldn't like what they found anyway.

Chapter 21

Brock Bardal had been registered as a sex offender in Illinois since his release from Tinley Park's Mental Health facility. He could function very well when he took his medication and had held his job for nearly two years. His employer, a regional non-profit thrift store, had been giving Brock very encouraging performance appraisals.

He no longer wanted to hurt himself or others.

Brock's medicines were first withheld two weeks ago. His demeanor started to change with no treatment.

The black demons had come in to his home and hurt him.

They said he wasn't done healing.

They flushed his meds down the toilet and made him watch, saying medicine was just keeping him from what he was meant to do.

They told Brock that his mother would be coming back for him. Dr. Rubins had told Brock in the hospital that his mother had died years ago. Now Brock was not so sure.

The demons had put Brock in the basement. He hated being alone. It was dark in the basement and he was scared. They played the movies a lot. He wanted to touch those girls. They had taken him out and let him have the girl in the big building, and he liked that. She was pretty like the other girls he used to watch and touch.

The men told him that he should be proud of himself. If he was good, the demons may even take him to see his mother and let him have more girls. He wanted that ever so.

Harrison Mann gave Brock a knife and a laptop computer. Brock was told to put the computer under the mattress upstairs in the girl's bedroom to the left of the stairs. The back door didn't need to be picked and Brock had been quiet as they slipped through the shadows of backyards and dimly lit streets.

Brock was instructed to sit on the floor and pull the knife over his wrists to let out the poison. It had to be all out before his mother would come for him. She would see that he was trying to make things better and she would love him again.

If Brock did it right, they could go back to his home. No more hospitals. He could go back to work and get his medicine back. No more basements. Brock wanted to make this demon happy. The demon told him that after he cut his wrists, if he really wanted to, he could try cutting at his neck to let all the bad thoughts come out from his mind. Brock was indeed having bad thoughts. It would be good to let them go.

This demon was always nice to him and never hit or yelled at him like the others who came into the basement at night. Brock was going to do a good job.

Harrison knew the alarms would be off in the Havens house. He had been told that investigators would no longer be coming to the house and that Havens, while in town, would be at the hospital. Harrison would send Brock in, confident that Brock was now on his own delusional jihadi mission to enter the heavens of mommy. *Fucking freak this kid is.* He gave Harrison the heebie-jeebies.

With little experience dealing with the mentally ill, Harrison figured he could treat this guy like an interrogation detainee. Keep him in the dark. Keep him in his shit. While surrogates of the Activity had handpicked Brock for the rape from some police reports, when they learned of his delusions of beasts from the underworld, the value of this ticking time bomb increased exponentially. A little reading of his stolen file and some psychology tips from the internet, and they were on their way to augment tradecraft that was already developed for making people do things they would not normally do. Exploitation was their business. Brock was yet another of their helpless unwitting pawns.

Harrison disrupted Brock's sleep patterns, exploited fears, used a lot of carrot and stick (mostly stick) techniques to push the buttons on this guy's psychosis. It didn't take long before the guy had completely lost it. It had been fun for a while, but lately Harrison was having to babysit so Brock didn't kill himself before being tasked. Harrison was not going back to square one if this lab rat croaked.

Upon opening the back door in the darkness of night, Harrison had sat Brock down at the kitchen table. Harrison turned on his LED flashlight and asked Brock to lay the laptop down on the table and lay one wrist up. Harrison instructed Brock on how he was going to make the cut. Harrison wasn't taking any chances and had decided to get things going. Brock pulled the knife across his wrist under the pressure of Harrison's grasp.

Like a kindergarten teacher instructing a student how to cut out his first outlined paper shape, Harrison's gloved hand re-guided the knife over Brock's wrist with increased pressure cutting the vein that started the drain of Brock's life.

"Good Brock, I am very pleased. Do it just like that back and forth and criss-crossed down. Good, that is perfect. Your mom will be so pleased. Now go upstairs and put the laptop under the bed."

"No."

"What?"

"I am scared."

"Scared of what?"

"It's dark up there. The demons will be waiting and they will lock me up and hurt me."

Harrison leaned in closer to Brock. "No, Brock, the demons are not here, but they will be if you don't get your ass up there."

"No, I'm scared."

Harrison grabbed Brock's shirt in his fist. "Fine, I will tell the demons it is time for them to eat your mother's eyes out so she can never see you again you fucking crazy shit!"

"No!" Brock yanked the knife away from his wrist and slashed at Harrison, catching him completely off guard. When his motion reached arm's length it retracted back towards Harrison's side, the knife tip catching Harrison's black nylon jacket and entering just enough flesh to make him flinch.

Harrison's instinctive movement to jump back drew the knife in further. He grasped Brock's hand forcing a guided spear thrust a half inch into Brock's neck and twisted back and forth to rupture the jugular. Blood pulsed but Brock remained in an altered state.

Wasting all this damn time creating a puppet when we could have just done this ourselves and dropped off your dead body. Stupid idea, Draeger. You twisted fuck. Now you have me caught up in this crazy ass shit.

From outside, Harrison heard a car door slam.

"Brock, the demons are here. They are bringing your mother. Hurry, run upstairs and turn on the light. They won't go in there with the light on and your mother will be able to find you. Run. Then get your other wrist. Go."

Brock looked down at the blood on his hands and wrist.

Brock now leaking life quickly, ran through the kitchen up the flight of stairs.

Harrison looked around at nothing in particular.

Who the fuck is coming to the house? Shit!

"I can't find a light," Brock called down.

Fuck it all to Hell.

"Hurry, they are coming. Rub up and down against the wall and try to find a switch."

Light shone down.

"Get started and don't talk anymore or they will hear you."

Harrison had seen enough blood loss in his days that he figured Brock had less than five minutes given the parallel knife cuts to the vein and the arterial nic that was evident from the decent spurt of blood illuminated by the flashlight.

As an insurance policy, Harrison had given Brock a drink earlier laced with Coumadin, an anticoagulant blood thinning medicine. Best to poison the lab rat a bit.

Time to bail. Shit, the laptop.

Still calm, Harrison could hear the front door unlocking; he opened the laptop on the table and turned it on. He laid the computer on the floor with the computer screen and keyboard laying face down before exiting the back door. He hoped the girl had a password protected system that may have looked like her rapist had returned, for some reason tried to get on to her laptop, became frustrated and threw it to the ground. Then, due to the mental anguish of the whole thing, killed himself.

This is such a stupid idea. Holes in the whole operation. Draeger, you or these guys are coming up with shitty CONOPs and CONPLANs all around.

On the other hand…maybe that was a good thing. Run the cops in so many directions it is easier to just leave it as a complete head-shaker making no sense to either the hunted or the hunters. A very untidy cold case. Maybe Draeger does know what he's doing.

From Harrison's perspective, their small unit would still be clean of any association. They had accounted for loose ends, left clean sites, and short of a small stab wound, which Harrison had decided he could fix on his own as his personal secret, they were in the clear yet again.

As he ran through the backyard he shook his head at the quiet neighborhood unaware of the mayhem transpiring while they went about their dull lives.

You people are so clueless.

The evening's moisture on the grass brushed and wiped evidence of the blood droplets from Harrison's boot sole—save the two imprints on the Havenses' kitchen floor.

Lars entered the foyer, flipped the light switch on, and could immediately see the blood stains on the stairway carpet. He assumed from the murders. It was his first time in the house since his sister was killed. He took a deep breath.

Same ole same ole every time.

With some variance to the scenes, certain elements of murders always looked the same to Lars after more than twenty years in the police force.

Hello? What is this?

Lars saw fresh blood trailing from the ceramic tiles in the hallway through the foyer and up the stairs with smears on the banister rail. Wrong color for old blood.

"Hello?"

Lars never carried his police issue sidearm. For him it simply got in the way of his work as an investigator. He always rationalized that everyone he looked at was already dead, and when he was investigating potential suspects, he always had an armed uniform with him. There simply was no need to carry anything big.

Still, Lars was a practical man. He watched enough TV shows and B movies to know that some criminals may still be on scene and could come after the bachelor cop sitting in a La-Z-boy chair in a lonely apartment.

Bowing to the genre that would kill the lone unarmed detective stereotypes, Lars kept a Smith & Wesson 6-inch CS45 with a 3-inch barrel. It was small enough for Lars to keep in the small of his back, a pocket, or even boot if he needed. It was also a bit too small for his big mitt hands and looked like a child's chrome squirt gun when he held it at the ready. It was just backup for emergencies.

Lars creaked all the way up the stairs.

I'll be damned. I'm giving myself away. I told Christina to fix these stairs and she insisted that they tell her when Sean is coming up or when Maggie could be sneaking down. Damn creakers are going to get me killed.

Brock saw the giant demon king come up the stairs to the lit room. He had been tricked. They were coming for him.

Brock lunged for the demon, but with the blood loss his strength had left him and the knife fell short. As it grazed the knuckles on Lars' gun hand, he instinctively lifted his hand up losing grip of the gun which was stuck on his trigger finger but now facing up to the ceiling.

Lars re-gripped the gun and hammered it down on the assailant.

Lars knew who this was now in the house. He had pulled the mug shot on his own, having transferred Maggie's rape kit and file for his own team to handle. Lars had initially withheld the findings so he could be on the arresting team.

I'm going to break you in half, you little piece of shit.

Still on the floor, Brock made another slash at Lars' legs, but anticipating the move, Lars lifted his right leg up then crashed it down on Brock's shoulder.

Brock screamed in agony.

Filled with rage, Lars lifted Brock by the shirt and threw him into a dresser.

"What are you doing here?" Lars bellowed as he moved in pursuit.

Brock's eyes were rolling back due to the blood loss and physical shock. Lars shook Brock like a ragdoll yielding no response. In a fit of rage Lars reached down and grabbed Brock's neck with his left hand and with his right grabbed between Brock's legs, the gun still stuck on Lars' finger.

The gun cracked, splintering the wooden frame of a closet door. The shot startled both Lars and Brock. Brock made an effort to claw the demon again. Before Lars lost hold, he hurled Brock towards a windowed wall. The momentum and force of the throw shattered the double paned glass and broke the window framing right out of the wall as Brock sailed through the air onto the ground below. Glass and wood followed on to the lifeless body after it hit the paved patio eighteen feet below.

Harrison had remained in the vicinity to watch and see if there was further movement in the Havens house or from Brock. He panned the scene with his FLIR Scout thermal handheld and caught a falling and landing Brock.

Interesting. See ya, Brock.

Say hi to your mom, you crazy son of a bitch.

Chapter 22

The police officer was escorted by the same nurse who had brought Havens up; he knocked on the door frame of Maggie's room.

"Thank you. I can take it from here. Uh, sir?" the officer said quietly as to not wake the sleeping patients.

Havens had positioned a chair at Maggie's bedside so he could hold her hand and keep an eye on the door for any roving doctors.

The neurosurgeon had come by and checked on Maggie before going home and had offered little aside from her condition being stable for now but critical. They would know more in the coming days. For now she had been medically induced into a coma to help with the swelling and overall recovery.

The doctor and nurse had encouraged Havens to go home and get some rest, but for the time being Sean refused to leave his daughter—in part to avoid having to cope with the loss of his wife. He knew that if he tried, he could compartmentalize the loss for now and could avoid the emotional acceptance, but it wouldn't be true to his love for Christina. He owed her more than being tucked away and hidden from his heart and soul. Avoided and abandoned. He had already done that to her over the years and the guilt was eating him from within. He had to let her out and make amends. Alone with his daughter, he embraced his vulnerability and wept.

Havens released Maggie's hand, now hot and sweaty from his grip for the past two hours. He stood and walked to the officer who had stepped back into the hallway.

"Yes?"

"Mr. Havens, there has been another accident at your home and…"

"What do you mean accident? Nobody is at my home."

Lars is.

"Lars Bjorklund," he continued. "He's a cop. Was he there? Is he there? He was going there."

"Yes, sir, he sent me to get you. Said you needed to get home but that you didn't have a car at the hospital, so I am here to get you. He's OK. He would have called but said you didn't have a phone with you either and didn't want to worry you by calling the nurse's desk and have to explain then still get you home."

"What happened?"

"Well, I can tell you that there was a break in and there is a body."

"Did Lars, do it? Did he shoot the person breaking in? Who in God's name is breaking in now?"

Havens was red with rage.

"Um. No."

The officer covered up a grin and suppressed a slight giggle that was increasingly difficult to contain, knowing it was highly inappropriate given the situation. *The guys at the station will talk about this for years.*

"Well, what is so damn funny…there is a situation with a dead guy that Lars didn't shoot but I have to come home for?"

"The suspect fell from a window, kind of to his death."

"Kind of to his death? What the hell does that mean? How did he fall?"

"Well, um, he was thrown out the window."

"Thrown, oh, sheesh. Did Lars do it?"

"Well if you ever saw him stone put or caber toss the wood poles at the city's Scottish games, Lars, um, Chief Bjorklund, probably lofted that guy a good ten feet out from the house, and that includes the resistance of the window frame. You have a hole in your wall. I'm sorry. I know you have been through a lot, it's just, I'm sorry. This isn't funny."

"No, it's not. Let's go."

"Of course."

Havens looked back at Maggie as they left the room.

"I'll be back soon."

"He really threw him out the window?"

The officer broke a smile again. "I kid you not. I didn't get the full picture, but understood some whack job was in there with a knife carving himself all up. Chief came in and the guy went after him."

"Why didn't he draw his gun?"

"He did. Got stuck on his finger. About shot himself in the head too from it going off on accident while he tried to subdue the perp. He should probably call Smith & Wesson and get one custom made for his paws. Chief insisted on them getting his statement at your home. Said he had a lot to do helping you make final arrangements for your wife. Sorry to hear that, Mr. Havens. Understood you were away on business?"

"Are you making conversation or questioning me?"

"Just making awkward conversation in an awkward situation. You can sit up in the front with me."

"Thanks."

"So, I hear you were in Greece. Couple guys around the shop and I were wondering if there is a big Albanian population in Greece. You know much about Albanians?"

"Afraid I don't know much about anything anymore. I'd kind of like to be alone with my thoughts right now."

"Understood. I can get you home in just a few. Not a word from me, not anymore. I'll just keep quiet."

"You do that."

"I can. Some of the older guys in the shop used to have me do the same thing, and they never even had to go through something like you're going through. They would just have me see how long I could go. Went pretty far. One day made it almost to lunch without talking."

"How about you try it now, starting right now."

"OK, I gotcha. Just don't usually have someone riding with me now that I have my own cruiser."

"Right now."

"I gotcha."

I know Maggie is a smarter kid than all this is showing. Christina has no baggage that would materialize like this. That leaves just one of us.

What has followed you home, Sean?

Chapter 23

As they pulled around the corner to his house, police lights could be seen in the driveway and along the road. A few neighbors had been out on their porches to see why there were police at their neighbor's house again.

Must have been the dad, some surmised. Seemed like a regular guy. Nice enough, but you never know. Came home and they caught him perhaps. So sad. That Christina was a sweet woman.

Havens got out of the car. He saw a couple neighbors who had concentrated on the sidewalk. It was late. Gossip was running. Havens gave them a wave.

"Sorry."

Sorry. I've probably heard that word a hundred times in the past twenty-four hours. What a word. Something you say when no one can do shit about a mess. It never makes things better but everyone expects it to be said.

Havens entered the house with the officer.

The day's events had so consumed his mind that he never had time to think about what the crime scene would look like in his home. Old blood trails, new blood trails. The stains looked so flagrantly obnoxious to someone who had lost a family member and who may lose another still. The stains were not just a reminder of his failure, they were a haunting image now burned into his mind forever.

Looking down the hall to the right of the foyer he could see a reflection in the sliding glass door mirroring the kitchen. One of the sliding glass doors was taped up with heavy construction plastic.

Lars was sitting with his back to the window. Officers were facing him.

Havens heard voices, but no one was laughing about Lars' feat of strength and anger. Havens entered the kitchen to find police officers circled around the table. Lars was hunkered down with a fork over a jar of pickled herring. Cold fish was an understood staple of Lars'. A supply was stored in a special section of the refrigerator for this regular guest of the Havens family.

In his other hand was a bottle of wine. Condensation on the bottle told Havens that Lars had likely gone to the fridge, grabbed his fish, and decided he needed a drink—fast. Fast enough to take an open bottle of white and forego the glass.

Lars had a gauze dressing wrapped around his hand.

What a week this has been for you too, Lars.

Lars looked up at Havens. The anger from the hospital had left. Lars looked different. He seemed disconnected. He looked spent.

"Hey, bro. Heard you did some redecorating around here."

Lars gave a snort, forked another piece of cold herring, put it in his mouth, and took another pull.

In a fraternal gesture, Havens edged in to a seat at the table as if the officers were not there. He opened his hand for the fork, pulled out a piece of herring for himself, then handed the fork back to Lars. He reached for the bottle. Lars didn't look up, but opened his hand, releasing the wine so Havens could take a chug.

"So, mind telling me what happened? I assume you are OK?"

Lars just nodded. Still chewing. He looked up at the officers and swallowed, "You guys get everything you need?"

"Yeah. Body's gone off now and kits all going to the lab."

"You let me know what you get on the floor print. It didn't match the shoe of the perp. Doesn't make sense that you have a whack job and a crony. Makes sense that you have a babysitter if that whack job was someone's wind-up toy. He didn't have the sophistication in his state to be here alone and playing with computers."

Lars took another pull and passed the bottle to his brother-in-law who obliged.

"Call me when that gets in and do a quick canvass. I also want that fiber on the knife's tang and hand guard. Didn't look like anything that I saw on the perp. Directionality on the knife upon initial inspection looked like a different flow. Not sure what that means if anything, but put an eye on it."

"Chief, you can't get involved…"

Lars slammed his fist on the table.

"I am involved! If not in the investigation, then fine. Consider it a fucking fairy whisper in your ear or something. I don't know, pretend you had some divine intervention dream if you need. Just don't screw it up and take a tip for what it is. Now leave me if you all are done. I have some other matters to attend to."

The officers headed off, some giving Havens a nod before leaving. One informed Havens that he would have to follow up in the morning to see if anything else needed a report for insurance or if something came up in their investigations. Havens confirmed that he was not going anywhere.

When they all had left, Lars looked up at Havens.

"So we have some sorting out here. I don't blame you for not being here, I do not blame you for anything that happened, but here is how I see it."

Havens hadn't seen this side of Lars, now much more assertive.

"I made some initial arrangements for Christina. Sean, you will need to make some final ones. You need to have a visitation in two days and the funeral in three. We can't wait any longer. She needs to be at peace now in a final resting place out of that damned cold metal locker. Also, it appears that some foundation has paid for everything. Silver Star. Something about taking care of military folks. They thought I was the husband when I called back to inquire about some details. Now, that doesn't make a whole lot of sense to me given what I know of your background not being in the military. So we will get to that next."

Lars took another pull before continuing.

"This whole thing of poor Maggie being raped by some guy who threatens if she goes to the police to having gangbangers come in, to now seeing that this nutcase is here killing himself and googling on her computer or something isn't making a shitload of sense to me. Those are different worlds and don't mirror your daughter's world in any way. All of it is too random. What's really chafing my balls is how none of this has ever happened until the couple weeks that you are gone, all hell breaks loose from all sides of the world on my sister and niece. This isn't about her having a boyfriend who slaps her or tries to get to second base and gets shut down so he eggs a house or slashes a tire. This is all out Gang unit, Special Victim unit, Homicide, Cyber...We have all arms of a police department in this shit. Real life doesn't work this way."

Havens interjected, "Lars..."

"Now you hear me out."

"No, Lars." Havens stood up breaking Lars' attempt at dominance. "I will listen to you so you can get out whatever you need to get out. But you know this... I had nothing to do with this. I am just as confused, and have been equally—no offense—but if not more devastated by this whole thing that happened to my family. My wife. My daughter. In MY house! And if I'm not showing you enough emotion it's because I can't anymore. I'm broken."

Lars raised his hand, closed his eyes. "Wait."

Recomposing himself, Lars continued as if he had only extended a courtesy break in the conversation for another voice to have some time. That time was over.

"Seany, I know you didn't do it. I know you didn't have someone do it. All I am saying is this stink of shit isn't following what I know to be my niece's behavior. It isn't something that my sister is involved with. It isn't a mistaken identity or random act. That leaves one thing. In my experience in law enforcement, it means the stink is on you, and I need to find out what. Not to bust you, but to help you. Because if it is what I think it could be, you could be next, and you are all I have left. I look at you like my own brother. I believe Maggie will get better, but that is going to be a long road if she makes it."

Sean nodded without uttering a word. He started to move away from the table. Indeed he did look like a broken man to Lars.

"Now, Sean, hear me out and then it will be all you. You have never treated me like a guest in your home; you treated me like your own. I don't take that lightly, and I would never want to disrespect you, especially not in your home. But I made a promise to Christina that I would never snoop around you and sniff under stuff that I have no business sniffin' under. That time has passed and I can no longer keep that promise. I know you don't work for some bullshit business consulting contractor doing some bullshit whateverthefuck you all call it. I did a full BI on you, and you hardly exist. You aren't a normal profile. Your profile is eye candy."

Lars took another pull of the wine knowing Sean wasn't going to walk away.

"I am guessing you are CIA, and if you aren't, you're something damn close to that type of business. I don't even know much more about your past aside from little bits and pieces. You have been pretty good at keeping me away from any real details by just giving me little nuggets here and there until you can change the topic away from you. I want it all out on the table now. The time has come to let me in. Keep out all that classified mumbo jumbo on how you bugged the Queen of England's toilet or something to see how many times she shits in a day. Just spare me the stuff where you say all dramatically, 'If I told you I'd have to kill ya.' I've had enough of this cockamamie outlandishness for a while. You owe me."

Havens turned and walked away.

"Where the hell are you going? We had an agreement."

"We never had an agreement, Lars. I am going upstairs and I am going to see what you did to my window. I am going to see where my wife died. Then, because we have finished that wine, I am going down to the basement and bringing up all the beer I can grab in my arms, and I will tell you what you want to know to the best of my abilities. And then we will have a proper wake and funeral for my wife and your sister. Then I have to find the best specialists in the world to make sure Maggie is OK. In the meantime you can find out what happened. I trust you with that like no other. Is that a deal?"

"Deal!" Lars shouted back. "One more thing, after we talk and get a couple things done tomorrow, don't make plans tomorrow night."

Havens leaned over the banister, "What's tomorrow night?"

"You go upstairs; take all the time you need. I'll go down and get the beer. Then when you tell me everything first, I'll share my surprise."

Part II

I am the nightmare, right where the soldier
Overstands warfare, caught in the crosshair
The moment when focus becomes more
Than what's noticed by the starving locusts

The burning of the pride, turning of the tide
Searching through the fight
Snuck in with the shadow that broke the castle
Escaped the cell, let hell out of the capsule

—X-Ecutioners,
from "(Even) More Human than Human"

Chapter 24

Sean Havens had witnessed a great deal of violence aftermath in his career. He had been responsible for creating such blood-spattered scenes in rooms throughout the world—but none so personal as this. Never children.

Seeing the room where Christina and Maggie were shot was unbearable. It looked to Sean as if a fifty pound bag of blood exploded, touching red to all corners of the white room and soaking the thick pile carpet. Sean replayed the scene in his mind of what must have happened. He sobbed at a blood smear on the carpet, imagining Christina crawling across the room to be beside her daughter cowering against the wall. A dark red mass remained surrounded by lighter red misting where Maggie took the head shot and the round exited. Havens walked over to the bullet-pocked walls and put a finger through one of the holes. He rested his head on the wall willing it all to go away, then recognizing the futility of this, moved to his daughter's bed for comfort. Bedtime stories and tickle fights. He willed the happy memories to cloud his visions of horror.

After an hour in Maggie's room, Sean retreated downstairs to evade the ghosts echoing his failure as a protector and provider. He took a deep breath upon sitting down at the table then cracked a can of Guinness and slowly poured it into the glass.

"You're three behind," said Lars, reaching for another can. "I decided to get a head start while you were upstairs. It's horrible up there."

Havens deflected the last statement. "Don't you want to put those in the fridge?"

"I put a bunch in the fridge. These are the ones we are working on now. I don't expect mine to get warm. I am in the fourteen beer stages of grieving."

Havens raised his glass to Lars. "To Christina, the best wife a man could ever wish for."

"And sister. I love you, sis."

The two brothers in marriage clinked glasses and drank to their loved one.

Havens looked around to a cupboard reserved just for him. He opened the door to retrieve a bottle of Dalwhinnie Highland single malt scotch.

"Going for the good stuff are we?"

"This was recently given to me by a British SAS soldier I did some work with. I could use a little bit of extra power."

"SAS, huh? Best fill me up." Lars put his glass down. "In my business, the bad guys get killed in their homes when they have product in there. In your business, it appears that you are the product. And you live here with my sister and niece. Now let's have it; spill your beans."

Havens wasn't sure what he was going to share. He thought a little fabrication here and there would be necessary. Lars really didn't need to know about Havens' life, training, capabilities, and expertise. He would give him just enough.

"So you know how you said if we told you we would have to kill you?"

"Yes," replied Lars, not sure if this spilling of the beans was such a good idea now.

Similarly, Havens wasn't sure that that was the best opening for discrete disclosure.

"In the units I have served with, we would have responded, 'No, we wouldn't kill you, we would kill your family and make life so unbearable you would wish you were dead.' In my case, I may help them set things up so we know what family or person to kill, but we'd have someone else do it."

"Kind of like what just happened to you."

Havens paused. A look of bewilderment frosted his face. For the first time since getting the news of his family's tragedy, he took a look at his life. Maybe Lars was right about the past coming to haunt him. He needed Lars' help after all. Lars had great instincts and could see both big and little picture.

Havens decided then and there to share it all.

Chapter 25

Sean Havens' father had been an Army drafted Vietnam veteran whose war souvenirs of empty ammunition magazines and clips, canteens, hats, and canvas pouches managed to fall into Sean's toy box. The military items provided Sean hours of fun when he was old enough to play soldier or cops and robbers. He was a decorated war hero by his eighth birthday. The number of imaginary confirmed kills Sean had achieved by that age rivaled entire infantry platoons' kill stats.

By the age of ten, Sean's fascination with Vietnam led him to write almost all creative school papers on U.S. Army Special Forces, the Ho Chi Minh Trail's strategic importance, and the history of Unconventional Warfare. Coming from a conservative Republican family with a long history of military service, Sean was simply a young patriot in the making.

The neighborhood that was Sean's battlefield proved to be complete with allies. To the south of the Havens home was a street filled with actual WWII Jewish concentration camp survivors and a mix of refugees from Poland.

Mrs. Lewicz in particular was especially kind to Sean. The number tattoos on her arm intrigued him. She tried to cover them up most of the time, but one Halloween Sean saw them through her sleeve as she reached to put candy in his plastic pumpkin. Seeing his discovery, she pulled her sleeve up to show Sean. Her husband, who wore his as a badge of honor, invited Sean back to talk about it sometime.

Sean spent hours with the Lewiczes in the summer as Mr. and Mrs. Lewicz encouraged him to go after the neighborhood's imaginary Nazis instead of the imaginary Viet Cong, who they described as simply protecting their homeland and being used by other bad people. Sean liberated the Lewiczes on a number of occasions. Mr. Lewicz took a break from mowing the lawn to hide while Sean swept the countryside and gave an all clear. He saved Sean on more than one occasion by pointing out a sniper in a crow's nest and a Nazi bastard still hiding in the brush.

The Feldbaums, just behind the Havenses' house, had also escaped Nazi Europe. At least the sisters had. They too took an interest in Sean's inquisitive nature and on occasion invited him and his family to their Passover and Rosh Hashanah celebrations. They preferred not to join in the war games and demanded that Sean check his weapon at the front entryway.

Sean blew the traditional shofar horn and tried his hand at reciting the Jewish prayers and blessings that he had heard at both the Feldbaums' and Lewiczes'. Sean's father, a staunch Baptist, chided his son about having a Bar Mitzvah before his confession of faith in the church. Sean would laugh and continue reciting the Jewish prayers he had learned. That Christmas Sean received another bible from his father. It didn't have the effect that Sean's father had hoped for. Young Sean had shaken the box. It had to be the Crossman CO2 BB pistol he had asked for. But it wasn't. Sean didn't want to be armed by "the sword," he wanted the hardware.

Just north of the Havens were a number of other Jewish families but next door was a Korean family, the Kims. Their children were much older, but from time to time Mrs. Kim would babysit Sean and his sister. They would eat lunch at the Kims' on those occasions. Mrs. Kim would make Sean's sister a grilled cheese sandwich while Sean would eat whatever Korean food Mrs. Kim was making for dinner. She even gave Sean a bottle of Korean garlic hot sauce that he would put on his eggs at home. This too received an eye roll from his father who would receive a good morning from his son in Korean. Sean could now construct greetings and short phrases in three languages.

Another half block over were his parent's friends, the Singhs. The Indian family had a daughter in Sean's class. The two got along well and in time the Singhs were also on the circuit of Sean's cultural interests.

Sean would often trade sandwiches at lunch with their daughter, Prithi Singh. Prithi was embarrassed to eat the cucumber chutney sandwiches in front of her predominately white peers, who found the food to be just as different as she, and Sean was sick of PB&J and the requisite mushy bruised apples that everyone at his table ate. Prithi's mother became suspicious when her daughter started asking for two sandwiches a day, but realized that Sean was growing and obliged.

The Kims moved suddenly. Evidently, Mr. Kim didn't just have a laundry business. According to Sean's dad, the police had said that Mr. Kim would lend money to people and hurt them if they didn't pay when he wanted it back. Sean thought that was pretty cool and made perfect sense. Sean was angry that the people who Mr. Kim had helped ratted him out to the police. It wasn't the reaction Mr. Havens was hoping for.

Pakistanis moved in to the Kim house. Mr. Fatani, the man of the house, was a short ugly man who was always cross with his wife and her sister. In the warm months when windows were open the Havens could hear a lot of yelling coming from the Fatani home. They had two very young girls who would sometimes come over and play on the Havenses' swing set. One day Sean asked why their dad was always so mad. They said he was just like that all the time and shared with Sean that both of their mommies slept in the same bed with their dad. When Sean asked his dad about it, he smiled and said it was "cultural."

With other moves came other neighbors. All had something that Sean could learn from. When a boy named Kent moved in, it changed his life.

Kent DuBoise and his family moved to the area in the summertime. They went to the same church as the Havenses, which made it the duty of Sean's father to push his own son on them as a potential playmate. It was perfect. They were Christian and they spoke English. Enough of this foreign influence on the boy, thought Sean's dad. The family would serve as a good foundational role model for Sean in the eclectic neighborhood.

Sean wasn't too pleased with the prospects and shuffled his shoes over to Kent's house one day on orders from his father. Sean heard mouthed explosions and the rapid fire gun rapports sounding off through the backyard. Kent was holding a black plastic M-16. When Sean asked what Kent was doing, he replied, "Killing VC."

The two boys killed most of Chicagoland's VC in the backyards and alleys that summer. Kent was a bit off personality-wise at times and didn't get along with many of the other kids with the exception of Sean. When school started Sean found himself having to protect Kent from the other kids. It cost Sean friends, but every time he got in a fight and his parents were called, Sean's dad stood by his son. He was proud that Sean was standing up for something and someone.

Sean was appreciative of his father's pride and understanding but it still didn't help the situation. He remembered coming to his dad, who was reading a paper, and presented the dilemma.

Sean's dad never lowered the paper, and just said, "If you can walk away from it walk away. The words will make you stronger as a man if you can take it. If they are picking on you physically, you hit them hard and hit them often."

"What if they hit back?"

"Then, Sean, you hit them harder, and you hit them faster, and you don't stop until a teacher pulls you off. Go for the biggest one. Don't hit the chin. Hit the nose, hit the lip. If a teacher pulls you off try to get in a last kick to the kid's privates. Overall, make whoever is hurting you bleed and make them regret it. You are still young, Sean. Big kids will still cry at this age when you make them bleed. Heck, if you make them bleed enough at my age, they back down."

"What if they make me bleed?"

"Then you didn't hit them hard enough and you probably deserved it. But never ever let them see you cry."

"Will you be mad? The principal may get mad if you aren't mad at me."

"Good. I'll make him bleed."

Sean smiled. "Thanks, Dad."

His dad kept the paper raised. "Why don't you go see what Kent is doing?"

Fights ensued for a few months. Sean's dad was right. The fights came, the blood flowed, and in short time few would pick on Sean Havens. The students still didn't like Kent, but they allowed him to hang out. It was better than a bloodied nose.

Backyard wars continued after school, on weekends, and throughout the summers for Kent and Sean. Innocent neighborhood games like kick the can and ghost in the graveyard became opportunities for Sean and Kent to demonstrate their unconventional skills to the local indigenous forces.

By age thirteen they had hidden homemade sniper ghillie suits in the bushes that they would don to free jailed neighbors, then run back to their safe haven in the camouflaged attire. Stealth, freedom of movement, decisive action, and Hi-C was their formula for success.

Parents started to caution young kids against playing the neighborhood games after a kick the can incident when Kent and Sean covered their movement by lighting a homemade smoke bomb made of cooked potassium nitrate and sugar made in the Havenses' kitchen. The smoke bomb had been cooked in an old pot that Sean's mom had given them. They made three pounds that was laced with a waterproof waxed rocket fuse from the hobby shop. The smoke had filled an entire cul-de-sac and fire engines were called. When the smoke cleared, the kid who was "it" had been renditioned by Sean and Kent and tied up by the can. A fire truck had braked just in time.

Sean and Kent escaped to their forward operating base under a neighbor's canoe. Their SERE training failed them as their adversary parents beckoned them home with the false flag of dinner. The boys were each confined to their bedrooms over the weekend. Escape was not an option. Kent broke before dinner was over. Sean's mom, the unwitting accomplice who provided initial support and enablement to weapon's manufacturing in her kitchen, broke the grasp of the boy's hearts and minds campaign. They suffered the hard labor of making Christmas cookies with her—until she found a pan of dough shaped into AK's, triangle straw Vietnamese hats, and Claymore mines. Mr. Havens destroyed them over a tall glass of whole milk.

Sean's life changing moment came three years later on Kent's sixteenth birthday. Sean, still his only friend, was invited over for a small party. Sean's parents had been told that this could be an emotional day for Kent due to a family present that they had to give their son, and they were hoping he could have a friend over.

After hot dogs, cake, and the start of a Rambo movie, Kent's mom and dad came downstairs to the basement with a box. The TV was turned off and the box was opened. Kent's mom started to cry.

"Kent, I have some news that I have to share with you. It could be upsetting, but I hope that you will understand that nothing changes. Your father and I still love you and your father will always love you."

"What is it? What is in the box?"

"Your biological father's name was Robert Laughlin. He was an officer in the United States Army Special Forces. He was killed in Vietnam due to a series of what they called intelligence failures, but his actions led to him saving his entire team. He was a hero."

Sean's jaw dropped as Kent's mom lifted the triangular folded flag from the box and set it on the long coffee table. She reached back into the box and pulled out a purple heart, a bronze star, a bronze statuette of a Green Beret soldier, and Robert Laughlin's green beret, laying them on the table for Kent to take in.

Wow, Fifth group. Sean recognized the flash on the beret. *Daaamn.*

Kent looked up from the memorial display on the table. "I don't understand, why didn't you tell me before?"

"Kent, your father, well your father Jack, and I thought it would be best if you were old enough to understand a little better."

"I can't believe you hid this from me and that you are not even my dad."

"I SURE THE HELL AM YOUR DAD YOU UNGRATEFUL...YOUR DAD LEFT YOUR MOM TO RUN AROUND THE FUCKING JUNGLE AND GOT HIMSELF KILLED!"

"JACK! Language for God's sake! We discussed this!"

Kent stormed off upstairs as he started to melt down. His mom trailing behind.

"Shit." Jack kicked at the air.

Jack, a hippie in the '60s and '70s who still played his share of Moody Blues and the Grateful Dead, picked up the statuette and read the inscription.

"Nice job, LT Laughlin, KIA 20 March 1968 SVN 5th SFG B-52, whatever the hell that all means."

Sean, still sitting in a chair ten feet away, was stunned.

Jack picked up the beret and put it on his head. With his beard and glasses, he looked more like a French artist. He pulled up his hands and fingers as if he were holding a machine gun that he fired in automatic mouth bursts at Sean.

"Take it off," Sean said.

"What? Why you want it?"

Jack took off the hat and frisbee'd it over Sean's head into the wall where it fell behind the TV. Sean looked at Jack in horror. Emotions were building. He felt like he could cry. Sean got up and walked to the TV where he wedged his body and stretched his arm as far as he could to grab the green beret.

"Leave it, Sean!"

Sean ignored Jack and continued to stretch. He retrieved it by willing his body to conform to the tight space, lengthening his digits by sheer heart. Sean tried to pull off the dust bunnies and lint that had adhered to the fabric behind the television stand. He couldn't get it off. He rubbed and the dust and cobwebs only seemed to go into the green felt fabric more. Sean couldn't hold back the tears, the frustration, and the hurt. He was panicking. The beret symbolized everything he wanted to be. To this point he had only dreamed of what it would be like to hold a real green beret.

"How could you?" Sean questioned Jack in utter contempt and ran towards the door with the beret. Jack picked up the Purple Heart award still encased in the jewel box and hurled it at Sean's back.

Sean continued to the door but Jack had caught up while Sean fumbled with the lock latch. Jack grabbed Sean's right arm pulling it away from the top chain.

Sean spun.

With a left open palm heel strike Sean connected with the lower part of Jack's nose and upper lip. The surprise and pain caused Jack to release the grip and in no time Sean was running home clutching the beret to his chest with both arms.

Sean's father had just come home and nearly collided in the entryway of their house with his bawling son.

"What's gotten into you? Stop crying. SEAN! What's wrong?"

Through sobs and heavy breathing, Sean managed to gasp and form words between breaths conveying to his father what happened. His mother came out of a room to see what was going on.

"I have it under control, hon. Go back to whatever you were doing."

"Sean, come with me."

Sean followed his dad into the laundry room where his father pulled out a clean white hand towel that had been recently folded, ready to be put away in the off-limits guest bathroom. Sean's dad dabbed some water on the towel and gently stroked off the debris. Moments later the green beret was clean. Sean's dad folded the towel so only the dry end was exposed and he continued to brush Robert Laughlin's beret so all water droplets were off. He admired his work and showed it to his son for final approval.

"Thanks, Dad."

"We're not done yet. How's your wrist?"

"Red. Sore."

"Get in the car."

Though only houses away they drove to Kent's and went up to the front door. Sean's dad knocked on the screen door frame and within seconds Jack, his wife, and Kent appeared. Kent's mom had her arm around her son. Both of their eyes were red and swollen from crying. Jack had a fat lip. Dried blood was visible in his nostrils.

Jack was still furious and immediately went on the offensive.

"Don, your son just stole my boy's hat and nearly ripped the screen door right out of the frame. I tried to stop him and he took a punch at me. This is unacceptable, and I am afraid he is no longer welcome here."

Ignoring Jack, Don Havens, his own son also under his arm, said calmly, "Cheryl, Kent, while I know this is hardly timely, please accept my condolences for the passing of LT Laughlin in the line of duty."

"Don, you don't have to..."

"Please, Cheryl, we had no idea. I'm merely here because Sean was concerned with your husband's lack of reverence to this symbol of service and honor, which we have now restored to a more proper condition."

"Thank you, Don, but..."

Don continued his little speech now back in a formal military voice, "Please accept my apologies for Sean's heartfelt motive to flee and seek safe haven in our home. He only meant to rectify the situation. I'm sorry he wasn't able to better communicate his intentions. We didn't mean to add to this rather heavy day."

Cheryl knew there was no stopping Don and appreciated the formal words that had seemed lacking when she first received the news of her late husband's demise so many years ago.

With that, Don Havens opened the screen door and handed the folded green beret with its flash patch up to Kent. Don snapped back, heels together, and saluted Kent who was holding his late father's beret like a ring bearer holding a silk pillow.

"Kent, you are still welcome in our home whenever you wish." As Don turned to Jack his demeanor changed. "Jack, as a former serviceman myself, if your wife and boy were not standing here, I'd pound you to a pulp. You owe my boy an apology. Now."

Don Havens wasn't a big man, but he was a righteous man. At that moment in time, Don Havens represented himself as a father, the military service, and LT Laughlin KIA. Even Jack could not deny the force and power emanating from Don and Sean and offered them both the most sincere apology of his life.

"And Jack, you touch my boy again and I will rip your arms right from your body. Mark my words. Never question if I would."

Sean and his father walked away while Jack closed the door in shame.

Sean wondered what Kent's birth dad would have thought of the scene. Because he was killed in the line of duty, some asshole got to marry his widowed wife and raise his son. Would LT Laughlin have approved of how life moved on after his death? Sean concluded no. Sean decided then and there that someone needed to protect the men in Special Forces and he would be that person.

Chapter 26

Sean went to the fridge and pulled out some more beers.

Lars had slowed his drinking. He really knew nothing of Sean's childhood and now a lot was making sense about his brother-in-law's personality and interests. He still needed the bottom line of his profession. Lars remained silent and looked around the room feigning boredom.

Sean knew what Lars wanted and continued.

Soon after the incident with Kent's father, Sean heard about the Police Junior Rifle Team program. Having been a crack shot with a pellet gun he received the Christmas before, the .22 caliber match rifles felt natural.

Detective Doug Shiller, an ex-Marine sniper in Vietnam, was in charge of the police program and took Sean under his wing. Havens won every match he entered.

Shiller tried his hardest to recruit Havens towards a career in law enforcement, but understood Havens' passion for special operations.

Havens shared with Lars a particular conversation he had with Doug that was yet another stepping stone to who he was today.

"Sean, special operations may seem glamorous, but I think you have something different to offer the world."

Havens just shrugged. His father had said the same things. So did his beach-landing Iwo Jima uncle. "Yeah, I've heard that before, but it's what I want to do."

"Why? Do you like the guns, the adventure, the foreign lands, the idea of killing?"

"No. I want to help the other spec ops guys like Kent's dad."

"Why do you think you could help other team members better than someone else?"

"I think I may be smarter and more adaptable than some. I want to be Special Forces so I can speak a lot of languages and get good intel to make sure everyone is safe and we kill the right bad guys."

"Hmmm. That's pretty noble. And who do you think is going to give YOU the right intel so you can do your job?"

"I'll get it."

"It doesn't work that way, Sean."

"Well you did it, Doug, when you weren't shooting guys."

"Yeah, I did plenty of recon and close observation, but here is the thing. Sometimes we traveled in decent sized groups. My group was wiped out with the exception of me and a couple other guys."

"So who was giving you the intel?"

"The Navy and another observation group."

"And who wiped out your group?"

"The Navy and another observation group."

"Huh?" Sean wondered if it was a conspiracy theory of the government whacking its black hit team. He knew Doug had done some dark stuff with the Marines.

"They fucked up, kid. That's the thing about intel. Someone high enough up believes it is true, then it is. We got shelled from the ships at sea who were getting our position from another observation group, who in turn was cutting us down as soon as we tried to evac from our position."

"Fratricide, right?"

"That's a pretty polite way of saying it, but yeah."

"Sean, the down and dirty in the weeds stuff can be fun but I would much rather have had a guy like you telling folks where to point the guns. It's not always going to be fighting in jungles. And tanks are done. Someday it will be more about mixing with people and understanding them. We were starting to do that better in Vietnam. You could have done it well."

"So what should I do?"

"If you want to help cops and catch crooks and killers, I'd rather see you with the Bureau. If you want to help soldiers and still see the world and speak your languages and eat nasty food in nasty places, be a spook."

"CIA?"

"Shhh. Don't ever say that out loud. They can hear you." Doug lowered his head and shoulders and looked around. He raised his eyes slowly to the corners of the room.

Sean mirrored the same subconsciously. "Really?"

Doug smacked Havens on the side of the head and walked down the firing range.

"Your birthday's coming up. I'm not getting you anything, but you can still blow out your candles. Load up."

Doug lit four small cake candles down the range, dripping wax on the ground then seating them to stand up. "Two prone, two standing. You have thirty seconds. Wait for me to get out of here."

There were ten seconds left when the last light was shot out. The candles remained standing. Perfect shots.

When the time came to start planning for college, Havens knew he wanted a university with an ROTC rifle team, a foreign language and study abroad program, and a social psychology program. The school counselor came up with three schools: Princeton, Ohio State University, and an in-state public university. Don Havens came up with one: in-state tuition.

For the first two years at school, Havens excelled. He thrived in the academic environment, participated on the ROTC Rifle Team and Ranger Challenge team, picked up French and Spanish, and started on Modern Standard Arabic. He decided that he would contract with the Army. It was still his dream to qualify for Special Forces. He told a member of the cadre Sergeant Major Jones, and ex-Special Forces officer about it.

"Havens I think you could do it but you're the one who had to stop during the field training exercise because you lost your contact lens."

"Yeah, but I couldn't see."

"You can't call time out if you are in combat. How bad are your eyes, boy?"

"Minus seven."

"Shit. Can you even see me standing here?"

Havens just looked down. This was not happening.

"SGM Jones, I have to qualify. I have unfinished business."

"What are you 19? 20? What kind of business haven't you finished except tappin' some little Suzie Sweatpants?"

Havens gave the Sergeant Major an abbreviated version of LT Laughlin and Kent. He said he felt like if Special Forces were supposed to be the best, who was protecting them? And if something happened to a Special Forces soldier, who was protecting their family? If Havens was Special Forces qualified, he could protect them all.

Jones nodded. "Nice story. Almost made me sniff, but you still ain't getting in with those Coke bottle contacts unless you get surgery on your eyes. Maybe you can try Military Intelligence and go the Infantry route. MI can deploy with SF. An S-2 can be attached to an A-team and support them with intel."

"I only want to do Unconventional Warfare."

"Son, don't you think SF has to learn Conventional before they learn Unconventional?"

"I already learned it in lab and class. I did all that basic maneuver stuff. That was all old school. If I was Infantry, I'd get killed in a week if a war broke out. Only those Huckleberry Central Illinois kids want Infantry."

"Uh huh. Why they haven't already asked you to be a general is a wonder to me," Jones remarked. "Havens, I am beginning to think you wouldn't last in Infantry or any other military function, but not because they are old school, but because you don't know when to shut up and check your attitude. What makes you think you are better than those men? You are not a team player."

"Sir, I didn't…"

"SERGEANT MAJOR, BOY! I work for a living!"

"Yes, sir, sorry, Sergeant Major, sir, I mean. Now you got me all flustered."

"I think you were flustered before."

"I am not better than those other guys. I'm just different. I know what the right situation will be for me. I can't be constrained by all these rules. I want to be more autonomous."

"Autonomous, huh. Boy, where do you come from? God help me, but I am going to do this. Havens, don't join the Army. You need to run from the Army before the Army runs you out. I have a friend coming to town next week. His name is Jerry. He is going to be at the University recruiting for the Department of State."

"I'm not going to sit in some embassy."

"Shut the hell up and do not interrupt me again! Damn you are impertinent, boy. He doesn't work for State. He works for someone else who may be able to use you. I know you have a couple more years left here, but..."

"I'm leaving next year for Europe. I am studying abroad." Havens cringed, realizing he had interrupted the Sergeant Major again.

SGM Jones was the blackest African American Havens had ever seen. Jones was six feet tall and seemed to be four feet wide at the shoulders. Havens loved SGM Jones and often came across as too familiar. Jones had reminded him of Doug, who let Sean get close. Jones did not.

"Dammit Havens, shut up! If you want help let me help. I don't give a shit if you are going on some all expenses paid Eurail trip. Go find Jerry at the recruiting event. Tell him I sent you. Tell him I hate you and that I am offering him payback. He will take care of you. Just shut your mouth when you talk to him. Shut your mouth when you listen to him, and shut your mouth if he asks you a question. Whatever you leak out, since you can't follow directions, will be a good enough answer. The man is a legend, but keep that to yourself, and understand that it means if you screw this up I will thoroughly wreck you, boy."

"Thanks, Sarge." Havens gave a playful slap on Jones' arm. "I know you like me. Hug?" Havens smiled and outstretched his arms.

"Havens, drop and give me a hundred. If Jerry was here, I'd say he's going to love you. If you weren't such a smart mouth you could be one of my best. I'm giving him a mustang 'cause Lord knows I've tried to break you. And don't get me wrong Havens, if I wasn't confined by this school, you'd be all busted up and tamed."

"What are you going to buy me for my graduation, Sergeant Major?"

"Faster Havens, you loud mouth four-eyed spoiled irreverent piece of shit! Every one of those push-ups is how much I hate you. Shit, I hate you so much that if you did as many pushups as the amount of times I wished I never met you, you'd look big and handsome like me. And you ain't pretty enough to look like me. Don't bend your back and keep your ass lower. You trying to cheat me, Havens?"

"Sergeant Major, I see a smudge on your boot. Hey, looks like maybe some popcorn stuck on the side. You go to the movies in these?"

"Start from the beginning, Havens." *Good luck, kid.*

Havens found Jerry at the career day by hovering around the State Department booth and looking at name tags. Jerry was an older fellow. Much different than Havens expected, especially if he was a friend of SGM Jones. Jerry looked more like a professor or even a carpet salesman. He was just a regular guy. Maybe even less. The type you would never notice if you passed each other on the street.

Jerry was talking to a young coed who was sharing her future plans as a political science major and ideally working for the Department of State. Jerry was attentive and appearing interested. When the girl would look down nervously in her pitch, Havens watched as Jerry scanned the crowds in just enough time to meet the girl's eye contact again.

Fuckin' A, this old guy is a pretty cool hawk.

"Can I help you? Are you interested in a career with the Department of State?"

Havens turned to an attractive African American girl who could not have been more than twenty-five years old.

"No, thanks. I just need to talk to Jerry."

"Oh, well perhaps I can answer some questions for you."

"No, thanks. I am not looking for a job. Just need Jerry."

"I see. Does he know you?"

"No. He knows a friend of mine. Well a friend of mine is a friend of his. I mean, I was referred to him."

"I'll get him."

Glad to have an excuse to save Jerry from the coed, the State Department representative excused the interruption and nodded towards the young man wishing to speak to Jerry but not wanting a job. Jerry excused himself to attend to Havens and outstretched his hand. He had a huge gem-adorned college ring on his hand that Sean couldn't make out.

"Hello, I'm Jerry. And you are?"

"Sean. Sean Havens. I know SGM Jones. He said to tell you I should talk to you and that you would be happy he did so."

"Nice to meet you Sean. Yes, I do know SGM Jones. You must be in the ROTC program here."

"Yes, sir."

"And what exactly did he say to you, can you recall the exact words?"

"Exact words in the conversation or exact words when he referenced you?"

"What do you think would be most appropriate, Sean? This isn't a test, relax. I just want to make sure I don't miss anything."

"He said, 'Go find Jerry at the recruiting event. Tell him I sent you. Tell him I hate you and that I am offering him payback. He will take care of you. Just shut your mouth when you talk to him, listen to him, and answer his questions."

"Thank you. Indeed that is the man I know. He must like you."

"I like him, but I am not so sure he likes me. I wouldn't say that if I wanted a job, but thought if you were helping me, you should know everything."

Jerry smiled and patted Sean on the arm. "He likes you if he sent you. Years back I sent him one of my best. I really liked the kid but thought he would flourish more with Jones. The kid needed structure and wanted discipline."

"That's a good fit with Jones. How could you just send someone to the Army from, um, State?"

"I sent him to Jones when Jones was 'special' Army. He is returning the favor, I would imagine."

"So what do you do?"

"Let's take a little walk. We can get some fresh air. I have been inside all day and could really use a stretch of the legs. Don't suppose you have a Scotch on you?"

"No, sir, but I'd have one with you if I did."

"You like Scotch, Sean?"

"Never had it. Plenty of whisky and Coke, but I am open to new things."

"Good ol' Sergeant Major Jones." Jerry took a moment to gaze at Sean as a proud teacher would. He made an assessment right there that he liked what he saw. Jerry pulled out a small stack of 3x5 note cards and jotted a few things down before securing them back in his breast pocket.

Before Sean Havens went abroad to the south of France, Jerry gave him a contact number. He had told Sean that if he ever needed anything or wanted to earn some extra cash while away, he could call his friend Rick in Europe. Jerry said that if Sean didn't need anything he should call Rick anyway after a couple months in France so he could at least take Sean to dinner.

Sean did as he was told and called Rick after only a few weeks in Marseilles. He left a message and Rick called him back a couple weeks later at the student housing number Sean had left.

They agreed to meet in an older part of town at a small café. Rick was much more of what he had expected Jerry to look like. Rick was in his mid-thirties to early forties, judging by the flecks of grey in his dark hair but younger chiseled face.

After Sean told Rick a bit of his day to day routine abroad, Rick started asking about the students that Sean hung around with. He inquired about their ethnicities or whether Sean was just sticking to Americans or Australians to make communication easier. Sean was proud to say he had befriended a group of Algerians, Tunisians, Moroccans, Saudis, a Turk, and a Lebanese Christian named Stephen who smoked hash like a fiend. A detail Sean immediately wished he had left out. Rick complimented Sean on moving outside the normal comfort zone, to which Sean had replied that he was even learning Arabic with consideration to their different dialects.

Rick told Sean that he worked for a cultural group within one of the State Department's French Embassies. He expressed interest in knowing more about these Arabs at Sean's school, especially those who were dating or sleeping with American students. Rick asked for names to be written down. Sean was surprised at this, for he had just learned that a number of his new Arab friends had a thing for American girls. They settled on a price for Sean's discrete information, which meant Rick offered a modest sum and Sean accepted it.

The two met periodically, about once a month. Sometimes, Sean would simply receive a small package at his school apartment that would include a travel ticket to Italy, Spain, and once, Austria. The note would say "Enjoy a trip on me, but if you can, please do a little shopping for me while you are there. Call me when you arrive." Sean found himself shopping for a number of shoes or boots in various sizes, jackets, sweaters, etc. It seemed a bit odd, as sometimes those orders could be for five or six pairs of shoes and as many clothing items. They would need to be boxed and shipped to another address that Rick would provide over the phone.

Sean shipped clothes to England, Canada, and Mexico. Then, with extra spending cash, he would enjoy a nice weekend getaway seeing sights. If that was what they wanted him to do, he was happy to oblige.

One of the oddest tasks, however, was a list of streets in a particular city. Havens was asked to walk up and down the streets and count how many houses or apartments were for rent. Another time he was given cash to purchase a car then asked to park it at a different location and leave the keys next to the tire underneath the car. In Bari, Italy, he paid a year's rent—cash—for an apartment. Other times he was given cash to buy various plane tickets, train tickets, and a ferry ticket from Algaciras, Spain to Morocco. He turned them over to Rick.

By the time he had left his study abroad, Sean had unwittingly helped to discover a number of Middle Easterners impregnating students to gain access to the U.S., he purchased cover clothing made in foreign countries for a number of special mission units, and helped identify viable safe houses and modes of transportation for case officers and intelligence assets. Most importantly to Rick and Jerry, he never asked questions and kept his mouth shut.

For Havens, he had earned close to five thousand dollars in six months, had seen the better part of Western Europe, and had gained additional language and cultural knowledge.

It seemed to be a win-win for everyone.

Upon his return, he met with Jerry one evening at the Palmer House hotel bar in downtown Chicago. Jerry had found a small table in the back out of earshot of the patrons.

"Welcome back, world traveler. I thought you might like to try your first Scotch."

Havens laughed. "You should have gotten me one when we first met. I have been partying with Saudis who were away from home. Not too Muslim when they are in a discotheque. I have had all the 'Macs' and 'Mc's,' Johnny Walker Blue label, Green label,

Black label, Red label, Pink label, whatever. They make it, I drank it."

"Well good for you. This is a 25 year old Scotch in the "Mac" category. It is quite nice. Tell me what you think."

Sean sipped it. "Good." He took another gulp.

Jerry closed his eyes for a moment appreciating his protégé's naiveté with a thirty-dollar glass of Scotch. "We'll work on that. So, did you have a good time? Learn anything?"

"Yeah, where do I start? I saw a ton of things, did a ton of things, had a chance to do some weird stuff for your friend…" Sean looked to Jerry to see if he was on track and keeping his banter in check.

"How did you like working for Rick?"

"Good guy. Bit of an over-the-shoulder peeker to me. He kind of fits the profile of a spook."

"Excuse me?" Jerry put down his scotch. "Rick is part of the Department of State. What makes you say that he is anything to the contrary?"

"Look, I don't really care who he works for or who you say he works for. I just figured he thinks he's James Bond or something. I could always spot him a mile away."

"How so?"

"Well, he isn't like you, but he would also pick a back table, do the back to the wall thing like cops do in movies. He walks down the street and crosses, then goes into shops and stuff and comes back out to go the other way."

"Where did you see him walking, Sean?"

Sean, realizing he had opened a can of worms, thought of lying, but he trusted Jerry. He wanted Jerry to trust him too.

"I followed him."

Jerry took in a deep breath. "Continue," said Jerry as he sipped his scotch and signaled the server for another.

"Well, one day I took the train north and met with Rick in Paris. I left and he left, then I just decided to walk around town a bit. I saw him driving in a nice Alfa Romeo a few miles away from where we had met about two hours later. He parked and did some walking around and stuff. That's when I saw him all zigzag-y and looking over his shoulder and stuff."

"What kind of stuff."

"Well first off, it was pretty warm out. He was, like, the only guy wearing a coat. He sat down on a bench, but when he sat I could see his jacket didn't just have a regular drop. It had something inside like a book or a package that made it bend and stick out more than how a jacket is when you just sit. Plus, his left arm was kind of tight like it was holding the thing in place. He walked past some people and dropped his hand down over the coat pocket area like he was protecting it. He kinda dropped and opened his shoulder up and pivoted just a bit to avoid a bump. Didn't seem real natural."

"That's very interesting, Sean. Anything else?"

Sean paused in thought. Jerry could sense Sean was deciding what to share if anything at all.

"Sean, before you say anything. I think you are a really bright kid. Rick thinks so too. We think you have some great potential. SGM Jones wants me to look out for you. So you have to also trust me a bit to help you. Anything you say is just between us. Understand?"

"Yeah."

"So what is it that you are holding back? Don't be embarrassed or think you are getting anyone in trouble."

Sean took a drink of the Scotch. He grimaced through that swallow. "Did you hear anything about Nice?"

"Can you refresh me?"

"A bunch of my Arab friends were going to Nice for Carnival. I decided that I would go with. I mentioned it to Rick, who asked where I was staying. I told him a youth hostel. He gave me some money and told me to stay at a particular hotel and that I should tell my friends that I was staying with a friend. I told him that I had plenty of cash and there would be no need. I'd rather stay with my friends so I wouldn't offend them and I would have more opportunity to practice my Arabic and the dialects. He thought I was too close to them."

"So, anyway, we came back to the hostel that night and it was locked. We knocked on the door but no one came down to get us. It had closed, like, an hour or two early. We went around back to see if there was a back door. I was climbing up a fence and was pulled down. I looked up and it was a French cop. The other guys scattered. The cop was yelling at me, asking what I was doing and why I was with Arabs. You know, 'cause the Arabs in France have to deal with the same prejudices as our blacks."

"I am well aware. Please go on. So far it just seems like a misunderstanding."

"Well that's what I thought. But instead they drive me to a small police station. They ask for my passport, put me in a room, and this guy starts giving me the business—pushing me and slapping me and talking about Arabs and drugs and stuff."

"I see."

"So after a bit he lets up, but see, the thing is, he isn't asking me anything. He keeps talking about drugs, but never even asked to check my pockets or have me strip and show that I have nothing."

"Did you?"

"No, and neither did the guys I was with. One of the guys was this rich Saudi out sowing his oats. He was buying bottles of $120 booze for our table all night, but we were pretty sober. So, anyway, the guy leaves me in the room. It wasn't a cell or anything. It had a window to a back parking lot. So, I look out the window and I see Rick's Alfa in the parking lot. I get all excited because the cavalry was coming to get me out of that mess with the cops."

Jerry raised his hand to signal Sean to pause.

"One, there are a lot of Alfa's in France so I am curious how you knew it was Rick's, but before you answer that, did you mention Rick at all to the police?"

"Why would it matter if I mentioned Rick? He's State, right? State is my foreign advocate." Havens gave a coy smartass smile.

"Touché. Did you mention it, though?"

"No, so that is why I thought it was so weird when I saw him sitting in the damn car. After a couple minutes he got out of the car and I couldn't see him anymore. Then the cop came in and started beating on me again."

"Perhaps he was not aware that you were even there? Have you considered that possibility?"

"Jerry, with all due respect, I don't need anyone playing devil's advocate with me. Do you really mean for me to completely avoid challenging the natural act of an American Embassy representative coming into a random-ass precinct in the south of France, when Rick is supposedly working from Paris, and yet there is an American who is being detained and that doesn't come up in any conversation with him?"

"Maybe he was protecting you. Or maybe he was protecting himself. Have you considered this?"

"Jerry, I really like you, so please don't play games with me. Rick shouldn't have even been there. This wasn't about protecting. This was about punishing."

"Punishing for what?"

"For me not taking his advice and staying at the hostel. He had no right."

"Hmmm. I see where you would feel that way. It sure could have been handled differently."

"So you agree he was trying to punish me?"

"No, I agree with the fact that you have a right to be angry and you could have handled it differently."

"But you don't see it as a punishment? Are you serious?"

"No, Sean. I see it as part of your training. Your initial selection. Welcome. Now comes the hard stuff if you think you are up for it."

"Wait. So that was all set up? You mean I can work for you?"

"First, you need to finish your school. Then you come to my school."

Chapter 27

Jerry worked with Sean to pick the rest of his courses so they could be of value to his future profession. With the change to the new administration in the early '90's, Jerry told Sean that he had two options after completing an initial four months of training. Plans had changed some.

"Sean, the administration is making cutbacks to field ops. President Clinton will be finalizing things shortly that have been set in motion. I know you wanted to come work for us along the Mediterranean, but Arabs are not our concern. We still have a need dealing with Russia and a need for Chinese work. Arabs are not a threat right now. I can get you a desk analyst's job in Langley or I have another option. It would be rather unconventional."

Deflated by the news of another obstacle in the way of realizing his dreams, Sean was all ears. *What does it matter anymore? Let's hear who I'm going to be handed off to next.*

"I have some friends who are leaving the Clandestine Service. They don't want to stick around and see the changes or the cutbacks to their activities. They want to stay in the same line of work, but they will be contractors. This solves two problems. They are no longer on the payroll, and they are subject to less oversight."

"Okay, I'm listening."

"The non-official cover programs have some problems. Companies don't want to get in trouble if a CIA-covered individual gets in a jam that could blowback to a host company. By the same token, a lot of NOCs end up having to do their covered job that pays a lot more than the government job and they still have to do their government job in between and during off hours."

"The new program that they are putting together has the group going to work for a bunch of separate companies that would give them placement and access to do their work while providing them larger base salaries. The fact that these companies they will be going to work for are one hundred percent unwitting to their activities provides better insulation than they currently have at the Agency."

"I think this could be a great opportunity for you to get some training and they will help you find your first job out of school. The market is tight and I suspect that many of your peers will be taking any job that comes around. You, however, can just let me know what could interest you commercially, I will run it by the group, and they will come up with something suitable. What do you think?"

"Actually it sounds kind of cool, but will I get to work overseas?"

"Once you are properly trained we will have tasks for you from time to time that will coincide with your job. The nice thing about this is you can also operate domestically. No oversight, no rules. You are like an international private investigator, but you don't need a license. You also won't have to worry about a clearance. At the level you will be working, you won't need to know who the client is or what the end purpose is of your task. You will be an unwitting asset. This will also enhance your security. Some of these guys can't go back to certain countries because of Aldrich Ames and other traitors who gave secrets to the Soviets, Israelis, and whoever else that we don't know about."

"So. . . will I still get to go to the Farm?"

"No Farm for you. You will go to the Barn."

"What's the Barn?

"You will know when it is time. Barns, the bay, and pond for you, son."

"And what about Rick?"

"Rick is getting laid off. He is going to go work for a technology company. They gave him over a hundred thousand dollars to start."

"Man, next time I see him, we are going to have words."

"Your words should be thank you if you have the privilege of seeing him again. He was a big advocate for you."

Havens took a moment to process this.

"So, is he legit for them or doing this group thingy that I am being invited to?"

"First of all you are not being invited. You had been recruited and are now selected. You could still wash out just like any other special operations selection process. I believe Rick's new endeavor is legit, but one never knows in this business. Remember that."

Months later Havens tried to check in with Jerry. The phone extension was disconnected. Havens mailed a note to the P.O. Box that he had been instructed to use previously. The mail was returned to sender. No forwarding address provided.

From that point on, Havens received only a Christmas card each holiday season. The postal locations were always different. Nothing was ever written below the card's embossed holiday wishes. They were simply signed —*Jerry*.

Chapter 28

Still sitting at the Havens' kitchen table sucking down beers, Lars pulled his hand down his face. It was getting late. The day's oil on his face felt grimy.

"So let me get this straight, Sean." Lars breathed in deeply through his nose. He was feeling the drinks a bit. "You were working for a bunch of ex-spooks who were still working for the CIA but off the payroll?" Lars was shaking his head in disbelief at the concept. He downed the rest of his beer and got up to raid the refrigerator again.

"I assume so, but the beauty of it was I never knew. I could never really confirm it. That is how they designed it. I think we have a frozen pizza in the freezer. I can pop that in the oven if you want."

"I want."

"So what was that Barn shit all about? You wrestle in the hay and shoot cows?"

Havens knew Lars was eliciting more, but his defenses were down and he fully intended to share more. "Had to shoot a goat. Had to patch him up and keep him alive. They said it was my makeshift corpsman goat school. Guess there is really a school like that for medics. Maybe they were screwing with me."

"Did the goat live?"

"For a while. I did a pretty good job bringing him back to health."

"So how did it die?"

"I had to kill it."

"More medical training?"

"No, I had to learn how to make it into a goat curry. I learned how to make a couple forms of bread in clay and brick ovens and I had to learn how to make tea in the custom of about five different countries. They would blindfold me, make me tea, and I would have to tell them what country it was from. Then I had to replicate it. That's one of the reasons I don't drink it now. Coffee's my bag. Hate tea. All dozen or so ways I can cook it."

"Guess you only have to make coffee one way."

"No, about seven for coffee."

"You are a puzzle. Glad our taxpayer dollars are hard at work so you can go to CIA Cordon Bleu. Guess when you are done killing people you can open a restaurant with all that fancy beverage and goat training."

"Learned how to do that too."

"Open a restaurant?"

"Yep. And a trucking parts company, an import and export company, learned how to deal with foreign tax laws, open and register a foreign or local business, move money around, you name it."

"Damn." Lars just shook his head and swirled his beer. "I had no idea. You are a jack of all trades."

"That was the point."

Sean figured there must have been about eight "Barns" over the course of his three-year training. Barns were both formal and informal sites where he learned his tradecraft. According to his numerous instructors, he was not receiving the same tradecraft that was taught in the "spy schools" and special operations schoolhouses. The instructors had decided that certain foundational skills such as eliciting information and subtly asking questions were the craft of a number of professions and still had strategic and tactical importance. The idea was to keep Havens, and he assumed others somewhere, from standing out as a traditional spy or clandestine operator. Just as he had picked up Rick's countersurveillance movements, Havens was instructed that other security and intelligence apparatuses throughout the world would pick up on the operational tells that were common to the trade.

Much to Havens' disappointment, he did not initially learn how to blow up bridges, slit sentries' throats, or fire rocket-propelled grenades. He did have the opportunity to learn this later with some paramilitary forays, but more from the standpoint of showing others and not doing the acts himself.

The instructors were a myriad of ex-SOG warriors from Vietnam, ex-CIA Special Activities Division operators, and old timer OSS men who had served overseas. Aside from the common thread of the operational training that these men possessed and were able to share with their new trainee, each of these men were also successful business owners or held key leadership positions in global firms. They had been successful both on the battlefield and in boardrooms. They matched a dual competency model that suited their overall craft.

Havens had been taken on a number of discrete operations as both an observer and participant while using true name covers under the protection of legitimate company bona fides. If he ever got into a jam that his skills could not get him out of, he was to immediately revert to the methods that a normal citizen would use: panic, demands for U.S. assistance, and an assertion of wrongdoing. In short, play the Ugly American but keep his mouth shut about everything else.

His jobs lasted two to three years at various global firms where he could get lost in the organization at lower level jobs as a sales support researcher, market researcher, competitive analyst, etc., That way he could put in twenty to thirty hours of work a week and also get involved in other discrete operations work.

Domestically, Havens was assigned a number of tasks that involved investigating Asian front companies. Many of these companies existed legally in the U.S., but they were stealing intellectual property and trade secrets from pharmaceutical, technology, and defense companies. Due to the fuzzy nature of arresting and prosecuting the theft of information, many of these firms and individuals could nimbly alter their corporate ownership, address, and business names to avoid the Federal Bureau of Investigation and other prosecutory agencies.

His involvement was limited to roles as a singleton autonomous operator gaining access to computers, individuals, and information to stop companies that were actually foreign government and military cover-ups or legitimate subsidiaries of these. On more than one occasion Havens was involved in liberating computer hard drives or locked files and then setting the place ablaze. Municipal departments could then enter the building and others at a federal level could enter based on an anonymous tip.

There were a number of close calls, but it was an operation against some Israelis at a software company in Silicon Valley that gave Havens pause. He had been working on an assignment when he accidentally discovered involvement of the Israelis in a partnership that would give them informational access to most of the Fortune 500 companies and their employees. By innocently chatting up one of the Israelis at a tradeshow, he learned that a number of these men in the company had served in an electronics unit of the Israeli military. A very discrete electronics unit. Few would mention their name.

Upon further investigation, Sean learned these men had been, and in a few cases still were, part of Sayeret Matkal, an elite covert action unit within the Israeli Defense Forces. He informed his handler and was instructed to resign from his current company and move to New York City in order to avoid a potential problem.

The night after informing his employer of his discovery, Havens came home to find his apartment had been ransacked. The intruders were still in the apartment and immediately neutralized Havens, who was no match for the Krav Maga-trained fighter. Havens was knocked out cold and awoke to find himself duct taped to a chair. Two masked men stood over him.

"Who do you work for Mr. Sean Havens?" a man demanded in a heavy Israeli accent.

Sarcastically, Havens replied, "I work for Benjamin Netanyahu. Call him and he will validate this information."

The blow was forceful but the sting of the open hand slap actually brought water to Havens' eyes. It hurt worse than a fist.

You are a corporate employee. Act like a corporate employee. An employee would not name the former commander of the Sayeret Matkal commando unit to members of Sayeret Matkal. Bruce Willis would do that if he were in a terrorist movie, but not you, Havens.

Havens coaxed himself into crying, which was less difficult than he would have liked to admit given the slap and his growing fear. *Dad would be so pissed at me.*

"Stop, please stop. I work for our General Counsel. I work in copyright infringement. I know some people have been using our training material in Israel, Turkey, and India. Please don't hit me again."

"Copyright? Why would you say the name Benjamin Netanyahu?"

"Because you sound like my old neighbor who was from Israel. But she never hit me."

"You are a smart ass American. What do you even know of Israel?"

"I know this…"

Before the masked intruders could answer, Havens sung in his best Jewish cantor voice a holy Yom Kippur blessing that he had learned in the neighborhood.

"Baruch atah adonai eloheinu melech ha'olam asher kid'shanu b'mitzvotav v'tzivanu l'hadlik neir shel you hakippurim…"

When Havens finished, one of the armed men pushed a leather bound portfolio pad into Sean's mouth.

"Your prayer just saved your life. Bite down," the assaulter said calmly.

Doing as instructed, Sean Havens bit into the leather as hard as he could before the gun butt smashed against his head and he was jolted into unconsciousness.

Chapter 29

"You did not really sing a prayer to them," Lars said, digging into the pizza. Lars was easing up on his attitude. The stories mixed with booze and food helped.

"I'm afraid so. Seemed like a good idea at the time. As soon as I got free I called my handler to tell him what happened, then called a florist in my home neighborhood and had them deliver flowers to Mrs. Lewicz's resting place."

Havens was telling the truth while carefully inserting himself back within Lars' circle of trust.

"Sean, I had no idea. But how is it then that you are doing so much overseas work?"

"Things changed after 9/11. Christina and I were married, Maggie was in pre-school. We were back in Chicago and I was at the Sears Tower working for a different surrogate company when Christina heard a second plane had hit the World Trade Center in New York. She called me on my mobile and asked if I was still at work."

"Were you?"

"Yeah, in a stall on the 37th floor taking my morning shit." Havens laughed.

"She was frantic about me getting out of there right away and thought Chicago might be next. I was getting a bit nervous myself."

"What did you do?"

"Wiped and ran down thirty-seven floors in record time. Took a bus home where she and I sat on the bed watching the towers come down."

"Yeah, bad day. Horrible. Never forget it."

"Right. Well that is what got me more directly involved. The phone rang and it was my guy. I didn't say anything, but Christina just looked at me and said, "Go get those fuckers.'"

"Christina said that?" asked Lars, with a look of utter surprise.

"I kid you not. First time I ever heard her drop the F-bomb."

"No shit. Good for her."

"And that is when you left for a bit, right?"

"Yep. I was made a contractor for a tier one military slash Agency counterterror task force, sent to a two week intensive training, and found myself in Iran and some other places."

"Iran? Not Iraq or Afghanistan?"

"Nope. What I said. And you will never speak of it."

"Who would I tell?"

"Doesn't matter."

"Anyway, I think you get the picture. A lot of missions, a lot of other stories for another time."

"You ever have to kill anyone, Seany?"

Havens took a deep breath.

"Anyone who was ever killed had to be killed. If not by my hand, by another's."

"Christina asked me once about people who can't sleep. She said you had a hard time once about something."

Havens was surprised. He told his wife next to nothing. It was understood. Sometimes he would come back from a trip and need time to decompress before engaging his family. Christina would give him a knowing look and suggest he go down in the basement to do his trip's company expenses for a few hours. She knew that her husband lived in a world where he was surrounded by people who he would interact with but had to keep outside his wall. She could see how lonely he looked at times. What she didn't know was that while there was excitement, boredom could still set. It was necessary to remain vigilant in spite of this in order to stay safe and keep others around you safe. If you slipped up, that was when the hordes would penetrate the operator's mental front. Your only choice was to run, fight, or submit. For some, a safe haven was the only answer to take pause, gather ones thoughts or emotions, and focus on the desired end state and act.

Sean began to realize how much he had depended on his wife as a baseline for reality outside of the battlespace. The emptiness he felt without her was beginning to eat at him from the inside.

"No worries. I see that look on your face. She didn't say anything. Well, she said you were sleeping on the floor for a bit. She was worried that you were sleeping with a gun. She was concerned for Maggie's sake. Should she have been worried about something else?"

"Sean?"

"Sorry, no, I just slipped away for a moment. Well, I guess she *would* need to talk to someone. I just needed to work something out from a trip or two. I don't see victims' faces or anything. Well, not victims, but you know what I mean. I am not haunted, but there are times when the high stress of an operating environment is so intense that it takes a while to unwind and decompress. I know you know what it's like to be in high risk areas, but you have learned to adapt to it by being in the same area. I go from worrying if someone is going to kick down my door one night and the next coming home to Mayberry. It takes some time to recognize a bump in the night is just one of the girls taking a late night whiz versus some storm troopers coming to drag me to some basement before burying lead in my forehead or making a home video of my head getting Ginsu'd."

"No, I hear what you are saying."

"So we good? I can't think of anyone who wouldn't want to kill me if they knew who I was or where I was, but I have been so careful with my trail and use so many cutouts that I can't see who would associate me with anything."

"How about those Israelis?"

"No. That is in the past and I can't see them doing something like this. If anything, I would have been shot or blown to a million pieces from an explosion. They would be honorable and not take out my family. Plus, I may have done some work for some people over there that puts me on the no-kill list for the time being. They actually owe me a favor."

"OK, I agree. And, no, I don't want to know."

"I'm not telling you anyway." Enticing Lars, Havens added, "But it is a good story." He smiled. Havens was a bit drunk now. Lars was the first person he had told most everything to. The feeling was liberating. But Havens was careful, and remained sure he hadn't gone too far in disclosure.

"Screw you. Don't play games if you can't pony up. You're drunk."

"So are you."

"But I don't have to worry about keeping secrets. I am not that drunk, but I do feel it a bit." He smiled and gave a long yawn.

"I'm done with secrets. I need a break. I don't want to do this anymore. I am not sure if I am really making the difference I set out to do. I'm just not sure about anything anymore. I just need to focus on getting Maggie back now."

"OK, bro, time for you to get some sleep. You are getting on the drunk box now and I'm going to stop you before you go on blubbering about how your life is worthless."

"I can't go up there to sleep. I can't be up there without the girls being there."

"Go downstairs and sleep on your sofa. I will assume my usual position on the recliner up here."

"Should we even be staying here? Isn't there evidence we could be messing up?"

"They have everything they need from the first incident. I got the OK for a cleanup crew but haven't had the time. This last one they also have captured for evidence exploitation. Everything is pretty cut and dry from my statement and the evidence. My biggest interest is a partial footprint that didn't match the perp. There was also a blood droplet I want checked. The perp was cutting up his wrist pretty good but then I saw some droplets outside of his action spot. In some cases of psychos, they are talking to themselves or voices and get all wigged out, flailing their arms about. Sometimes that throws off blood spatter beyond their immediate zone."

"So you think someone else was here too?"

"Yeah, I got this Spidey-sense tingling that there was someone else. Had some of the lab rats taking swipes and photos and had the boys doing some canvassing of the neighborhood. Got one guy to get the K-9 out while they walked the backyard to see if there were some remaining ground compressions still present. I'll see what they have in the morning."

"Well at least they got the guy who killed the crazy in the house."

Lars gave Havens the finger with only a hint of a smirk on his face. "That guy was off though. I recognized him right away."

"How could you recognize him? I thought they didn't know who he was?"

Lars pursed his lips. He had half-meant to slip in his disclosure about being involved with the case. Lars liked to keep a handful of secrets.

"Sean, I somewhat diverted the rape kit with Christina's approval."

"You what?"

"No biggie. I wanted to make sure it got a rush but also got the proper attention to detail. We got partial prints from the perp off of Maggie right away and a few full prints with some work. I have this new little gizmo that can suction prints off fabric. State of the art. But we were able to pull this guy from some past arrests."

"Did they put out a warrant?"

"Yep, but they couldn't find him. Had a few leads, but nothing came through. This all happened very fast. Plus, I had to do this while I was away. Christina didn't want me to come home but still wanted some help, so I did it all remotely until I got in town. By then I was making funeral arrangements."

"Thanks, Lars. You shouldn't have had to do that."

"I know you are her husband, but I couldn't wait or trust there wouldn't be delays. I tried calling you a number of times but it went straight to voice mail."

"Sorry about that."

"No need. A lot is cleared up now that I know you were doing special mission unit stuff in suits and what not. I suspect more, but that'll work for now."

"Thanks."

"So, what is this about tomorrow night?"

"Technically, it is tomorrow now. Still have enough energy to go for a drive?"

"I'm not so sure I can drive. Can you?"

"Who's going to pull me over, a cop? Plus I can just hit the autopilot on my car. It is only about fifteen minutes from here."

"Where are we going?"

"We are going to flip over some dead gangsters in their coffins. Good for the soul."

"I thought you were just angry when you said that."

"I was. But I was also serious."

"They probably aren't even buried yet. Won't they be at the funeral home?"

"Nope." Lars continued to gather his personal things lying on the table. Rather buzzed, he patted himself down for car keys.

"Lars, it's stupid to take that kind of risk. I'm not sure what the point is. We have no plan."

"I have a plan."

"Lars, seriously, if we really want to do something, let's give it time so we can send a message, but one that won't get us busted. Cop or not, they would look to us first for the crime. We have the motive."

"Careful Sean, you are using cop words now and that's my lane."

"I have an idea. Let's get some shut-eye and sleep this off. I'll check on Maggie first thing and get some arrangements made. I want this carpet pulled up and walls cleaned and painted tomorrow. I don't want Maggie coming home to this."

"OK, Sean. Go get some sleep. I'm going. I know the guy who works the backhoe at their cemetery and he said he isn't covering them until tomorrow morning. Sean, these guys are a dead end. There is nothing left to do other than disgrace their remains." Lars shrugged his shoulders, thinking it made perfect sense.

Sean found the idea to be ridiculous. It was dangerous. It was careless. It served no purpose other than some stupid way for revenge. Havens knew how to exact revenge on men and this was trivial. Amateurish. He brooded for another few seconds and realized it was the only thing they had in their power to do at this time. They were drunk. They were hurting inside.

"Let's go. Wait. I have some gas in the garage."

"Now you are with the program."

Lars smiled and gave a little mini dance. He walked to a kitchen drawer and retrieved some wooden matches.

Part III

I am the hunted that stalks my aggressor
I am neurosis, I am the measurements used
When it's time to choose which tools are proper
For the opportunity to break it loose

When it breaks, it'll all come together now
Armageddon, just a change in the weather now
I am the one, I've come to let the pressure out
More human than human, so you can feel better now

Yeah, more human than human

—X-Ecutioners,
from "(Even) More Human than Human"

Chapter 30

The new orderly arrived for his first day at work in the intensive care and trauma ward. He showed the security guard his badge with an unfriendly demeanor of annoyed accommodation.

"New guy, huh? ICU I see." The guard inspected the badge while sizing up the new employee. "Well, alright, Mr. Whittington. Do you know where to go?"

"Yes, sir." The orderly looked around and down, not making direct eye contact with the security guard.

"Alright then. Have you worked in a hospital before? You look a little sharper than most of our orderlies. Better shape too. Military man?"

The orderly looked up. "Sir, if you don't mind, I don't want to be late."

"No problem. I was in the Marine Corps for thirty years. You sure look like a military man. I'm sure I will be seeing you around then."

The orderly nodded and continued walking down the corridor making the hard left that visitors and new employees typically miss on their first time to this wing.

"I'm impressed. You do know where you are going. Pretty good, new guy!" the guard called out down the hall. "I'll see you around."

A maintenance man approached the guard to check in. "Hey, Jose, man, just saw a new big ass orderly. Military man. No Marine. Looks Army. Probably fresh out. Think I will pay a visit this week to Meredith in HR upstairs and see who our new friend is. Be a good excuse to say hello. Wonder if she is still sweet on that new administrator. She still sweet on him?"

"Yo no se."

"Mmmhmm. Well tell me this then. Why they starting a new guy at midnight shift? You ever seen that happen?"

"Man, I don't see nothing. That's your job."

"Mmmhmm. Every soldier's a sensor, Jose. You're my soldier and sensor."

"I'm just a janitor, boss."

Harrison Mann tended to the wound he sustained from Brock then finished cleaning the basement of the rental home where he held his crazy captive. The wound wasn't as deep as he had thought, but it still needed some stitches. He had a small kit with med supplies in the trunk. Harrison looked around the house. All traces of Brock's short stay were gone. The bungalow was perfect for their ruse of frightening Brock as his meds had worn off and his mind reverted to its diseased state. Despite the success, their work was getting sloppy. Harrison didn't like having to assume that Brock had bled out or broke his neck. He also didn't like playing with nut jobs. He knew Brock was a freak and wondered if Draeger was as well.

This operation needed better tactical intelligence and more time on target. No more of these seat of the pants operations where they depended more on luck and fate. No more of these surprises like unexpected guests. That was for amateurs. It made Harrison feel like a criminal, not a soldier.

Even if they were supposed to look like amateurs, time constraints in planning would get them caught. He decided he would have to discuss this with Draeger. Harrison returned his focus to the situation before him and scanned his memory of the unfolded events. What else needed to be done to wipe this op from their hands? What traces could later come back to haunt them?

Confident that all had been taken care of, Harrison turned off the lights. Perfect tenants. The cash paid month-to-month lease would expire in two more months. Better call the landlord tomorrow to let them know the property was now vacated. It would be better to get someone else in here as soon as possible. No, he thought. Better to find some squatters to come in here. He could pass the word through a contact of his on the street. He had plenty of drug snitches still running around the area from a DEA stint he did locally. That would do the trick in less time. The landlord could keep the deposit.

Chapter 31

Draeger tossed and turned in his bed. There was a loud knock at the door. Moments later it became a pounding. Draeger could make out the verbal sounds but didn't understand the language. He tried to move but couldn't. Something was binding his legs. His head was foggy. He heard a crash as the door caved to the unrelenting visitors. Where was his gun? He remembered leaving it on the night stand beside his bed. He just needed to break free somehow. The men surrounded him now in swivel chairs, laughing. Draeger's mind raced. Was it Iranian security? Lebanese Hezbollah?

An explosion blew the roof off over his bed. Men in white robes and black assault uniforms rappelled down the walls from the helicopter above. Draeger watched the metal casings cascading from the assault rifles. The woman beside him in the bed gyrated from the impact of the bullets. Her blood, exiting her body like liberated peoples, joined in the dancing.

A masked assaulter continued shouting in the foreign tongue as he unraveled plastic wrap to cover Draeger's face. Draeger struggled to lift his hands into his line of vision. They were now bound by flexicuffs. The woman's cold arm flopped onto his naked chest. Another assaulter began lighting a propane torch. Draeger couldn't breathe, couldn't move. The men in chairs cackled harder. Left with no other outlet, Draeger opened his mouth to scream.

"Shit," he muttered, at last escaping the blanket tangled between the couch cushions.

Draeger, with arms now free, wiped his sweaty face. His heart was racing. He ran his hands through his sweat-soaked hair and scratched the back of his head. A security panel on the wall still showed a steady glow of small red lights in a descending trail of secured zones. He looked at the clock on the cable box. It read 2:45. He had hoped it was much later but knew it was unlikely.

Great. A whopping hour of sleep.

To Draeger, this meant a number of things. First, he had had a bad dream just after entering REM sleep. He would have a few more short sleep sessions before sunup. Second, the night terror had not come yet. Most of the night terrors he could not recall. They were less vivid than his recurring dreams. His night terror would likely be next before he hit REM sleep again. His hands continued to perspire. His heartbeat was still strong but the stage-4 sleep cycle terror wake-up would send his heart racing to maximum output. He would awake disoriented and panic-stricken. He hated the night.

Draeger shut off the television's muted flashing and closed up the main floor after making a cup of valerian root tea to put him to sleep.

He went upstairs a soldier, ready to engage his enemy on the battlefield of his mind. He tried to process the dream as he climbed while reflecting on his day for potential triggers.

Shit, my whole damn life is a trigger. Gotta change the ending somehow. I can change it. I can train to win this. I have the training to beat my own head.

I'll take the Prazosin pills tomorrow if I don't sleep.

Draeger downed the tea, grabbed a pillow, and went to the guest room. He slid a heavy wooden chair under the door knob and assured it was a snug fit. He looked at the blankets on the closet floor and felt a sudden pang of shame at his situation. He was afraid that if he sought help the medical records and payment coverage would signal instability to someone. He'd lose his job and clearances. Fluffing his pillow and pulling up the blankets, Prescott Draeger solemnly closed his eyes with the same mental preparation that he would in a high altitude low opening parachute jump to go behind enemy lines. He closed the closet doors and felt secure in the tight space.

Chapter 32

Havens dashed the mobile phone against the concrete sidewalk in front of the hospital. The rugged OtterBox case bounced the phone onto the small strip of city grass. The sight relieved Havens, but he immediately regretted his impulsive tantrum.

It had been days since Christina's funeral and burial. Maggie was still unresponsive and the doctors were concerned about her continued low brain activity. Now Havens was being told that in order to keep his job he would have to deploy yet again to the Middle East. Killing America's top terror suspects had opened a Pandora's box of seemingly random actors who were now targeting any key westerners that were within their reach. Libya was a concern and the boss needed him to go on an exploratory mission east of Tripoli. When Havens declined due to his daughter's critical condition, to his shock, he was terminated. Jason had apologized but said it was beyond his control.

Insurance benefits would revert to COBRA continuing coverage but only for so long. With no job, Havens would have to start using his savings. Like many public sector employees, Havens had planned on moving to the private sector to take advantage of the higher pay rate in order to fill his coffers. For some reason, those coffers never seemed to fill as much as he'd like.

The phone rang from the grass. Havens could read the incoming caller's name, CABLE GUY.

Prescott Draeger.

Havens picked up the phone and accepted the call by the fourth ring.

"Hey, buddy."

"Hi Sean, how have you been holding up?"

"Bout as good as expected."

"Sorry I couldn't make it to the funeral. I just got back CONUS. I'm so sorry for Christina's death, real shame. Sean, are they closer to finding anything more about the whole thing?"

"Thanks, Prescott. No worries. I understand. They have some hunches and the two or I guess three guys who were involved are now dead. Whole thing is crazy. The guy who killed them was some random Latino gang member who ended up getting shot too. Story is these guys were involved in drugs and the Latino was looking for them. After he found the two black gangbangers and shot them, their guys must have gone after him and killed him a few blocks away. Probably never get answers to everything. There was some other twist and I ended up getting another body in my house. It's just all fucked up. None of it makes sense. Cops suspect the crazy guy paid some street thugs to kill her but they left something behind and he had to go back to get it."

Draeger was surprised to hear the latest update. *Well, now there is an interesting twist. Nice work CPD. Keep busying yourselves with the nonsense.*

"And how is Maggie doing? I hear she is in a coma?"

"Yeah, they don't even know if she is going to come out of it. Doctors keep saying we just have to keep waiting and monitoring her progress. Clearly it means they don't know either."

"Probably so, but I know they are top notch over there."

"I suppose. Guess I should give them more credit."

"I think asking questions and keeping them on their toes is always best. I am sure you are doing the right thing. How is work, they give you some time off then?"

"Yeah, just spoke to them. I have time off…permanently."

"No way. You didn't quit did you?" Draeger was loving this.

"No, they gave me some time but since I am foreign tagged I have to be able to deploy when called. They called and I can't deploy. That violates the contract so they need someone else."

"I thought you were government, though."

Havens lowered his voice as if it would really stop someone from hearing over the unsecured line.

"Pres, I don't know how they ended up spinning the thing. I was govie then not govie, signed all these crazy papers that made me an employee of some company, but then it still counts for some things and not for others. I think we outsmarted ourselves to cover our tracks and now I don't even get a severance."

"Can't you raise that to the boss or program director?"

"Well, that too is a great example of our genius compartmentalization. I don't even know who I report to. I have a handler that I report to but I only know people along the horizon of my group and no tiers above. I am tasked unwitting to the client or intermediaries. It was a brilliant idea until I got canned. I don't have time to look for a job. And now Chicago is like the worst possible place I could be to find a job for the work I do."

Havens sighed over the phone.

"Sorry, Pres, I didn't mean to shovel my shit your way like some sad ass pathetic guy who lost everything."

"Well Sean, you are a sad ass pathetic guy who lost everything, but fortunately for you, you did manage to keep a couple friends along the way."

"Thanks, man. So what can I do for you or were you just calling to say hello?"

"Just calling to see how you're holding up and to tell you I am coming through the area today. Can you break free for a bit? I can even meet you at the hospital if that is easier."

"I could use the company, actually. I wouldn't mind getting out of the hospital for a bit. I've been here every spare moment between attending to the funeral or making sure the house was getting put back together."

"The shit you must be going through…I feel for you. Well I land in about five hours over there. Do you want me to meet you somewhere near the hospital?"

"Sure, there are a couple decent places we could go to. How long are you in for?"

"Just the night. I will book over at the old Palmer House. Always liked that place."

Havens smiled having recently recollected his times with Jerry there in his younger days.

"Sounds good. You sleeping any?"

"Not much. Let's talk when I get in. I'll call you when I am about 10-15 out from your position."

"See you then."

"Out."

Havens walked back in to the hospital to sit with Maggie some more. As Havens exited the elevator he saw the orderly standing at the door of Maggie's room peeking in from the side of the frame.

"Can I help you?" Havens asked hoping to startle the lurking orderly.

"No," the orderly replied, unperturbed. Walking away he added, "Just checking for linens," without turning to Havens.

Satisfied, Havens sat back in his chair where he would wait until the evening when Draeger would arrive. He brushed his daughter's hair with his fingers.

I'm just glad your mother didn't see you like this.

He would sit for hours holding her hand hoping for a squeeze or any sign of movement. Looking for some sign of life.

Prescott Draeger finished his meeting with Harrison in his hotel suite at the Palmer House. Havens had introduced him to the hotel years back and found it suited him. He would call Sean in about thirty minutes from the hospital's main entrance to start the pitch and hook process of recruitment.

Over the past few days during his restless evening hours he reminisced about being at the Havens home. Christina was always very kind to him. Of all the men she was ever introduced to by her husband, Prescott was the only one she called by his full first name and not a nickname as the others would be called. She once told Draeger in one of their few exchanges before the guys headed down to the basement how she liked his name and enjoyed saying Prescott. Prescott, in turn, liked hearing her say his name. She was a beautiful woman with a penetratingly charming voice. Yet he maintained no illusion that her demeanor and attention to him was flirtatious. Christina Havens was just a sweet woman who was innately kind and devoted to her husband.

Their daughter, Maggie, was the same way. Maggie would always extend a casual hello from the kitchen table where she did her homework. Draeger had only engaged her once when he saw her writing a report on the significance of President's Day. Prescott praised her for the topic choice but was chagrined when she responded that it was just assigned. Havens laughed, knowing how patriotic Draeger was, and chided him on it being simply a nice day off. By that time Maggie had disconnected herself from the conversation and continued on with her studies in another room.

On weekends when the men came by, it was not uncommon to see Maggie and her mother watching a movie together in the family room. They were a nice family and Havens was both appreciative of it and deeply attached. In Draeger's mind, Havens was too attached to fully maximize his natural talents to rid the U.S. of its adversaries. Draeger would miss seeing Christina and hearing her say his name. No matter, he couldn't have her. He could, however, have her husband. Draeger estimated that he would have Havens in his pocket in a matter of hours. He smiled as he rolled his shirtsleeve cuffs up.

Draeger called Havens twenty minutes early from the admissions area with the intent of flustering Sean a bit. Not expecting Draeger to be at the hospital so early, Havens rushed to the elevator so he wouldn't keep his friend waiting. Havens lightly jogged through the long corridors navigating the labyrinth of paths and found his buddy, Pres.

He and Draeger got along well, being more intellectuals than hard men. Draeger had the formal ex-military pedigree but rarely acted like a former soldier. He was amazing at his work, but horrible on a team.

In the mixed presence of operators and analysts, Draeger and Havens fit somewhere in the middle, which most of the time meant they didn't fit in with either circle. Like their status amongst peers, they were grey men. Like their jobs and their covers, their color of grey was blacker than coal.

While capable of extreme violence, both men would prefer a good conversation to an operational takedown. At least on most days. They preferred the hunt over the capture, the game and chase over the kill. After a surviving a close scrape in Iran together, Draeger and Havens had the makings of a deep friendship, but for reasons unclear to Sean, Prescott Draeger preferred to keep his friend at arm's length. He pushed him away even more after Iran. Havens wondered at the time if Draeger wanted more of a full-time friend. Not one that was shared with a family.

They greeted one another with the requisite bro hug and started the short walk to a nearby restaurant.

"So Sean, I know you've already got a lot on your mind right now, but I was doing some thinking on the plane about you losing your job and your current situation."

"That makes two of us."

Draeger smiled and nodded in affirmation of the obvious. "Right, well what exactly would be an ideal situation for you?"

"Yeah, I have actually been giving a lot of thought to that and can't come up with anything realistic given my location and constraints with Maggie's needs. A perfect world would be a blend of what I have been doing. Unfortunately, I can't tell you too much about that."

"Look Sean, I have a pretty good idea that you are not trading bonds. We both know who we are and what we do. So, if I understand you correctly, you would do some type of hybrid operational intel collection or support work domestically that would give you flexibility for Maggie?"

"That's about it, but not even domestically. It really would need to be here. I know that the FBI or some relic of CIFA, maybe Secret Service or even the DEA may have something, but I don't know where to start and don't think I would have the flexibility with a government job."

"Yeah, that is a bitch. I don't think anything would give that type of freedom given your limited skill set outside of your niche. Can't see anything that would turn you loose on Chicago. You'd burn the damn city down."

"I'd be happy to burn some of this city down. That whole personal side of everything just makes me want to get in and take out the trash. Never thought I'd say it, but I feel like those spec ops t-shirts that say 'Kill 'em all and let God sort them out.'"

"Have you looked on Monster.com for anything in Chicago that says killer for hire?" Draeger elbowed Havens in jest as they walked the city streets.

"Nah, that's on Craigslist now," Sean joked back. "There's gotta be a Homeland Security program or something out there. Turn right up here on Michigan."

"Now that I think of it, Sean, there may be. I don't know much about it but may know a guy who is in the city here doing work for them. Too bad I don't have more time to find out for you."

"What is it?"

"I think it's called Silver Star. They have a Chicago office."

"Silver Star? I think they were part of the funding for Christina's funeral."

"Oh, so you have heard of them before?"

"No, but they offered to take care of everything. I didn't look into them. I figured there was some involvement with my employer and I knew not to ask too many questions."

"Alright, well you may be closer than I am to this."

"I don't have a contact or anything. But I'm not sure I want to do a USO-type thing. It might be a bit of a stretch."

"Well that is what I thought when I first heard of it, but the guy I know isn't doing Honor Flights and Welcome Home events. Let me make a call. How about I have him call you direct. Can I give him your personal mobile?"

"Sure. Just have him leave me a number to call back if I have it off or miss it in the hospital. They have all these no cell phone signs up in the wing. I need to change out my phone number again but I can wait until we at least speak."

"Will do. Let's see if there is anything to this. See, things are looking a bit brighter anyway. I'm glad you prompted me to think of this. I had totally forgotten about Silver Star."

"I'm telling you, man, we would be dangerous if we ever worked together again."

Draeger put his arm around Havens' shoulder as he opened the door to Ditka's. "I agree. We should partner up sometime. We'd sure clean up a lot of dirt."

"Shit, we'd probably get ourselves arrested."

Draeger took in the sports memorabilia with little personal interest. "We'd just have to be careful. Do they have ribs here?"

"Awesome ribs. Awesome pork chops. Good red wine for you. Just don't say Da Bears. Hate that."

"Daaa…"

"Don't make me kick your ass, Pres. Glad you called."

"Two please, somewhere in the back kind of away from people. Need to discuss a presentation for the morning."

"Come this way gentleman." The brunette hostess, hardly in her twenties, motioned her guests to follow.

"Absolutely," said Draeger fixated on the young hostess' firm buttocks. "You have a very nice voice."

"Is that the best you've got?" The hostess turned around with an appreciative smile to Draeger who rapidly looked up. "Thank you, no one has ever said that to me before."

Draeger, his brow aggressively turned down, eyes assessing like a predator to prey, wet his lips with a subconscious shallow lick. *I could have you in my room tonight and kick you out before going to sleep.*

"Is this table alright, gentlemen?"

"Perfect," they said in unison.

"Your waitress will be with you momentarily." She handed each man their menu, smiling at Draeger as she released the menu. He noticed a small-stoned engagement ring on her left hand.

Bitch. And marrying some poor sorry ass loser. I could break him. Maybe I should so you can learn everything that comes so easy to you can be taken away so fast. Whore.

Stuffed from food and wine, the two men walked a block south on Michigan Avenue before Draeger hailed a cab back to his hotel. The two parted with a handshake and loose embrace as Havens thanked his friend.

"Anything to help, buddy. I will call my guy and see if there is anything there."

"Sounds good. Who should I expect to call? Do you have a name?"

"Let me see if it is cool first. You know how it is."

"Indeed I do. Take care and stay in touch."

"I'll be close. By the way, you still keep in touch with Red, right?"

"Yeah, he was just asking about you, wanting to know if you were up for some soccer. Did you want his number?"

Draeger made his fingers into a gun gesture. "I got his number alright. Six in the six. Two in the head for good measure. Just seeing if you still stayed in touch. I know you were tight."

"Should I worry that it will affect my candidacy?"

"No. What is between me and Red is between me and Red. It's all good."

"You know it was an act of a young adrenaline-driven pilgrim and not malicious, right?"

"We've gone through this before, Sean. It isn't sour grapes. Red never respected me but we were always able to work together."

On some things we agreed. Like how you would have been better off in the field with us instead of staying here with your family.

"He just never understood you, Pres. You are a bit of an onion. If you don't like the smell after peeling the first layer, you stop peeling."

"Thanks…I'll be in touch, Sean."

"I'll tell Red you said hi."

"Tell him he is still number one," as Draeger raised his middle finger.

Havens pulled out the cut cigar he had purchased in the bar for the walk back to the hospital. He struck the match preparing the tip and inhaled his much needed treat. *Good to see another friendly face. Seems like Draeger is keeping it together a bit.*

Draeger pulled out his mobile phone and typed a text to Harrison. GUD 2 GO. Draeger deleted the message, feeling more like a tween texter than experienced operator. He typed again. GREEN. *Much better. Wonder if there will be any wounded antelopes drunk at the hotel bar by now. Have to check that out before trying to turn in. Can't sleep anyway.*

The reply came back from Harrison almost immediately. RGR. GUD2GO.

Draeger smiled seeing the GUD2GO that he had considered, immediately glad that he took the professional highroad and put away his phone. He looked out the cab window and marveled at the city. How he was going to enjoy turning it upside down. He glanced at the back of his driver's head and then looked to read the name on the placard below. REZA SHIRAZIAN.

"Reza, huh? And where may I ask are you from?"

Draeger knew the answer before it came.

"I am longtime in Chicago."

"But where were you originally?"

"Detroit."

"And before that?"

"New York. You been to New York?"

"Yes, I have been to New York. Where were you born?"

"Why you like to know?"

"I'm just curious. I saw your name and knew a Reza once. I was curious as to where you were from, originally, where you were born."

"Ah."

"And?"

"I am Persian."

There we go. "So you are from Iran."

"Yes. You have been? I don't think so maybe."

"No, I don't get out much."

"So how long are you in Chicago?"

"I think I just decided that I will try to leave tonight."

Of course you continue to haunt me. Why did I even ask? Persia, Iran, my personal Hell. Why won't you let me sleep? Havens, you don't even have half the training of our old teams. How can you possibly sleep with no trouble to your soul? Maybe now you can't as your own horrors have come to roost. I'm just getting started.

Draeger continued to gaze out the cab window at tourists walking the streets. With a finger to the glass, he double-tapped each pedestrian in the head. Willing them all to die. Women and children first.

Sean exited from the elevator. He could still smell the smoke on his clothes despite the nice breeze outside. The halls were dimmed to let the patients rest. Visiting hours were over. Havens was an exception. He watched from afar as the orderly walked down the hall. When the orderly approached Maggie's room, Havens noticed he slowed and started to turn his head. Assuming the orderly might be shifting to look behind him, Havens stepped back into the water fountain nook between the men's and women's bathrooms. Havens scanned to see if he could find anything with a reflection. He spotted a polished handle on the fire extinguisher box fixed to the wall. He could make out the orderly's back, now turned to Havens. Havens emerged to see the orderly stepping into the room.

Havens rushed down the hall quickly and quietly taking long strides, his feet meeting the linoleum tiles briefly with the outsides of his soles. He wasn't taking any more chances on the oddities occurring in his home world.

As he approached the room, the orderly quickly exited.

"Hey, what are you doing in there?" Havens demanded with an air of authority.

"Nothing," the order said as he exited from the room, not even looking at Havens.

"Hey, wait. I am not done." Havens reached for the orderly's shoulder. When Havens' right hand touched the right shoulder of the orderly, the man spun around and already had Havens' hand in a pressure lock twisting at the joint and simultaneously squeezed pressure points in order to incapacitate Havens.

The offset size of the large orderly and Havens' slightly smaller frame provided an opening. Havens flowed with the movement increasing its direction. Ducking and stepping in through the twist of arms Havens got behind the orderly grabbing a hold of the man's larynx.

"Now let's try that again."

The orderly managed to communicate through a suppressed airway, "Just seeing if she was doing any better."

"Why the fuck do you care?"

"I just do; it's my job."

"That's not your job. That's for the nurses and doctors."

"Sir, it's my job. I am supposed to protect her."

"What? From who? Who are you?"

"Let go and I will tell you."

"Tell me and I may let go."

"Sir, I can take you out. Please let go before I make you let me go."

"If you can take me why am I holding your throat?"

"I am supposed to keep an eye on you too. Make sure you were safe."

Guardedly, Havens released the orderly.

"Who are you?"

"Name's Whittington."

"And Mr. Whittington, why are you the fairy godmother orderly assigned to watch me and my daughter?"

"Because I work for someone with your interests in mind, given your prior employment in government."

"Are you government?"

"Not exactly. I am a contractor."

Everybody is a contractor these days.

"Why are you wearing an orderly uniform and badge?"

"So I fit in."

"And what if you had to perform medical duties?"

"I do. I was Special Forces 18-Delta. I'm a trained medic."

"So what other things can you do, Mr. Whittington. Brain surgery, banking?"

"I paid for your wife's funeral arrangements on orders from my boss."

"OK, Delta, you've got my attention."

Two cups of coffee later, Havens had learned all about Whittington's deployments to Iraq and Afghanistan. He hadn't noticed the burns on Whittington's arms until his sleeves were rolled up. Whittington had been medically discharged from the Army with a broken vertebra and severe burns to his upper arms and torso from wounds received in battle. Due to his limited physical abilities, Whittington was no longer eligible for service but had been identified by the local Silver Star chapter as a viable candidate for their Family Protection Program.

For the past year, while undergoing rehabilitation and therapy, Whittington was assigned various tasks to protect or assist the families of servicemen who were overseas. Initially, Whittington assisted some wives who needed to go to the police for various harassment claims or instances of neighborhood or family abuse cases. In most cases he assisted spouses who were negligent in their parental duties due to situations that had occurred while the other spouse was deployed overseas.

"Why haven't I heard of this program before?"

Whittington looked at his watch and downed his coffee. "You wouldn't have unless you needed assistance. The process is this: if a soldier overseas is having personal problems during his or her deployment due to an external issue affecting their family back home, they let their superior officer know. The superior officer can pass that information on to a readiness and deployment entity that then makes a judgment call and triage evaluation. If a local military support group can handle it, for example their house burned down, someone lost a job, or their house was going into foreclosure, the 'ticket,' as it were, doesn't escalate."

Havens nodded in understanding.

"Now let's say a soldier is deployed, his wife is back home and her brother or the neighbor is beating on her or harassing her but the authorities have not been called or are not willing to do anything, we can act as an advocate. If something happens that is not to a high enough level that cops would get called for 911, we can help. Like, perhaps we escort the woman home from work, check out her house when she arrives, and make sure no one's there waiting for her. That sort of stuff."

Havens sat quietly looking at his cup of coffee. "Sure could have used you guys."

"Well, actually we were involved. See, you were not technically government or military, so we had to jump through hoops from an internal billing process standpoint. I know that sounds horrible, but that is what went down. When your daughter was threatened, she actually found us on Facebook. She said her father was in the military or government but we couldn't find your records."

"I see."

"Later when we got the authorization, we were too late. But in this case, it likely would have been handled by law enforcement anyway since they were already involved. We could have made an introduction to assist in an augmented role to the police though. I suspect that is why we felt compelled to pay for the arrangements."

"Who pays for all of this?"

"I don't know exactly, but it is a blend of DoD funds and private estate and corporate donations. It's very low key so it doesn't become a requested service or taken advantage of. Also it gives us some latitude as to how we think a situation should be handled. We prefer to dispatch ourselves for the right situations. It also seems to be favoring those service members of the special operations community."

"Why is that?"

"Well, it isn't very politically correct, but some feel that general purpose forces may already be inclined to have some domestic issues based on studies of demographics, economics, social status, education..."

"Alright, I got your legal disclaimer. I won't hold it against you."

"Bottom line, for the soldiers the United States has already invested so much time and money into training, this is a benefit designed so elite forces can focus on the matter at hand as opposed to matters at home. We have a motto, 'We Have Their 6," which means the family's back. We know our brothers have each other's backs in the field."

"This is amazing. So why are you still here?"

"Well I have been trying to leave for the last ten minutes to make my rounds so I don't get fired."

"No, I mean why are you looking out for me and my daughter if I am back?"

"Bit of work, bit of personal. Your daughter seemed like a good kid. I felt bad that we couldn't help in time and I felt like I should look in on her from time to time."

"Bullshit."

Whittington looked from side to side and lowered his head. "Well, frankly, your home situation was pretty messed up. Cops were going in a bunch of directions. We looked at it from a team perspective and thought it didn't make sense. Looked like someone was doing all this because of you, not because of them. Since there wasn't much information on you, it seemed like we should check it out. If you work in a team and you were being targeted for something you did in the so called line of duty, we figured shit rolls downhill and someone else could be in cross hairs next."

"That's pretty intuitive thinking."

"We do a lot of predictive analysis based on indicators and scenarios for better warning. Not so much in my group, but we have a national support unit that spiders out to the regional and local level."

"And can you carry firearms if you are on a protective detail?"

"No, sir, not unless we already had a license to carry. We have some off-duty cops that help us from time to time, licensed P.I.s in the ranks, stuff like that."

"And you will up and go when I am cleared from this being a so called expanding issue?"

"Probably not. I am doing this job part-time while I am doing the other. It was a perfect fit. I may consider going into medicine even though I am a bit older. I saw some pretty bad shit in the sandbox. I need to clear my head and see how I can help people best and still make a good living in case I ever have a family."

"OK. Makes sense. I think we can all use a little help clearing our heads. Sounds like you have your shit pretty squared away. Thanks for cluing me in on all this."

"You really think you could take me?" Sean asked.

"I really wasn't sure, sir. Just didn't want you to hurt my back. I felt you pulling on my new skin. Grafts took pretty well and I didn't want to have to go through that stuff again."

"Fair enough."

"What's your first name?"

"My friends just call me Whitt. I gotta go. I'd like to hold on to this job for a while. I may transfer over to Loyola though. Trying to get there by the end of the week."

"Well good luck." The two shook hands.

As Whitt left, Havens cleared the table and finished the last drop of coffee. He was slowly getting hooked tighter and never saw it coming. *This Silver Star group is all over. Could be a good gig for a bit.*

Whitt left the cafeteria area and headed back to the nurse's station to check on the rest of his tasks before heading home. He stopped by the bathroom to take a quick piss. The door opened as he was finishing up.

"Ah, hey, Tom, um, I don't think we were properly introduced."

The orderly, Whitt, turned around to see the security guard from his first day.

"Oh hey, yeah, good to see you again. I'd shake your hand but my hands are full."

"No problem." The old security guard kept his eyes at shoulder level or higher. "I'd say Semper Fi, based on what I saw on your application. Say, I've got some questions for you. I had you pegged as Army. But when I called up the University of Chicago Hospital, which you have listed as your former employer, they had no record of a Thomas Lawrence. Being a good Marine myself, I had to chuckle at the thought of Thomas Edward Lawrence. Don't get to meet a man with the namesake of Lawrence of Arabia every day. You even a Marine? I know you ain't Lawrence of Arabia."

With that the orderly whipped his leg out, catching the security guard off balance and sending his feet into the air. Twisting in the opposite direction, the orderly threw his arms around like two baseball bats hitting the guard in the chest. Unable to catch his fall, the guard was flung backwards and slammed his head onto the floor. The orderly quickly put on a pair of latex gloves from his pocket and gave a forceful death blow to the guard by raising his head and smashing the back of the skull to hemorrhage the brain. The orderly then pulled his own sleeves up to the shoulder and balled a fist into the toilet while repeatedly flushing. Water cascaded from the bowl onto the floor. The toilet water flowed to the security guard. The orderly, careful not to get his shoes wet, picked up the guard's torso and bent the knees quickly to ensure the soles of the guard's shoes were wet. Drying off his own arms, he pulled down his shirtsleeves and exited the bathroom, leaving the victim of an accidental fall behind on the floor.

Chapter 33

Instead of staying at the hospital for the third night in a row, Havens drove home to take a hot shower and check on the status of the cleanup and repairs. Oddly, Lars' car was not only at the house and parked in the driveway as opposed to the curb, but he had backed in. The lights were off. Havens came through the garage door to the family room where a fluorescent glow illuminated Lars staring at the wall. The TV was not on. Also unusual for Lars.

"Lars, what are you doing…What the hell is that?"

On the shelved entertainment center were two glass cubes. Tanks. The glow was emitting from the tanks. Aquarium tanks.

"It's a long story."

Havens walked up to the tanks. He leaned down, first looking at the one emitting the neon blue light.

"Is this what I think it is?"

"Sort of."

"Why is there an octopus in my family room?"

"Alright don't get mad, but I thought maybe you needed something to cheer you up a bit. So I got you a pet."

"You got me an octopus for a pet?" Havens asked with a mix of irritation and disbelief. "And are…are these scorpions? You bought me a pet shop of exotic animals to cheer me up?"

"Hear me out. I was trying to do a good thing. I found a guy on Craigslist who was selling a blue-ringed octopus. I was thinking, you know, like from Octopussy, the really poisonous one that James Bond threw at that guy's face. Or like that Michael Crichton book. Some ecoterrorists took the poison from this type of octopus. So, I thought, you know, you are kind of like this James Bond…"

"James Bond ecoterrorist? And this isn't even a blue-ringed octopus. Those are tiny and this is larger and brown." He stooped to examine it further. "Or grey. Lars it isn't blue or ringed."

"I said, hear me out. The guy said it was a big one, which made it so rare, and when I asked the same question he said it was because in a domestic setting it camouflages itself to grey."

"And you believed him?"

Getting defensive, Lars shot back, "Well I'm no marine biologist or anything. What do you expect?"

"I expect you not to give me an octopus! This makes no sense. I mean what purpose does this serve? And what's the story with these things?"

"Well I looked up a little something about octopuses, or octopi rather. Anyway, I saw that maybe this wasn't the cool danger pet that I thought it was. So I went to the pet store and got a deathstalker scorpion. I thought that could be real badass."

"This is big and black. That's no deathstalker. It's an emperor scorpion. And why would you get me a pet that could kill me?"

"Now, Sean, that's just it. When I got it, and if you look close you will see the smaller yellowish white ones could be deathstalkers, but when I got it there was just that toilet paper tube and the emperor must have been under it. So, I'm not really sure what they are and I'm not sure if they could kill us or not."

Havens burst out laughing. "Lars, that is the kindest and dumbest thing anyone has ever done for me."

"So you like them?"

"No, I hate them. Please get them out of my house."

"Well, I already named the octopus, and it kinda looks cool there."

"Then bring it to your place."

"But I got it for you. See the guy I got it from was trying to mate her. She kept killing the males, so he wanted to get rid of her. I named her Cougar. Get it? Like the single women who go to bars to…"

"I get it. I need a beer."

"Here, I just got two for myself."

Havens shot his brother-in-law a frowning glance.

"So I don't have to get up." He twisted the cap and handed Havens a beer.

"Are you going to be a permanent fixture here?"

"Just until I know you are safe." Lars took a sheepish drink from his bottle, giving a sideways look to catch Sean's reaction.

Lars, you damn big Baby Huey. I think you may be more screwed up over all this than I am. Who buys another man killer pets for therapy purposes? Distraction is right. Totally left field.

"You feed the pets. I'm going to go check on the place."

"If you have a chance when you get back I want to talk to you about something else."

"OK, I can wait." Havens sat down on the arm of an overstuffed leather chair, crossing his arms and tilting his head in expectation of more unexpected news.

"I am thinking of selling my apartment and retiring. I found a place in Arizona that will put me near spring training and golf and I can still link up with a police department for part-time work to close the gap between my retirement benefits and some play money."

"Wow." Havens nodded his head solemnly, but at this point really couldn't care less. "So where will you be? Are you sure you can't wait a bit longer for your full retirement?"

"Scottsdale will be my main location but I was also able to pick up a fixer-upper not far from Glendale near Camelback."

"I wasn't aware you had that kind of money set aside. That's great."

"Yeah, well not too long ago I was at a seminar and there was a small booth in the exhibition area looking for some advisors for Hollywood writers. I thought it could be kind of fun. I had to have a big background screening and, believe it or not, a mental health test—or at least some questions about loyalty and stuff. Then after a lengthy contract process I was one of a few selected."

"I had no idea. That is great. I never had heard from you or Christina that you were going back and forth to California."

"That's what is so great about it. They ask me about some ideas from a crime scene perspective and I tell them how a perp would probably do it. There are about five of us, from what I can tell. I never talk about it because I was under a strict non-disclosure agreement. I have probably written about twenty or so scenarios and they pay me very, very well, especially if it's really detailed."

So why the hell are you telling me all of this now?

"And I take it the gig pays very, very well as in thousands?" Havens felt like a scrutinizing parent to Lars. He was actually more jealous that Lars could land a job like that for some supplemental income.

"So far I've gotten about four hundred thousand."

"Dollars?" Havens asked incredulously. "Why would they pay you so much? I mean no offense."

"They pay well for technical advisors I guess. Anyway, I just thought you should know. Timing has been weird but I just wanted to share some good news."

"Yeah, that's great. So is it one of the big production houses?"

"Nah, they are just a niche writing house. I don't know much about them."

"Well, hmmm, did you ever think of maybe using some cop skills, detective?"

"They just have a few guys. That's why they don't have much history to check up on. They must be well connected. The firm is actually set up off shore in Dominica. Easier to keep their holdings to themselves so they can pay their advisors a little more. They don't have to deal with overhead like buildings and what not either."

"Are you telling me what you found, what they told you, or are you convincing yourself of this?"

"Nah, it's all good. The guys are real nice. It's just one of those small little gigs you would never think about that can make a ton of money."

"And CPD is cool with it?"

Lars scratched his ear and looked down sheepishly.

"Well they really don't know, and that is, ah, one of the nice things about the offshore side. I, ah, converted some of that money into real estate out in Arizona. Got a better deal on the property too since I could close with no financial or home sale contingencies."

"Your deal man. Who am I to judge?"

Stupid ass, you are likely going to get your ass put in jail for tax evasion or get CPD Internal Affairs on your ass for living beyond your means. You will be lucky if this place lasts another year. Then again, you probably got what you needed out of it. Not a bad little deal if you would go about it a bit smoother. That is actually a pretty good scheme to use as a future cover for status course of action. Have to remember that one.

"Thanks, Sean." Lars raised his beer to his brother-in-law. "And you, and, um, Maggie, will always have a place to stay. Nice place right by the mountains. Kinda rustic, but some real nice homes that are spread out from each other for privacy."

As soon as he got the words out he put his beer down and wiped his eyes. Lars sat forward, his head bowed down in sorrow, and pressed his fingers to his eyes.

"Thanks, Lars. I am going to have a look around at the repairs."

Without looking up, Lars nodded his head.

Havens left the room to check on the new carpet and window work.

Man, this is tough on him. I had no idea how broken up he would be. Glad he has something he can look forward to.

When Lars sensed that Sean had left the room he slowly peeked up from under his hands. Seeing Havens had left, he sat up, downed his beer, looked at his watch, and checked his phone.

That was easy. And no more questions.

Chapter 34

Havens woke from a deep sleep on the basement couch to the phone ringing. He fumbled to see which phone it was and saw it was a DC number.

"Hello?"

"Sean Havens please."

"Speaking."

"I was told to call you about some work you may be interested in. My name is Harrison Mann. I am with an outfit called Silver Star."

"Right. Thanks for the call. I'm surprised to hear from you so soon."

"Well, we just received some funds and new projects with the budget passing, so I need to do some staffing pretty quick. I heard about your background and a little of your story. I think we may be able to find some mutual benefit. When can you talk face to face?"

"What type of time frame are you looking at? I see you have a DC number, will you need me to come out there or are you in the Chicago area ever?"

"Number is DC but I am here in Chicago. This is my territory. I can do something as soon as today."

"I will be downtown for most of the day, but any time after 11 works."

"OK, do you know where the Union League Club is?"

"Sure."

"Meet me there at 11:30."

"Who am I looking for?"

"I'll find you. See you then. Out."

"Out, OK, bye." The line was dead.

Dumb ass. Make up your mind, Mr. Amateur. You a military guy or a civilian?

Something as simple as hanging up the phone had a certain tell about who you are or what you did by how you ended it.

Out, over, bye bye, tootaloo, cheers. Out and bye worked best, but who is this Harrison—government, military, a business guy? What translated best for all three? Cheers? Bit old to be figuring this out now.

Havens shook his head laughing at himself.

Cheeriooo old boy. Red could pull that off, not me. Red's a real good operational chameleon, despite the carrot top.

Havens put his phone away and reoriented himself with his surroundings. He hardly remembered coming downstairs last night. He recalled an overwhelming feeling of exhaustion. The house was getting restored and was almost to the point of looking as if nothing had happened. Still Havens couldn't bring himself to sleep in his bed upstairs without his wife. With his daughter away in the hospital, there would be a deafening silence in the home were it not for the comings and goings of Lars tending to his circus menagerie of freakish pets.

Havens was pleased with the news of Lars moving to Arizona. While he enjoyed Lars in moderation, this Felix and Oscar setup in the house was not going to work. Most of the time, he and Lars just sat and drank beer while watching TV. Always sports. It was Christina who could stay up talking with Lars after the games had finished. She was Lars' rock, and until she had married Sean, Lars was her protector as well. It wasn't until this past week that Havens realized that the relationship he had with Lars was pretty superficial. He wondered if that was his own fault. Lars always tried reaching out to Sean, but he always seemed to reject it. In hindsight, Sean wished he had nurtured his relationship with Lars a bit better. It would have been easier to already be fully included in his circle of trust than trying to subtly break in now.

Sean could see how Lars would be an easy target for inducement. Messed up, no family to speak of, and few people really knew his patterns and proclivities to tip off any new unusual behavior. All of Lars' behavior was unusual. Now this routine Lars described about receiving a consulting fee on a private basis to provide innocuous information sounded like the classic work of developing a contact. Lars could very well be developed for financial motive, getting him into the habit of doing things for a fee even if it was outside his comfort zone or meant looking the other way. Lars was a brilliant investigator but the death scene didn't affect him much. He too was numb to normal events that should bother the soul. The question Havens now had to worry about—as if he didn't have enough on his plate—was why this group would want to exploit Lars. Lars was already past the testing phase of assessing his inclinations. Havens wondered how much privileged information Lars was sharing about his crime scene expertise or about CPD. With over four hundred thousand dollars in his pocket, Lars was now deeply past assessment, development, and initial recruitment. With others evidently doing the same thing as Lars, he was a trusted source, fully recruited.

What have you done, you big lout? Now I have to get on the offensive side of you too. Maybe you could just move to Arizona tomorrow and I can leave it as your mess. Shit. How do I keep you close and still at arm's length from me?

Chapter 35

After checking in on what was now determined to be a lack of progress in Maggie's recovery, Havens caught a cab and headed south of the river to the historic Union League Club. The doorman greeted Havens and signaled an already rising Harrison Mann who was seated nearby in an antique reading chair.

"Hello, Sean. Pleasure to meet you."

"Likewise, Harrison."

"Let's go upstairs to the library where we can chat comfortably."

"Sounds good to me."

"Have you ever been in here before?"

"A few times. I used to know a member, Jerry."

"Well I'd need to have a last name to know who he was."

"Oh, it hardly matters. Just an old business contact. Have you been a member here long?"

"No, I am here on an agreement with another city's club. It is private here and I can come and go as I please. The room is small but comfortable."

"I take it you have seen the paintings then?"

"Yes, quite a private collection."

"Had a few glasses of the Opus One as well?"

"Mmmm, yeah. Despite the clubby surroundings, I'm no Ivy League guy."

You don't seem like the Yale type. More military and out of your element but trying to fake it here.

"I'm sure we will get along fine."

The two found a square of cognac dyed leather couches and chairs with mahogany wood arms and tastefully studded leather backing. The area was set aside from members in the quiet library with no one within ear shot.

"My daughter is coming along, I think. Thanks for asking and thank you for the generous act to take care of the arrangements. It was certainly nothing I would have expected any organization to do. But frankly, I am somewhat concerned that I was tagged as military or government service."

"Well, not to sound dramatic, but we have our way of knowing and our reach is supposed to be able to touch those in our brotherhood. Sounds kind of corny in this club atmosphere, like we were Skull and Bones or something, but the gesture was in the right spirit, and those who reached out to us disclosed little. It was Lincoln who had the interest to care for those who have borne the battle, his widow, and his orphan. I'm paraphrasing of course."

"Well, nonetheless, it was concerning, but appreciated."

Who do they know and how? Draeger? Red? Turner? They certainly wouldn't say anything.

Havens continued, "So what should we discuss here? I'd be interested in knowing more about this organization, but I am not sure of the fit based on what little I do know."

"Right. Well before you talk yourself out of a job, let me give you a bit of the behind the scenes pitch…unless you have some other job offers I don't know about, Sean. I will also need to know a bit of your behind the scenes experience too, to see if we can make this work."

"I take it not many get this pitch."

OK, let's see what you've got. First you hit me with some quid pro quo niceties, and then you throw out such a provocative statement. You know about me, and I know nothing about you, so you are going to bait me into a conversational hourglass to elicit responses from me.

"That's true. Are you good to sit for a bit and chat before we grab a bite?"

"Let's do this."

"Much of this work is similar to your international work, from what I understand, unless you were just a cutout gopher?"

"I'm still listening." *Strike one. You won't get me to correct you.*

"We rely heavily on denial and deception cover for our activities. I am basically going to read you on to this informally because I know we will have an agreement at the end, and because I know as a man of honor you recognize the need for secrecy, correct?

Lobbing it back to me after trying to draw me in.

"I am still listening, but would be interested in knowing how many others are read on and if it is such a clan org, why you would still be so casual with OPSEC."

"Understand the concern." *Cold fish.* "That being said, because it is a skunkworks program, it isn't even classified at our levels and does end up being more of a secret society for the ground troops. Does this make sense to you? Again, I don't know that much about what you do. How does your past work coincide with what I have started off with?"

"Listen Harrison, this sounds like a very interesting program. If it fits, I am happy to share plenty about what I do, have done, and can do as it relates and as appropriate. But I sense some Elicitation 101 going on here and some basic level enticement for recruitment. That surprises me if you are some elite group that can operate in the dark worlds. Maybe you all are a bunch of family babysitters with P.I. licenses. Either give me your best shot or let's recognize each other as brothers in the community and cut this play shit out. If you want me, talk to me. If you don't want to have me step away, keep this Huachuca first day stuff out."

"I never went to Huachuca. I wasn't Military Intelligence. Sorry if my presentation style doesn't meet your approval." *Way to take the bait, champ.* "Let me start over." *You want back in the game since you see this other work as beneath you.*

"Please do." *Nice dodge but I am still on to you, chump.*

"Under a domestic program linked to Homeland Security and some DoD soldier wellness programs, we have constructed a cellular network form of law enforcement that leverages small, dispersed, mobile teams that can be used against a wide array of crime, violence, or terror roots that either reside on U.S. soil or have key sanctuary, support, and sustainment mechanisms here. We face off with these foes through surrogates to extend our reach and minimize our direct involvement, for the obvious reasons. At present, law enforcement in major cities is trying to fight an unconventional war conventionally. They have uniforms, sirens, legal constraints, political constraints, ethical constraints that allow an enemy to predict, anticipate, and adapt before a confrontation with, and I use this term loosely, a 'superior force.' Take, for example, those guys involved in the Mumbai attacks from Chicago who are untouchable due to various extradition loopholes. Should they just walk? We know they were complicit and so were their associates. Who can do something about this? You with me so far?"

"Yeah, you have a domestic shwacker program that use these autonomous units—and this is where I would fit in—that can converge assaults domestically by targeting the nexus between crime and terror or violent extremist supporters. We target in the form of destroying or disrupting their cohesion and then at times we can instigate a fight so they attack each other in the denied spaces of closed dark networks underground, blah blah, just like every other small war doctrine is saying has to be done."

"You are a skeptic?"

"No, I'm tired of people who want to set up these programs that end up being poorly run, horribly orchestrated, and staffed by people who come from white SOF and just think black SOF would be gee whiz cool. It is like the recruiting surge of Navy SEALs now that OBL was whacked. Those guys think they are signing up for night raids until they have their tenth stand down mission aborted."

"You are a bit of a prick, aren't you? This is supposed to be an interview, not a rant session."

"Harrison, I have been doing this for a long time. I'm sure you have heard of those who are no longer with us such as Russian spy Alexander Litvinenko, Egyptian billionaire Dr. Ashraf, Stefan Zielonka, General Yuri Ivanov, Imad Mughniyeh. I was the guy that was sent to make things happen so they didn't look like we did it. Now I am not going to give you a big sob story of my life of late, but if you have the internal mechanism and a mandate to do things domestically, I can help you out. I can teach you how to do this viral type of targeting where the disruptor spreads to places that we don't have placement and access, and I can flush the underground out so you can send in additional people to kill whatever I cannot from a viral spread from within."

"Now *I* am listening."

"If you are set up as a hub and spoke with daisy chain networks as cutout offshoots, you may have a chance, but not a great one. Use autonomous agents with two layers of low connectivity funneled up to only one or two with medium connectivity that can take problem assertions and not taskings from the authority. Try not to have a functional hub. Only use a hybrid hierarchy for budget and top down information. Taskings should not be orders, they should just present a problem that needs to be solved. Local or regional cells will establish their own protocol and techniques without overhead monitoring and counterintelligence stopgap. Empower your cell so they can be a fluid and dynamic network based on terrain, opponent, and mission."

"And now that you have just hired yourself and taken over the world, how do you propose the cells develop proper courses of action based on just receiving a problem statement?"

"Oh shit, you were a trigger puller weren't you?"

"That sounds like a booger-eating hobbit intel weenie speaking, Havens. Sorry, thought I was speaking to a hard man. We can be done if you are just a concept guy. I don't need donut eaters on my team."

Havens laughed. "You are a bit of a douche bag yourself, Harrison."

Harrison smiled. "So, smart guy, how do you operationalize problems at a cell level?"

"Harrison, I take it you were a military man, so this should be classic. It's textbook OSS Strategic Services. You have your sabotage, direct contract with and support of underground resistance groups, and the conduct of special operations not assigned to other agencies and not under direct control of theater or area commanders. That's like 1944 classic field manual stuff. Each cell knows their environment. It follows the same typical long stay Special Forces mission set. They know all the tribes, chiefs, political, informational, you know, the PMESII—political, military, economic, social—framework but they think of it as an interconnected ecosystem. From there, they can map the problem according to the battlespace's patterns of life in an operational design to identify respective complex situations and connected reference points to explore for potentials, trends, relationships, and tensions that can be exploited. You can look at it like a massive supply chain of financial business flows, cultural enclaves, support networks, informal and formal economies, etc. Then they are identified for strengths and weaknesses, criticality, etc."

"I'm with you. I remember reading something from that general officer who wrote about learning and adapting in complex missions. Then you add a CARVER model but attached to each area of disruption."

"Bingo. I knew you were a PowerPoint Ranger underneath, Harrison."

"Ha. So when can you start?"

"I can't."

Surprised at the sudden loss of momentum, Harrison readjusted himself in the chair. He stretched his leg in anticipation of how he was going to close Havens on the job. "Why not?"

"Because I would be working for you, right?"

"Is that so bad?" Harrison replied, a bit put off.

"It is if you haven't thought of all of this. If you are not structured this way, then it means you have to upsell it to your bosses. The chances of them buying in is slim to none."

"And what if they knew I was already talking to you and that you were an integral part of this building process? And what if you could do it from Chicago as your Forward Operating Base? And what if we gave you a choice of being a formal employee at the government level with all benefits, or we let you be a contractor and let you put together your own company, payment means, and even alias if you wanted to control your segment? For the first few months and maybe longer, you just need to prove yourself with some light setup stuff. No action on your part. That way you can focus on your daughter. You just help us out with some planning and validate courses of action that we can be taking." *C'mon Havens, come to the light. We custom made this for your role. You better be right, Draeger. It was your profile.*

Havens continued the game even though it sounded too good to be true. *Sounds like Lars' gig.* "How much does it pay?"

"Because we have funds from government and private, we can pay like a major prime contractor. We can start you with a hundred seventy thousand plus pay your COBRA for a year until you get other care up and going. We will pay for the health insurance as a separate line item expense to you. You will have a personal operational budget for your mail drops, throw aways, travel, etc., of two hundred thousand a year. There will be a team operational budget that rolls up to me. You just request and justify, and I hand it over to you."

"Sounds pretty reasonable. Generous at that."

"Let me sweeten the pot." Harrison reached into a small brown leather attaché and retrieved a file. He held it up but close to his chest signifying something important but not yet for Havens' eyes.

The infamous manila envelope. Ready to fully compel me to action. Blackmail? Can't be. I never strayed on my wife and don't do stupid things.

"Sean, I hate to blend personal with business, but I think if I were in your shoes I might welcome something like this. We will call it a mutual interest gesture. I have in this folder the Chicago Police investigation on your daughter's attack, the home intrusion resulting in your wife's death, and the latest home invasion with the original attacker."

Havens' face looked broken, but Harrison continued. "What I also have is separate files on the three gang members involved and the gang unit breakdown of their cadre that ties to something even bigger."

"What is bigger that involved my family?"

"The bigger part doesn't seem to involve your family. But aside from empathizing with you, this is where we are willing to also help fund you before you potentially start with us. Within the gang, higher levels involve other criminal syndicates. The narcotics and money exchange flows are intertwined with other financial activity such as interstate cash flows, pass-throughs, and funnel accounts. We have found through our treasury and law enforcement contacts that a lot of the deposits and withdrawals have little business and legal purposes. These flows branch to Italian mafia, Eastern bloc mafia, Somali traffickers and gun runners, and Middle Easterners that have ties to Panama, Venezuela, and Lebanon, from what we can tell so far."

Havens exhaled loudly in response to the overwhelming amount of information tying back to his personal situation.

"Sean, if you want to join us, we can let you go at the bottom feeders fully funded. We'll even give you some local surveillance support from the street electronics and can add some other technical overwatch, be it infrared, heat, time lapse. We have a lot of toys at our disposal."

"May I?" Havens reached out for the file. The first few pictures were of his wife dead on the floor. *You assholes are playing me.* He thumbed through the photos of the dead gang members. Reports had come from the Chicago Police and FBI.

"Why was the FBI involved?"

"For your case they weren't. We have just created a comprehensive file of everything involved or related."

So maybe that does rule out Lars from this group if they can get files from anyone. Maybe my imagination is running a bit crazy these days, seeing ghosts everywhere.

"And how do you all get these files?"

"They give them to us when we ask. In this case, we had a contact within the district attorney's office procure a bit of everything. If you are interested in going after that gang and the leaders who tasked your wife's killers, we can have your file closed and sealed. That further secures you as a suspect if people start disappearing or whatever it is you want to do with them."

"And you think they would consider me as a suspect, why?"

"I don't. Just trying to think what you would be thinking. Frankly, CPD and the Bureau could really care less if they know an authority is whacking these guys who are out of their grasp. It is easier to kill than to prosecute and lock up with a bunch of other like-minded thugs so they can all plan more elaborate activities when they get out of jail. The worst thing about your wife's killers is that these guys couldn't have cared less about you and your family. They did it for status. Their taskers were doing it for other reasons and likely could be tied to your overseas work."

"Why do you think it is tied to my stuff overseas?"

"From what little I know of you, and the names you dropped of those who are no longer with us, you have focused on your own orchestration and hunting of proxy actors overseas. You hunt Iran's Qods Force, Republican Guards, Hezbollah, and a smattering of AQ around the world. Chances are pretty good since you are dealing with ideological groups that a supporter or empathizer may have marked you as a problem child for their work. Really, with all the surface level cleared personnel that our intelligence community sustains, do you really think you are covered well? Didn't you just get out of a little scrape overseas due to shoddy work and no solid backing?"

Someone is talking. He's right; I'm exposed. "I suppose. The sad truth is you just don't know at the time. Let me ask you this..."

"Shoot."

"How does the parent organization Silver Star get involved and why would they want you all part of what they do?"

"Great question. Short answer is they don't. We receive lists of individuals who are threatening the families of our guys and girls overseas. The overall organization does a bit of a triage. Low level may be walking with a wife or daughter to work or school if there is light harassment. Another level may be to help get a restraining order. When beatings, threats, rapes, and even amber code abductions happen and prosecution would involve more resources, time, or even just the mental involvement of one of our deployed guys who is in sensitive missions, we just want the problem to go away. In those cases, it goes to a door down the hall. Our door. It just says Electrical/Mechanical on the door. You need to go through two doors to get there. That type of thing."

"I see where you are going."

"Exactly. Everyone is happy when a problem can just disappear and our special mission operators can focus on their tasks at hand without domestic distraction. Those ones are slipped under our door, so to speak. And, in most all cases, those targets are pieces or shit that are bothering other citizens around them. We are taking out the trash for our brethren while also cleaning the streets. In that folder you have there are gang members who are tied to your situation but they are also involved in the families of local servicemen, whether they're trying to recruit a service member's kid to a gang, pushing drugs, shooting up a neighborhood, maybe sexually assaulting a serviceman's wife or daughter."

"We whack them and problems go away. When problems go away politicians are happy and police chiefs are promoted. If our guys are caught, someone can turn a blind eye. Been there done that."

"Exactly, we just stay clear of media or use it to serve us by creating situations that they will exploit unwittingly to facilitate our desired courses of action."

"How long have you all been doing this?"

"Our group? Just a couple years. Part of that was an evolution and framing. We had a couple trial profiles of team members that we tested and are finding we needed more guys like you than guys like me. Things were starting to get sloppy. Frankly, things are still a bit sloppy. The framework and concept are solid, but as you know black ops are better constructed in the mind and on paper than they are in real day-to-day planning and execution. Sometimes what sounds good at the time is pretty stupid once you are carrying it out. Backstops and top cover aside, we have to be professional and not create any awareness to our activities. We are all seasoned, but frankly, we are pretty close to acting like amateurs in this arena."

"Makes sense. I am all for the basic concept of the program, but these types of things end up taking on a life of their own, and most often the ring leaders start getting a bit of a God complex."

"So do you want to think about it?"

Havens flipped back to a picture of his wife contorted in her own blood. He could imagine his daughter watching as her mother fell. He imagined the fear she had before the gun was fired at her crashing a bullet through her skull.

"Think about it? That's all I have been thinking about since I got the news. I am in but want to know who is running things at the top."

"Excellent. I will be back in touch with you in the coming day with some details. You start thinking of accounts you want money put into and other housekeeping items. Keep the file. It is yours. Let me know if you want them to close the file."

"You never answered me on who is flagging this group. Who does this boil up to?"

"I've shared everything you need to know. The details you are asking about are not your concern. Just like your old line of work. You work through me. You see me starting to act like I think I am God, you come to me."

"How can I contact you?"

"I will give you a number when I call you next. In the meanwhile just get some things in order."

"When do I start?"

"You already did."

"Sounds good. We have a deal then." Havens extended his hand to his new boss.

"Great." Harrison looked down at his Suunto Vector watch. "Still have time for a bite?"

"No, I'm going to start working. Thanks."

"I'll show you out."

"I am assuming we don't need to do any of the planning and communicating in a SCIF?"

Harrison grinned.

"Brother, if we don't exist, we can't get a secure compartmented facility certified out in the field. You will buy or rent your own facility and a small fleet of vehicles to suit your needs. Ideally, you can do the same to support our ops. Our communications will be like any other friend or business associate just talking but we will establish some protocols and use encrypted commercial phones for designated communications. Most, however, will be up to you. We hope to get the encrypted phones in soon. There was a procurement hiccup. We can use burner phones no problem, but the reality is, who's going to pick up on us anyway? And from what I have been told, if we get picked up, having the encryption may draw more attention."

"That's true. I use an iPhone 5 and pull out the SIM card since I can't take out the battery. I figure no tool out there can pull data off a 5 right now and with a PIN and PUK code, it would take a court order and a few days to get the info. By then, I'd be using another one."

"Shit. I figure no one is even pulling from our airwaves, and I don't keep contacts or things, so I keep it unlocked so I don't have to put a passcode in when I drive."

Loose lips. Not real smart though I get the concept. Whatever.

"And I will pick the teams or be assigned?"

"Sean, you will have little interaction with the guys that do the work in the field. I will be the primary interface."

Havens processed the information.

"I will provide you the targets and you will come up with the courses of action and to some degree the operational plans. You can go in the field as you see fit on your own for recce and source development. Chances are, for the first number of months, you won't need to develop sources and go underground. Just help us check the boxes."

"What is your background, Harrison?"

"Let's save something for the next time."

The men parted with another handshake. Havens thanked the doorman again as if he had just been a guest in the man's home.

He walked out the revolving door with a new sense of purpose. The emptiness was filling again. He couldn't wait to go see his daughter. He hailed the first cab he saw.

Harrison went to the restroom and then gave a last look around the club as he retrieved his light overcoat from the check. He could see actually being a member of a place like this. A bit stiff and he probably wouldn't like the people, but he liked the thought of a nice upscale wood-trimmed officer's club. He had been to such clubs with his SAS counterparts in the UK years ago and often stayed in the Special Forces club while in London when he wasn't trying to disguise the purpose of his visit. Until then, there were plenty of other clubs and discrete meeting places in the city that could be obtained with the right amount of personality and green dead presidents. Harrison handed the doorman another two hundred dollars and thanked him.

"Thank you, Mr…"

"You're welcome."

"We hope to see you again sometime."

"Doubtful. This old place just served its purpose."

"Please consider us again."

Yeah, please come back and tip me four hundred dollars for two hours use of your space.

Harrison walked out the alleyway exit and headed south to a parking garage a block away.

A job well done, Harrison. Double tapped Havens without him even knowing. It will be win win though. Havens could be good to work with even if he is a bit of a prick.

Harrison relished the idea of working with elite professionals again.

It was a beautiful day and he loved his work.

Chapter 36

After circling the block, the taxi now thirty feet back from the club pulled back into traffic. Havens hadn't seen Harrison leave the front way and caught a glimpse of him in the alley. "Take a right here after the alley." Is there a large covered parking garage down this way?"

"There is one a building over."

"No, that's no good. How about one maybe a block or two down?"

"Yes, sir. There is one just off Congress. Four levels. Why do you ask, sir?"

"Just take me over there but keep going past it on this street. Then make a slow loop around it so we can get there in five to seven minutes."

Havens had no intention of following Harrison. He suspected if Harrison was cautious he would be running some surveillance detection routes of his own, which would end up costing Havens a fortune in cab fare and ultimately end up somewhere that he couldn't enter without risk of exposure. No, Havens just wanted to see what kind of car Harrison would be driving, whether rental, utility, luxury so he could make note of its general purpose or track it later if need be.

It was Havens' city and now he was working it. He was back in the game. He still was uncertain if he liked playing in his own backyard. This was different from imaginary Nazis and VC in the backyard. This was a killer game and he just volunteered to play.

Chapter 37

Draeger turned the dial of the SCIF safe. He kept turning. Missed his spot. Spun the dial again.

Pain in the ass security. These fucking safes are so temperamental.

Finally the lock clicked and the door popped open. Draeger signed the access document under a different name and pulled the Special Access Program file he was looking for. Despite this being a protected program, they had made a number of administrative adjustments to ensure a greater sense of anonymity and plausible deniability.

The folder contained what he expected. There was a list of a number of names and tagged offense subject descriptions organized by city. Judgment had been passed by others and these individuals were to be eliminated as a further threat to U.S. security or interests. He would relay the names in a benign manner to Harrison via RSA standard encrypted email, and now that Havens was on board, a plan would be forthcoming in weeks. If the phones would get here, it would be more ideal for timing.

Harrison had expressed some concern as to how on board Havens would be for exterminating such a wide base of people in his home city where even the most careful planning could have blowback on his own domestic foundations. Havens was used to working abroad where he could keep distance from his life. This was one of the reasons Havens never moved to Virginia, Tampa, North Carolina, or Maryland where his business associates and clients resided.

Draeger, however, had assured Harrison that he had a plan. If Havens was able to help them knock out this list, that would buy DOSA enough time to find his replacement. Their newest recruit would be the perfect scapegoat if something fell apart and would be an ideal backstop once he was dead. He would be a fucked up head case who decided to take apart a city over his grief.

Under the current administration the longevity of this project would probably be less than a year as the bureaucrats involved would no longer be able to stomach the political risk of any fallout from such a program on their careers. Draeger's orders were to move this quickly to get some defense funding back into the budget. Cuts would make the U.S. weak. Cuts would make people who were promised riches to question alliances if they weren't paid.

Yes, even in its infancy stages, this program had a very limited shelf life and Draeger would need to start planning his next gig in short time. In the interim, he had another idea as to how he could nudge Havens just over the edge of sanity and transform his former colleague into a homicidal maniac—or at least create evidence that would support such a claim. It would close the loop on Harrison and the entire Chicago operation.

This is going to be fun.

Now Draeger just needed his contractor to finish the new panic room and life might get back to being more enjoyable again.

His mood darkened quickly as he recalled his last mission with Havens, being forced to kneel alongside him in the corner of a Tehran apartment bedroom. Draeger had slipped up and missed a surveillance tail when they rotated spotters. The Iranian authorities had followed them to the apartment and surprised them. Two highly trained IRGC operatives now each had a gun to the heads of Draeger and Havens who were kneeling executioner style facing the cracked plaster wall. Draeger was pleading in Farsi while Havens remained quiet. Draeger looked at Havens who was fixated on something beyond the wall as if he were a million miles away. Draeger had continued his frantic negotiating when Havens interrupted, also in the armed men's native tongue.

"Excuse me. We are indeed CIA spies. If you please, as fellow soldiers we would like to kneel before you, our captors. We will accept the bullet so you may know that power of Allah will prevail in this lost war."

Havens further admitted to being sent by the Americans to kill the Supreme Leader despite that not being their mission. Havens gave his real name as well as Draeger's. "Glory to the destroyers," Havens had said in Farsi.

Draeger knew Havens had lost it.

Great, Sean, not only do we die but you just outed us and linked us to a cockamamie mission that will be a PR coup for the Iranians.

Entertained by this admission and the idea of making these weak Americans bow to the Persian power now before them, their captors all too eagerly honored the request as Havens was now denouncing his God and praising the almighty power and mercifulness of Allah. As Draeger was about to emit a final plea to save himself and stop Havens from talking, Havens started retching violently and vomited.

His captor, in disgust, cursed this dog, and instinctively looked for the reaction of his other IRGC comrade. In that instance Havens executed an attack with a Krav Maga left hand grab at the gun barrel and a right hand wrist wedge. He pulled back on his adversary to use the foe's counter motion as a momentum lever to raise himself up and turn the man's gun fire on the second operator while delivering a series of furious kicks to his first victim. Havens' last action was firing off two more rounds into the heads of the now former IRGC members.

Havens shouted at his companion to get up, but Draeger remained motionless.

"Get the fuck up!!! We have to move now!!!"

"I can't. I shit my pants."

"You what? Who gives a fuck? Get up and move. Are you afraid someone is going to laugh at you, you pussy? Move it or we are both dead again with you lying in shitty pants. What the hell, Pres?"

Their escape and evasion had been successful due to Havens' cool head and pre-deployment preparation, notwithstanding his use of some well thought out tools provided by "X" and an extraordinary amount of luck. It was apparent to both that God understood Havens' ruse as a distraction and granted the men amnesty as they fled. And yet Draeger felt more humiliated by Havens than bound to him for a life of repayment. The two never spoke of the event's personal aspects, and while Draeger demonstrated his own acts of heroism during that time as they retreated to friendly confines, he would never get past the embarrassment or the shame of his cries of self-preservation while selfishly questioning the actions of his protector's operational mind still engaged in the last seconds of life.

You're dead, Havens. And your little dog too. Draeger writhed his hands in his fantasy depiction of himself as the wicked witch in *The Wizard of Oz*. He took pause in the moment of comic relief, knowing that little Dorothy from Kansas lived in the end while the witch died.

Note to self. Stay out of Chicago while that asshole is still alive. Fucking Havens will find a way to drop a house on me or melt me with a cup of coffee to the face. Fucking black ops Captain America. Hate you. I hate you, I hate you.

Chapter 38

Days later Havens met Harrison at a greasy spoon restaurant for a cup of coffee where the tasking orders were exchanged. Using an overkill of tradecraft, they split the bill with cash, and Harrison insisted on paying the tip with a few dollars and some change. He remarked that Havens had paid too much and pushed the change across the table. Havens noticed the fifty cent piece, which in his experience meant a micro-SD card was inside. Havens took the change, put it in his pocket, and parted with Harrison like old buddies just playing some early morning catch up.

"Hey, Harrison, you know no one uses 50 cent pieces anymore, right? I've got a guy who can make one with a nickel when you are ready to play with the big boys."

"Budgets, Havens. Talk to your Intelligence Committee about it. Now maybe they can free up some cash with that roadblock bureaucrat dead in Missouri."

That's who that guy was in the paper. He was on a funding subcommittee who wanted more defense cuts.

"You can buy a quarter on eBay for about twenty-five bucks." Havens watched Harrison squirm under the open chatter.

This guy is wound pretty tight. Not a lot you can do with a regimented shooter unless you have more stuff to shoot. Although there are some good JSOC intel guys who were Ranger shooters first. Who put him in charge of a program like this? He had to be an officer prior.

At home, Havens pushed with the edge of his thumb on the back of the coin's America letters and the piece opened revealing the tiny storage device. He popped it into the larger adapter card he had on hand and viewed the benign list. With the context removed, it looked like a number of individuals who had made over a hundred dollars in contributions to a local arts campaign. To

Havens it would have been a year's work to really put the plan in place with airtight contingencies. Now Harrison had notified him the deadline was being pushed up by eleven months with no explanation.

Why is he keeping me at arm's length about this? Harrison isn't even finger pointing bureaucracy or some bullshit reason. I should be included in these kinds of decisions if we're going to be working together. Unless there are no plans for extended interaction…

The time frame was unrealistic as it always was in this business. Timelines are often artificial and decisions are made by people who are not the ones doing the actual work. With no comprehension of the difficulties involved, operational dates are set like the planning of an ad hoc family get together that would be better done sooner than later due to other more important commitments that may arise. Why should this job be any different?

Havens resolved himself to this being his fate until he could find something he was more suited for. But he had no idea how he could do anything else in life at this point. He knew that he needed the money for his daughter, but he knew money was tight in this budget climate and that the defense and intelligence committees were recommending a pinching of pennies, especially the guy who…*yeah, that committee member that Harrison mentioned. He was killed with that Lincoln thing I glanced at on the plane. I have to check with Red on that. A lot of people are going to be out of work if that budget doesn't pass.*

He reviewed the names. All he knew was that the names would be intermingled. High value targets were mixed in with some lower value targets, all of whom had apparently committed some offense to the families of soldiers now abroad. Based on his initial discussions with Harrison, efforts to cease the infractions by the accused were not working and it was starting to stress the family situation and operational effectiveness of the soldiers.

Havens considered Chicago's most violent communities like West Englewood, Austin, Woodlawn, Greater Grand Crossing, Humboldt Park, South Shore, West Garfield Park, and looked to tie them to other areas with lesser violence such as Rogers Park, West Ridge, and Lincoln Square. With most of the violent communities experiencing between fifteen to twenty-five homicides in a given year, that gave Havens only one to two bodies per community without raising a pattern or concern about the rise of violence. As a crutch, Havens had the luxury of an additional one to two killings in each community, violent or otherwise, with some accidental deaths, suicides, or manslaughter. If they were able to spread the victims out over eighteen months, their operation would be that much safer. It was fortunate for Havens that so many of these criminal cartels had become transnational organizations performing just as many astute business transactions to solidify their power as they had acts of violence.

Havens would also hit core elements of Chicago as an important drug distribution center that connected groups throughout Asia, Africa, Europe, and Central and South America. He would have to gain an understanding of specific neighborhoods in order to learn how the cartel leadership and traffickers blended into their neighborhoods without arousing suspicion while still interacting with the lower henchmen gang members who handled the retail aspect of drug sales. The nexus of instigation would have to be within the trafficking of heroin, cocaine, marijuana, and methamphetamines. With an increased presence of AK-47s on the street, there would also be ties to munitions flows as well as the sex trade through human trafficking. Gangs would be easy to identify with their open air drug markets and untrained lookouts making overt signs to their counterparts.

Havens thought it over. He had also heard of some ruthless cartel assassin squads that were reported to have committed killings of rivals in and around the city. Perhaps they could be used somehow. Havens pondered how he could use the roving bands of Somalis who moved drugs across the upper Midwest. With between six to seven identified Somali gangs, that gave him some room to play with, especially since some of them were connected. The fact that many were involved in the trafficking of minors to engage in sex acts meant Havens had no issue with inflicting both pressure or death on those gang members or their associates.

Since the Somali gangs didn't protect territories, it would be feasible that they would interact with different communities around the city and be in competition with new market entrants as well as established groups. The fact that the Somalis didn't identify themselves publicly with typical gang attributes and generally kept a low profile only added to their utility. Havens could find the volunteer agency contracted by the State Department to determine where Somali refugees were resettled. Havens started to make notes and Google various social services, charities, and relief agencies in Minnesota. He thought he might be able to tie that to the local mosques and some of the recently reported sex trafficking.

With ties to mosques, Havens could extend to the greater Muslim community, of which a select few were on the list. With Minnesota banks ending the transferring and routing of money to Somalia, Havens suspected that Chicago ethnic communities would pick up the new business of informal value transfers in their back office hawala remittance system. Their incited or planted attacks would typically be honor based and not well thought out. Such murders were typically one individual carrying out a shooting or knifing, but arson was also a common method of avenging a grievance.

Havens also tied the assaults to the notion that pedophilia was more acceptable in pockets of Islam. There were reports of attacks on non-Muslim children where well-organized networks of like-minded rapists preyed on pre-pubescent boys and underage white girls. The community of cohesion granted the offenders immunity from prosecution when discovered. In these cases, the offenders were most often Pakistanis and Moroccans, which would also widen the aperture for Havens to work by leveraging the Middle Eastern liquor and convenience store ownership within the various ethnic enclaves where Havens would be targeting gangs. Those ties could be broadened to the Lebanese and Persian communities who had targets on the list for suspected Hezbollah ties with links to illicit free trade zone commerce and funding schemes in Venezuela.

The trick was to identify catalysts so strong between the differing groups of targets that Havens would luck out and have some random domino effect revenge killings that would taint any potential link to the Activity's movements. Havens would have to ensure in good conscience that the second and third order effects and unintended consequences would not take out a single innocent.

With notes strewn all over the table and nearly eighteen hours of straight research, Havens had created his recommended courses of action to cover his human shopping list. What Havens didn't know was that some of the targets selected would be used to place other groups in power who had the funds, community connections, and access to influence U.S. political elections, while others could be framed to start a domestic conflict for Prescott Draeger and the powers he supported.

Chapter 39

A simultaneous doorbell ring and knock at the door startled Havens from his thoughts. Glancing around at all of the notes and printouts strewn across the dining room table, Havens closed the lids to his laptops and scooped up the papers and stuffed it all into the lower kitchen cabinet reserved for a couple of big pots that the Havenses only used for chili, gumbo, and boiling mountains of pasta for family birthday meals.

Through the peephole Havens recognized the two police officers who had harassed him about Albanians and Greece.

Not in the mood to deal with these idiots again.

Havens opened the door. He grimaced at the thought of another round of questions.

"What do you two chuckleheads want?"

The two men smiled.

One said, "We probably deserved that. If you have a minute, we'd like to start over. I am Detective Neil and my partner…"

"Bob," Havens interrupted.

"Kneel and bob, ha ha," the detective responded stoically. "Daniels, did you hear that? The kneel and bob joke again."

"So normally, Mr. Havens, I'd get up in your face when I am trying to extend an olive branch and it's shoved back in my face, but really, we could use your help and would like to take a much more collaborative approach this time where my partner, Detective Daniels, and I don't play the slapstick Mutt and Jeff routine and work with you as a professional."

"Can we come in for a moment, Mr. Havens?"

"Did you catch the Albanians?"

"Look, Mr. Havens, we came at you with a little game that we used to play when we were deployed overseas together in our reserve unit. Sometimes it works here, sometimes it doesn't. We really don't think Albanians or street gangs had any involvement in this. We have a lead on the guy who attacked your daughter and Lars spiraled out the window. Doesn't make sense. Sure, he had been involved with sexual assault and stalking, but he was too hot and cold. He was never involved in drugs and I can't see him making contact with street gangs to put out a hit on your family. Too many mutually exclusive parts that don't connect well with daily life around this city. Pattern of life for these events won't add up unless you force them."

Surprised at this approach and at their new demeanor, Havens invited them in. He led them to the kitchen and offered some coffee still hot and fresh in the pot.

"You know, Mr. Havens that Keurig coffeemaker you have does the same thing by the cup. You must really like coffee. How you been holding up?"

"Yeah, I used up all the cups and haven't gone to the store. My wife used to order them online, but as the man of the house I am a bit lost now that I really am the man of the house. I just keep walking around in here fixing up things a bit."

"I hear you, Mr. Havens. We are again very sorry for your loss. How is your daughter doing?"

"She's hanging in there. I have to head over a bit later to check in. Thanks for asking. So, while I'd like to know what you are doing here, I'd also be interested in where you were in Iraq or Afghanistan."

Daniels jumped in to answer the question while pouring a cup of coffee and handing it to his partner before pouring his own. "I was SF tasked to do CT, but had to do COIN. Sorry, I forgot you're a business guy. I was Special Forces tasked to do some counterterror work in Iraq. I ended up doing counterinsurgency and was assigned to a taskforce with this jarhead who was a reservist up in Michigan. We did Fallujah and then got a call from the powers that be that they needed some more guys to collect intel and who could survive in isolated areas. We were sent to Kunar and Nuristan in northeast Afghanistan. Special…"

Havens interrupted. Something was off. "From what I have read in the papers, that area was an awfully violent and rugged area for two detectives to be running around while on reserve duty. I mean no disrespect but…"

"Yeah, well we are leaving out some of the details so we didn't bore you, but suffice it to say, we both were deemed as capable of dealing with the feuding clans, understanding the long history of fighting outsiders, and how insurgents move freely with the help of many local allies." Neil gave his partner a knowing wink. "Probably something an accountant wouldn't know much about."

"Oh, speaking of which," Neil added, "we need to figure out what to do with that dog."

"Shit. You're right."

"Whoa." Havens was struggling with the situation. He held up a hand. They knew something. "What's going on here?"

"Whattayamean?" Detective Daniels had a smile across his face protesting innocence like a sibling caught picking on his younger brother. "Want a dog?"

"No, I don't want a dog. I just got rid of some pets." He paused. "What kind of dog?"

"Belgian Malinois rescue dog. Still gun shy from Afghanistan."

"I don't care about the dog."

"You just asked about the dog. Getting frustrated, Mr. Havens? Sarandui ta khaber warkri?"

"What did you just say?" *Stay in character, Havens. They are baiting you, asking if you want to call the police in Pashto. They know something.*

"Ah for geez sake, let him off the hook before we both end up in the hospital."

"Fine."

"Sorry. Just meaning we know you can be a badass. Havens, Detective Neil used to work with some folks you used to do some work for. He had seen your picture in a file before at a particular compound and heard of some of your exploits."

"Dick, that would be classified," Neil scolded his partner. "I told you that in confidence."

"Is it worse to violate your compartmented read-on or that I told a secret? Confidence doesn't meet your DSS obligations." Detective Daniels turned to Havens, "Sure you don't want a dog?"

"Enough! What do you want?"

"Fine. I'll come clean. I knew your name the first time I read it in the reports. It was confirmed once I also saw that you were connected to Red Peterson whose name I saw on a report notation in the station. Since I didn't know much about you, we had to see how you stood up to the travel cover that you were no doubt using. I was a detective before joining the Army then took up a job here when I got out. Even though I wasn't privy to the work you were doing with a particular squadron, loose lips still made you a bit of a legend. Not many Clark Griswolds roll with our kind and can make us look like a couple of pussies. I know some of the shit that you've done. I certainly know of Red and the teams that he was on. It's two and two math."

"So you just came by here to play the name drop game with me or what?" Havens got up and poured himself more coffee to keep busy.

"No. I played the name drop game so you know we are still working your case and that the shit doesn't smell right. CPD is still on it, and you need to know we are personally handling it since our fear is there is some evil shit that could be on your proverbial shoe."

"And why do you say that, detective?"

"As they say on TV, it just doesn't add up. And the circle of events that surrounded the attack with you as a primary objective spinning down to no one to question, dead ends, and more dead ends with the look of everyday random or half-assed planned violence but with a degree of backstopping that kills trails? Frankly, Mr. Havens, it's the kind of shit you or…shall we say…your likely former associates—who do not officially exist—might do."

And what I am doing now. Good point.

Havens sat and said nothing for a while. For such a small community, it could be so big sometimes. No attribution was supposed to mean no one would know. So how do people know? People talk. And people who like to keep secrets and compartmentalize their activities and personal lives hate talk. Was there more to this?

"How would you guys know I would understand Pashto? It isn't in my records."

"I guessed."

"And where does this dog fit in?"

"It doesn't. We told someone who couldn't take care of it any longer that we would ask around the station to see if someone would tend to a furry retired soldier. Had no intention of mentioning it to you, but for a second there it struck me that you could probably use a friend. At the very least a distraction. But you seem like a decent enough guy and that distraction would turn into a kinship. You look like a dog guy. Plenty of room in the backyard."

"That's a pretty big dog. They also have quite a spirit and I am not going to just leave a dog like that around in the house all day."

"Actually, well she is huge, but she has some non-physical war wounds and doesn't do much. Likes to go for a walk every now and again but only in the morning when it is light and there are not many people around. Pretty much happy with just a place to sleep and a pat on the head every now and again. Good dog, but the owner is moving to an apartment. The dog was used to rolling around in the sandbox and being in a crate most of the time. Seen some bad shit too."

"I can't deal with a dog right now. Tell me more about your hunches on what happened here. Does my brother-in-law know any of this?"

The two men looked at each other. "Told you."

"Mr. Havens…"

"Sean is fine."

"Sean, your brother-in-law is a great guy, but he is too close to this and he's already breathing down people's necks."

"Well that's good, right? For chrissake, it was his sister."

"Yeaah," Neil responded, dragging the word out. "But he is more interested in trying to direct us where to go and where not to go."

"I don't see the issue. He is a brilliant criminologist."

"That's the point. Some of his direction...He's all over the place these days. Asking questions, getting his nose in other people's cases. Looking at past evidence."

"Re-direction is what it feels like," Daniels interjected.

"Right, re-direction."

"Guys, what are you implying?"

"We are not implying anything. We are just saying he is being a pain in the ass and it isn't helping us. It would be good to maybe not mention we were here. We are on your side and just wanted to say we are on it. If there is anything that comes to mind which would help us or make sure nothing else happens..."

"OK."

The men nodded.

Havens rose. "Look guys, I appreciate you coming by. I really want to get to the hospital and have some other things I have to do."

"You have our cards?"

"No, I threw them out. Do you have another?"

"Sure." The detectives handed Havens their cards again. He regarded them as if the names should mean something now, but nothing came. He tucked them in his back pocket.

"You sure you don't want a dog? Might keep you out of trouble. You don't happen to know anything about two charred bodies?"

I knew that we should have covered them ourselves.

"Heard something on the news about it. I heard there was some rival gang stuff trying to add insult to injury on those guys. They were the same ones who were in my house right?"

"I'd have to check, Mr. Havens. It's not on our radar. CPD isn't pursuing it at all. They buried those guys to avoid more vandalism. Family decided on unmarked graves too now. Looks like they were just erased from this world. Suppose what goes around comes around."

"Suppose so."

Daniels walked to the door and turned around. "Alright, brother, call us if you need anything." Daniels reached out his hand in an upwards motion for a hand clasp.

Havens looked at the extended hand and glared icily into Daniel's eyes, hands still at his sides. "I'm not your brother, detective. Thank you for coming by. I will call if I need anything or if I have something I think you can use."

He shut the door behind them as soon as they hit the stoop.

"So how do you think that played?"

"Fine until you did the brother shit."

"Yeah, well I thought we were all good, knowing we are all on the same team and had served."

"Havens serves those who serve. He doesn't fit in with us. He is an anomaly. He doesn't fit in anywhere. The guy pretends to be a business guy, but really doesn't embrace the commercial community. He supports the military, but would prefer to be away from the military apparatus. He turns it on and turns it off. Guy is a fuckin' chameleon robot. I actually feel sorry for him. A guy like that needs a wife that will leave him alone and deal with his shit, no questions asked. He's got none of that now and he probably is really struggling with who he is and what he does. The man wants to be left alone on his own terms and now that he really is alone, it probably scares the shit out of him. But I'll tell you what, you should hear of the shit he has done. Can't ever take that away from him, but he doesn't wear it on his sleeve. He just does it and puts it behind him. If he was real military, he'd have a full breast of metal on his uniform."

"Like, what's he done? You never really told me aside from getting out of some scrapes."

"Well clearly you can't keep your mouth shut."

"Clearly you can't either, so don't go bustin' my chops. Give me something."

"Pretty much this guy was considered a surgical instrument mold for the future. Dudes like me fit more of the conventional profile of covert smash and grab door-kicking operators and usually had to get jammed into discrete operating platforms. What that means was the country didn't do as many black ops when they thought too big of a footprint would get us pinched."

"So Havens doesn't get pinched?" Daniels raised his eyebrows suggesting that maybe Havens was more involved in the murder.

"Nah, bro. This isn't his style. Havens works ops that are considered 'unacknowledged' and 'waived' status for clandestine intel, ops, and support stuff. That way he and the program details and funding don't get linked to the actual programs. Only a small handful of guys even have access to the same programs, and if they do, they really don't even know the true purpose of the program or mission."

Daniels whistled. "So this is a bad dude."

"He's bad, but mostly he's smart. Thing that I never liked about black ops stuff is you are in the middle of it, don't know about all of it, and you can't let that bother you. So to me, it means you are really trusting, a bit off, or your moral compass is spinning at light speed. Most guys can't do the work for too long. Havens has been at it a long time.

"I see. So why do they do it?"

"The thrills probably. The black can be pretty fucking exhilarating. You see firsthand that things get done by your direct efforts. About as tip of the spear as you get. But I think of it like black ops are fought in some dark abyss. You have to trade your soul to play. Dedication, honor, and all that jazz drive the priority of the mission. Fucked up thing is those who emerge from the abyss may come out alive but are real casualties. Kills their souls."

"Man, you're giving me the chills." Daniels shook his head in disbelief and just stared out his side window.

Neil continued. "Bro, blind ops mean you have to trust the program is real and within the law. What is cool about Havens is he has to totally trust that someone has his back and that there is total integrity from all who play their parts. If you ask me, someone didn't do their part on this one. I don't know what that's going to mean."

"So can you call in some favors to your bubbas?"

"And say, what? This shit Havens is into is unknown and disavowed. You just sign your name, social, and date, and the dudes with the forms don't always know what's up. All closed door shit. I'm not sticking my nose anywhere near it. Leave that world to those guys. Chi-town's our shit. Let's leave it at that. If this guy finds out who took out his wife before we do, there is going to be a hell of a mess for someone to clean up and you will never even know Havens was there. It will either be up close and personal for someone or they will just get randomly smoked by someone or something that makes no sense to them."

"He is a pretty cool cat."

"He's a damn death dealer who thinks he is beyond it because he can hold down a family and likes to mow the lawn on Saturdays. Pissed off some of his old team members too. Clearly he didn't do as good of a job as he thought he could do and sad as it is to say, may have gotten a taste of his own poison."

"Dude probably sat on the edge of those graves of the gang bangers roasting marshmallows as he toasted those guys up."

"No doubt. Surprised he didn't go kill their crew. Means he could still do it or he is actually leveled enough to think this whole thing out."

"Do you think he will tell Lars we came by?"

"Not sure. He will probably sit on this for a bit unless he can use it to get inside Lars' head. I don't know if they are close or not. He and Lars are both a bit standoffish, so who knows? They could probably sit in the same room for a week and not say anything to each other and have a great time. But either way, if he does say something we will know soon. Maybe the shit with Lars is his personal situation, maybe it is political, maybe that dude is just all fucked up. But Lars is acting sketchy, that's for sure. Even more of a prick lately. And if he doesn't say anything, maybe Havens will keep an eye on him too. Win, win."

"I dunno. I think both of these guys have just seen some personal shit and they are not as used to it affecting them. Think about it. You see dead people all the time, maybe even have a hand in it most of the time, but when it happens on your side of the fence, they probably are a bit conflicted emotionally. Don't know if they should shut it out or if they should deal with it like normal people."

"Maybe."

"What would you do if it was you?"

"Hmmm. I'd want someone to pay dearly." Detective Neil pounded his steering wheel in emphasis.

Though he didn't have a family he could put himself easily in Havens' shoes. His whole move to the police department was so he could spend more time in the states and less time in shit holes around the world. He also had a great reserve commander who had gotten the whole team some help after their last tour. His ODA came to love their circle time for some emotional decompression. They were tighter than ever and dealing with their demons very well. Life was good again for those men and their families. They were among a growing group of men who realized they had to deal with some shit inside if they were to lead normal lives and have healthy relationships.

"And what if you were involved somehow. What would you do or how would you be acting?"

"I'd be sad on the outside, play the support card, and then think of distancing myself from it all until the coast was clear and start over."

"My money is on Havens just sitting tight and being pretty screwed up over this whole thing. Agree?"

"Agree. If his people did it, he will go after them directly. He'll do more than burn up a couple gangbangers. So that leaves us with Lars."

"I don't think Lars has the criminal contacts to pull this off. Even if he had gambling debts or some shit like that this whole mess isn't a loan shark thing. It's more black, like that Will Smith movie when the NSA was trying to kill him for getting some spy disk or something."

"That was a cool movie. Gene Hackman blew up his own place after he got his cat out. I hate cats. What are we going to do with this dog?"

"I don't know. I kinda thought Havens would be a good person for that dog."

"The dog is a frickin' monster."

"No shit. Feel bad for it, but I think it severed the nerves in that kid's hand. Just hate to see them put that beast down. Dog did good work. A fucking hero. Just messed up now. Not its fault."

"Damn thing could eat a hero. Oooo. I could eat a big hero sandwich."

"Just need to find it a safe place before they put it down."

"See, perfect for Havens. Two peas in a pod. Ooo, or Chinese food with pea pods."

"That guy is anything but safe."

"Same goes for the dog. Hot dog would be good too."

"Dude, let's get you something to eat so you shut up."

The two men chuckled at the thought of the man and beast together, both damaged goods.

Havens remained standing for a moment in the entryway. He turned around and slammed the back of his head against the closed door. The artisan woodwork edge pained his scalp. Christina had looked for over a year to find this specific door. She didn't know what she wanted but said she would know it when she saw it. And when she saw it they bought it. It was a lot for a door. He thought it would bleach in the sun. It hadn't yet. This is not how he had expected his life to be.

He thought about what he needed to do today. Only a small part of it consisted of what he wanted to do which was spend time with his daughter. He was starting to lose hope for her recovery. But he knew he would still go to the hospital. That was a given. He knew he needed to talk to Harrison. And he needed to call Jason and Rusty to see how many people had been read on to his programs over the years and who they were. Was there anyone who could have a score to settle?

Ridiculous. I only accept my tasks, do my work and hand it off to someone else. My work is good and no one has ever been burned on my advance ops fixing the space for their work. Even my hits were clean.

He looked across the room. So quiet. So empty. He spotted a cordless phone sitting out of place on the arm of a sofa in the sitting room. Havens reached into his back pocket and stared at the detectives' cards. If he was going to get out of this mess he would need some help.

Detective Neil fumbled for his ringing cell phone while maneuvering through the drive thru lane.

"Bring over that dog tomorrow. Sometime in the evening. I want two bags of food, a 20′ foot leader nylon leash, a choke collar, and a size 3 soccer ball."

"You think you're Oprah?"

"You want me to take the dog?"

"Done. What is a size 3 soccer ball?"

"You are a detective. Figure it out. What's its name?"

"Jeez ok. So dog, leash, collar, food, and you get your own size 3 soccer ball. And give it whatever name you want."

"Done. I am also calling my old CI guy to see if there may be anything that can help you guys. Will keep you posted. Out." Havens hung up the phone. *Well that was dumb. I wonder how big this dog is anyway.*

"Don't tell me that was him asking for the dog."

"Yep."

"Shit. It was funnier when I didn't think it would happen."

"That's what I was just thinking. Hope it doesn't eat his hand."

Chapter 40

Harrison called Draeger while driving into the city. Draeger was on his third cup of coffee, which meant he was behind his usual amount for this time of day. A routine that went on nearly 24/7.

Harrison said, "Havens and I are going to meet up today. I have given him some time to look over the requirements so he has been nugging pretty hard to come up with some courses of action. How are things in the ivory tower?"

"All good today. I assume you are still juicing his daughter so there is no effective recovery process?"

"Correct. Old DEA days contacts paying in dividends. She's getting her fix like a little shooting gallery whore."

"Good. That will keep Havens focused on the job. Push Havens to ensure he is not just putting some creative thoughts down, but also putting some courses of actions together that are actionable sooner than later. I'm getting a little more pressure here for some heads to be delivered and they really don't understand the intricacy to these things. Havens will get jacked up about a moved timeline, but he can make it happen even if it isn't perfect. We have enough top cover to make any slight imperfections go away. Plus, with a seat open on the committee, we need to shake some things up to get some defense spending back in the budgets. That may well take precedent over other projects if it comes from the top or if the opportunity presents itself. I am working that end too with one of the targets. Havens did some work a year or so ago that never saw the light of day, but I can use that and attribute it to him. Best of all, if someone at the federal level does some real hard sniffing, this stuff was loaded on JWICS and points to his direct access and another one of his team guys who isn't living anymore."

"Don't suppose you are going to tell me who 'they' are yet. Who is running this whole show?"

"In time. Need you to get the field work all in order. And frankly, you would hate the desk jockey politics stuff anyway, so why would you care? Shit, I'd rather be doing what you are doing. I miss the dirty work. Soldier on Harrison, no need to know what's really going on at this stage of your career. Just be a SEAL and kill something."

"Roger that. But this hinky shit always makes me squirmy. Especially ones like this where full operational shut down can happen with shifts in the administration. Shit. Lower Wacker Drive is closed again. Hang on. Let me make this…"

Harrison's mobile phone dropped as he moved it from hand to shoulder while making a quick lane change and simultaneous blind spot check. The phone hit the plastic wood grain trim with a loud crack in Draeger's ear. Harrison scrambled to grab the phone before missing an exit.

"Sorry about that. Draeger? Draeger, you copy? Shit. Call you back in a couple."

Chapter 41

The sound of the phone cracking against the car interior reverberated on the other end, transporting Draeger without warning back to Operation Cherokee Spark in Mogadishu. Draeger could smell the stench of the late afternoon heat mixing a fishy smell with burning garbage and some unknown combination of filth that permeated the air. He heard the cracks of the various rounds outside of his door. The unique sounds of CAR-15s and AKs competed with each other. M-60's were chiming in to the chorus. An explosion resonated in the background. And another.

U.S. soldiers from the base by the airport were on the ground now in the city. Black Hawks and MH-60s were overhead flying around the city. He could hear the mini-guns sounding off. *Fuck! They are not supposed to be here today. Fucking Rangers.* With his hand tightly gripping his government issue ceramic coffee mug, Prescott Draeger was back in Somalia. The sounds, the smells, the sights.

Draeger gripped a small Gerber flick-blade in his oversized pocket as the rounds sounded off closer and closer. There was pounding on the doors. *Don't come knocking here. Nobody's home. And I'm not finished.* An RPG exploded meters from his door. *What the fuck is going on out there?* He resisted the urge to look out the front door and decided to climb the stairs and get a better view from the balcony. First, though, he needed to check the device he was calibrating to the new specifications. It would sit behind the false wall plate without even a hum for another month until he, or someone else from the team, would come back for another calibration and check-up. The rent would be paid and a local tenant would be back in to keep up appearances of normalcy. Another dull day in Mogadishu.

As Draeger reached the upper balcony door he could hear another Black Hawk roar by overhead. The bedlam outside continued. Draeger cracked the door only to see a Somali youth also on the rooftops hurling objects and taking shots at what Draeger assumed to be American soldiers running through the streets below. He heard the noise of a small Humvee convoy racing down the road. Plumes of black smoke lifted from the streets.

Shit. Need to ride this one out. Should I make a call? Probably not. Wouldn't matter anyway.

Draeger saw more youths jumping from rooftop to rooftop. Some entered unlocked doors to gain a better vantage point.

Shit. This is not good.

Draeger heard glass shattering back downstairs as rounds riveted the walls from shooters taking blind shots behind cover.

What to do with the box…If this blows over we are all good. If shit goes to hell, the box needs to be taken care of. Fuck it! NSA, Agency, whoever's toy this is can buy a new one. I'm not taking chances.

Draeger retrieved a small tool kit and proceeded to open the false plate and remove any core parts or telltale technologies from the device. Downstairs the front door crashed open. Draeger stopped unscrewing and froze. He heard American voices below.

"Thompson, you go check the rooms. I'm staying with Reed and will try to stabilize him. We can hook back up with the rest of the chalk later or he isn't going to make it!"

"Roger that Top!"

As the soldier mounted the stairs, Draeger called out, "American serviceman here!"

Thompson demanded that Draeger come out slowly and identify himself. Draeger approached the staircase with his hands raised.

"What the fuck is going on out there?" Draeger inquired to the soldiers below.

"Well, we had a surprise op that didn't end up so surprising. Go figure. I mean, it's the middle of the fuckin' day, right? Can't possibly see us coming."

"Thompson!"

"Sorry, Top. Just sayin' the town loves Aidid and that kinda tilted the scales in their advantage. Govie up here. State Department."

"Thompson, go back out and get a look at where we stand right now. See if we have any vehicles coming our way. You! State Department guy. Come here and give me a hand. Who the fuck are you anyway? You sure as fuck can't be on vacation and you sure as fuck ain't one of us."

"Top, one is coming our way!"

"Flag 'em down, but mind your cover LT!" Sergeant Major, let it trail off, "…fuckin' wet nose green leaf."

Among the sporadic snaps and echoes of fire, a particular rapport seemed to sing above the rest in that moment. The supersonic lead met with Thompson's flesh and bone and hurdled his body back through the entryway. Thompson's eyes were wide but saw nothing in his death throws.

Draeger got up to move from what he saw as pending death for the soldier now collapsed next the blown out door frame. He wanted to finish decommissioning the device and find a way out quickly. It was critical to his National Security initiative. He needed to move northwest of the city where he had another potential safe house on the outskirts. It would buy him time to establish communications and figure out his next move.

The Sergeant Major gripped Draeger's wrist tightly, preventing him from getting up. "You willll follow my orders and assist me with this boy."

"Sorry...Top…. this ain't working for me. He's a goner. I have work to do and then have to get the hell out of Dodge with my own troubles."

The Sergeant Major's grip held fast, and the stronger man pulled Draeger closer to him. "Sir, you willll assist me."

"You have two dead dudes right here. I can help you get them to the street so your other boys can collect them. I have to go."

"Negative!"

"Sorry, Top, but this is bigger than you. You just became collateral damage."

Draeger flicked the blade surprising the soldier, and thrust it into his carotid artery with the tip moving towards the brain stem. Another push and a slight turn of the wrist. The seasoned combat soldier fell back dead. Draeger moved quickly to take the various clean uniform pieces off the three fallen men to cobble a relatively unbloodied uniform of his own. Fortunately, he was wearing his mid-height camel-colored boots that would suffice for his new appearance without having to take the time to try on shoes and risk undue exposure. He outfitted himself with the battle kit and made for the door.

Upon his exit, he was immediately picked up by another passing Humvee full of soldiers stopping for a map check. They motioned for Draeger, now visible as a U.S. Army Ranger, to hop in quickly.

The phone rang.

The ringing seemed curiously long and Draeger picked up.

"Hey, you there? Where did you go? I tried calling you back a half dozen times."

Draeger's gaze was fixated on a point beyond his office wall. He blinked. "What?"

"I said I was trying to reach you after I dropped the phone. What are you doing?"

"I'm busy now. Have to call you back." Draeger ended the call and sat back in his chair.

How did I get so fucked up?

He put his head in his hands and closed his eyes.

I'm so damn tired. Shit. How did my coffee get cold so fast? I'm fucking losing it.

Chapter 42

Sean Havens sat across from Harrison Mann. Havens was giddy with anticipation of sharing his plans.

"So this is how it is going to start. Roughly, anyway. And high level so you get the gist. Robbery and killing of a Muslim store owner which will be set up to look like Latinos did it. That is then going to piss off some of the black gangs and some crime bosses when heat comes into their area due to the heightened violence as an excuse to make some opportunistic crackdowns. Some hot head in the black gangs will end up killing a few Hispanic gang members. You bring in your team to get the top Hispanic gang leaders and make it look like African American gangs. This gives you a week to knock off some key individuals on both sides and get inside the books of the Middle Eastern targets by investigating the shop owner murder. You can get some secondary effects of community outrage with editorials about the dead Muslim man to be inflammatory towards police and the Hispanic community. While you're investigating the Middle Easterner you have the opportunity for INS raids and you can detain any other Muslims that could be of interest. The next leg is tied from the African American gangs to this Somali guy you have up in Minnesota. He obviously will have a number of Somalis wittingly or unwittingly involved in his affairs of gun running and trafficking that you guys cite here on this page. I see it ties in to that military spouse who is being harassed in Minneapolis. Depending on where you mix in the drugs, that can be the link to this Rockford drug dealer that you have listed here with the heroin trails going down the major highways in a star formation to other Midwest states. I took into consideration each specific gang, the family details that you had, logistics, and how to make the hits according to area patterns and frequency. It solves your prime targets, the ancillary ones, and most importantly covers all the military family issues immediately so they are safer right away. I could easily work the military family issues in the area. Frankly, I'd like it, but I didn't see that many of them. I was under the impression there would be more."

Havens sat back for some answers and the overall impression of his summary while Harrison digested it all.

"Havens, in theory it works but how do I orchestrate it for my guys?" Harrison was shaking his head. "You have us running in a ton of different directions in too short of time."

"You don't orchestrate it for your guys. I will. How much real time do I have and how much money and men can I have? I will do all the recce and find a business with a big lot in a shitty part of town where folks won't notice a small fleet of vehicles and some dudes coming and going behind chain link fences. I can have that done in a month while you go after the threats to the spouses, and over the course of a few months we unravel the rest."

Harrison's eyebrow rose. "Months?"

"I found a storage business on the west side of the city that is for sale. Place is pretty run down with some decent abandoned equipment, and I suspect that due to the neighborhood and lack of activity, the business plan was not too well thought out and they don't have a solid customer base. Probably had loans for the equipment that are in default. That gives us cover to do some stuff and move some vehicles around like we are fixing the place up. I figure we have a month to shuffle stuff around while neighbors try to see what the business will be. By then we bug out to a sub site and start executing on these targets."

Harrison readjusted his posture and leaned in with greater interest, but his concern still dwelled on the timing. "I'm listening."

"Not much more to say at this point. I just need some cash to buy the place, some cash to go out and buy some vehicles and equipment. I plan to set up camp in Englewood and Garfield Park. Streets are empty during the day so no one catches a stray bullet. There are fewer formally run gangs to shake us down too. CPD has been really pressuring the organized aspect of their gang leadership structure so there are more cliques of a handful of members that are loosely affiliated to a parent gang. We just need to be mindful of the cameras they have all over the city."

Harrison cut Havens off. "We have vehicles. We got a deal on some surveillance vehicles that were dinged up and repurposed."

This time Havens waved off Harrison. "No way. They won't look local. I want local inner city cars and vans that come off the street from each of the ethnic areas. That includes all the shit they have in their backseats, on their windows, Bondo, mismatched hubcaps, and most importantly local DNA that can be used. Fingerprints, hair, the whole gamut. Pure native. It will take a little extra work on my part, but if I can even get the vehicles from homes with known criminal offenders, it just solidifies the stories that we plant. Plus, some of these folks will recognize the cars from those neighborhoods and give them a pass, which will buy us some time. If I don't change over all plates and paperwork, that buys us more time and if we need to ditch a car, keeps the pattern of life intact. We just dump it somewhere with the keys in the vehicle. I want to be able to slap a plumbing, electrical, painting or landscaping logo on any one of them at any time to best mirror the situation. And I want some of the real stuff that goes with them. A lot of businesses are going under, so I may be able to buy one with a real phone number and logo with a legitimate bonding number for one stop shop use."

"How much do you need?"

Havens pulled out another sheet of paper and handed it to Harrison.

Harrison reviewed the spreadsheet.

"How do you know the businesses can be procured for this little?"

"I found out that the warehouse and its lot is going into foreclosure. The amount you see is what they owe to the bank. Taxes have been paid. The owner is an old city worker who just wants to get out from under it. He has some good equipment on the property too that will solidify our cover. If we wanted to, we could probably sell some of it off and recoup operational funds. The other items on the budget I found on Craigslist and in the newspapers."

"I suppose you talked to the owner?"

"'Sean Havens' didn't but 'someone' did. It's legit. Don't tell me that you can't get that kind of money for an op. It's cheap. I can pick up these cars and vans for under $30K total. Probably half that."

"No, Havens, I actually think this is realistic. What is this incidental cost? Fake moustaches, sunglasses, and trench coats?"

"Doesn't matter. It's whatever I need it for. Pocket money to make this work. I'm sure you can get the amount. It's a tenth of what I would normally ask for of any entity that is serious about getting something done. Call your boss and make it happen."

"Draeg…" Harrison stopped himself short. "…pery truck for sale down the road from Roosevelt and Halstead that I just saw today. That might look good, right?"

Harrison hoped his near slip would go unnoticed. He held his breath and could feel his heartbeat. Havens was looking at a few pages of his plan and noticed Harrison's hand flex out while he was talking about the drapery truck.

"What? Sorry, I was looking at something here I have to fix."

Shit. What did I just miss? Something just happened. What did he just say or not say?

"Nothing. I was just trying to help, but you seem to have this under control. I think I can work with this budget. Remember, you also have a budget for your incidentals. Let me give you an account for that. You figure out how you want to clean the money. We have it linked to some LLCs from Delaware and Nevada for now. I will leave you a message and tell you where to pick up the cash in the next day or two. Good work."

"And what about my team?"

"Ah, we don't really work like that. I told you that before. We will coordinate the tactical. You plan it and design what we need to do and we will handle everything with our contractors to your specifications. I am sure you can appreciate that."

"Yeah, as long as you don't deviate I am ok with that. They better be professional because I don't like my plans screwed up. They go down to the very detail if they are going to work and if the course of action seems to miss the desired outcome, I don't go to a contingency plan as much as I dynamically shape the situation to get back on track. I will need to be somewhere near there with comms to direct or redirect."

"Havens you just worry about your end. I will worry about the rest."

"That's not really how I work best."

"Well, frankly, I don't give a shit. You do your job and I will do mine. Be the professional I hear you are and follow orders. You needed the job, right? We gave you a job. Orders are orders."

"I'm not much on orders."

"Yeah?" Harrison got up from the table. "You will get your cash and in one week we will speak next about your plan of action for execution a day or two after."

"Fine. Where will you train them for the pre-execution?"

"What don't you get? I will handle it." *We don't train, we do. No one needs to know anything beforehand.* "You just make sure your CONOP reads like a fucking Hollywood script."

"Sure, Harrison. Like a B action movie it is."

"And like I told you before, cut the time frame down to a month for everything. Not another word. Just do it. My orders were changed to step things up quickly. The winds have shifted in Washington."

Chapter 43

Eight days later Havens had procured the operating platform of a secure site and vehicles were being purchased throughout the city. He had received the financing on time in cash. Through a number of unrelated transactions, Havens laundered the funds in the event that the monies were marked by some governing authority to which he was not privy.

While making these purchases he donned the garb and look of the areas he was entering and paid careful attention to the times of day when light was dim and traffic was heaviest. He made little small talk unless not doing so would have been noticeable. And the small talk he did engage in remained brief, often employing a plausible excuse as to why he had to move on. Havens made use of public transportation and congested pedestrian areas where possible. His end of the plan had come together with few trails left outside of the ones he intended to leave.

Harrison, for his part, was able to obtain the finances with little prodding. Draeger knew the basics of what Havens would plan and had prepared to facilitate the requests, doing his own routine of transferring funds and receiving cash monies to stay under the bank regulations established to detect suspicious activity like money laundering. Harrison shared that the first leg of the operation would go down in three days. He hinted that the first assault could occur later that evening if they got the go ahead.

Following his discussion with Harrison, Draeger decided to call Havens under the pretext of inquiring about Maggie's health. While they were on the line he steered the conversation towards improvised unmanned aerial vehicles and whether Havens thought they were a viable threat to military aircraft in the Middle Eastern theater. Prescott Draeger took a chance with the detailed topic, but then again, he wouldn't hesitate the pull the tail of a mean dog just to get a thrill. Havens proved to be rather knowledgeable about the topic, having written a homemade UAV threat piece a year prior, and he was pleased to have someone solicit his opinion. Draeger, however, zoned out during the more technical part of the conversation having already gotten exactly what he wanted from the interaction.

Havens remained concerned about the operation being compromised if preparations were not being properly made according to his strict guidelines. If the team accomplished its mission it would be with a lot of luck. This approach was using too little advanced work. Havens fretted over it at night. He was losing sleep and had a hard time concentrating on anything other than the plans. During the hours of tossing and turning, he started to think of Christina, Maggie, and the past. When his eyelids became heavy enough to drift into sleep, a detail would pop into his mind about the operational planning. Another hour of sleep lost.

He would have liked to have run the issues past Draeger just as Draeger had recently bounced a few ideas off his friend, but knew OPSEC was paramount to Havens even if both men were on the same side. Despite being compartmented to need to know, which could mean the program, the tasking, and target, to name a few, Havens didn't like to take chances with disclosure. It was a line people just didn't cross, unless of course, they were using hypotheticals as a workaround, but even that was done by only the closest of trusted agent relationships in the business.

Havens was always a proponent of advance operations that were less tactical and more a gauge of sociocultural considerations in order to better appreciate the holistic environment in which they would be engaging. Havens found Harrison's approach to be sloppy and sloppy didn't happen if operations were planned with the appropriate consideration to the ancillary effects and scenarios that could manifest themselves with little warning. He was being forced to cut corners, put his stamp on things, but not be involved.

Havens would have to recce the sites again on his own and just keep it to himself. Precision in planning required the utmost attention to details to ward off potential surprise. Or so he told himself. In truth, any time that he let up on the gas his thoughts would shift to Christina and Maggie.

Havens pushed himself to keep busy despite complete fatigue and self-induced sleep deprivation. Having a new dog in the house also kept thoughts of his loved ones tucked away. The dog, Cougar, named after his temporary pet octopus, had been leaving plenty of trails of waste and wreckage around the house, providing a perfect therapeutic distraction for Sean. The two quickly developed a love-hate relationship as they vied for dominance and space in the house now filling with off-limits rooms.

Chapter 44

Lars had been out of pocket for the past twenty-four hours. He had explained to Sean that a lot of cases needed to be finished up and that he would be mostly away over the weekend and out of touch packing and what not. Havens paid little mind considering he would make a last run to some sites in the evening with a focus on the Middle Eastern shop owner.

On the surface the shop owner appeared to be fairly benign. He ran a business that had been established at the same location for eight years. The man sold second rate electronics, could provide prepaid stored value debit or credit cards, and likely also supported some informal monetary transfers, often termed as hawala.

While Havens didn't have the luxury of time or a mandate to investigate, his distrust of the list troubled him. He would have to pay a visit to scratch this itch and decided to drive to the shop for an onsite inspection. *What to wear so I don't look like a cop or a fed…How do I play this out? Why would I be stopping by this store in this neighborhood? Ah. Need that sport coat and glasses. Get the other wallet. Cash.*

Lars pulled up to the storefront he had been directed to. He gave it a quick glance to confirm the address and went around the block again. He scanned the nearby parking lots, street parking, and restaurant parking to see where he could camp out this evening. His tasking tonight was rather out of the norm for him. He was to be called in to support an undercover government raid if any casualties occurred. An unfamiliar admin from a nearby precinct had left a message on his voicemail to give him the tip. His presence now could put the raid at risk if anyone grew suspicious, so he made sure he would only pass by the site once and remain at least a few blocks away in a manner that would not cause alarm.

Perfect. A burrito storefront with side building parking. Hmmm. Maybe a taco or two now just to see if it was worthy of a return. It may also provide a plausible reason to come back tonight. Big cop type with the munchies while working the area. Not absurd.

Havens rounded the corner and scanned the streets. It was a nice looking Latino area with a typical amount of gang tagging and graffiti to show who ran the area and who should stay out. If he stayed on the main drag at this time of day it would not rouse any suspicion. He had selected a white 1998 Toyota Corolla from the fleet with a University of Illinois-Chicago sticker on the back window. With a brown suede sport coat and some trendy but affordable spectacles, the getup was a bit overkill of the poor academic role.

Hello?

Havens spotted Lars stepping out of his car as he raised his head in time to momentarily lock eyes with the passing car's driver.

Holy shit that guy could have passed for…

Lars walked out from the parking lot and into the street, his eyes following the passing car.

Havens looked in the rearview mirror without moving his head. He watched Lars step into the street.

Shit. What are the chances? I know his head is spinning now.

Havens pulled out his phone and dialed.

Chapter 45

"Doctor, we got the results back from the labs you ordered on the patient in 416."

"Thanks, Brenda. Leave the charts up on the desk and I will take a look after lunch. Hey...who brought in pizza?"

"Some drug vendor. If you want deep dish, there is stuffed spinach in the second box. Can't pass up Giordano's. Plus, I wouldn't mind getting your opinion on the labs while you're here."

The doctor grabbed a paper plate, reached for an end slice of the thin crust sausage pizza and stuffed it in his mouth while opening the second box.

"Mmmhmmm?" the doctor murmured as he pawed apart two deep dish pieces tethered by strands of cheese.

"Well the cell count was lower than you were thinking. I saw a trace of something else but it would need a toxicology test. I'd need your approval and then I'll code it."

The doctor had another mouthful, this time of the stuffed pizza. As he spoke the tomato and spinach on his teeth moved with his tongue like wiper blades cleaning bugs off a windshield.

"There's no need for a tox," he said dismissively before biting off another piece of pizza, cheeks still bulging with previous bites.

"Doctor," the nurse said rising from her chair. "Look at these numbers." She held her gaze and handed him the report.

The doctor rolled his eyes knowing she was not going to let this go unless he gave her a couple minutes of his time. He put his plate down on the makeshift buffet table and grabbed a napkin. He wiped his face and wadded the napkin in one hand as he began looking over the report. He stopped suddenly mid-chew and spit out the glob of dough and toppings in a nearby trash can.

"Just a sec." He moved around the nurse station desk, eyes trained on Maggie Havens' room. "I want to have a look at her."

Chapter 46

"Hey Lars, was that you?"

Lars' suspicions were confirmed the moment he saw Sean's name appear on the caller ID of his phone.

"Yes, and what, may I ask, are you doing… not being you? Whose car was that?"

"New job thing. A soldier's wife is getting harassed while walking home from the high school down the street. Just checking the area out before I meet with her. I was just over at the school trolling a bit. How about you? Thought you had a mountain of paperwork?"

"Yeah, I had some follow-up questions in the neighborhood and stopped by for a bite. They have a fleet of cars for you guys to use? That seems like a lot of overhead for a non-profit."

"Oh, I just asked to borrow one of the admin's cars who was coming into the office late since she couldn't find parking near the building. She thinks I had to run out for a minute and didn't want to take my car out of its spot. I said I'd park it for her in my place afterwards since I had some more errands to run."

"So why didn't you just change it in the first place? Where is the office?"

I don't trust you, Seany. You are a shady dude. What are you doing in this area?

"I was parked a couple blocks away and figured she could just pull up. Anyway, just wanted to say hello since I saw you and figured a good sleuth like you would be wondering if that was me or not since we appeared to have had a moment."

"Well, I was wondering."

Havens jumped back in, "Well I was wondering why you were looking so close into the eyes of another man. Have something to tell me Lars?"

Lars wasn't in the mood to be teased.

"Sean, I gotta go. Talk to you later," he replied shortly and hung up without another word.

You're growing colder, Lars. What's going on in your head?

Convinced that Lars would actually be eating for the next ten minutes or so, Havens made a few more turns and parked on a street behind his mark's store. He quickly walked along the side of the building and then lingered out front, hoping to be spotted by the proprietor. After making brief eye contact through the front window with the man behind the counter, Havens opened the door to the sound of jingling bells and walked in. The merchant placed something under a stack of papers and moved his phone from the counter to a drawer underneath.

Chapter 47

Harrison was briefing the team north of the city in a GSA-leased building that Draeger had found. It was paid and devoid of a tenant. A product of government waste perfectly suited to such activity.

Over time Harrison had made a number of adjustments to the team. A few became a bit frenzied after one particular job staging a Mexican drug cartel hit on a family. It was one of their first and Harrison thought it best to eliminate the entire team. Others had simply gotten too close to each other. Some needed to serve a higher purpose. Those men who were no longer needed were sent on a long journey in a COSCO container by sea while others found their way by rail. They would not require accommodations such as air holes.

Given the similarities of disposal, it could be easily construed as the M.O. of traffickers. In actuality, the men had done their jobs well, but a few slip-ups and a sharp detective almost blew their cover with the drug cartel crime scene. It was good to have that detective on the payroll now to avoid such inconveniences. When possible, the Activity put such astute individuals on the payroll, but in a couple of instances detectives had to be eliminated to ensure a less seasoned one would take over the case and produce less effective results. Even those added to the payroll were eventually eliminated once their usefulness expired. The jury was still out as to how long Lars would remain useful.

With a pause in the rundown, one of four Hispanic operators asked, "So who is this guy we are going after?"

"He is a known money launderer for Hezbollah. He is being monitored by OFAC but due to some jurisdiction issues, there is little evidence obtainable at this time without probable cause or something like that for Feds or law enforcement to enter his premises for a search. However, we know from our assets that he is involved in lethal aid logistical and financial support through his network. Our intent is that with our operation tonight law enforcement can come in and do site exploitation while investigating the crime and find some items that can link this man to other criminals and agents for Hezbollah.

"And what if they can't?" another operator inquired.

"That's not for you to worry about. At the very least it will open up some opportunities to expand investigations to some of the criminal elements in the area. If you look around, you can probably tell why you were selected, and it's not just based on skills."

"Hey, chief, my parents are Greek. I just look Mexican. I'm starting to feel discriminated against. Where is my HR rep?"

The room chuckled as the operator put his hands up in mock protest.

"With a flat nose like that you're practically Mayan," another operator retorted. "You must have gotten your ass kicked a lot growing up."

Harrison raised a hand. "Gentlemen, please. Game face time. This mission is not to be carried out in military style. Precision, yes, but style has to be street. It can't look like a robbery either; we need it to be a signature gang hit like this shop owner did something to cross someone."

"Rico, you are locks and picks. I need you to put this collateral in any filing cabinet or moderately well hidden place in the store so it doesn't look like it was left out, but not locked up either. CPD evidence will need to find it, but our orders are to leave room for proper chain of evidence collection to show the where and how of discovery to be realistic. I have a sheet for you to review from our J35 of Plans on how I want this to look. Copy that?"

"Roger, sir."

"Then you're all going to scatter as planned. Your vehicles should be left outside another designated shop a few blocks down from where you will be."

Harrison showed the driver and team lead a map point signifying the location.

"Meet back here for a debriefing tomorrow morning and we'll discuss the next leg."

"We going to have to get our homies in more trouble?"

"Nope, we get to rattle someone else's cage next time. Review the board and the plans for the next few hours and work out your roles. Make sure, Rico, to get the shop owner's prints on the files. You also need target in position for execution style if possible. He has to be hit by 21:45."

Harrison wondered who he was going to pick to beat the corpse with a bat or two by four to further stage the crime. This zombie crew was selected by their military files for their aptitude but also for the low psychological scores for remorse. They were less professional than other teams that consisted of men like Havens and Gunny Gonzalez who were driven by acts committed against their family. These goons were just driven.

"Hey, boss, why 21:45? You trying to make the news?"

"Exactly."

Chapter 48

The shop owner walked to the door to greet his customer. He was wearing a traditional sleeved tunic over slacks. His graying but trimmed moustache and designer glasses signaled to Havens that he was a man of traditional values who likely had money and some education. Given the neighborhood, Havens surmised this man either made a decent living before and may have lost work, as many PhD cab drivers can relate, or he was making more than he should at such a location given the economic status of the area and the type of goods on display.

"Hello, sir. Thank you for coming to my store and seeing us today. How may I be of help to you?"

The man cocked his head slightly to the side while smiling and clasping his hands together. Havens always appreciated the graciousness of Middle Eastern hospitality. It warmed him slightly despite the likelihood that this man was up to no good.

Havens gazed around the store processing his surroundings and trying to retain as much as possible, noting anything that could be of importance later.

"Well, I didn't actually intend to come here, but when I saw the store, I thought perhaps you may have a few good deals on some electronics. I am in need of a small inexpensive radio with an alarm. Mine just shorted out. But I also see you have some remote control toys that my nephew might like for his birthday."

The merchant reached out to Havens and grasped his upper arm firmly but without hostility.

"Yes, sir. You will be very, very pleased with what we can provide you. We have the best that I personally select. I am expert in this area of electronics with three masters degrees in electronics. Three!" the merchant chortled.

In typical bazaar merchant fashion, he drew Havens over to a number of random clock radio boxes that had worn edges and dusty plastic wrapping with cords hanging out of the cardboard encasements. The merchant threw open his arms in proud presentation as if it was the finest the world had to offer. A treat for this customer alone.

"You see, I have much for you here, my friend. Panasonic, Sony—I have the best! Which would you choose? I take it to the front for you while you look some more."

"Oh, I suppose the Panasonic is just fine. Does it have a snooze button?"

"Yes, of course it has the snooze." The merchant drew out some reading glasses that were likely a $5 pair in a $100 case. He switched his current glasses out and put the readers on, drawing the box near in order to see the actual product capabilities. The action demonstrated to Havens that the owner spoke first and verified his claim later as a mere technicality. A common cultural trait. "Yes, yes, sir, it does indeed say it has the snoozing for you. I will let you buy this one for you. It's very, very good one. Very good quality."

"How much?"

"This one…" The man moved the box around as if there would be a price tag. "This one is thirty dollars."

"Thirty dollars?! That is a ten dollar clock at best!"

"No, no, no, sir. This is a very good clock. Panasonic does not make a ten dollar clock. I already give it to you for a good price of thirty dollars. What would you pay?"

"Maybe twelve." Havens couldn't resist haggling and it also bought some more time to look around the store.

"Please, sir. Can you pay twenty? It has the snoozing."

Hmmm. My guess is that if this guy was doing something really shady, he probably would just want me out of the store as fast as he could. Let's get towards the back of the store and see how he feels.

"I'm not so sure. I still have to buy a gift. Let me look around a bit."

"Yes, sir. Please look around. The toys are by the register here." The merchant motioned towards the front of the store.

"What is your name?" the merchant asked. "I am Adeel," the store owner said, extending a hand to Havens.

"Alex," Sean replied, meeting the man's outstretched hand.

Adeel clasped Sean's hand with both of his and vigorously shook it with exaggerated honor and salesmanship. "Alex. Alexander the Great! You are a great man. I can tell. You look very smart. Please. I will show you some more, Alexander the Great."

I really didn't want this much interaction. "That's OK. I kind of want to look around. You have some interesting things here."

"Yes, sir. You may look around if you wish, but over here is food items that you may not like unless you can cook. This is for our women customers."

The merchant again cast his arms out to what did indeed look like food stuffs to include sacks of rice, canned goods, and a small produce area of mangos and assorted nuts and dates.

I think he really is trying to be helpful. No one else appears to be here. This does not seem to be a dark hawala shop at first glance. What could be going on?

"So, what got you into the retail business with all the electronics degrees you have?"

"Ah, very good question, sir. I am happy to tell you. I have the degrees from Pakistan, and from Penn State, and IIT. I am programmer for telecommunications controllers at Motorola for many years, but they sell off my group. I work for the railroad to make controllers for the switches and train controllers but then these bastards too have me to go away because I am too rich for them to pay. It is the bullshit, man. You know what I say? The bullshit! What is it that you do?"

"I'm just a teacher down the road. Subbing now, trying to find something. Hey, do you have any remote control cars that aren't too much?"

"Yes, sir, they are right over here, but do you want to see something? I have the remote control helicopters. They are my specialty and I make them myself. A teacher. This is a very good job. Not good pay. Let me take you over here, Mr. Alex the teacher. I will teach you something!"

Chapter 49

Lars ordered another glass of milky white horchata. He was stuffed but wanted to sit tight with Havens in the area. Best to order some more chips to clean off the remaining pieces of carnitas, adobo carne asada steak, and globs of guacamole and salsa in a pool of chorizo oil that had not quite held together in the last bites of the two pound Burrito Gordo.

He'd give it another thirty minutes just to be sure he wasn't within contact. Lars remotely accessed his cloud files to review a number of scenarios the consulting firm had sent him. At this point Lars was convinced he had been duped into working for a criminal organization to cover up hits. Lars' mind was like a sponge. He noticed random events on the news and read cases at the department that pointed to scenarios he had advised on. This is not what troubled him though. He figured if they were criminals they were likely going after other criminals and he was getting paid to have bad guys fight it out with each other. He just wanted to make sure he didn't become a loose end to someone's security.

Slowly munching on the last bits of his dinner and flicking through the files on his phone, Lars considered the situation. He could put his new house in Arizona in a trust so he couldn't be traced and then have all his mail sent to a PO Box, but he would have to look into things a bit more before finalizing his plans. It would be a pity to retire only to be killed shortly after.

Chapter 50

Adeel, the shop owner, pulled down a 47-inch long helicopter with a 34-inch rotor span. He explained that he was particularly proud of this model because it had incredible lift and was capable of supporting nearly a pound of additional weight. The design would be complete later in the day. He was in the middle of welding what looked like a piece of rebar from the frame to tail.

"What's this piece?"

"This is a special metal with great strength but is much lighter than steel."

"Why do you have it on there?"

"Mr. Alex, this I admit I do not know. They have asked me for more of these kinds."

The shop owner proudly bragged about how he had augmented the 3.5 channel transmitter with his own electronic recipe of configuration to ensure no interference to also meet the specifications of the customer.

"So what kind of customer buys one of these homemade units? Do they cost a lot?"

The shop owner grinned.

"I have collectors from all over the states and I have even made some for the U.S. government." He lowered his voice and looked around cautiously although the store was empty.

"I can protect the homeland security. They have called me for the special ones like these with the bar. I am very, very good. Someday, I hope to be a big defense contractor, you know."

Adeel laughed.

"I don't think this makes my friends very happy if they know, but it is American dream. A success! I sold six so far. For how much you think? Twenty thousand dollars! In cash too."

Oh shit, the plot thickens.

"Good for you. I wish you great success."

Wonder if that Homeland Security guy looks like Harrison. Fuck! Wonder if he looks like Draeger? He was going on about these things not long ago. Maybe the detectives are right after all. There are too many coincidences these days.

Chapter 51

Havens was reeling at the possibility of Draeger's involvement with the store owner and was fighting to process what the doctor was saying on the other end of the phone.

When his mobile phone rang, Havens excused himself from the store to take the hospital's call, but not before the courteous store owner could relieve him of twenty dollars in exchange for the unneeded alarm clock. He made a mental note to do some more research on the store owner once he got his arms around the new developments from the doctor regarding Maggie's toxicology report.

Havens wrestled with his findings at the electronics store. While Havens was still not convinced of the store owner's role, much less his innocence, he knew it would be senseless to try to intervene with the take down at this point. He reminded himself that it was part of the job. You must trust that someone higher up has done proper due diligence in targeting and vetting, then follow orders. If the targeting was bad, then a review would be conducted and trust would have to be earned back. Accidents happen when dealing with dark networks and surreptitious affiliations. It just seemed different on American soil. Somehow the black seemed that much dirtier. The work was that much more nebulous. He questioned whether they had the authority to conduct such operations. In his gut he knew they didn't.

This is all starting to turn into a bit of a shit show again. What the hell is the doctor talking about—an abnormal presence of a toxin in her bloodstream and lack of muscular responsiveness? Shit, what else does she need to be going through? Once again I'm not 100% there for her. Fuck! Move cars!

"Move!"

Havens worked the horn as he maneuvered through the city traffic.

And what about Draeger? Is this a coincidence about the RF helo? Remote coincidences like this are not likely. Draeger is secretive but how could this tie in to the hit if this guy is providing hardware to the government? Unless the government isn't officially using him. He said cash. Probably too much cash which would keep this guy quiet. Paying a Pakistani to build stuff for government…that is potentially cutout…and using frequency channels that can't be disrupted. We used disruptors for IEDs. And that thing back there can carry a small payload. This could be leveraged to implicate the guy and to further another objective. Fuuuck. This guy is whacked so he tells no tale and we cover it up. That protects buyer but also starts additional conflict where this guy is a terrorist. It also leaves things open for retaliation or a dead end two to three layers down in an investigation. Shit. I may be covering up the lower layers to something bigger. And he's an engineer…that could play into any number of threats and infrastructure vulnerabilities. Shit. I designed a ton of them myself. Oh fuck. Oh fuck oh fuck oh fuck. There would be blowback to me if someone dug far enough in classified systems. CPD couldn't do it, but FBI or ATF could. And then there is Lars. He too is part of some consulting scenarios as cover-ups. Shit, that plays to the back end of all my front ends. Oh damn, this is a disaster program. I have to get with Red and pick his brain a bit.

Havens' phone rang again.

Blocked number. Harrison. How much does Harrison know of this? Ok, be cool.

"Yes?"

"Hey it's me. You getting next phases together? I have guys heading to the storage lot you bought to check the vehicles and make necessary preparations. You sure no one will be paying attention to who comes and goes?"

"I already discussed this with you and all environmental details are in the COAs."

"Yeah, I can read your courses of action but you can also assure me that you have considered everything, intel weenie. Is this neighborhood the black area or Latino one? Hate to get all shot up before we even get out."

"Harrison, I have to trust you, you have to trust me. Should I trust you?"

Dumb. Don't play games and tip a hand. Harrison may not be the sharpest guy, but he is a seasoned operator.

"I am sending you to the one you all will fit in best with. Except you, white boy, so dress appropriately."

"Thank you."

With heightened op tempo everyone could get a bit jumpy. This was the first one he had planned for Harrison. Harrison's neck was on the line as well as his men's.

"Look. You are my boss. If you need me to walk you through it so you can appease yourself or your superiors, I can walk you through it."

"Where are you now?"

"On my way to the hospital."

"Hospital?" Harrison's brow furrowed. He needed Havens to be available, not back in a hospital where he may not have a reliable connection. "Who's at the hospital, you hurt?"

"My daughter."

"Havens, I'm all for you visiting your daughter, but we have…"

"Harrison, there is something wrong with her. The doctor called."

"Shit, what happened? Is she OK?"

"I don't know. Doctor didn't say much except a toxin in her blood."

Fuck. Gotta get to Draeger. No, get Whitt. This is my show. "I see. Well hope she is OK. We can take it from here. Obviously I will be out of pocket in a bit. Leave me a message and let me know how things are and if you will be delayed. I also want to catch up tomorrow. 1330 at UL Club. Can you make it?"

"Sure. Talk to you later."

Shit, what's Whitt's number? Maybe it's time to work that nurse. Harrison scrolled through a coded contact list.

Chapter 52

While the doctor could not identify what the foreign compound was without another full lab report, he could tell that it had to be introduced into Maggie's system proactively—and by another party. Given the exposure of the Havens incident, the doctor initially wanted to call police since he suspected something abnormal, but without proof he was required to consult the family first from a liability standpoint. He needed to show that if something was wrong it was not negligence on the part of the hospital. Even if he suspected a family member might be to blame.

Havens shook his head in disbelief. "OK, have you inspected her for sites of injection, is there another way she could have been exposed, like IV?"

"Mr. Havens, I have the lab checking a number of the past draws to see if we can do a time trace, level of the toxin, etc. She has no identifiable physical markings."

"Can I go in and see her?"

"Of course. We should have some more information for you shortly. But Mr. Havens, we will have to contact the police if we find evidence of any foul play."

"OK, thank you. I'll be here."

Havens opened the door to see his daughter. He noticed how thin and frail she was getting. She looked horrible. He took a brush from her bedside table. As he stroked her hair, large clumps came out and accumulated in the bristles. The shaved part of her head was barely growing stubble. It seemed like she had just been a pre-teen. It seemed like she was just a toddler. He had missed quite a bit of her life and he was losing more. He kissed her forehead.

"Hang in there kiddo, I'm still here."

Havens checked his smart phone and saw there were a few bars of connectivity. Enough for a search. He should be jumping IP addresses if he was searching a target, but figured the risk was acceptable if he deleted the trail and ensured that his mobile wouldn't get into the hands of a digital forensics technician. Right now he was more concerned about the whirlwind of thoughts going inside his head than the data on his device.

The search yielded little about the store owner with the exception of some public records for property ownership and past addresses. Ohio, Michigan, Illinois. Pretty typical. Havens searched a few of the addresses to see who or what else would come up. A first name Zahed matched Adeel's family name and address that Havens spotted on a bill sitting out on the store counter. Havens found a newspaper article indicating Zahed was a high school track star before joining the Navy. *He has a son.* As he read on and strung out a few more search parameters, Havens discovered that Zahed was a Navy electronics specialist currently deployed. *Military.* Zahed had a LinkedIn profile and Facebook page. It appeared that Zahed was a typical young adult with no odd affiliations and mostly white American friends, a white girlfriend, typical interests, and age appropriate photos and wall postings.

What is this kid going to do when he finds out his dad is dead? How is he going to react? Who is going to tell him and what will they say? And what if his dad is linked to…an attack? This kid could be bent in so many directions. How would he feel? Would he feel responsible? I know I would…I did…I do…I need to revisit the Somali hit and the Rockford drug hit. What am I covering up? What kind of drugs does the Rockford hit have again?

Havens' eyes darted to his daughter then to a blank wall. He began going over all the strange events and a sickening realization slowly emerged from the fog of his grieving mind.

Christina…Maggie…gone, taken. The unbearable grief. Then I'm fired…destitute. Suddenly willing to entertain new options without considering the ramifications.

Havens' insides began to boil. His eyes were shooting everywhere and nowhere. He looked down to see his palms had begun to sweat. His heart raced. He knew he was being played.

But who? Why? Someone is on the other end of this attack. Someone like me…Draeger? But why? Draeger would have the ability. And the stomach. Where was Draeger working exactly? Exactly. He never says.

A nurse called out to Havens as he headed towards the elevator bank. "Mr. Havens, the doctor is coming back up. He has some results."

"So do I. It's a narcotic to keep her from recovering."

"How did you know?"

"Call CPD and ask for Detective Neil. Tell him everything and that I told the doctor to call him with the details. Have Detective Neil call me afterwards."

"But sir, there is a note here that I am supposed to call a Lars Ba…jor…"

"Bjorklund. Call Detective Neil!" The elevator doors opened. Sean took a deep breath and checked his watch.

16:20. I can make it home and grab my kit and still get to Lars' place with plenty of time before he gets back. But if Lars is by the shop owner today, could that mean they moved up the timeframe on me? Why else would he be around there. He's no beat cop. He's involved too.

Chapter 53

Harrison failed to get a hold of Whitt. He called Draeger as a last resort to find Whittington and was informed that Whitt was moved out of the area shortly after the accident with the security guard and replaced with a female nurse on staff.

"You can't leave me out of these types of decisions! Is this the nurse I was working already? I was doing complete backgrounds before I put her in place."

"It was a small detail. Nothing to concern you with. You still handle her."

"It concerns me now!"

"Well when you are running things you can have it your way. Until then, consider them orders. I owe you only the information that you need to know to do the job in a manner that I want you to do your job."

"When will you be back in town? You either need to let me run things in this AO or you need to be here to drive things and keep us all informed on your decisions. We aren't running a company here where we can just video conference, email, and call each other. Shit, a secure VTC would beat the shit out of how we have been running things. And where are those damned Type-1 secure phones you promised? At least get some encryption packets."

Harrison had made a living following orders, but as an officer himself and the respected leader of his men, he couldn't stand idly by under a weak superior who didn't respect his officers in charge.

"I won't be back anytime soon. As a matter of fact, things will be ramping up here pretty quickly and that will require more of my time and attention. From here on out, I will simply fund accounts, give you names, and you can run your show. Fair?"

Surprised at Draeger's willingness to delegate responsibility and grant more autonomy so readily, Harrison simply replied, "Fair." *Fair unless the carnival is moving to another town and I am left holding this bag.*

"This whole initiative, as you likely surmised, has a number of facets to a greater cause. Up to this point, we have been laying groundwork. I'm finding that my initial thoughts of gaming these groups is taking too much time, effort, and planning. There are too many variables to assess and as much as I would like to think I could pull this off with Havens and these others, it's not worth the time and effort. We are going for a more direct approach now and where we need to we can shape our battlespace after the fact."

"So I am guessing you don't believe in long stay counterinsurgency doctrine where you pay attention to the hairball of inter-related possible effects?"

Draeger knew Harrison was being glib, but he came to a realization about this setup. If he had had Havens doing the job of Harrison, Havens would have been able to play it off. The massacres had their purpose and set the foundation for where they were now. Vision and reality were separate. Even Draeger could see this.

Best just keep Havens as a patsy fall guy for this given his background and situation. It's plausible enough, especially if supported by proper Information Operations and momentum in the right channels. Maybe Havens would even take care of Harrison…

"Harrison, I know you are pulling my chain, but frankly, I know where you are best skilled and I know how your teams need to operate, and this just isn't working. I'm getting pressure from my superiors and time is running short. Don't pretend you are a planner. Just execute your tasks."

"So we done fucking around with Havens' kid and all this Silver Star bullshit? I'm playing games around here with my thumbs up my ass being your piece of shit pawn so you can play with kings."

Draeger liked the thought that he was playing with kings, but he too was a pawn. He aspired to be a king and needed to do something more king-like.

Time to put the bow on this.

"Your part in Silver Star will be cutout as mine is through DOSA. Asset mode for you and your teams now. That kid of Havens' is probably a vegetable now anyway and it's best we drop the matter and back off. Let's just cover our tracks. Seize opportunity where you can. Do as you see fit."

"And Havens?"

Draeger sighed. He'd love to just kill Havens at this point but still needed him around. Draeger wrestled with need and want. Havens was a threat to Draeger's career and the operation if he found out too much. Not that Havens would ever take Draeger's job, but they knew each other and had worked together. Havens knew his history and could potentially question the fabrications that Draeger used to bolster his career. Havens was an inconvenience and Draeger would love nothing more than to discredit him and pin him as a scapegoat for subsequent plans. There was never a real plan for Havens; Draeger just wanted to mess with him every way possible like a toy.

"Hey, what about Havens?"

"Keep him on task for now, but pull him back a bit. Keep him away from this next bit of activity aside from his planning. Tell him to ramp it up more or get him frazzled or something. Do not let him near any sites. That asshole will jump light years ahead piecing this all together if he gets a sliver of reality. No telling how he will fuck it up. No, we will pin part of the end game on Havens. He will be very much in an unsafe place. Then you can take him out. If you have to do it sooner, so be it." *Who gives a shit? Just keep yourselves busy and out of my way.*

"Roger that." *Good. My call.*

Chapter 54

Cougar had eaten a chair leg and was mid-cushion when Havens entered the house and caught her in the act.

"Hey!" Havens shouted, half wondering if the dog would attack him. While a vision ran through Havens' head of the beast pouncing on him to take a death bite from his throat, Cougar laid down in a sphinx position and put her head on the ground in submission.

"OK, girl. Let's get you out quick for a piss, then I need to get my gear and we'll go for a ride to Uncle Lars'."

Cougar rose with guarded excitement and nuzzled Havens' hand, emitting a deep affectionate growl.

Havens grabbed his EnCase, FTK and Cellebrite UFED data forensics kit and headed for the door. Cougar bolted out the door before he could change his mind, but turned immediately to await further instruction.

"Smart dog, Cougar, but damn you are a horse."

Chapter 55

While Cougar waited in the car parked a block over, Havens ran up the flight of stairs to Lars' apartment. The hallways were always dark and there were few other residents. Lars rented two of the units which cut down on foot traffic—something Lars valued, and now so did Havens.

Sean was prepared to use his custom pick set. Lars hadn't changed locks in this older unit so the standard lock rake and tension bar would suffice.

Fuck it. We're in a hurry.

Havens reached for his tried and true Lockaid gun. Some chose the Cobra Electronic, but Lockaid never let him down when time was critical to pick a lock.

In.

It had been some time since Sean was at Lars' place. Last time he had come by to help move a new couch in, but Lars had beaten him to it and moved it on his own. Instead, Lars coaxed him into staying for a few beers and a Cubs game.

Havens looked around the bachelor pad scanning for anything unusual. Sean was surprised that Lars never invested in a security system, but then again, he made sure everyone in the building knew he was a cop.

Eyeing Lars' workstation, Havens pulled out his phone and took a number of photos to ensure everything would be put back in order when he was ready to leave. If anyone would sense something out of place, it would be Lars. What else did he have to do in here aside from watching the games and admiring his shrine of Chicago sports memorabilia? Above Havens was a framed 20x24 photo of a tattooed and pierced Dennis Rodman of the Chicago

Bulls Dream Team. Rodman had his tongue sticking out. It read, "To Lars from Dennis."

To the right was a signed photo of Michael Jordan walking with Charles Barkley. "Friends. Brothers." Lars had given Sean the same framed photo for Christmas about six years ago. Lars had said at the time that it reminded him of Sean being like a brother. Lars joked that of the two of them, Sean was shaped more like Sir Charles. The whole family had a good laugh over it that morning.

Good times.

OK, user name up. Password. What else, Lars…C-U-B-S-W-I-N.

In. OK, let's just mirror image your hard drive so I can review this all at home and...Hello?

Havens lifted his fingers from the keyboard. He hesitated before resting them back in place. Inside of Lars' C drive was a My Documents folder named "SHhh." No doubt, the capitalization was intentional—SH for Sean Havens.

Havens opened the folder to find files attributed to link analysis software applications and geospatial overlays. On a map overlay, Lars had placed a pin with a date where—or where Christina may have said—Sean was traveling to. Nearby there was a correlating pin for an incident in another location with a date. There were trails all over the world where Sean supposedly was and where newsworthy events occurred during that time.

You knew all along, you motherfucker!

Shit. Why did I open that? Now I have to scrub most recent files opened. I don't have time for this. Damn. I could have had X just do this remotely. Why didn't I think of that? God I need sleep.

Havens opened more files.

Fine, you want to play it that way, I'll fucking trash your place and stage a break in. Then I don't need to fix your computer.

Havens found a number of the consulting responses Lars had written for crime scene hypotheticals. There were dozens. They ranged from discrete assassinations to full out massacres. Havens recognized a number of incidents that had hit headlines across the U.S. in recent months. He noticed that in the murders of families the father was almost never home. In the other scenarios, the targets generally resembled someone Havens could be targeting, but this would provide more of a road map as to the staging from the crime scene perspective forensically. Havens even read an assessment that mirrored this evening's targeting of the shop owner.

Havens opened a subfolder to these scenarios that was simply entitled "Questions."

Similar to the layout on Havens, Lars had pinpointed spots around the country on a map where these acts had been carried out. There were other pins that did not seem to be associated with a crime. He double clicked some of the pins to read the notes. They were color-coded. Black pins appeared to be for ethnic individuals. Detroit. DC. Tampa. Virginia Beach. San Diego. Minneapolis. Springfield. Lake of the Ozarks. Arlington. He clicked on blue. They were for families, labeled by last name. As he clicked through the notes, he found that a file link attributed to the surviving husband showed they were a military or government worker in all cases. He clicked on the one he was avoiding. Chicago. Havens.

Chapter 56

Sean Havens leaned back in the leather office chair and rubbed his eyes. He had to get moving but still had not checked the red pins. Unlike the other colors, when a red pin was selected a radial appeared with connections to larger cities or landmark locations. A number of cities were linked to Reagan and Dulles with question marks. Others linked to O'Hare and Midway International Airports. There were other red pins along Chicago's Burlington Northern railroad and Metra rail lines as well as the Acela on the east coast. Again with question marks.

What are you trying to figure out, Lars?

It came to him suddenly.

"Shit, you're targeting."

Havens heard the apartment door open slowly with an initial creak.

"Lars?" a male voice called out.

Havens remained silent.

The creak grew louder as the door swung open.

"Hey, who are you?"

A dark silhouette filled the entryway. Sean's phone began to ring—it was Detective Neil.

Now scrambling, Havens decided to carry on and work the story. "Hello?" He answered the phone and beckoned the individual in the doorway to come in.

"Mr. Havens. Detective Neil here. You have a second?"

"Yes. Can you hold one second? I have someone here with me. It will just take a moment."

"Sure, but have to chat with you quick."

"OK, one sec."

As the man approached him, Havens saw he was in his mid to late twenties, early thirties tops. He was wearing a t-shirt and jeans with an unzipped hoodie and flip-flops.

"Bit cold out for flip flops, huh?"

"Dude, who are you? Why are you in Lars' apartment and on his computer?"

"I'd ask the same of you, kid. I know I am supposed to be here. Not sure why you are just marching in."

"Dude, I always stop by when Lars leaves the top bolt undone. Then I know he is home since the door won't close. Now, who are you?"

"Sorry, man. I'm Sean. I am his brother-in-law."

"Oh, dude. Shit. Oh, I am sorry. Was that your sister? I mean your wife and daughter, his niece?"

"It was. Thanks. How do you know?"

"Dude, I know all about you. Lars and I watch games together and shoot the shit sometimes. I just moved here a few months back and don't know many people. He talks about you the entire time saying you fly all over the world for accounting stuff. Sounds cool even though I'm not in finance, but I am in computers. Work for IBM consulting too. He was really a mess when your wife was killed. Sometimes he just sits and looks at that picture of her and your daughter."

The kid motioned to the wall with the flat screen TV mounted. It looked odd right next to the television. It was indeed a picture of Sean's wife and daughter, but Havens didn't recognize it. Perhaps shot while he was traveling.

"He says you guys are all real close and you are like a brother to him."

Alibi. Nice Lars. Way to sell the sob story.

"So, like no disrespect, but why are you on his computer if he isn't here?"

"It's kind of a secret. And I can't be long because I have to take this call. I suppose I can tell you. You must know how lonely he has been without his sister, so for the holidays I am going to make one of those photo albums that you can order online that look just like a book. I know he has some pictures I don't have, so I snuck in to copy them."

"With an imager? That's for copying a whole hard drive. The one you have you can't even write to. That's a forensics tool."

"Yeah, I had to get a lot of high res graphics and my external storage is about full. I don't have much time and just wanted to copy it then I can look through."

"But you will take his personal files too doing that."

Havens was getting pissed. This kid was asking to turn up missing, but killing him wasn't a good option despite it being an appealing notion.

Seems like a good kid. I am feeling a bit nasty though.

"Hey, you know, you are right, so I will go through and deselect them, but I have to take this call. I'll be leaving shortly, but please, I don't want to wreck this surprise. Don't let him know I am doing this for him or that I was looking at his pictures. OK?"

"Sure, man. I know he will really appreciate it. That's cool of you to do for him. My mom made one for our grandparents and they loooved it."

"Cool. Thanks." Convinced he was in the clear he unmuted the phone as the kid left. "Sorry, you still there?"

"Yeah, but barely. I need you to authorize something. I can bring it by your house."

"What's that?"

"Well that doctor story kind of scared me, so I think it may be best to move your daughter somewhere safer. Another hospital. We can use a different name if I can get an approval from my guy up top."

"Good idea, thanks. What do I need to do?"

"I already got it in play. Just need you to sign off that it was OK. They are bringing her bed down now and will transfer her to an ambulance and take her to a…well I don't want to talk more on an open line. If you are close, you can come by here. And don't worry about insurance shifts. I already cleared it."

"Cleared it how?"

"I pulled a little clout. I saw Silver Star was handling it, so I called them. They made a couple calls and got me a bed."

Havens heart dropped.

Oh no.

"Stop the transport, Neil. Go stop it now. Get her!"

"Why?"

"That's who is behind this!"

"Fuck!" Detective Neil sprinted towards the elevator bank. "Don't let that door close!"

Chapter 57

Detective Daniels was waiting in the car at the hospital's ambulance bay having just returned with some food for himself and Neil. As much as he would have liked to have had the monstrous Al's beef sandwiches dipped, years on the job made him think better of it. Their beefs would still be moist with sweet peppers and cheese but would not have the full immersion in the broth. A sacrifice of public service. Neil arrived shortly after, having run down the stairs and sprinted to the exit.

"Where is she?"

"I have been out here the whole time. She never came down."

"Impossible."

For the first time since the shooting, Maggie Havens' eyes opened. The nurse looked down at her and held her hand.

"Well hello, Sleeping Beauty. We've been wondering if you would wake up. Unfortunately, I am probably the last person you would like to have standing by your bedside."

The nurse pushed the trigger on the IV and Maggie closed her eyes again. Her breathing and heart rate started to slow. The nurse continued wheeling the gurney down the hall making a few more turns down the corridor. She pulled the IVs and settled her now limp patient into a wheelchair near a side exit. As instructed, the nurse wheeled the patient out to the side lot behind the maintenance area. It was an area unknown to her and was not covered by security cameras. The white Family Plumbing van sat running with the back doors open. Harrison Mann was there to receive the patient.

"Are you the man I am supposed to meet?"

"Why yes, I am."

"OK, here she is. I did everything you told me to do. Now when can you get David out of jail?"

"Oh, sweetie, I'm sorry, but I don't have that type of clout. I'm afraid I had to spin a bit of a tale."

The nurse's eyes widened in astonishment.

"But he has never been to prison. He's got to be scared. You said he was being beaten every day, but if I helped you could move him until Silver Star got him out!"

If she could be even more shocked, it would have been about the time that Harrison raised his Ruger Mark III Hunter .22 with integrated silencer and fired two soft Aguila SSS rounds into her forehead. The rounds entered narrow and exited wide ensuring the target was fixed. The nurse immediately folded to the ground.

He loaded Maggie into the back and sped off the hospital premises.

Nice van, Havens. Your kid fit in it just fine.

Chapter 58

Havens pounded on the steering wheel. As he stomped on the floorboards willing the lights to change and the traffic to part, he gave the wheel another good pounding. Rage boiled inside. Cougar gave a whimper and lifted her head but decided it was best to lie back down in the backseat.

Daniels called Sean to explain what happened while Detective Neil continued directing CPD to scour the hospital and a perimeter of five miles. More men would be put on alert once they knew what to look for.

Daniels told Havens about the dead nurse they had found. Sean immediately knew what had happened. Someone at the hospital was working for Silver Star and alerted the higher ups. They came, got Maggie, and closed the link. This was too small of a city to have a bunch of assassin killer types with military training. Harrison's reaction about Maggie and the drug toxins gave Havens the impression that he was less shocked about what was happening and more shocked that it was discovered. Havens figured if Draeger was involved then this whole nightmare was most likely for leverage against him. Maggie would only be useful if she could be held as bait and control.

But leverage against what? This is unforgivable. Draeger is a friend. If he needed me as an asset and the mission was legit and the authorities were complied with, I would have been more than fine with working a domestic project and staying closer to home. What would Draeger need me for? First things first. Maggie. If they don't need her or me then we have a really big problem. Think PACE: Primary, Alternate, Contingency, and Emergency. What are they thinking now?

A man like Harrison would think about the attack. A man like Draeger would think like an attacker and consider the defender. A hybrid intel strategist and operator like Havens would act like a red teamer and think about the attacker, the defender, and how they were each thinking of each other. He would model the system and as many permutations as he could in the time allotted. Which wasn't a lot.

Where would Harrison take Maggie, though? His crew has to be heading to the hit so he wouldn't have them with him. If he has one of the cover vehicles and knows I am on to them then I am a link to be cleaned up. He's got to be heading to the warehouse in the hood. Last stand. Shit. I'm no action hero. Man to man, Harrison will kill me. You only fight the way you practice, and I am out of practice. Out of shape and not moving too fast mentally or physically. OK, work the problem. Maybe Harrison isn't as honed either. Hospital is northwest, traffic is heavy, and if he thinks cops are on lookout, he will take side streets. He has proven to be fairly regimented so he will probably go to the one he knows best. I can get there first. Just have to confuse him a bit first.

Havens sent a text to Harrison.

"Problem here at hospital. Will be out of pocket. SH."

Need to get to Red. He could help with back up. No. That could put him in a bad spot. Have to see this through solo. My shit. My cleanup.

"Cougar, wish you could hold a gun. I'm sending you to training if we live through this so you can back me up."

Chapter 59

Harrison passed under the Dan Ryan Expressway and was nearing his turn to the warehouse when he received the text.

WTF?

"At the hospital?" *Havens must not know I have Maggie. That gives me some time.*

Instinctively, Harrison wanted to consult with Draeger, but when a man asks for autonomy, it's best not to then need the boss's help. Harrison questioned whether he made a mistake. He never liked the idea of stringing Havens along with the kid and thought it best to sever all loose ends. With the op going down, he had already changed up the plan by not being present to ensure things went according to the vision and directives he had set. He crossed his fingers that the men could handle it.

He was also tying up the second vehicle that they planned to use. It was going to be a backup and primary storage for site exploitation material, removing evidence that could tie the target to any DOSA communications.

"Shit!" Harrison realized that he had the van with all the storage cases and equipment.

Too close to the warehouse now. Fuck this. Smoke the girl. No. Smoke Havens, keep the girl 'til he is smoked in case I need a backup plan. Then kill the girl. Smoke this team and screw it all. Screw Draeger. OK. Drop the girl at the warehouse and secure her. Then drop off the van with the team.

Harrison looked at his watch. Still time.

Harrison pulled into the lot and wound around the back entrance way. The streets were calm for the most part. Hooded apparitions stood in dark entryways and about twenty feet from any street corners. They would stay in place. Question was who they could send out if they wanted to. The van bumped up and down over the worn gravel and weather-induced potholes. He exited the car and scanned the night. It was cool and quiet. No movement. No sounds.

So far so good. Need to move the van in so Havens or anyone else has to come inside to know I am here. Havens you could have at least bought a place with a garage door opener.

Harrison walked to the metal door. He unlocked the deadbolt and door handle and walked in to hit the lights.

As he reached toward the light switches, Harrison was struck by a powerful bear paw punch to the ribs. A balled fist next cannoned his abdomen. Havens shoved Harrison's shoulders to the metal door slamming his head against the hard surface. On the rebound Havens' open palms simultaneously slapped against Harrison's ears. Havens quickly turned his wrists in for a quick eye gouge with both thumbs and slammed Harrison's head into the door again. The combination effect was as disorienting and disabling as a flash bang device. Havens' left elbow swung up with full force, catching Harrison's jaw and cracking it. With his right hand and now a rejoining left he grabbed Harrison's head and brought it down forcefully to his bent knee.

Havens left nothing to chance and quickly bound Harrison's hands. Confident that Harrison was out cold on the concrete, Havens raced to the van and flung open the side door. Maggie was still unconscious. Havens quickly assessed her vitals. He had to get her back to the hospital, but first needed some answers. Second, he would release some more energy and tension on Harrison. Havens' adrenaline was piqued now and the audacity that these men would go after his daughter again would mean death to anyone responsible. Harrison would be atoning for anyone Havens couldn't immediately reach.

Chapter 60

It wasn't until the second bucket of cold water was thrown that Harrison regained consciousness. He groggily fought to gain awareness of his surroundings.

"There we are. Shit, Harrison, you were more of a pussy than I thought. Must be that Navy blood I found out you have. Do you realize you just got your ass kicked by an intel weenie? A non-government, non-military, commercial intel weenie."

Harrison's eyes blinked. He tried to mouth something but felt incredible oral pain. Havens watched Harrison's tongue probe where teeth once were.

"Yeah, you are going to be on a liquid diet for a while, buddy. Bunch of those teeth are gone. I'll make you a smoothie in a bit, but first we need to talk a little. You're lucky my little girl is OK. That really pissed me off, Harrison, really pissed me off."

Harrison, sounding like he was coming out of numbed root canal surgery, managed to get out a garbled and bloody, "Fuck you."

"Yeah. I thought that may be the case. So, here's my issue, notwithstanding my daughter. This whole domestic black op thing you have me involved in has been a shit show since the start. I have been able to have a little backstop in that my techie buddy, X, has been able to trace my calls and my whereabouts, and from your calls to me was able to pull your logs too as of about an hour ago. Now that I have your phone, and you should have at least password protected it, your call history shows some interesting locations and dates. All said and done, with proper chain of custody of this evidence, it probably would be sufficient to prosecute you."

Harrison was now able to get out a more convincing "Go to hell," but lost intimidation credibility with the enunciation of "Habens." Blood and drool continued to leak from Harrison's mouth.

"Well, I suppose we both may end up in Hell. You sooner than me at this rate. But I suspect I won't be far behind you. I have been feeling a little bit frisky these days. I think it suits me. You'll have to let me know in a bit. I see a few phone numbers in here that I recognize and that has been quite disappointing. But for kicks and giggles why don't you tell me which one of these numbers is Draeger's."

The telling motion by which Harrison looked up at Havens ended the discovery process. Havens had suspected it to be true, but this new reality left him without breath. He had wanted it not to be true. He had even saved Draeger on a couple of occasions. The guy actually owed him.

Harrison saw the look on Havens' face. Amidst the pain he was feeling, Harrison found great enjoyment in the thought that Havens was experiencing a little of the same pain, albeit of heart and soul. Harrison's broken toothed grin amidst the blood and the bruising was like a demonic vision. As Harrison started to cackle, it made Havens shiver in the way a child may fear a fanged Halloween clown. Sean grasped at his own pant leg looking for some sense of security. The discomfort and fear was not from the man before him. It came from Havens' core as he questioned his base strength to take this all in. His soul was darkening and he didn't care. As he rubbed up on his leg, he felt the other phone he had taken off Harrison. It wasn't a smart phone and only had one number in the memory.

"My guess is Draeger's number is this one. Should we try it?"

Harrison had ceased to care about anything at that point. The number wasn't Draeger's. *May as well see where this can go from here. Couldn't get much worse.* Harrison wasn't sure if Havens planned to kill him. If he got the chance, Harrison would definitely kill Havens. *Wait for the opening.*

Chapter 61

Havens looked back on the smart phone for longer, more frequent calls. They would likely be tasking and management calls. Whoever had been running this show clearly thought they were untouchable using commercial phones. Maybe that was part of the plan too. It wouldn't be out of the question to maintain multiple commercial phone lines with the disposability many telephone carriers now offered. A group seeking anonymity could actually keep things out in the open to blend in or so they could be "officially" investigated later if they wanted to leave tracks. Havens selected and dialed the number that showed on the display the greatest time durations. As the phone rang, he had a confident anger that kept the rising queasiness in his stomach at bay.

Sean Havens recognized the voice immediately when it was answered.

Draeger.

"Did you end up going after the girl yourself, Harrison? Naughty boy, dancing with a devil like Havens." Draeger exuded an air of nonchalance that accompanied the norm of messing with people's lives for a living.

"Hi, buddy. Looks like you got another phone number. Guess who I'm with?"

It took Draeger a moment to register that this was now Havens calling from Harrison's phone. The situation registered and he knew that things had gone very, very wrong. A narcissist at his core, the surprise was just as rapidly suppressed to the point that it hardly mattered to Draeger. It simply became part of the plan.

"Well, aren't you just the sneaky little fucker of the year. Congratulations."

"Thanks, Draeger, but I think you claimed that one all on your own."

"You just called me Draeger and not Pres. Is something wrong? Where do we stand with this all? I have to admit, I am at a bit of a disadvantage not knowing what you know, if you have been told truths, or if someone is setting me up. A lot of strange things have been happening and I am not sure who I can trust, Sean. Can I trust you?"

"Nice. Try to create some doubt to give me pause. Don't oversell the victim card."

"No, Sean, I wouldn't do that. We have built our careers on taking orders and understanding that there is a higher authority at work. This situation is no different. The fact that I knew you were in trouble and chose to help you out should have no bearing on the fact that I never told you I was your superior. For that, I won't apologize because I know you would have viewed it as charity. Hell, Sean, I have been your boss for well over a year now. Yemen job. Mine. Venezuela, mine. Lebanon. Guess what? Me there too. I've been looking out for you."

"Cut the act, Draeger. Harrison spilled everything about the military family murders to the killing of my own wife, notwithstanding this fucked up war you are trying to start so we can inflate defense spending with false legitimacy. I figured it out. Sorry to say I had blinders on at first, but I have been tracking it since you capped that politician in Missouri. Cemented it with the symbolic Lincoln attack. That's got you and your self-proclaimed patriot ass all over it."

"Like you are some bleeding heart liberal? We're in the same position, Sean. None of us have jobs or worth if there are no wars and no spending. This is bigger than us. I am a freakin' hero for doing this. Taking the responsibility to spill the blood of our own patriots for a greater cause? Who could bear the weight of that? Certainly not you! I sacrifice myself to uphold this nation."

Deep in the bowels of the Pentagon's benign white on white doors sat Prescott Draeger in a small darkened room. He closed his eyes as he took a breath and waited for a response from Havens.

Draeger's head was starting to pound. He squeezed his eyes tighter as if springing his eyelids open would flash this all away. The situation was a nuisance. He didn't owe anyone an explanation even though he was caught. Worse, he had betrayed the man who was capable of being his only true friend. Worse still, Havens was going to make him pay dearly.

No turning back now.

He was furious that Havens couldn't see the weakness of the U.S. and the threats that loomed the way he could. He couldn't under why people didn't get that cutting defense spending due to a weak economy only makes the nation weaker. It occurred to Draeger that he should have staged some attacks at the U.S. foreign embassies to get other nations to pony up some funds and stomach for this war of ideologies. The thought reinvigorated Draeger with new ideas for the future. This wouldn't be his end. It was his debut. He had the connections; he could fully commit to the Pond.

"Sean, I was just following orders."

"Orders? Are you shitting me? There are no orders. This is your fucked up little scheme. You are a sick little man. You needed help so you fucked me and fucked up my life!"

"Sean, I had nothing to do with that. My superiors were aware of our friendship and cut me out of your personal situation. I had no idea of what they planned to do. I was just responsible for getting you back on track and on our side. I demanded it. That is the God's honest truth. You have to believe me." *Get off my trail, Boy Scout.*

Havens listened intently. The worst part of living with a family of liars was you had to assume someone was lying but never really knew how much or when. Their world afforded little humanity and the typical physiological and psychological lying 'tells' couldn't be found in the hunter machines that they had become.

God I want to believe you, man, but in the wilderness of mirrors, it's best to shoot all of them.

What am I talking about? Draeger knew Harrison had Maggie when he answered.

"Who do you report to, Draeger?"

"It's complicated, Sean. It's not one man."

"Well uncomplicate it for me."

"Let's meet Sean. I can't do this over a mobile. You know it's not secure."

"I'm a civilian Draeger and you are going to be dead when I come for you. Either way, I don't think you will be needing references from them. Give me the names."

"Sean, please. It's a panel of leaders. Someone is running this program through a bigger one. It's a cutout snuggled into Silver Star but it goes higher and into other areas. Some of our old bosses even."

Until I can take care of Havens, I need to take care of myself and get this fucking bloodhound on the scent of someone more expendable. I still have work to do on this or the Pond will come hunting for me too.

Chapter 62

Less than a hundred miles from Draeger's cell tower, two men were summoned by the listening post's head technician who was tapped into the conversation with Havens.

"So what's the situation, boys?" the crusty old two-star asked, looking at his watch as if he had somewhere better to be than mixing with the techies.

"The phones we have been providing the teams, even the throw aways, all had their subscriber identities logged into a tracker so we could pull them up at any time. Sean Havens has been hard to locate and track since the guy pulls the SIM and battery all the time on his phones. Anyway, sir, we have been keeping an eye on Draeger's crew since they are carrying the biggest load. Unfortunately, it appears that Draeger is on the ropes. Chicago is a mess. Sounds like you were right. Having Havens as a wild card unraveled things."

"How much?"

"Enough. The program could be at risk."

"What specifically?" The old man took a sip of hot coffee while he awaited the answer. He blew the steaming brew and never lifted his eyes from his cup. "I would argue that our wild card has been Draeger and not Havens. I've worked with these boys before. Havens is no dummy. Draeger's just willing to get his hands dirtier. The question is how much of it serves a purpose and how much he just gets off on. It's like sending a porn addict in to manage a strip club."

A man with round glasses and an ostrich egg in the nest of his balding hairline made a subtle gesture slitting his throat to the old man signaling the technicians didn't have the need to know.

Pulling the old retired general to the side, the program director defended his selection of Draeger.

"Sir, Havens wasn't eligible for executive service in a government role. He is more qualified than Draeger, but he's a contractor. Draeger is govie that we have covered under another community element that sought our assistance. The program therefore is simply an understanding. We can roll it up somewhere else. Start moving the books."

"I don't give three ape shits and a monkey turd about bureaucracy. What's going on and how do we reach our damned end state. I won't have you blemish my career cause these two bunk buddies aren't willing to work together to see this through. Am I clear?"

"Sir, Havens knows Draeger was responsible for the local operations, the Havens family, and the target cover-ups."

"Well, that's your mess. Not mine. And what about Silver Star? We put a shitload of resources into that puppy."

The balding man looked around the room, trying to be as discrete as possible. There was so much that should have been left unsaid already. "Havens appears to be aware that some superiors here in NCR have interests in preserving our security by these rather unconventional means."

"I see. And did Draeger mention anyone in particular?"

"No, but seems like that is the route he is going."

"Well, fortunately, Draeger only knows of you by name and he has a few other regions that are hopefully in more control." The old man blew his coffee again before slurping another sip.

"Yes, sir. That is true. But he knows of us all."

"No, he knows you and assumes he knows us all, correct?" The old man raised his watch again and looked around uncomfortably.

"Correct, sir. He knows of the greater us…in theory. But remember we are DoD. He is now more intel. I don't know where his loyalties lie."

"I don't see loyalty mattering if he knows to do his job and keep his yap shut." The old man raised an eyebrow signifying he was done and that nothing more needed to be said. He finalized his comments, "Well then, I think you best deal with your problem straight away and I entrust you to keep the shop in order. I trust the other aspects of our program are going forward as planned?"

"Yes, sir. They should be hitting the news by tomorrow evening at the latest."

"Hooah! Now I suppose you will be sending a team or someone for Mr. Draeger?"

"I will handle it, sir."

"Yes, you will, Conrad."

"And Conrad," the old man floated his hands towards the technicians, "I suggest you find a way with your cyber guys over here to get this phone call to end immediately. Just a thought. I'm sure you had already thought about that but out of respect to me you did not wish to interrupt. Keep me posted. I have dinner plans with our organization this evening. You've already made me late for another meeting."

"Yes, sir. Sorry, sir."

"And why are these shitheads on open lines?"

"We had a problem procuring the secure ones through a required GSA contract."

"We had all the cash we could spend."

"The contractor insisted so they wouldn't fall out of procurement favor. They said invoices were already running at 120 a day payables and they didn't want to put money up front since it was too hard these days to get add on dollars without jumping through hoops."

"Fine. Just cut that damn line." The old man poured his coffee in a nearby trashcan and stormed out of the control room.

Conrad, a former Air Force one-star general, tapped one of the technicians on the back. "I need you to cut that conversation off now and make sure it does not reconnect."

"Roger that, sir. On it."

"Oh, and tell Passport to clean up his own mess with the wife he's wanted kept on life support. I'm not paying for that insurance policy after we shut this down. Too many loose ends."

Chapter 63

From the warehouse floor, Harrison was able to anticipate what Draeger was saying on the other end. He was saving himself. *Why does that not surprise me?*

"Draeger, you have some service related stress issues and I should have been there for you. I will not forgive myself for that. You, on the other hand, also tried to kill my family and did kill my wife. For that, I will never forgive you. But in this whole mess, you are my brother and you served your country alongside me. That would have gone further if you had served honorably though. Maybe part of that came from your prior service. God knows we have seen shit that today's men should not bear witness to. Or maybe you were always a narcissistic asshole with sociopathic tendencies. I am not here to judge. I am here to solve the problem."

Harrison rolled his eyes. *This Havens is a piece of work. What an idiot.* Harrison worked his bindings.

"What are you getting at Sean? You are going to help me after all of this?"

"I already have. Good bye, Prescott."

Wait for it...

"Wait, Sean! What do you mean you have? What the fuck are you talking about?"

Harrison became more attentive again, thinking he may have underestimated the man.

"You'll see. It's in your home. In your safe room to be exact. There you will find a geo location on a red piece of paper placed on the underside of one of your items in the house. It will lead you to one of your personal items stuffed in the mouth of a dead Harrison here in Chicago. After that, you need to get some help for yourself. Call me when you find it."

"How the fuck were you in my home, Sean? How do you know about my room? No one even knows where I live, you fuck! I've got remote sensor motion activated IR cams, alarms, UV powder…No one can get in!"

"Fuck!" Draeger exclaimed again. The line had cut out and a disconnected message displayed on his phone. Draeger knew he was screwed now.

Havens has been in my house. But how? When could he have flown out? Did he have someone else do it? Shit. In my safe room? How did he breach my security?

When Havens' call ended, he assumed Draeger had hung up of his own accord to hurry home. Havens turned to Harrison.

"Why so perplexed, Harrison?"

Harrison remained still.

Havens circled around his captive and grabbed a three-foot length of pipe. Harrison cringed in anticipation of another beat down or worse. Havens had changed since the first time they met. They had killed his wife and taken his heart. It was supposed to break him, but Harrison knew now that Havens was only simmering. The daughter being alive wasn't enough. Havens was capable of doing anything now. Not to follow orders, but because it drove him to fill the emptiness and the guilt.

"This? The pipe? Remember *A Few Good Men*? Tom Cruise liked to think with a bat. I'm just thinking. No worries, Harrison. See, Draeger's on his way home. As we speak. As I speak. You don't need to speak. I really have no idea where he lives."

Harrison struggled.

"Harrison, don't make ligature marks on your hands or I will be forced to cut your arms off at the elbows to hide my tracks. I plan to let you go. I only have you bound so you can't kill me. Me being a donut-eating intel guy and all and you being a badass snake eater."

Relief passed over Harrison's face. Maybe he would live through this after all.

"Draeger is going to hop in his car where I had my buddy X put a tracer. I knew he would find it but not before I tracked it to HQ. I also had X put some secret sauce in his coffee. You see, he always leaves coffee in his car. Draeger drinks half on the way to work hot and the other half cold on his way home. It'll kill him in a couple hours, but not before he tears apart his own place. I wish I could see him smashing stuff and panicking. He'll go into cardiac arrest after he tries to call me a half a million times. In the end it will look like someone tossed his place. Worst case it will look like he went berserk. No, I have no intentions of answering his call. That just enables a guy like Draeger. I'd like him to die without an audience. And since no one knows where he lives no one will come looking for him. That gives me plenty of time for the toxins to dissipate. Not that it matters to me because the number on the cell phone he is using is your number. It doesn't make a difference that they are throw aways. The idea is you need to throw them away more often, Harrison. But I'll make sure your phone stays with you."

Havens smiled at Harrison. Harrison returned his gaze with wild eyes.

"So now you wonder why I am going to let you go. Frankly, I don't dispose of bodies. Too much risk. And why am I telling you this? It's not for you. I am grieving still and opening up more. I'm getting in touch with my feelings, Harrison. Even got a dog."

Shit. My dog is still in the car down the street. Not that anyone would steal it. Dog or car with dog in it. Need to get Maggie back soon too.

Havens was now behind Harrison and cut the flexicuffs off. "Don't move, Harrison. I am going to back away and exit stage left with Maggie. You will wait for a bit to let me go. I know you want to distance yourself from all of this too. Go ahead and rub off or shake out your wrists." *Let your mind think you are going to be safe. Resist the urge to escape.*

As Harrison brought his arms forward in a stretch, Havens swung the pipe at Harrison's head aiming for the upper brain stem. Havens had expected to hear the sickening sound of solid impact before Harrison collapsed forward but realized Harrison had moved slightly in an attempt to execute a last ditch offensive. The strike was only enough to knock him out.

Harrison, you are a bit of a sneaky one as well. I was all for letting you go Chicago style with another beat down with your wrists free...

While Havens took no pleasure in post-consciousness brutality, he finished the story by swinging at Harrison's elbows, ribs, and knees. His mind blended pent up vengeance with a crime scene course of action that would solve a problem, create effect, and mitigate additional risk to Havens. It was business—mixed with pleasure.

Twenty minutes later he had completed the staging in the warehouse. He would soon light some papers and toss them onto the car seats of the small fleet they used for recce. Only one small truck was missing from this location. The other site may look like a chop shop or drug distribution center. No worries. He doused a bit of accelerant to spread the plan. Once each of the vehicles was lit, Havens would depart the scene. If the kill crew came back, the place would be locked and blazing inside. Not his problem what they did at that point. Even though Harrison had paid Havens through the shell company accounts, Havens had ensured that he used Harrison's name for new accounts. Call it a gut feeling, but he wanted to make sure he had an insurance policy and someone to take the fall if this Silver Star was shining him on.

He looked at Harrison lying lifeless and walked over upon hearing some weak moans. Leary that his victim might wake from the dead and make a grab for his foot, Havens stood at Harrison's feet out of reach.

You piece of shit.

Sean thought of Maggie and his wife. Harrison's death would not make things right. It wouldn't bring them back. It was just part of the solution to a problem.

Harrison was broken now. A bad soldier. Dead he would regain honor. They would be able to check his prints and give him a full honor guard burial. Would he have requested Arlington National Cemetery?

As he regarded Harrison wondering what to do, Havens thought of something his own father said about combatives. "When you are fighting hand to hand, you can grab a guy's ear and rip it right off. Then step on it so it makes the guy feel bad." Havens had just smiled at the time, not sure whether to believe it or not. Had he made Harrison feel bad enough? He didn't think so. Havens reared his foot back and drove it straight into Harrison's groin. He was certain that wherever Harrison was in near death consciousness, he'd feel that. The air escaping Harrison sounded enough like a grunt for Havens to savor the moment that much more.

Suddenly laughter began to well inside of him. For the first time in months, Havens started to really laugh. He thought of the tree brush chipper in the back lot that came with the building and could hardly contain himself. That would get rid of fingerprints. Harrison couldn't have a funeral if there was no Harrison. Havens knew it was dangerous to deviate from a plan. But it was more dangerous to test a man who had practically lost everything. He sensed that he was losing self-control. It felt good.

Oh, what the hell. Things haven't been exactly according to plan this past year anyway.

Havens opened the large service door and sprayed a quick Latino tag on the outside. It was a cliché set up, but it's always easier for the public to dismiss acts of violence as gang related. He headed towards the back lot to get the industrial tree chipper that was left over from the lot purchase along with some other landscape equipment. Having gassed up all the equipment for potential resale to self-fund further operations, Havens now had an ideal disposal solution. He would need to hurry as he'd already spent too much time at the warehouse. Havens recognized that his time spent with Draeger and Mann was putting his daughter's safety at risk, but rational thought was long gone.

Chapter 64

"Hey, ese, whatchu doin' in there, man?"

Caught up in the events with Harrison, Havens neglected to consider the danger of the surrounding environment that made this site so perfect for his activity. Clearly, there were others in the area who also found the location to be perfect for crime away from the prying eyes of the law and nosy neighbors. He had wasted too much time letting his ego and revenge drive his negligent actions.

Havens sized up the situation for a moment before being struck from behind. Searing pain exuded from his lower back as he collapsed to the ground on all fours. He had counted three hooded individuals in front of him yet missed the consideration of another from behind. Mexican gangbangers. *Cholos.*

Before another blow could come, Havens spoke.

"Wait! I need your help. I'm new to this area and knew I needed to pay some respect. I'm looking for a crew that may want in on some action."

The Latino who spoke earlier stepped up to Havens. He appeared to be motioning to the man behind to wait for a second.

"Whatchu mean action, man?"

"Well, my crew is no longer useful to me and I am looking to hire some guys looking to make some large cash. Fast."

"Keep talking, man."

"Actually, I need to keep moving. I have a dead cop in the warehouse. Need to chop him up and get rid of the body."

The men each stepped back a pace at the mention of police.

"There's cops in there, man? Dead?"

"Why you bringing 5-0 in our hood, ese? Man that's just wrong, man. You gonna do somethin' bout that man now."

"I know. I'm trying to get him out of here so no one comes around."

"Whatchu do, man? Got drugs? You talk too Harvard for drugs, man."

"Drugs? No. I deal with paper."

"Yeah, all books and shit, professor. What kind of paper, man?"

Havens saw the guy was reaching for something under his sweatshirt, likely a pistol in the waistband.

"Money!"

The third man spoke up. "We like money. Whatchu need help with for money except giving it to us, pinche."

"I need help circulating it. You probably have guys in your organization that need help moving their stuff too. How would you like to pay for your stuff with fake cash? I'll sell it 10% on the bundle."

Havens hoped they knew nothing about counterfeit money as he had no clue what going rates were and just wanted to buy time.

"Let's see it, man."

Havens turned around to see the man behind him was likely no more than seventeen.

"Someone help me up?"

Haven extended his hand towards the hood who had been reaching towards a gun in his waistband. He knew that as the man leaned forward the weighted handle of the grip would slip back some and raise the barrel. It would be a third out of the waistband.

As the hood automatically reached for Havens' extended hand, he clasped the wrist pulling up while simultaneously pulling the man off balance and taking another hand to find what Sean hoped what was a gun under the sweater.

Bingo! Coming right out to papa. Not as heavy as it should be if it's fully loaded. Hope I have enough.

Pouncing up, Havens shot the leader in the forehead then swung the weapon around and fired at the second man's temple. As the third reared back to swing the metal bar at Havens he was shot in the chest. The man who had landed on the ground was now devoid of a weapon and equally devoid of hope and pleaded for his life.

"Get up and get inside. Pick up that bat."

"Man, I don't want to fight you. Just lemme go."

"Grab the bat or I *will* kill you."

The hood picked up the bat and upon entering the warehouse looked down at Harrison who was moaning and gaining some lucidity. "Man, is that really a cop?"

"No. Sorry, I lied." Havens shot the youth in the stomach twice. The slide remained back. Empty.

The perfect end to the story. Thank you, boys.

Killing the young men left no emotional scarring on Havens. To him, they were killers. Indeed he had chosen the location based on local gang and crime surveys. He knew that if they were not yet killers they soon would be. There was no hope for them in this area. He felt bad that the community was such a death trap and personally believed in social programs for improvements. They were just surrogates in this battle. Gang members who would have easily killed Havens if they'd had the chance. As a citizen, he wished there was change. As an operator, they were adversaries in his area of operation. Now he had taggers to match the sprayed tags. *Preparedness meeting opportunity wins again.*

Havens ran back out of the building to get the chipper. A few thousand pounds pulls easier with wheels on asphalt. The gravel was going to be murder. His lower back was badly bruised from the assault, but he had to wrap things up quickly. Havens unhitched the chipper and rolled it into the small warehouse with all his might. He started up the roaring Cummins diesel engine.

Havens read the warning above the chute, "105 fpm. Keep all hands and arms away from opening."

A now groggy, broken Harrison was close to going into shock. Havens looked across to him.

"Harrison, good news! This does a hundred and five feet per minute, if that's what this means. Since you only have two feet, this should be over soon!"

Havens smiled as Harrison regarded him with a new found horror.

"Harrison," Havens continued to shout over the roar. "That was funny! Why aren't you laughing? Two feet…aw, never mind. You're not going to laugh. You're no fun."

Havens could see Harrison was trying to say something and shut down the engine.

"Huh? I can't hear you. Your fate is too loud. Say again?"

Harrison was defeated. He wanted to say a big fuck you to Havens but knew that would seal his fate.

"There's more I can tell you," he gasped.

"Do tell, Harrison. Time waits for no man and I am just about out."

"He's doing it through planes and trains I think." Harrison's eyes rolled back. Havens bent down to slap him awake. The hood's blood was closing in on Harrison's head in an expanding slow dark tide. Havens watched it, mesmerized. He visualized Christina in a pool of blood.

"I figured," he said, snapping back to the task at hand. "But sorry, I have no intention of saving you to go find a needle in the haystack of some train or plane on schedule somewhere in the U.S. That's someone else's job."

"Chicago. Soon. Other places too."

"Shit. You had to say Chicago. Where?"

"Don't know. The phone."

"Your other phone?"

Harrison closed his eyes and tried to nod.

"It will call the team. Call it when they pull in. Identify yourself on the phone before they get to you face to face. They can stop it." Harrison knew he would not be saved from the shock and decided that if he could succumb to it, all the better. He tried to let himself go.

"Harrison! Where are the other spots?"

Fuck. He's out. Question is, would he know or would Draeger have told him? Draeger would want to be here if it was something like that. If Draeger is dead then he can't tell me. Shit! OK, clean up this mess and get your pound of flesh, Havens, then move on.

Havens started up the chipper again and saw Harrison's eyebrow rise at the sound.

C'mon, Harrison. Open your eyes. You playin' possum?

Harrison couldn't resist the fear of the roaring machine. He had seen tree trunks chipped away in seconds. He opened his burning eyes wide to see what Havens was doing. Havens was crouching right over his head almost nose to nose.

"Hi, buddy! You up? You awake, my brother?"

Havens smiled down on Harrison. This time the demonic look came from Havens.

"Chipper time. Or do you have more for me? Up to you. I got what I came for."

Harrison licked his lips.

"Your…brother…big guy they are too."

Havens wasn't a killer. He was bluffing. Harrison continued to convince himself of this.

"OK, Harrison, thanks. I know all about Lars. Sorry, but I have to get rid of you. Never wanted to be a cleanup guy, but in light of what you have done to my family, seems only fitting. Now that I am in a rush though, I'll have to reflect on the moment instead of enjoying it now."

The convincing was not working. Harrison struggled but his broken and damaged limbs would not respond. Havens hefted his limp ragdoll body up and Harrison screamed in both excruciating pain and protest.

"Last chance."

"Fuck you!"

"Well fuck you too, Harrison. It's been a peach. I figure this will either cause me years of therapy or save me from a lot of therapy. Anyone's guess. Probably save you some too. And since you killed all the guys I would like to have killed, this will make me feel like I am killing you with a thousand cuts. I just wish it could last longer. Anywho. Ta ta. Ah, let's go toes first so we can both see this for the best view. Give you a good seat. Box seat right in front."

Havens looked over at the van to ensure his daughter, by some miracle, had not woken up and gotten out to see what her father was about to do. No daughter.

Swinging the body up into the chute, Havens slumped enough of Harrison into the opening for the grinding jaws to catch enough foot to start pulling him in. As Havens grabbed the second leg that was about to get hung up on the safety guard he noticed Harrison's billfold was starting to come out of the pocket as its owner thrashed about like a fish out of water. Havens did a quick grab and caught a piece of paper that was walking out too. Havens jerked his hand back just in time to avoid the roaring monster of metal that was now spitting Harrison Mann out on the warehouse floor like a snow thrower of dark multi-textured slush.

"Nice screams, Harrison. Is this how my wife and kid screamed? Were you even there? Man has a guy's daughter raped, emotionally scarred, shot, kills the guy's wife, kidnaps the helpless daughter. Fuck, man. I can't kill you enough times. This is just going to have to do."

Havens tripped the safety switch to give the moment a lasting picture in both their minds. The machine had Harrison up to the abdomen. Harrison had a blank stare. Blood frothed from his mouth.

"I'd love to take a picture of this for Draeger, but I know that sick fuck would just be entertained. Poor decision cost you your life. And mine. How do you feel knowing that you were just a pawn too? Another disposable soldier. Should have asked me. Draeger is about as dirty as they get. I always chalked it up to the business. Not really even sure why I considered him my friend, huh? Thanks Harrison, you are a great therapist. Very thought provoking."

Havens lifted the guard back in place and the rolling jaws went back to work, spun effortlessly by the belts and wheels. The raised metal gnawed its prey. Havens turned away as the rest of Harrison was consumed by the machine. The loud roar drowned out any sounds of flesh ripping and bone crunching as the gears and wheels became lubricated with Harrison's passing life.

As Havens stood beside the humming machine, he realized vengeance wasn't so sweet after all. Although he had brought the man responsible for his wife's murder to justice, it was a feeble sense of accomplishment. It couldn't bring his wife back and his daughter still needed a lot of care. It didn't reverse time. It actually took more away. Havens felt not remorseful, but ashamed. His wife would not have approved.

Sorry, babe, not feeling quite like myself these days. Man's gotta do what a man's gotta do. I just don't know what I can do to make it right. I suppose nothing. I miss you.

He blinked and filled his lungs with a deep breath.

Speaking of which, I'm going to need to mix this DNA to buy some more time.

Havens looked at the bodies of the gangsters.

Sorry, guys. Two of you boys are going to have a really bad day.

Babe, if you are looking down on me, you're really not going to like this either.

Chapter 65

Havens finished the last bit of staging and started dialing the number on Harrison's other phone. Before hitting send he looked at his watch.

21:45. Team should be coming back. I missed it. Shit. Oh well. Not my fault. Someone up high wanted it done. Not my business. But that kid…Shit, my kid. What was I thinking? Need to get Maggie out of the van and down to the car. Hope that's the last of the neighbors.

Havens pulled Maggie from the van, relieved that she would never be aware of the macabre death scene that had surrounded her. As he held her in his arms and looked about the room it seemed surreal even to him. This was done with his hands. The same hands that held his helpless child. Once Maggie was outside, he'd light up the place. As he exited the building, the van of the hit team was just pulling around. He knew they would be armed and held up a waving hand.

He was met in the face by a Glock 9mm out the window of the driver's side.

"Harrison is inside. He wants you guys to pull the van in and will debrief you. There's a mess inside from the project he put me on, so hold your noses."

"Who are you, man?"

"You can put that away. I'm just one of the crew. 'Nother team. I don't ask. You know the drill."

"Fuckin'A. That chick dead too?" He asked, nodding towards Maggie. Others in the van started peeking out the front, craning their necks for a look. Havens knew it wasn't to see a dead body, but instead to see if "the chick" was cute.

"Harrison doesn't want much living."

The man nodded to Havens in understanding and started to pull in. Havens shouted ahead to the still open driver side window.

"Um, there are a couple guys left on the ground in there. As long as you are in there, how about you start up the hopper and take care of them too."

Need more time. Sorry, Maggie, we have about four minutes tops to get to our car.

Havens rounded the building and saw the streets were still clear. He shifted to a light jog. As he rounded a corner, he saw some silhouettes had gathered by his car. There was some sort of commotion. He assumed he would hear Cougar barking but heard nothing.

Damn. Best not be messing with my dog now. No more trouble tonight. That hit crew is also going to come looking for me in a minute when they don't find Harrison and they smell the accelerants on the place. Maybe I can buy a minute or two and say I am Harrison pulling around the corner in another vehicle.

Havens reached into his pocket and hit Send to dial the number.

The warehouse a block over erupted with a fantastic explosion.

Holy shit, Harrison. Was that for me?

The group of young men eyeing the car focused on the fireworks display flaring into the sky from down the street. They started walking towards Havens or the lights.

"Excuse me guys, this girl is hurt. I have to get her to a hospital."

Havens handed the detonating signal phone to one of the young men. Please, dial 9-1-1. There are a number of people dead in there and some valuable electronics outside in the delivery trucks. I can't let them catch on fire."

"Yeah, man. Get going to the hospital. We'll call the cops alright. S'all good, man."

"Yeah, we'll take care of things real good."

The kids looked back at the car.

"Say, man, that your dog?"

Someone was in the driver's seat of the car. Havens got closer to make out the silhouette behind the wheel. He saw broken glass on the street from the driver's side door. As he neared a voice cried out.

"Help, man. Get this dog off me."

For the second time that night, Havens had a good laugh. Cougar had her jaws around the teen's entire head from the backseat. She was giving a low growl, her incisors pressing firmly on the boy's skin.

Good thing I taught her to play fetch with a big soccer ball. She hasn't popped too many of them.

"Release, Cougar!"

Obediently the dog released the boy's now saliva-soaked head.

"Get the fuck out, kid. Go join your friends."

Havens got Maggie into the passenger seat and feigned thanks with a cursory wave to the young hoods standing around, now torn between seeing what they could liberate from the fire and what their buddy was going to say now that he was safely out of the car.

Havens reached back and patted Cougar on the head.

"Meet your sister, pup. Sorry I'm late. We still have work to do."

As Havens drove past the blaze, he was pleased with the outcome. His staging would be that much better now. What was left of it, thanks to Harrison. But he was especially pleased that the funding accounts, transactions for cash washing, and ownership on record that Havens set up were attributed to a now dead Harrison Mann.

X had been able to trace the funds to the origin from which Harrison had paid Havens. The account had over six hundred thousand dollars in it. X could find no legitimate ownership as it was tied to a series of offshore accounts and international companies intermingled with a law firm or two. Classic clandestine funding scheme. Havens sent an electronic signal to X. X was to then obfuscate the disappearance of those funds to an account that could not be traced for quite some time. The funds were to be used as needed by the two men "for the good of the cause." Both agreed that it was tax payer money and should not be used personally, but they would divide it in a way so both could use it as their own operational kitty. Neither man had plans for early retirement.

Chapter 66

As Sean made his way to the new hospital where Detectives Neil and Daniels would be waiting, he called Red. He would need some help but this was someone else's watch now. Once Maggie was settled into a room secured under a false name, Sean, Red, and the detectives met in the hospital's empty coffee room.

"Guys, I know you realize something has been going on around here. I am not fully aware of everything or everyone involved. I no longer know what is real or what isn't. Frankly, I think we need to leave some of it alone. What I need your help on is this. Something is going to go down in Chicago and perhaps other parts of the U.S. It will likely be orchestrated by surrogates who are supporting their own cause, but may have been manipulated to do the acts. Their resolve will be true and they will have been supported and enabled to carry out their deed. All I know is it will likely involve a mode of civilian transportation. Train or air. Probably both modes in some simultaneous manner."

"Like another hijacking?"

"I don't think so. Something I heard leads me to believe it could be done through cyber or RF helicopters—homemade suicide UAVs."

"Sean, can you elaborate? That's a pretty big space."

"Maybe you should call in Lars Bjorklund for questioning. I think he is at a crime scene now. That's all I can say."

Daniels looked at Detective Neil.

"I don't even know where to start."

Neil concurred, "Right. Sean, if it could be anyone manipulated to do a deed, witting or unwitting, there is no way we can look for suspects or figure out an attack time. It's futile."

Sean nodded in agreement. This was a rather daunting task. He rapped his fingers on the table in thought.

"We know this. For a terror attack on aircraft using UAVs, we have Midway or O'Hare airport. My guess is O'Hare is too far removed from most access with the exception of the Hilton hotel right near the terminals. Window access is limited so the rooftop is the best option. That means it has to be a witting player."

"I'm following you. So how about Midway?"

Neil was starting to think along the same thought pattern. Daniels still looked puzzled.

"Dude, you look lost. You write this down, I'll do the thinking with Havens," said Neil. "Red, what do you think?"

Red, who was busy texting didn't look up to answer. "Guys, this is a Bureau thing. Sean you should just stay with your daughter. I'll put out an alert through FBI. You guys and CPD should wait for our assist."

Neil wasn't willing to let it go. "Havens, what about Midway?"

"Right. Midway, as you know, has parking garages closer to the terminals than O'Hare, and it has all those apartment buildings under the landing flight path. If I were doing anything, I'd do it there. Rail, no clue."

"We need a profile."

Havens looked at the men. "Us. Me, Red, Neil. Soldiers. Narrow it…Me. Someone who was a soldier who just experienced a tragedy. Can you run a profile like that? News headlines of all slaughters, domestic, that didn't have the husband home. Pull all of those and find whereabouts. Canvas the apartments at Midway for the same. Residents and recent renters. Railroad the same. Any military veteran workers who would have access. That has to be our first stage profile."

Red still typed away on his mobile device. "And time or day? How do we figure that? Too many variables, Sean."

Daniels stopped writing and nodded with Red's statement. "Red's right. From what I can tell, we don't know if it's tomorrow or next week or next month."

"Sure we do. Just thought of it. I have a license plate for a rental car. Find out when it is going to be turned in. Also check airlines. Look for a reservation under Harrison Mann."

Red looked up at Havens but didn't say a word.

Chapter 67

Sean remained at the private hospital continuing the bedside vigil while nurses hooked up IVs to balance Maggie's lost fluids and toxins. The detectives and Red had left to spread the word and dig up whatever intel they could on potential suspects. Red called shortly later to inform Havens that raising the FBI terror alert required him to fly out to Washington right away. Sean was again left to his thoughts of Christina, his guilt for the price his family had paid, and the rage against those who brought it to his doorstep.

With nothing to do but sit and wait, father shifted back to operator. Havens called Daniels periodically with more thoughts about the Middle Easterner's store. Daniels dutifully took down Havens' comments and called back once they had some additional insights.

"Sean, FBI took over jurisdiction, apparently at the request of Red. I did get some insight from one of our officers who's banging one of the on-scene Agents. She relayed to our guy that there were schematics found in the murdered guy's store. As the Assistant Special Agent in Charge, Red personally oversaw that his agency confiscated all materials due to the national threat. The man in the store appeared to have been beaten and robbed for small electronics but based on evidence retrieved, he had what looked to be terror ties and plans for unmanned aircraft to fly into the engines of passenger jets preparing to land or take off. Sean, that follows your hunch and narrows our target."

"Anything else?"

"Yeah, plenty. Other plans the officers found indicated the store owner's electrical engineering skills were used to enable some communications instructing how to breach the rail community."

"I am guessing we don't know who the owner was communicating with? Any forensic techs working on it?"

"No. Right now the powers that be are giving media interviews hyping up how it was so fortuitous…I know, big word, I'm reading a release here…that such a random act of violence could uncover a plot and trove of information pointing to nefarious networks of terrorist cells hidden within America."

"Idiots."

"Get this. I also learned the terrorist's son, who is a naval serviceman, was also called in for questioning. He's in transport from wherever he is stationed. They think he is a plant in the military to obtain classified technical information."

"Poor kid. He's getting set up."

"No doubt. What do we do now, Havens? If I don't task myself with something, I could get roped in to something else here at the station."

"I understand. Any specific targets for the trains?"

"Seems like a few of the majors. One on the East Coast I can't remember the name of. I don't see it on any of the notes here. Seemed like the East Coast one was the foundation of operations for the others."

"Acela?"

"Yeah! You know it?"

Havens chewed his lip and wiped his face with his hand although he was not sweating. "Daniels, you need to find out some info on the plane or car rental dates for Harrison Mann. If they do the Acela, it will be a real disaster."

"Sure, I'll check back on Mann. What's so bad about Acela?"

"I fucking planned it! My name is on files of planning it. It was a red team exercise I did showing where the threats and vulnerabilities were. It's my play book."

"It could implicate you given all the other shit going on."

"Damn. I've gotta fix this. I brought this on."

"Sean, it's not your fault."

"It's my world. It's my people. These two worlds were not supposed to meet."

"What can we do about Acela?"

"We need to get to Red. I don't know if he's going to be checking messages. Do you have any clout with someone on the East Coast?"

"I can check out CPD liaison. We have Feds in all the time."

"Perfect. Here's how Acela will go down. Even if security is heightened, it could be too late to assess any computer system breaches. Part of the issue is going to be that the Department of Homeland Security, the FBI, and the Department of Defense won't come to an agreement on how to coordinate or respond to civil support for a cyber-incident. We have to go direct to the railroad."

"OK, what else you need? I'm not sure I know what to tell them."

"If the bad actors did this right, all systems will show normal on the monitoring grid. The trains will have been targeted by a cyber-attack against a combination of SCADA industrial railway control systems and communication protocols to fault the logic controllers and altering it to create train derailments, system shutdowns, switching, and traffic light intersection disruption. This is true of Metra lines here in Chicago too."

"OK, hang on, I'm writing this down. Say that again."

"Here's what you need to know. The Acela has three core vulnerabilities that can be exploited: speed, curves, and structural weaknesses, all of which can be open to a hardware hack to throw off the yaw damper assemblies and continue the propulsion blocks while sending a false signal to the hydraulic system that normally receives a sensor signal to tile the cars on turns."

"Dude, seriously. Slow down."

"Write faster. You don't have much time if this is going live. I think we only have a couple days at best. Wait. Today is Wednesday. They are not going to do it Friday since people leave work early or telecommute. The weekend won't have many passengers. Monday is the best day, but it's too far out."

"Shit, you think it's tomorrow?"

"I think so. Not only is Monday too far out, but a lot of people don't go in as early on Monday as they do mid-week. More commuters pack in mid-week. Yeah, you need to tell the liaison all this stuff and put a speed cap on the trains for the next week if we are wrong. The tangos are planning a route stretch where the train reaches a speed of 135 mph between New York and Washington. That is what I selected due to the likely target passengers and the combination of speed and a key turn on the tracks that is risky due to surrounding terrain and civilian housing. What the train IT folks need to do is block anything that will trip the system so the speed is locked. In my report we wanted to ensure that the gyroscope sensors were tricked so they failed to adjust lateral force through the hydraulic system."

"Holy shit, Sean."

"Holy shit is right. If we can't get to Amtrak we can expect over two hundred fatalities and at least three hundred people seriously injured if the train derails near top speed."

"How about Chicago? We don't have turns like that."

"In Chicago the Metra rail line could experience something similar, but if they are following this attack pattern, signals can be switched electronically to collide with another express train. I'd say easily one hundred and fifty passengers could be killed. The Middle Easterner and his so-called elusive but fictitious network will get fingered for the terror act. That will start up more domestic security programs and funding releases. You guys will be busy chasing false flags. A lot of innocent people will be blamed. Minorities. That will cause finger pointing and domestic rifts."

"Dude, this is major conspiracy shit."

"Just business as usual. Let me know when the appropriate people have been contacted."

Havens stared at his daughter. He wanted to be in the field. He felt helpless here knowing his skills were needed, but he had resolved that he would not go anywhere. His daughter needed him here. It was time now to be both parents.

Sean found the television remote control and settled into a bedside chair and started flipping channels. The show *Diners, Dives, and Drive-ins* stopped his surfing. As a foodie, Havens knew this would be a good distraction. His phone rang within minutes. Sean recognized Detective Daniels' number.

"Hey, detective, what's up?"

"Sean, I think you may have something, but I'm not sure what you want us to do. I can task some officers, but Detective Neil just called and said you are right about tomorrow. There's also some shit on the news right now that leads me to believe it may have started."

"What's going on?"

"Not sure. It's unfolding now. Turn on any station. There is an attack in Minneapolis."

"Somalis?"

"Yeah, how did you know?"

Sean changed channels until he found coverage of breaking news at Minneapolis–Saint Paul International Airport. According to the news report, Somali gunmen had breached a runway access gate. The event must have occurred over an hour ago and the channel had obtained a video clip from an airport security camera feed. It showed a small non-descript rental truck smashing a back gate, driving towards the terminal then stopping abruptly. When police surrounded the truck, bewildered looking Somali armed terrorists were shown looking around the area and at one another in disbelief. Moments later the van exploded. According to the reporter, authorities believe the vehicle was remotely detonated by a terrorist still at large. Praise was being given to the airport police who had recently received a grant from Silver Star for special tactical training when their funds were cut in defense budget reductions.

Silver Star. You didn't have a proxy for this so you staged some unwitting locals. Clever. You showed the threat graphically but didn't kill innocent civilians. The van stopped long enough to be engaged by forces and captured on camera. That kept the focus on the terrorists and the threat, but didn't cloud the message with victims. News tonight will give a chance for commentary and tomorrow you will show how the interviews were spot on. Classic psy ops. Whoever is behind this will now get a congressional subcommittee to push for more domestic terror funding appropriations in the coming days. No doubt, the votes will be unanimous.

"Havens you have it on yet?"

"Yeah, Daniels. I'm watching it now. Unbelievable. It's just like you said. It's going down now. No one will get hurt until tomorrow. Tomorrow could be a shit storm. What info did you dig up?"

"I take it you have the inside lane on this one too, huh?"

"Unfortunately, I do."

"Well, what I learned is also unbelievable. Across the country, there have been dozens of situations like yours over the past few years. I don't want to jinx you, but most of these guys end up dead about a year after their families are killed in a robbery, mass murder, or accident."

"Not too surprising."

"Good news is I have four potential suspects left. No one is from Chicago, except for you. There is a guy in New York, a guy in DC, and one that is missing."

"Missing how?"

"Well, these other guys have proverbial radar pings in their areas. Traffic violations, credit card usage, bank accounts. Seems like they tried to go under the radar, but just had to hold on to a little something, which is what is popping up on our databases. I think we can put someone on these guys right away once we determine jurisdiction."

"Daniels, fuck jurisdiction. Get someone to put kiddie porn on their computers, call and threaten the president from their cell phone, pull a damn fire alarm in their apartment or whatever. Smoke them out and whack 'em!"

"Sean, c'mon. Really. I'll see what I can do. What about the missing man?"

"He probably has better tradecraft than the others. What's his name?"

"Roger Joyce. Family killed in a car accident while he was deployed. Just over a year ago. Meets the profile."

"Rusty. Shit. Fucking traitor." *No worse than me I guess.*

"Who's Rusty? Oh, like a nickname? You know this guy, Roger Joyce?"

"I thought I was getting to know him better. Figures. And you have no info on him?"

"Nope. Was in Bragg and DC area, but the guy has bugged out for the last nine months."

"Do a LexisNexis search on the Diligence database. You guys have access to that?"

"Sure. I'm at my desk now. I can pull it up. What am I looking for?"

"See if there are any known relationships. Should come up family. Look for anyone in Chicago area."

"Hang on. Let me get his name in here and last cities... Bingo! Damn. He has family in Cicero. Nope. Parents dead. Property was sold in 2009. Asian family owns it now according to the record."

"Call the Palmer House Hotel. See if he stayed there. If they don't have his name, print out a copy of his driver's license. Show the picture to the front desk, doorman, bar tender, anyone. He's a big ass red head. He was our counterintelligence guy and probably covered his tracks. Anything else?"

"Nope. I'll get on this. Why the Palmer House?"

"Seems like that's where my friends stay. Daniels, this is the real deal. I need you to do me a favor."

"What's that?"

"If you find that Roger Joyce is at the hotel, send Neil over there. And if you wouldn't mind, can you come back here to the hospital to watch my daughter?"

"Havens. What are you going to do? I need to help on this. Why Detective Neil?"

"Daniels, I trust you. Not many others I can say that about right now. Neil is better prepared to deal with Rusty. No offense, but it is what it is. I'll be the backup plan but have to get in position."

"Where are you going?"

"First, home to get something. Second, I'd prefer to keep you out of this part. Thanks in advance, Daniels. Maggie is all I have left. You have everything of mine in your care. Will you do it?"

"Well, if it's all…"

Havens disconnected the call. He knew Daniels would challenge him for leaving Maggie. And Daniels would be right. What father would leave his child again after all that has transpired?

Christina, you know I have to go. I have to finish this. One last mission.

Even as Havens expressed the words in his mind, he knew he had said them time and again to his late wife. Promises said, but never kept. He bent over and kissed Maggie on the forehead.

"Daddy?"

Chapter 68

Havens left the hospital with tears streaming down his cheeks. Maggie had finally woken up and now he had to go. She woke scared and confused and he hadn't helped things with his explanation for leaving. She did, however, understand when he said he had one man left that would pay for what happened to Maggie and Christina. He knew in actuality that it could be a lifetime of effort to eliminate everyone directly or indirectly responsible.

First things first. One man at a time.

Daniels had arrived at the hospital and relayed the news that a cop who was near the Palmer house was able to receive a text photo of Rusty and obtained a visual confirmation moments later. However, according to the Palmer House Hotel front desk receptionist, the identified man had checked out a few hours ago. Havens shifted to plan B. Father of the Year was certainly out of the question. His disregard for family commitment surfaced again when he found Cougar laying in the backseat of the car, forgotten.

In less than thirty minutes, Havens had dropped off Cougar, retrieved a pre-packed satchel with his tried and true Osprey Armament Glock 34 Tier One Recon pistol, and was now en route to where he suspected Rusty would be headed.

Havens figured Rusty would return to his parents' home and kill the current owners in order to gain access. The home was located along Midway Airport's runway flight path. Close enough for Rusty to launch the UAV towards commercial airplanes. Whether Rusty would actually use the unmanned aerial vehicle to attack the plane or simply scare the pilot didn't matter. He assumed that Rusty would launch during the morning so news coverage would coincide with any simultaneous train attacks. At least that was how Havens would have done it.

Sean approached the house and recognized Detective Neil's car parked on the quiet side street in front of the bungalow home. As he slowed to park a few houses down, he noticed a body slumped on the front porch of the home.

Neil.

Havens threw the car into park in the middle of the street and raced up the lawn to Detective Neil. Hearing the car screech and door slam, Neil turned towards the fast approaching Havens.

"Hey, the cavalry's here," he said weakly. "Guess my hunch was right. Wish you would've beaten me here."

"How bad is it?"

"I'm bleeding pretty good. I just radioed in that I am down. I crunched up here so I could compress the bleeding. Door was open. I must have gotten here just after Joyce did. I saw a body on the ground in the house right before he popped me. Hit me hard enough to push me out the door. Nine mil. I surprised him though. He didn't hesitate, but the brief look I got on his face wasn't rage. He and I met before at Bragg. I think he recognized my face but couldn't place me. One thing for sure though..."

"What's that?"

"He sure didn't come out here and say sorry. He just shut the door. He needs to be taken out."

"Think he went out the back?"

"Not sure. I don't think he expects someone else to be coming for a bit. He may be figuring what to do next. You need to go in somehow and I need to throw up. Fuck this hurts."

"Yeah, this isn't how I thought it would go down. He's gotten caught up in all this shady mess too, but looks like he's playing for keeps."

"You going to try and talk to him?"

Havens pulled a stun grenade from his satchel. "No. I've had enough lies and dead guys don't lie. Can you throw this through the picture window?"

"Yeah. I can manage that. Drapes will probably catch fire."

"That's fine. I'm going around back and will throw one through the side window here on the right then hit the back door. Go ahead as soon as I round the corner."

"Roger that. Fire in the hole, buddy."

"See you in a few."

"I'll be here," Neil said, wincing in pain as he positioned himself for the toss.

The first concussive explosion sounded and the second was immediately pitched by Havens and detonated on the side of the house. Havens figured Rusty would stay on the main floor in the event that he had to flee. As Havens rounded the brick wall to the back of the house, Rusty emerged from the house and stumbled down the back stairs, disoriented from the blasts. Rusty still held the 9mm he used against Detective Neil. Rusty tried to orient himself to his surroundings but failed to command his senses.

Havens took a big swallow. He knew how this was going to go down. He believed that Rusty had been used but couldn't think of a fast way to improve the hand they had been dealt.

"It's Sean Havens, Rusty. You're safe! Just lower your sidearm! You're safe! I'm not going to shoot. This is all going down bad."

Rusty quickly leveled the firearm towards the sound.

Sean squeezed the trigger twice.

Chapter 69

Sean opened the front door of the Havens home to find Detectives Neil and Daniels. Daniels handed the small Sports Authority bag that he was holding to Sean and stepped inside.

"What's this, early Christmas?" Sean asked.

"It's not for you, Havens. We know how you accountants don't like to play sports. Too afraid of jamming your calculator fingers. It's for the dog."

Havens pulled the size 3 soccer ball from the bag and smiled.

"Gee thanks, but you guys haven't seen Cougar in a while. She'll choke on this thing now."

At the sound of new voices, Cougar bounded up from the basement gnashing her teeth and barking relentlessly.

"COUGAR! DOWN!" Sean barked back.

With a whimper Cougar got down on all fours, anxiously smacking her tail against the hardwood floor like an old woman beating a dirty rug.

"Holy shit, Havens. She did grow. And she's obedient. I'm impressed." Daniels knelt down for a closer look.

"Careful, I don't have her electric collar or thunder blanket on now, so she could go for your head."

Slowly Daniels rose. "Fuckin' beast."

The men all laughed.

"She ate a frozen pork roast I was going to cook the other night right off the counter. Gone. Strings and all," he added. "So you guys still rounding up the usual suspects in this circus show? I have been watching the news and sounds like you are making some progress."

Neil put his hands in his pocket. He continued to watch the dog as he responded. Havens could see that Neil was recovering well from the gunshot but had some residual stiffness and discomfort.

"Well that's the thing. I don't know what we are doing. We keep following these trails, and we find papers, computers, names, but it doesn't feel right. It's like things are being left in the open. It makes it so we can find it but not have it so easy that it looks set up. It's like a parent putting Easter eggs out for kids. Not too high, not too low, just within eyesight but not so you can see it directly."

Daniels nodded. "Yeah, but I guess scoring so many little wins in such a short amount of time is giving us more exposure as a city, especially with such big loss of life on the board now, is getting us a lot more funding. So, in one sense, it was horrible, but on the other hand Chicago Police has never had so many resources available. They even approved implementation of the social networking link analysis tools that Lars had been pushing for to follow the money and attack the network for organized crime. Even has geospatial layover I hear so we can do pattern predictive analysis based on crime indicators. Slick shit."

Neil nodded again in agreement and looked up at Havens. "Have you talked to Lars lately?"

Havens squinted at his new companions. "Is that an official inquiry or a friend inquiry?"

"Hey, you called us friends. Awww," Daniels said, tilting his head in mock adoration.

"Friend inquiry," Neil answered. "From our vantage, verdict is still out on that guy. Seems like he knew a bit too much. I know he was single and didn't spend much, but I just hope he wasn't on the take from these…whoever they are. CPD never did an IA investigation on him and his contributions got him a meritorious service award before he retired. FBI never checked on it either. Figures. I inquired about where all the intel we sent them on the trains went and they told us to back off. Did your friend Red ever say anything? I mean, we, well, you nailed it."

"Yeah," Daniels chimed in. "The Lars thing and Bureau thing don't add up. I really thought we were going to stop this."

Havens nodded and pursed his lips.

"It wasn't meant to be," Sean replied hesitantly. "Someone either called off or cut off everything we tried to disseminate. Red's been busy with all the fanfare and accolades. I sent Lars a note. Christmas card really. Just saying we are all good, but I haven't heard back from him. He left for Arizona in a hurry. I think he may be avoiding me for some reason. Not sure why. Something was off that's for sure. He could be in some sort of trouble. I do worry about him. He's too smart to have been played, and I can't imagine he was dirty. Seems to be pointing that way though. It wasn't the first time I was fooled this year though."

"Is he in Arizona for good?"

"He keeps going back and forth, but I know he is out of his apartment. I stopped by and the mailbox has changed owners. Lars never had a name on his unit. I know he likes spring training, but I also know he loves a good hunt. I wouldn't be surprised if he got involved with some law enforcement down there as a consultant, maybe looking into cartel stuff south of the border."

"I suppose. Well, I won't say to tell him hi from us. Can't say we were close, but, man, he was a god when it came to a crime scene."

"Let's just pray he doesn't become one," Sean added.

"Hey, here's a puzzler for you. Who do you think would win? Mexican cartels or the Albanians?"

Neil gave his partner a punch in the arm. "OK, Havens, we better get going. Have a good holiday."

"You too, guys. Maggie and I are going on a little road trip to see a specialist out west, but we'll be back for the Super Bowl if you aren't doing anything."

"May take you up on that if you have Cujo here locked away."

"Deal."

Chapter 70

Conrad knocked on the solid oak door. Despite the sterile feel of the corridor doors within the Pentagon, the quality of wood for the executive offices was quite nice.

"Come in, Conrad."

"Sir."

"Have you found him yet? Or the war chest of his that we funded?"

"No, sir."

"Have you searched his home, his records, everything?"

"We are still looking for Draeger's home, sir. The addresses we had ended up being abandoned homes in unincorporated areas. No utilities on, nothing. Mail was all sent to a forwarder and we lost the trail at a PO Box. Checked the security cameras and it had been him, but he paid in cash all the time. Trail is dead there. No credit card trails, money transfers, nothing. Draeger's gone, sir."

"How much did we lose from the approved funds we gave him?"

"Just over six hundred thousand. There could be more, but his guy Jason, the other commo whiz, is gone too. They moved the accounts so we can't access the funds. It appears they tapped into Silver Star too. Someone took a few hundred thousand. Draeger had another fund that is gone too. He kept the books on that."

The general sat in silence. He rubbed his chin, then his ear, scratched his neck. He began to nod.

"Conrad, that snake accomplished as much as we could have hoped for. I can't say I think he was the best man for it, and it was messy, but he succeeded in raising awareness and vigilance again in this country to an appropriate level. And we now have some resources back to keep our enemies at bay. To lose six hundred thousand dollars or six million dollars at this point is a shot of piss in the pot. It's a fart in the wind compared to what we gained. No, I think this ended up alright. Plus, I've been ordered by someone else to use him, so we're clear."

"So should we call off the hunt?"

"God, no. Do I have to do all the work here? Eliminate those motherfuckers from the earth, wherever they are."

"Sir, that won't be easy."

"My God, man, how did you make it this far? You make sure that man and his lackey cannot leave the country, cannot return to this country, cannot set foot in another country, cannot move by air, rail, sea, or dig under the fucking ground with the help of a million Chinamen. You trump up something bad and get it on all the wires. And if someone finds him…pffft pffft." The general made a pistol motion with his fingers.

"Yes, sir."

"Now go start me another war somewhere near Mexico or Canada. Let's get some more of that Canuck skin in the game. Those fur hat-wearing pussies. And get good people this time. We have more money now to hire good people. Get me the best. Get Havens. Let him pick his own team. We can clean up this little mess of his and expunge the records. Let him run the show. Shit, have him hunt down Draeger. And don't ask me how to do it. Just do it or find me someone who can."

"On it, sir."

"Close the door on your way out."

The general watched the door close before opening his drawer to pull out a royal blue folder. It was embossed with a corporate logo. He opened the folder and pulled out the top sheet. He looked at the figures in the offer letter.

850K plus 200K guaranteed bonus to run a homeland security business unit for this company? Wait'll I really get things fired up. Let's see what the competition will pay by summer.

Chapter 71

Two men shook hands in greeting on a mountainside in Arizona. While one unhitched a pair of mountain bikes the other went to the truck and extracted their rifles. Both agreed on the hide position and prepared themselves with their C14 Timberwolf sniper rifles arming .338 Lapua cartridges. They watched the target location through the lenses of the TrackingPoint precision guided firearm system until they marked their man. The PGF did all auto calculations through the scope, which was ideal for enhancing old sniper skills that had gotten rusty.

Lars Bjorklund was moving about in his kitchen. The panoramic window provided an excellent vantage for the shooters. Lars opened the refrigerator and grabbed a quart of eggnog. One of the benefits of being a bachelor was never having to hide when swigging right out of a milk carton. Swigging from an open carton of eggnog was one of those sweet moments in life for Lars these days.

"On two. I go head, you go mass."

The two professionals were perfectly in sync and had spent hours in planning while traveling to the hide site earlier in the day for the first and only recon. Final confirmations solidified the mission as a go. The selected round was chosen with consideration to the distance, angle, and need to penetrate the windowpane.

"Roger that."

"One..."

"Wait. I want to shoot the eggnog."

Havens took a full breath with a slow release to maintain his rhythm and keep his heart rate slowed.

"And why, Red, do you want to shoot the eggnog?"

"I think it would be funny."

"If I miss we have blown our shot—literally."

"Don't miss. Hurry before he puts it away."

"You are an idiot."

"Because I am here with you ready to commit murder? I'm a hero. Heroes don't kill cops."

"Ex-cop. Dirty cop. On two, I have head you have…eggnog. Don't miss. I'm gonna try using the hole you are going to make if he moves in."

"Here he goes. I get eggnog, wait a sec, and then go head through my entrance. I think you best go direct to glass and not catch an angle. Just don't start laughing. I'm going."

"The round is going to slow and tumble with contact to the glass and make a big hole in that carton. May blow off his hand."

Lars looked at his one and only Christmas card of the season. It was affixed to his refrigerator by a cheap magnet that said "Larry." There were no Lars magnets in the souvenir shop. The card was from Sean.

After all this shit, he still sees me as a brother and thought enough to send a holiday greeting. "Lars. Wherever you are, I'll be there for you. Merry Xmas. S."

Lars took another gulp.

"I'll try not to hit his hand so the coroner can fold them in his casket. Glad you decided to do this, Sean. It was the right move."

"Yeah." *It was your idea.*

The carton exploded in Lars' hand. Eggnog burst through the air. Red started giggling and dropped from his optic as Havens fired the second shot a fraction of a second later.

"Target down?"

"Target down."

"I thought it would be funnier."

"It was a little funny when eggnog splashed on his face."

"That was a little funny. Ready to go?"

"Yep. Let's go."

"Sorry about all this shit, Sean."

"I know. Thanks. Did you really want to shoot the carton or save yourself from life in prison? Either is fine. Just wondering." *I knew at the last minute you'd want to keep your hands clean.*

Red regarded his friend for a moment. He felt exposed.

"If you needed me to do it, I would have done it for you, brother. I could tell that you were going through with it. And I'll admit the thought crossed my mind about personal liability. I guess in the moment I just got a chuckle out of the thought of his face getting doused. Seemed fitting to humiliate him first. I know we don't laugh at a man about to pay the ultimate price."

"We don't. But his big ass did look funny with eggnog all over. I had to pull though before someone put us on *Funniest Home Videos*."

Sean's chuckle released the tension Red was feeling.

"I know. It'd be funnier in a movie."

"Tarantino style."

"Did I tell you that I kicked Harrison in the nuts after I killed him?"

"No!" Red scrunched his face quizzically. "Why?"

"I thought it would be funny."

"Shit, Sean, you are one fucked up dude."

"You too, Red. Real fucked. Your number was all over Harrison's phone. And your travel forays were all over Lars' computer. You covered all the federal angles of this and covered up some evidence while pushing other bits up the flagpole for national effect. You sat in the car while my wife was killed. I found out you and Draeger had been in touch regularly too. Guess you patched things up a couple years back."

Red paused just long enough for Havens to lift and fire a concealed .38 caliber semi-automatic pistol. The shot found its mark where Havens intended—just above the right eye a bit over the temple. It was enough to kill Red instantly without looking like a professional. Havens had encouraged Red's ride up the mountain by bicycle to mirror the Baseline Killer case of Phoenix or the Serial

Shooters incidents occurring around that time. Copycat? Third party? Either way it would have folks guessing.

The serial attributed kill saved Havens the chore of cleanup aside from the rifles which he simply cased and slid through the cutout in the mattresses and box strings tied down to the pickup bed. He checked Red's corpse quickly to ensure no pocket litter pointed to Havens. It surprised Havens to find that Red was also carrying a small Sig Sauer 38H .32 caliber semi-auto. The pistol was not Red's usual brand. To the best of Havens' knowledge, it wasn't even Red's gun. He took a deep breath in through his nostrils and exhaled slowly. Yet another friendship gone. He couldn't waste the time or energy wondering if Red was planning to kill Havens too on that quiet mountain. Red may have been looking to finish the story as well. Havens was running low on friends.

Chapter 72

After a quick call and a few minutes waiting at the front door, a rather rattled Lars emerged. He still had eggnog on his shirt. He cautiously let his brother-in-law inside.

"Sorry for the mess, Lars."

No response.

"I'll pay for the dry cleaning."

No response.

"I'll get you another eggnog."

Sensing no threat, but still on guard, Lars broke eye contact and looked down at the floor. His eyes followed the wet mess on his shirt to his shoes.

"It was the Southern Comfort brand. And I want two. I had just opened this one."

"Yes," Havens said, looking Lars up and down. "I see it was rather full."

Both men burst into laughter, breaking the awkward moment.

"Lars, I broke into your home in Chicago."

"I know."

"How did you know?"

"Two ways. One, I have a key light since the hall is so dark, and if I have been drinking I need to find the hole. I saw that the tarnish on the edge of the lock opening had a bit of polish to it. Like steel wool or a lock wizard."

"And two?"

"When I saw the lock was jimmied I really wasn't sure who would be in my home, so before I got myself killed I stopped by my neighbor's. I asked him if he had seen or heard anything and that I was concerned about someone potentially breaking in. He really didn't want to say anything, but figuring I have been through a lot, he assuaged my fears and said my brother-in-law stopped by just to check on me."

Havens nodded his head in understanding.

"Christina and Maggie had a key. You didn't."

"Sorry, Lars. Things weren't adding up."

"I understand. That's why I had to get all wiggy on you. Tried to signal you with the pets. Smart predator, dangerous predator, but it fell short. Made sense in my head. I was scared and didn't want to be seen with you so we could both stay safe. I knew I was in over my head and just hoped you would figure it out."

"When I called you, I hoped you would understand what I meant. That's why I said what I said."

"I know, 'Remember Seany, I am your brother. Red is not.'"

"It was a helluva leap of faith. But you got it." Lars started to tear up.

"I know. That's why I said, 'Sir Charles understands.'"

"I wanted to believe you, man. But boy, when that shot took out my nog, Crissakes."

"What were you thinking at the time?"

"Well, as you know, time stands still. I was aware that my nog exploded and my window had been shot, exploding the granite near the fridge. And then I saw your card. I figured, if that were Seany coming for me, he wouldn't have missed. If it wasn't you, then I prayed in that instance that you were going to be there for me."

"You said you didn't call the police. What did you do while I was coming down from the mountain?"

"It's embarrassing."

"I think we have been through enough where we can share."

"Well, the place had been cleaned before I got here, and I figured if indeed I was going to die, I knew the angle of the shooters had me pinned and I couldn't get to a piece."

"So?"

"I got on all fours and started slurping up that spilled eggnog. My Last Supper." Lars lifted his shoulders and shrugged sheepishly as only a giant can do. "So how is that baby girl of mine?"

"She's coming along and can't wait to see you."

"Well, I'll come back soon once I get this cleared up for you."

"You going to call it in?"

"Nah, not unless I need to. Shooter down?"

"Shooter down."

"Red?"

"Dead."

"Good. Had to practically wrestle the store owner's security tape from Red at the scene. Too much of a coincidence for you to be in the area earlier. If you had a disguise, I knew you were going into the store and they could put something on you as the initial recon guy before the killing."

"Thanks. Don't suppose you have the tape?"

"Long gone. Destroyed. Red was still asking me for it. Did you see my notes that Red was also in those locations where the families were killed? I hoped you would. He managed to be FBI on the scene even out of state, but no one ever knew who he was since he said it was always unofficial. He showed up when I was looking into a Chicago cartel hit. Something wasn't right. He had an awful lot of opinion about what was going on for someone unofficially there. I was surprised to see in the report that he was at your house too when Christina was killed. He was also at another site in DC that I was following up on. We had caught a picture of him while we were swarming the scene. I sent it on to one of my buddy detectives and got a match on him. I followed up on a few other scenes and every time there was that Red."

"I suppose somewhere in between they saw you as a threat."

"Just lucky they didn't make me out to be family when I first got the pitch."

"I'd like to say I designed that," Sean said, "but I think we need more pictures around the house of Uncle Lars. I just can't believe so many guys from my own crew over the years were involved."

"Sorry, buddy. I know you were close. I think they resented you, but respected your capabilities. They just couldn't pull it all off with you at arm's length. Or like you said, that one guy wanted to get you back for some stuff he had pent up."

"Yeah, we were all close, but not like my brother." Sean put his hand on Lars' shoulder and handed him a book that he had concealed beneath his jacket.

"What's this?"

"Merry Christmas. Maggie helped me put some pictures together for you. They were able to pull some from the hard drives that were impounded. Some good ones of the three of you in there."

Lars started to open the book and bit his lip holding back the emotions.

Havens put his hand on the book. "Why don't you look at this later by yourself when you have things cleaned up. I have to ditch this truck I have parked down the road and get back over to Maggie at Mayo."

"Maggie's at Mayo?"

"Yeah. Close to family. She's looking forward to seeing you when you can."

"She's talking?"

"Yeah, a bit. Slowly, but surely. They think she is processing everything but her motor skills need work. With the traumatic brain injury, she is going to need a lot of rehab for limb movement, balance, and of course walking again. Right now they are going to be focused on forming words better and with clarity. She passed a tower building test indicating memory and attention are coming around. Still going to be a long road to recovery as they say."

"Well, glad to know you guys will be near. Let me know if I can help."

"Thanks. I am going back home for a bit to get some things in order and probably put the house up. We'll move where there is care for her and work for me."

"Do you know what you are going to do?"

"I'm sure something will come up. I have some ideas. Just need to figure out how to get paid to do it. I liked the concept of the work I was supposed to be doing supporting military families that were having problems at home. I may see if I can get that going on my own perhaps. Could be a role for you if you're interested."

"Like I said, Sean. Anything I can do to help. I have a feeling I am going to need to do something to keep busy. So, we good?"

"We're good."

The two embraced again before Sean departed. As Sean was walking out the door, Lars called out.

"I am sorry about that train, Sean. Those poor souls shouldn't have died that way."

"We did the best we could. There are some bad dudes out there. Even the ones who are supposed to be the good guys."

"It's a black world, Sean."

"I am afraid this is just the beginning."

Chapter 73

The mild winters left some foliage to highlight the striking formation of the Albanian Alps. Prescott Draeger took in the familiar view as he crossed into the administrative district of Shkoder from Montenegro. The Mercedes M-Class hugged the turns, commanded by hands clad in leather CamelBak light assault gloves. The plush interior hugged Draeger's torso in style and comfort. The cowhide seat trim looked fitting next to the lambskin black leather barn jacket that Draeger sported. The Czech CZ 110 9mm would have made for a classy advertisement photo laying in luxury on the passenger seat beside its owner. A much classier owner than the last few men who had tugged on its trigger. He passed a small herd of sheep as he wound up a hill through the river valley. Today was a good day. No more migraines. No more coffee.

It had been relatively easy leaving the country. Each time an airplane hatch closed, Draeger's disposition improved. A signal from Jason meant he had gotten out too. In Prescott's opinion, Jason was still too uptight despite his time administering over discrete activities, but he did do as he was told. Draeger was amused by the thought of seeing how long Jason would survive in the field.

Driving home after Havens' call, Draeger realized his vehicle could be traced, his phones that he had so carelessly used could be monitored. For all he knew a hit team could be waiting for him there in the garage, the entryway, a room. It was too much of a risk. He had let ego override his training. That couldn't happen again.

Plans had not been perfect. Were it not for the satisfaction of seeing events unfold, Draeger would have internalized the shortcomings of his own performance. He would never reap the rewards in the manner he had intended, but perhaps it was fate. He knew his real employer would be fine with the outcome. Mission complete.

Draeger felt good about things now that he let it all go and fled to fight another day. He had attacked a weak apparatus and raised awareness for his cause. Havens had likely killed Mann. That was a nice convenience. Sure, Havens would want to kill Draeger, but with his daughter presumably alive, that harness would keep Sean in the U.S. for the foreseeable future. It would give Draeger time to implement his next plan and work internationally again. All it would take was a few keystrokes and Havens would be off running for his life. Draeger had plenty of funds to see it through and more than enough to start his new venture. It had always occurred to Draeger that operating in the black was illegal anyway, so why not reap the profits and go boots and knees together into crime and a completely deniable intelligence apparatus to secure the Homeland. He had just needed a little push to fully commit to the Pond.

Scanning the road, Draeger recognized some of the features and landmarks from the last time he passed along this way. He was only about eighty kilometers from his safe house destination. Another set of IDs, access to the web, plenty of kit, and plenty of underworld contacts still in lists from old jobs.

Yes, Draeger felt good about the future. He felt like he was driving to a new job grinning all the way. As he neared a small farm, an energetic dog ran along the road chasing the car. Draeger smiled as he veered off the pavement onto the side, overcoming the dog with his bumper and front tire and then rolling over the tumbling carcass with his rear wheel. It was good to be in control again. Havens had been right.

Until next time, Sean Havens. If we get a next time.

Draeger looked in the side mirror watching the canine roll broken in the road amid the gravel dust. He toyed with the radio buttons.

How about a little music?

Epilogue

On a freezing sub-zero Sunday morning in Chicago, the winter winds gnawed at the old man's hands as soon as he left the comfort of his transport's warm interior. The streets were quiet. The wind swirled lingering snow on the concrete. The metal handle on his cane bit his frail fingers as he slowly shuffled up the sidewalk glazed with ice. His gnarled digit pressed the doorbell. Chimes gave way to loud aggressive woofing.

"Oh my," he responded to the loud bark and reached up to tuck his scarf deeper into his black cashmere overcoat. He pulled his Irish walking hat lower over his brow and shrugged his shoulders up so the scarf would cover his ears.

The wooden door opened with the dog's master holding its collar with a combination of balance and force.

"Yes? Can I help you?"

The old man gazed into the barking dogs eyes. He slowly reached towards the dog with the back of his hand extended.

"Assez, assez," the man said, commanding the dog to sit and tilting his head slightly while extending to his full height. The Burberry overcoat extended the size of the frail aged man's shoulders some but not greatly. Nonetheless, the effect caused Cougar to lower her tail and head.

"Ici. Oui." She nuzzled up to his hand for a sniff and a lick. "That's a nice girl. Yeah, you are the queen of the house aren't you?"

Puzzled at this elderly beast master, Havens regarded the old man's translucent hand. Before the man opened his palm for Cougar to lick, Havens noticed a gem-adorned Yale graduation ring. Wrappings of yellow yarn now replaced what once was sized gold that met securely on a meatier youthful ring finger. It had been nearly twenty years since Sean Havens saw that ring. It was nearly 60 years since the ring was first put on the graduate's hand.

The old man looked up at Havens. A warm smile of clean dentures raised his red cheeks to meet pale blue eyes. Eyes that had once known a younger Havens. Eyes that had seen a lifetime of shadow wars.

"Hello, Sean. It's been quite a while. May I come in? It's rather cool out this morning. Good for the lungs, but bad for my joints I am afraid. She's a beautiful Belgian you have there. You should command her in French if you don't already. I don't suspect Flemish. Well, I suppose it depends on her youth. Never mind me."

"Jerry?"

The old man gave a laugh.

"I'm surprised you still remember me. I greatly hoped you would. I was quite realistic with myself that my appearance would not do much justice to your memory of me. Not that I was so young even then."

"I'd know you anywhere, Jerry."

The old man chuckled again.

"OK, well enough of the pleasantries out here. Let's step inside so my friends out here can read a magazine or something and I can die in my sleep instead of your entryway."

Havens looked up to see the two black Chevy Suburbans in the driveway and street.

"Who's that?"

"Oh, I am afraid all that fanfare is for me, and I suspect for you as well. Land's sake, I can hardly step down from my seat to the curb from those coaches. It's nearly as big as my first apartment in Prague in there. My I haven't thought of that place in quite some time."

Jerry walked in and propped his cane against the doorframe. Havens seated his CIA mentor at the kitchen table and offered something to drink.

"Well normally this early I'd have an orange juice or a black coffee, Sean, but I am not sure my bladder can hold it for the ride. These men are going to drop me at my sister's in Park Ridge for a bit after we talk for a few moments. I could be convinced to share a little taste of Scotch, if you would care to join me. Cuts the cold and good for conversation between friends," Jerry said with a smile.

Two glasses from the cupboard, two three-finger pours, and the two were toasting.

"Your taste in scotch is improving, Sean. I very much like this brand. Dalwhinnie. The Brits like it. MI-6, SAS. Very good. I suppose you know that."

"I've gotten your cards over the years. Have to say, they always made me feel a bit closer to you without really ever hearing from you again."

"I'm glad. You were one of my finest. I've been proud." Jerry sipped his Scotch and looked around in approval of the domicile. "I'm sorry about your family. I hear your daughter is improving."

Havens nodded. Clearly, Jerry had been informed and has always stayed informed. How was always a mystery, but it was not worth asking. It would be the least of this old spymaster's capabilities. Moreover, the least of priorities if Jerry was coming out to reveal himself again after all these years.

Jerry reached over the table and rested his hand on Sean's. "Sean, a bit of a storm is coming. We have word that some of your old files about those recent attack plans have been loaded on the Internet through WikiLeaks and are being attributed to you."

"Jerry, I..."

Jerry raised his hand. "Sean, you are not in trouble with us. There has been an investigation and it looks as though it points to some individuals in that outfit you were recently involved with. I looked into some of this as well, and found you know that Prescott Draeger. Those men, or Draeger, or some combination therein, tried to put much of the operational aspects on you. He's a dangerous man, that Prescott Draeger." Jerry reached into his breast pocket and retrieved a 3x5 note card. He scanned it and put it back in its former location.

"Great, so is there a warrant out for me?"

"Oh, no, Sean. That won't happen." Jerry patted his former protégé's hand. "No, Sean, you see, you won't exist anymore."

Sean pulled back his hand and loudly scooted back his chair startling a sleeping Cougar at his feet. "Why won't I exist? What do you mean? What have you done to me now?"

"Well, it's like a witness protection, but our people think it is best if no one has access to your information."

"Why can't they just clear it up? Why can't it just go away? They know it's all lies."

"Sure, Sean, we all do. But tell that to the world's stage who thinks you planned a series of domestic terror attacks. Defense wanted to let it go and make you the scapegoat. There could be a way, but it would take some big favors."

"Unbelievable."

"Well, Sean, you need to believe it, accept it, and move on."

"How am I supposed to move on, leave everything behind, and start over like a fugitive?"

"No, Sean, we will help you. You are one of us. We will take care of you. We will help you with your daughter's recovery. You will have the power to change your names and access an account set up for you. It's largely in your hands."

"Largely?" he said, shaking his head in disbelief. "Jerry, I have heard this all before. Same story, same we will protect you, your daughter, give you a job. I just lived through this. Barely lived through this. My wife is dead because of this type of care!"

"Sean, your reaction is perfectly understandable. Unfortunately, you didn't choose the life of an accountant or doctor. You are an intelligence professional, a clandestine asset. You are a hunter of men. While it was not my desire, you are now a killer. An effective one at that. If you want people to value you and pay for what you do, you either need to change your profession or embrace it and create assets, collect intelligence, and...well...kill. Forgive my bluntness."

"Jerry, why did they put you up to this? Who put you up to this? No offense, but you are still on the payroll? Don't they have mandatory retirement?"

"Sean, I was sent as a courtesy. I retired years back, but I still consult. With my knowledge of dialects and certain foreign places and people, I help these young computer kids that the Agency has hired to go in on those Internet jihadi chat rooms. I instruct them on how they should speak, reply, and interpret the conversations going on or how they resonate with readers. They have a comfortable chair for me and it keeps me busy. Just a few hours a day, and I get to see old friends. They give me free coffee," Jerry joked, trying to make the situation lighter. "My wife passed long ago, and I only had one child who travels around quite a bit. It's better than staying home waiting for my time to come. By the way, do you remember Rick?"

"How can I forget?" Havens exuded a sour look.

"Sean, you were young. You indeed were being tested at the time. You were not in a web of subterfuge. That experience has helped you survive this long. It helps you to question and trust your instincts. Rick, as you can imagine, never left the business."

"Why doesn't that surprise me? Sorry, I'm not trying to be a smart ass."

"Sean, Rick would like to work with you. You will need work. You will need flexibility. You will need someone who can trust you and that you can trust."

"How can I be sure I can trust him or anyone for that matter at this point?"

"Do you trust me?"

Havens gave thought to the question. He no longer thought he could trust anyone. Jerry, however, was more like a favorite uncle. Havens pictured some extravagant relative off traveling in faraway lands only to come back every ten years with gifts and stories for the kids. Unlike a fictitious uncle though, years had passed and Jerry never came back. Havens needed someone that he could blindly trust. He was too hollow inside to not have someone who could look out for him.

"Yes, Jerry, I can trust you, but I am not working for you. I'd be working for Rick. That's a different story."

"Same story. Rick is my son, Sean. Forgive the pun, but he will be your safe haven."

Havens put his head in his hands, trying to process the news. He knew he would need work. He knew his skills catered to only a few very select employers at this time. He still believed there was a need for a man like him, but he also needed to be with his daughter. He had lost so much for this country or maybe for his own aspirations and personal career goals.

"What's next? Maggie still needs to be in hospitals and therapy. Her mind is still repairing from the traumatic injury. Things are still broken in her thinking. She has to relearn how to walk. Her days are filled with speech and reading exercises. Shit, she still needs help eating, bathing, and dressing herself. In the coming weeks, they will have to do another cranioplasty since they left part of her skull fractured to get back in if there were more blood clots on her brain. Poor kid wears a hockey helmet 24/7. I'm putting the house up for sale. I have another banister up but think she would do better in a ranch and put special chairs and devices in the bathrooms for support."

Jerry listened attentively as a therapist would. He waited until Sean finished.

"You and Rick can come up with the plan. He is driving out here in the next hour. He does a lot of his work through a cutout holding company, Donovan Black Holdings, that you would join. It will keep you off the books."

"Why does this all need to be done today? Now? I've gone from one nightmare to another and have yet to have a good sleep. I'm beat, Jerry. I just need some time to breathe."

Havens put his face in his hands again. His outstretched fingers pulled down across the contours of his face moving back up in prayer form over his mouth and nose. He closed his eyes and expelled the air from his lungs along with the stress of the past few months.

Fine. I can do this. I went for months in the field with the same amount of sleep deprivation.

Jerry was swirling the last remnants of Scotch in his glass.

"That brings me to the second part of my trip. Prescott Draeger, or we assume it to be him. He certainly has the resources and capability from what I understand..."

"Say it, Jerry. What's going on? What next? He has a nuke aimed at my house? Screw it. Tell him to push the button."

"He has put out a rather extensive national and international hit on you tied to the release of your name and the attacks in the media. Evidently, Prescott Draeger has publicized a digital cash bounty through Bitcoin on the assassination market through Silk Road-type sites and anonymizing networks like Tor. You currently have one of the largest bounties as other users are donating Bitcoins to the pot. They are crowdsourcing funding for your death. The Secret Service and the FBI were unsuccessful at shutting it down the first time, and now, I am afraid, the anonymous network is that much more of a virtual apparition. From biker gangs to foreign assassins to someone looking to earn a rather lucrative fee, your life has just been put on the market. It will be very difficult for us to find Draeger and stop the momentum of this."

Havens felt numb with disbelief. "I suppose nothing anyone can do here either?"

"Sean, he has us on our heels with this one. The authorities are more concerned about the killing market than they are you, but rest assured, they are looking for encryption exploits and other more technical approaches to shut this down. You will need to get your affairs in order immediately though. The notices came out yesterday. We have done the best we can with system denials of service and disruption of postings online, but there is not much power that we have against this type of crowdsourcing I am afraid."

"How can I stop it?" *Clearly you aren't going to stop it unless I agree to this.*

"I believe you know the answer to that. You and Rick will need to find Draeger and those involved."

"Those involved? Who else is involved?"

"Draeger was somehow brought into this crazy Silver Star scheme, or shall I say placed. You see, once you moved away from some of our activities affiliated with the Agency, you worked dotted line against another one. Have you heard of the Lake? Perhaps the Pond?"

"The old G-2 Cold War group affiliated with Senator McCarthy?"

Jerry smiled like a proud parent.

"Indeed. And they still exist. They have moved on from Communists to Extremists. They were among the best at using corporate surrogates, unsavory character assets, and rather foul means. Aside from OSS, in our current community, they set the bar for cutout work and commercial cover for status and action. You did work for them for a few years. We had our rivalry but shared resources. We shared you. Draeger has been with them for years, but I suspect now more formally. You were from the onset primarily with what our joint leaders called the Bay."

"I thought that is just what some people called the Agency in the '50s."

Jerry raised his eyebrows and sent a tight-lipped smile across to Havens. He said nothing. While there were Agencies, there were still small societies within those agencies. Closed to all but a select few.

"Sean, Draeger has the reach and community anonymity of the Lake. Few know it exists aside from what is in the National Archives. Draeger may be on the run, but that will only play better to their hand. They love men like Draeger. We don't know who their sources are. We don't know where their safe houses are. We know very little. Rick has been involved with an Agency project as a bit of a national counterintelligence effort. Quite high level and discrete as you can imagine. You will be tasked to get our arms around the Lake. In some cases, where we know they have done harm to national security and national interests, we have authorities for extrajudicial...well..." Jerry sat up, shifting from a quiet and sly means of communication to one more befitting his image of himself. "As gentlemen here, let's just say we can go clean their clocks. I must say, if I were a few years younger, I'd very much like to be a part of this."

While it sounded like the kind of activities that should only exist in the fictional pages of a Nelson DeMille novel, it made complete sense to Sean Havens. He had been behind more than his share of closed door secret operations. It would make sense that Draeger would play on such a team as this Lake or Pond.

"Rick's work, that you will now be part of, will help with your situation as well. I would say it means you have two jobs. Well, three since your primary job is to protect yourself and, of course, that little girl of yours. I'd consider relatives too. Anyone with links to you is a trail that some may chase to get to you for their bounty reward."

"Cripes, Jerry. Where do I even start?"

"For now, Sean. . . run."

Cougar raised her head abruptly. Her ears twitched in concentration. She ran to the entryway as Havens spun around the table grabbing his mentor.

The rapport of automatic gunfire bursts outside erupted from the silent winter morning. The staccato salvo changed to a near constant barrage of ammunition, spewing the mixes of steel, Teflon, and lead that now raked the vehicles' metal in the driveway up to the beloved artisan crafted door of Christina Havens.

END

Made in the USA
San Bernardino, CA
23 July 2014